DARK

EYES

DARK
WILLIAM RICHTER

EYES

razOr
bill

An Imprint of Penguin Group (USA) Inc.

razOr bill

Published by the Penguin Group
Penguin Group (USA) Inc., 375 Hudson Street, New York, New York 10014, USA
Penguin Group (Canada), 90 Eglinton Avenue East, Suite 700, Toronto, Ontario
M4P 2Y3, Canada (a division of Pearson Penguin Canada Inc.)
Penguin Books Ltd, 80 Strand, London WC2R 0RL, England
Penguin Ireland, 25 St Stephen's Green, Dublin 2, Ireland
(a division of Penguin Books Ltd)
Penguin Group (Australia), 707 Collins St., Melbourne, Victoria 3008, Australia
(a division of Pearson Australia Group Pty Ltd)
Penguin Books India Pvt Ltd, 11 Community Centre, Panchsheel Park,
New Delhi–110 017, India
Penguin Group (NZ), 67 Apollo Drive, Rosedale, Auckland 0632, New Zealand
(a division of Pearson New Zealand Ltd)
Penguin Books, Rosebank Office Park, 181 Jan Smuts Avenue,
Parktown North 2193, South Africa
Penguin China, B7 Jaiming Center, 27 East Third Ring Road North,
Chaoyang District, Beijing 100020, China

Penguin Books Ltd, Registered Offices: 80 Strand, London WC2R 0RL, England

Copyright © 2012 by William Richter

ISBN: 978-1-59514-600-7

Published simultaneously in Canada

Printed in the United States of America

10 9 8 7 6 5 4 3 2 1

This is a work of fiction. Names, characters, places, and incidents either are the
product of the author's imagination or are used fictitiously, and any resemblance to
actual persons, living or dead, businesses, companies, events, or locales is entirely
coincidental.

For the Shaw girls

PROLOGUE

Valentina stirred awake and found Mrs. Ivanova leaning over her bed, gently squeezing her shoulder.

"Shh, little one," Mrs. Ivanova said in her most quiet whisper. Valentina could smell sweet tea on the old woman's breath. "Come along."

Valentina smiled, still half-asleep, and slid out from beneath her covers as quietly as she could, careful not to wake the other children with the sound of her squeaky bed. With Mrs. Ivanova's help, Valentina put on her robe and slippers and padded silently out of the room. The two of them moved hand in hand along the hallway of the main building, the faint glow of early morning light, cold gray, just barely creeping in through the high windows. They passed a low shelf on the wall where twenty small clay pots sat in a row, each with a single blooming flower, each with a name hand-painted on its side: Aniya, Mika, Stasya, Youri. . . .

No one else was up yet—not even Miss Demitra, the cook—and the privacy of their short journey added to the feeling of specialness that tickled inside Valentina's stomach. They reached Mrs. Ivanova's quarters at the end of the North Hall and entered the warm apartment together, the air inside rich with the aroma of blini and lingonberry jam and—most special of all—hot chocolate. A small table was already set by a coal stove.

"Sit, Wally," said Mrs. Ivanova. Valentina took her place at the table and Mrs. Ivanova served their breakfast, spreading sour cream on the warm blini and pouring a full cup of chocolate for her guest. Valentina waited anxiously for Mrs. Ivanova to join her.

"Okay, okay," the woman said with a smile as she took her own seat across the modest table. "Eat."

Valentina dug hungrily into her food, adding dollops of jam to each forkful of pancake and relishing sips of the hot chocolate between bites.

The two of them had shared such a breakfast five or six times before, each time a surprise for Valentina and, as far as she knew, a gift not shared with any of the other children. This morning, as always, the two of them ate in silence, Mrs. Ivanova observing Valentina's appetite with approval and then clearing the table once all the food was gone.

At this point in their other breakfasts the two of them had drunk tea together while Mrs. Ivanova told stories about someone named Yalena—Yalena Mayakova—who the old woman claimed was Valentina's mother. On those occasions the girl had listened carefully but without understanding; she knew only that a mother was a woman who cared for her children, and how could this Yalena, a complete stranger to her, be that? Valentina had no memory of her, or of any life beyond the walls of the orphanage. Where was this Yalena? Why had she left her daughter behind?

On this morning, however, there were no stories. Mrs. Ivanova sat in silence, drinking her tea and making the nervous *tsk-tsk*ing sound that the children recognized as a sign the old woman was in distress. Valentina observed this and became worried herself. What was wrong? None of their other private meals had ended this way. After many minutes of this silence, something happened that had never happened before, at least to Valentina's knowledge: Mrs. Ivanova began to cry, turning her head away in a futile attempt to hide her emotions from the girl. Valentina saw the tears anyway and soon she was crying also, upset and afraid but without knowing why.

"Are you sad, Babu?" Valentina used the shortened name for Mrs. Ivanova that the younger children in the home routinely used: Babu. Babushka. Grandmother.

"I am not your babushka." Mrs. Ivanova spoke with a hard tone in her voice. "I cannot be anymore. I am sorry, Wally."

"You *are* my babu," Wally said, wiping the tears away from her face, wanting to be strong. Crying was for the little ones. The older children in the home never shed a tear, ever.

"A young couple will come today from America," Mrs. Ivanova started in again. "A mother and father for you. A chance for a new life."

"No. I have a mother. You said. My mother is Yalena. If she comes to find me and I am gone . . ."

Mrs. Ivanova shook her head. "You must let go of the stories, Wally. I am sorry I shared them with you; that was my mistake. You must forget Yalena."

Overwhelmed, Valentina did not resist as Mrs. Ivanova led her to the private washroom and rushed her through a bath, soaping Valentina's hair with scented shampoo and scrubbing her body with a coarse washcloth head to toe. By that point, the old woman had composed her emotions, and Valentina struggled to do the same, hiding her tears of fear and confusion behind the clear warm water that rinsed the soap off her body and down the drain. When the bath was over, Mrs. Ivanova produced a pale yellow dress for the girl to wear, clean and pressed but well worn, with frayed threads at all the seams.

"Yes, yes," the woman said tersely once Valentina was dressed, adding the *tsk-tsk*ing sound involuntarily. "Very pretty. Beautiful girl."

Everything happened so quickly then that Valentina's heart and mind could barely keep up. Mrs. Ivanova held her hand tight and led her insistently through the Main Hall, all the lights on now and the place fully awakened. The other children—her brothers and sisters—were nowhere to be seen, but Valentina could hear them singing together behind the closed door of the main lesson room, the muffled sound of their voices echoing down the long hallway.

Mrs. Ivanova steered Valentina into a small office that she had never entered before, and there stood a young man and a woman. They smiled brightly at Valentina's arrival, the woman stepping forward and kneeling before the little girl so that they could see each other face-to-face. Tears began to flow from the woman's eyes and she twisted her hands nervously around each other, wringing them tightly until they were as white as the cream for tea. Valentina felt an urge to run away but found that she could not move, that her feet were planted on that spot of floor by a powerful and frightening force.

The woman reached out, taking Valentina's hands in her own, and the feeling was something overpowering, like an electrical spark passing between them that the girl did not understand; all at once, she wanted to embrace this strange woman tightly but also to push her away, the two emotions fighting a battle inside her that made her stomach turn. The woman looked deeply into Valentina's eyes and spoke some words in a language she could not understand. Whatever the woman had said, Mrs. Ivanova agreed.

"Da." The old woman nodded. *"Ochee chornya."* Dark eyes.

The other children were waiting in the hallway when Valentina emerged, each of the American strangers holding one of her hands as they led her along. The children broke into song and Valentina knew the tune; she had sung it herself a few months earlier when little Ruslan, just a year and a half old himself, had been taken away:

> *Puskai prïdet pora prosit'sia*
> *Drug druga dolgo ne vidat?*
> *No serditse s serdtsem, slovno ptitsy*
> *Konechno, vstretiatsia opiat*

How swift the hour comes for our parting
No more to meet, or who knows when?
But heart with heart must come together
And someday surely meet again.

When Valentina reached the door at end of the hallway, she began to struggle against the hold of her new guardians. In five years she had rarely left the confines of the orphanage, and at this threshold the reality of her situation became clear: once she passed through the doors this time, she would never return. She fought to pull her hands away from the strangers and succeeded in slipping the grip of the man, but the woman held strong, pulling Valentina close and wrapping her in her surprisingly powerful arms.

Valentina could see that Mrs. Ivanova had stopped at the end of the hallway, remaining in the shadow of the threshold.

"Babushka . . ." the girl wailed, but the old woman just turned her head away, her features knotted in anguish.

In the end, there was nothing to be done. Valentina's effort to resist proved only that she could not win, that the forces arrayed against her were too great to overcome. Within seconds she had been carried into the backseat of a waiting car, hulking and black, and whisked away into the bright new day. Twisting free of the American woman's grip with one final effort, Valentina turned and looked back through the rear window of the car, aching inside as she watched the only home she had ever known recede into the distance and finally disappear.

ONE

Eleven years later . . .

She called the Columbia boys on her cell phone and within minutes they ambled out of the dorm together, slightly drunk already, the four of them primped and preened for a night of adventure in the clubs downtown. They looked her over, briefly entertaining the idea that she might be available to them for more than just dope, but her eyes met theirs with a look of cold denial and the thought was abandoned.

"For one-fifty I can give you eight hits," she said, marking the price up since they obviously had money and were buzzed. "E or K."

"Both," said the tall one with curly hair. "Four and four." The exchange was made and the boys headed south toward the Red Line stop at 116th. She had intended to take the subway herself, but didn't like the idea of covering the distance along-side the drunken college kids. Paying for a cab would be the smart thing, but she wasn't used to the idea of spending money on herself.

Riverside Park then, on foot. She passed through the Barnard campus and across Riverside Drive, heading all the way down to the path below the Hudson Parkway, within view of the water. She followed the route out of habit, accustomed to traveling in a group that could protect itself through unity and numbers, but this time she was alone. Barely a minute passed before she heard the footsteps behind her: two men, both heavyset, quickly closing the distance to her but then slowing down, holding thirty or forty feet back. She could feel their eyes on her. She picked up her pace but they stayed with her, maintaining the same distance, plotting the timing of their move.

Shit. She scanned the area near the path, searching furtively for a route of escape, and only then did she truly appreciate—too late—the inherent dangers of the remote route she had chosen. The light fixtures above were in bad repair, with only one meager lamp still working on the quarter-mile stretch. A high barrier of blackened stone—the original foundation of the parkway—bordered the path like the forbidding wall of a medieval castle, preventing escape. Elm trees loomed overhead, their branches obscuring the view of the path from above. Traffic noise from the parkway filled the air with an ambient hum, muting sounds that might otherwise alert the residents of nearby apartment buildings.

Don't run, she commanded herself. *Not yet.* Her instincts for self-preservation had been earned painfully, all through the years of her childhood, and now those instincts were telling her that when the moment arrived, she would be running for her life.

The stone wall came to an abrupt end, and a fork in the path offered a route uphill toward Riverside Drive, a stretch of less than a hundred yards. If she could cover the distance before the men reached her, there would surely be traffic on the road—witnesses—whose presence would force her pursuers to call off their hunt. One hundred yards. The men behind her now recognized her opportunity for escape as well and picked up their pace, closing the distance.

Run, now.

The men were surprised by her initial burst of speed. Tired, scrawny, poorly fed, wasted away by chemicals and the ruthless attrition of life on the street, she gave every appearance of the runt, the weak member of the herd prime for culling. The pursuers' eyes could not measure her heart, however, her will to survive. Without that, she would have been dead years ago. And so she raced ahead, the roadway growing closer, offering the possibility of rescue.

The men were breathing hard now, spitting curses at the unexpected effort required. Thirty yards to go, then twenty— she could almost feel their hot breath as they came up behind her but . . . she *would* make it. She knew it now. The road was just ahead and she veered suddenly to her left, shooting up through a gap in the brush off the side of the path, and the abrupt change of direction surprised her pursuers. They cursed her loudly again.

She burst out from the path, across the sidewalk and out

into the middle of the road, bright in the glow of streetlights. As she sped across the road, a dark blue sedan screeched to a stop, just inches short of running her down. The girl stood frozen, paralyzed by the shock of the close call and the fact that she recognized the car. The car door opened and the driver stepped out—a familiar face, a friend. She felt the rush of relief that came with that welcome surprise, but then she read his expression. Her spirit sank.

No smile. No sanctuary.

Atley Greer grabbed a unit from the motor pool and reached the 79th Street traffic circle a few minutes later. He veered down a service road that led south along the Hudson River, toward the Little League baseball diamonds. The area was still in shadow, the November sun having not yet risen above the buildings to the east. Greer pulled up to the edge of the second baseball diamond, where a circle of ground was marked by yellow crime scene tape. He parked his unit beside two horses—Park Police mounts—their breath fogging heavily in the cold morning air, the early stages of their winter coats just coming in.

"Morning, Detective."

"Officer Carlin." Atley gave the young uniform a nod.

"Crime Scene is on the way," Carlin added. "They're gonna send more badges once the shift turns over."

Carlin led Atley toward the crime scene, lifting the yellow tape for the detective to pass underneath. Five other park cops lingered outside the tape line, smoking, looking cold and restless, eager to get back into their warm units or back onto their waiting mounts.

The girl's body lay at the foot of a cypress tree, on her back, still fully clothed in several dark, torn layers, a worn black leather jacket on the outside. The girl had short, spiky blond hair with a streak of blue on the left side and a handful of facial piercings. Street tats peered out from under her collar shirtsleeves and she wore heavy makeup, now badly smeared. Her face was battered and swollen, a trail of dried blood running down from her nose. The girl's knuckles were scraped and bleeding, probably from fighting off her attacker. Her eyes were open, pupils of deep gray just now beginning to lose their color.

"Run it down," Atley said.

"Wallis Stoneman," answered Carlin, holding up a clear plastic evidence bag, a driver's license visible within. "Her DL was stashed between her sock and the tights underneath. It says she's twenty-three, but that didn't seem right, so I called it in. It's a good fake, maybe two or three hundred bucks on the street. According to the DMV, the information on it is legit, except for the age—she's actually sixteen. I called her name in to Real Time. The kid had a long juvie record, but no felonies, no adult court. She's listed as a runaway, with a PINS warrant out on her."

A Person In Need of Supervision warrant meant that the girl had an active file with Social Services.

A dirty red messenger bag lay several feet away from the body, open, its contents strewn about the ground; there were a few pairs of underwear that looked like dirty laundry, a striped woolen hat, cigarettes, and some scattered pieces of individually wrapped candy.

"The bag," said Greer, "it was open that way when the body was first discovered? Everything spilled out like that?"

"Yes, sir. Money and valuables, if she had any, are gone."

Greer squatted down and examined the girl's filthy fingernails, her cracked boots, her torn leggings. There was dirt behind her ears, at least a week old. The clothes hadn't been washed in at least a month. Atley could see several old scars on her forehead and across the bridge of her nose. He pushed the girl's sleeves up and found more scars and hardened contusions on the outside of her forearms—old defensive wounds. Plenty of rich kids in New York dressed like punked-out street urchins, studied in their griminess and disrepair, but this girl's body and clothes told a story of authentic hardship and, somewhere in her history, physical abuse.

"This girl is street," said Greer, looking up at Carlin. "You ever see her around?"

"Maybe," answered Carlin dubiously, "but it's hard to say for sure. A lot of them hang along Riverside Park—they all kind of look the same in their tweaker uniforms."

Greer put on a rubber glove and reached for the girl's mouth, pulling her upper lip back to see her teeth; they had begun to decay from smoking meth.

"Tweaker," Carlin repeated his diagnosis.

With his gloved hand, Greer closed the girl's eyes, then rose to his feet. He scanned the immediate area, hoping to discover any detail out of the ordinary. There was random garbage scattered throughout the baseball diamond and the surrounding woods, plus the tracks of countless runners and bicycles and Park Police horses passing over every inch of the grounds.

"We'll do the canvass when the rest from Homicide show up," Greer said.

"You going to notify in person, Detective?"

"She's local?" Greer asked, surprised. He took the ID's evidence bag from Carlin and confirmed it: the given address was on West 84th, half a block from Amsterdam Avenue. Was he wrong about the girl being street? If the address was legit, she had died not half a mile from home. Greer took out his cell phone, selected the camera function, and held the phone close to the girl's devastated face. The flash ignited brightly as the camera recorded the image.

Atley Greer badged his way past the doorman at the fashionable 84th Street address and headed toward an empty elevator car that stood open in the lobby. He pressed the button for the 27th floor, assuming that the apartment number on the dead girl's ID was correct. As the elevator doors slowly closed him in, he saw the doorman picking up the house phone at the front desk, calling ahead to alert the Stonemans that a cop was on the way.

At the 27th floor, Atley trekked a long hallway of plush, cream-colored carpet to reach the apartment at the northeast corner of the building. The apartment door was already open. An attractive, well-tended woman a few years younger than Atley—thirty-eight, maybe?—waited there in anticipation of the detective's arrival, her hands clutched tightly in front of her. Her facial expression was a familiar one to any cop; over the years, this woman had met many police officers at her door, and of course they had always been bearers of bad news. There was a sense of resignation to Mrs. Stoneman, a determination to steel herself against the next, latest wave of heartbreak.

"Mrs. Stoneman?"

"Yes," the woman answered. "What did she do now?"

"I'm Detective Greer, ma'am. 20th Precinct. Could I have a moment of your time?"

"Come in."

The woman's apartment was tastefully furnished with a mix of modern and antique furniture, fine carpets, and original artwork placed throughout. On the living room wall was a large, professionally done black-and-white portrait of Mrs. Stoneman—several years younger—with her arms wrapped around a beautiful young girl: preteen, blond, smiling happily.

Atley heard sounds from the direction of the kitchen. Someone was moving around in there.

"Is your husband at home, Mrs. Stoneman?"

"Not for nearly six years, Detective. I'm divorced. My ex-husband, Jason, lives in Virginia."

Atley was sorry to hear that—death notifications to a single parent were particularly rough, and it fell to the notifying officer to be a source of comfort. He also wondered now who the person in the kitchen was.

"And your daughter Wallis . . ."

"We call her Wally."

"When was the last time you saw her?"

Claire Stoneman hesitated, looking ashamed.

"Three and a half weeks ago. She came on a Tuesday afternoon, for a shower and to do some laundry. I fed her lunch and we spoke for a while. She left after three hours or so."

She counts time, thought Atley. Days and weeks, even hours—waiting for her daughter to return. *Shit.*

"What did the two of you talk about?"

"These days, there are very few topics that don't result in arguments between us," she answered. "We keep the discussion light, or we stay quiet with each other."

"And as far as you know, her living arrangements are . . . what?"

"I hate to imagine. I've offered many alternatives to her, none of which she will accept. She will never take more than a few dollars from me, however much I insist. She's on her own."

"At sixteen."

"If you're suggesting that I have failed her, Detective, you're right."

"You have no thoughts about where she's been staying or who she's been with?"

"No, but she hasn't been alone, thankfully. Apparently she has a few friends in . . . in her same situation." Claire paused for a moment. "I used to look for her. After she ran away. For the first few months, I would go out walking the streets to look for her and I saw her once, near here. She hadn't run very far, it turns out. She was with others. Two boys and two other girls,

I think. I wanted to call out to her, but when I tried, no sound came out. Isn't that strange?"

Greer and the woman stood in silence for a moment, she wrestling with regret, he dreading the next phase of the interview.

"What has Wally done now?" Claire Stoneman repeated her question from earlier.

Atley could see that her demeanor had changed; the woman was even more anxious now, as if sensing from Atley's behavior that this notification would be different from the others. More serious—perhaps more final.

A woman slightly younger than Mrs. Stoneman now appeared in the doorway to the kitchen—domestic help, from the look of it, with cropped hard hair and dressed in something like a maid's outfit, pale green with an apron. She did not speak, but held her ground at the threshold as if waiting for instructions from Claire.

"Mrs. Stoneman," Atley said, "this is a personal family matter, so perhaps . . ."

Claire gleaned his meaning.

"No," she said, and looked to the woman, imploring. "Johanna, please stay."

Johanna dutifully stepped over and stood by Claire as if this was not the first time she had been asked to fulfill this role. How sad, Atley thought—tragic even—for Claire Stoneman to be so completely alone in the world that she had to rely on her cleaning lady for emotional support.

"Okay," Greer said, and took a breath. "Mrs. Stoneman,

this morning a body was discovered on the southern end of Riverside Park—"

"Oh God . . ." Claire Stoneman reached out toward Johanna, clutching the woman's arm as Atley continued.

"The body was of a young girl, around your daughter's age, fitting her description and carrying your daughter's identification on her person."

"No . . ."

Claire's agony was quiet, turned inward upon itself. She made a choking, gasping sound, which she fiercely struggled to repress. She let go of Johanna and clenched her hands into white, bloodless fists, pressing them hard into her abdomen as if punishing herself. Johanna, visibly moved by Claire Stoneman's anguish, wrapped the grieving woman in her arms and held tight.

Greer reached into his pocket and pulled out his cell phone. From the menu he selected the "photo gallery" command and the young girl's death mask appeared there immediately, battered and swollen and bloody. Greer realized then that he did not have it in him to present this sickening image to Claire Stoneman.

"I want to see her," Claire finally said.

"It's really not necessary, Mrs. Stoneman," said Greer. "Your daughter has a file. It's acceptable to use fingerprints to identify a victim."

"Victim?" She looked up at Greer, searching him, imagining for the first time the specific cause of her daughter's death.

"I'm sorry, Mrs. Stoneman. I'm a homicide detective."

The mother turned away from Greer, hung her head, and wept.

Atley drove Claire Stoneman to the Kings County Hospital morgue in Brooklyn and escorted her to an observation room, where she could view her daughter's remains on a closed circuit video monitor. Once Clare grasped the situation, however, she insisted on seeing the body in person.

"Fine," the coroner's assistant agreed with an indifferent shrug.

Greer led the mother to the gurney, gave her a moment to gather herself, then pulled the blue sheet back to reveal the dead girl. She paused, her own features in a rigor of grief, then leaned in for a closer look at the girl's battered face, wiped clean of blood and debris. The mother paused there, inches from the body, for a long moment. Mrs. Stoneman reached out and gently stroked the girl's hair, sobbing silently.

"It's not fair," she whispered to the dead girl.

"Mrs. Stoneman—"

Claire turned away from the body and faced Atley, not bothering to wipe away the tears streaking down her face. "This is not my daughter," she said unequivocally. "This is not Wally."

TWO

Wally Stoneman lay on her back, waking up slowly. Morning light spilled into the huge room, illuminating the colorful mosaic on the domed ceiling fifteen feet above her: a battle scene from the Trojan War. The room was surprisingly warm, even though the heat vents had been locked shut and the night outside had been cold; the single wool blanket of Wally's bedroll had been enough. She guessed that the building's boiler room must be located in the basement level just one floor below what had once been the lobby of a mercantile bank; the marble floors of the room were always a little warm to the touch.

For her private sleeping spot, Wally had chosen the catwalk along the north wall that overlooked the bank floor. The high ground gave her privacy, plus a ringside seat for the battle scene depicted on the ceiling mosaic: there were plumed helmets and tooled breastplates, charging stallions, and, of course, heroes atop their horses, poised to fight.

Someone climbed the stairs behind her and approached along the catwalk. She could tell it was Tevin by the squeaking of his sneakers; he was less physically mature than other seventeen-year-old boys she knew, just five foot eleven, but with ungovernable size-thirteen feet that constantly scraped the ground as he walked. He wore loose army-surplus cargo pants—always—and a heavy fleece hoodie in gray.

Tevin sat down beside Wally, and she sat up in her blanket. They leaned together against the stone wall of the walkway, gazing sleepily down through the railing to the ground floor below, devoid of any furniture now except for the row of empty teller's windows along the south wall.

"Morning." Tevin yawned, his sleepy eyes still a little droopy on his handsome face. The hair on Tevin's head was shaved close on the side, with the longer top fashioned into a frohawk that—along with the smooth, cappuccino-hued skin tone of his mixed-race parentage—gave him an exotic, otherworldly look. He had long, beautiful eyelashes, almost girlish in a way that Tevin definitely was not, and the detail was something that always gave Wally some pleasure to notice.

"Hey," said Wally, smiling to herself. Having Tevin next to her was always a good start to the day.

He looked up and studied the mural on the ceiling.

"Have you figured out yet what those guys on horses have to do with banking, or New York in general?"

"I have not," Wally said. "But I like it."

"Yeah. Not everything needs a reason."

Wally gave him a look. "That is *so* wise, Tev. Thank you."

"Eat me," he answered through another yawn.

The two of them sat quietly as some busy sounds echoed up from what used to be the bank's employee break room.

"Ella found some hot chocolate in one of the cabinets," Tevin explained. "You only need water to make it. You just put it in the microwave. It's pretty grody inside but still works."

"Good."

Now more sounds rose up from downstairs: Ella giggling, cooing. Jake laughing in response, quietly—then nothing. It was often like this in the morning between Jake and Ella—if they could steal a few moments alone—and frequently at night, of course. The two of them were in some version of love, breathless and grasping. Wally didn't mind; it was their business, and it seemed to make them happy. But the closeness of the couple sometimes left Wally and Tevin feeling awkward with each other, on the outside looking in, confused about the lingering tension between the two of them and what to do about it. Wally and Tevin were . . . what? Friends and family. But . . . something more, maybe. Something yet to be explored.

"What are we doing today?" Tevin asked.

"Taking in the machines," said Wally.

"To the smoke shop?"

"Yep."

Tevin was not enthusiastic. His childhood years in Harlem, some of them spent within a block or two of the 131st Street Smoke Shop, had consisted of one domestic nightmare after another, some perpetrated by his own family and some by the city's Department of Social Services. Harlem was bad memories for him and nothing else.

"You don't need to come," said Wally. "I'm fine with Jake and Ella."

"No, I'm going." But Tevin seemed distracted.

"What?" Wally asked.

"We should try to find Sophie," he finally said.

Wally sighed, impatient. "No."

"It's already two weeks now," said Tevin.

"We can't trust her," said Wally. "We can hope she gets her shit together, Tev, but she can't come back with us."

"What if it was me?" He forced the issue. "What if I was the one in trouble?"

"We'd help."

"Why me and not her?"

"Because you've earned it," Wally answered. "We didn't let go of Sophie, Tevin. She let go of us."

Before heading uptown, Wally and Ella went through their regular makeup ritual. Standing side by side in front of the bathroom mirror, they began with fingernail polish, layering dark purple gloss without removing the previous layer, creating a chipped and trashy effect that—weirdly—made them feel out of control but in control, all at the same time.

The two girls were almost physical opposites. Wally was fair-skinned with short blond hair and a prominent bone structure that came with her Russian heritage. Ella, in contrast, was petite and delicate-featured, an Amerasian with sleek black hair that cascaded down below her narrow shoulders. Their clothing styles had merged over time, though, to the point where they shared almost identical emo/scene kid mash-up ensembles: multiple torn leggings under tartan skirts or cutoff shorts, plus layered tops in whatever clashing materials and colors they could throw together from the bargain bins at the back of the Salvation Army shop, twenty-five cents per item or free, depending on which manager was working the floor. When the clothes got too dirty, they usually just tossed them and went back to the bins for fresh pieces. It was cheaper than laundry soap.

Once their nails were done, the girls started in on their eyes. They brushed a dense, crusty layer of mascara on their eyelashes, the application complete only when it was so thick that their lashes would hold no more and residue black crumbs flaked down onto the skin just below their eyes. They looked into the mirror, appraising the results—vampy, tragic, morning after. They never got bored of this routine.

"Twins," declared Ella, satisfied. "Princesses of the dark."

Jake and Tevin were mostly patient with the girls' primping process, waiting without complaint until the girls emerged from the bathroom. All four of them pitched in to move two large cardboard boxes out through the back door—the emergency exit—and into the narrow service walkway that stood between their building and the next. They loaded the boxes into a beat-up D'Agostino's shopping cart that they had hidden in the walkway behind one of the Dumpsters. As with all their exits and entries into the building, this process had to be carried out quickly, and only when they were certain no one was watching. The empty bank had turned out to be a good squat for Wally and her crew, and they didn't want to spoil it by alerting any meddlesome neighbors to their presence.

"It's a long way to the smoke shop," said Tevin as they moved west on 87th Street. "We could take a minivan cab."

"No problem," Wally said. "We're every cabbie's dream fare."

"Here's how we do it," said Tevin with a sly grin. "The rest of us hide, with the boxes and all, and you stand out there by yourself, flashing your legs and whatnot. That'll get 'em to stop."

"You can go ahead and stop thinkin' about my *whatnot*," Wally said, and Tevin laughed.

"I say fuck the smoke shop," Jake said, in a harsher tone than he probably intended.

Wally faced Jake. "What's your deal?"

"Panama gives me the goddamn creeps."

"He hustles." Wally shrugged. "What do you expect?"

"There's that guy I know in the Bronx—Cedric. I bet he'll give us more."

"That's too far," Wally said, "and Panama has cell cards to trade."

Wally's words seemed to leave no room for debate.

"Cedric is a good guy," Jake said, pausing to kick a dirty old pizza box off the sidewalk before continuing. "And I already told him we'd sell him the machines."

Wally shook her head and gave Jake a critical look.

"You shouldn't have done that," she said.

"Well, fuck it. I did."

"Huh," Wally said, trying to stay cool and evenhanded, mostly just feeling annoyed. She didn't want to embarrass Jake. "Then we'll make it up to him later, whatever next thing we have to trade. But today we're headed to Panama's."

"It's bullshit that you decide everything, Wally," Jake answered, pissy. "I'm sick of it."

Tevin and Ella stood by stoically, silently enduring Jake's rebellious outburst as a ritual that they had witnessed many times before.

"Okay, Jake. Screw it," Wally said. "You want to change things up, I could use the vacation. You take a few weeks running things. Figure out where our money is coming from without panhandling all day like every other skel on the street and where we're gonna crash so we don't have to go down into the tunnels and how to keep from getting ripped off when we have something to sell. Just make sure you have a good plan, Jake, 'cause if you remember, there was a time when we all followed Nick, and he almost led us off a damn cliff."

No one spoke for a while. Wally looked away from Jake, instinctively knowing that he needed some space. Jake shuffled around a bit, trying to walk off some of his steam. He kicked the pizza box again; it splashed up some puddle water as it skidded through the gutter.

Wally had always been drawn to guys who were on the sensitive side—brainy, even—and Jake was the opposite of that.

Everything was physical with him. Jake had the chiseled features of the all-American high school jock he had once been, with stormy blue eyes that were sometimes hidden behind what he called his "Samson hair"—dirty blond, unkempt, and grown way out from the military cut his coaches back in Ohio had always insisted on. He had maintained some of his linebacker/wrestler physique—sneaking in sets of push-ups and pull-ups and crunches when he could—and he even wore a letterman's jacket, purple wool fleece with white leather sleeves and a big varsity letter P on the front, that he had found on a Salvation Army rack for a dollar seventy-five.

Jake had no idea what high school the P stood for, but it didn't seem to matter. Wally and the crew could see that the simple article of clothing made Jake feel like himself, a call back to the warm, secure life he led before his parents and sister were all killed in a car wreck, leaving him to the custody of cousins who resented his presence in their home and never stopped letting him know it.

Jake had solved the problem for them by hitchhiking his way out of Ohio, never looking back as he made a solo journey to New York. He had mostly adjusted to life on the streets—and to Wally's authority within the crew—but sometimes there were flashes of his old jock mentality, some push-back against the idea of a girl making decisions for him.

"Whatever," Jake finally said, swallowing his objections. "Let's just go."

He started pushing the cart toward Riverside Park, muscling it on a straight course despite its loud, bent front wheel.

Ella walked beside him—always beside Jake—with little danc-
ing steps mixed into her stride, humming quietly to herself as
she moved along, following Jake's lead like a faithful moon in
orbit. Seeing them move together like that, in harmony, made
Wally envious. She had the authority and respect that she had
earned by seizing control of the crew from Nick, but with that
came a certain distance between herself and the others. At least
that's how she felt at times like these.

As if sensing her feelings of isolation, Tevin moved closely
into step beside her, giving her a playful little hip check that
bumped her off stride.

"It's a fine day," Tevin said. "A roof over our heads, money
coming in. We're doing good."

"Yeah, okay," Wally said, feeling only halfway convinced.

"I'm hungry," said Ella from up ahead.

"Surprise surprise," said Tevin.

Ella was *always* hungry. Like a hummingbird, she constantly needed to refuel her high-revving motor.

"We could dip into the emergency money for Mitey Fine, if
you guys want," Wally said.

"Yay," said Ella, and squeezed Jake's arm; the food truck
in Harlem served Jake's favorite fried chicken, and eating there
would clearly be a peace offering from Wally. Jake thought
about it—reluctant at first—but then he looked back at Wally
and gave her a small nod.

The crew made it to the top of Riverside Park in under
an hour and, with just twenty minutes more of walking, they
were well into Harlem. They found the Mitey Fine food truck

and stopped for the promised chicken; Ella ordered three large pieces herself and began carefully nibbling away the slightly burnt crust, savoring each greasy, spicy bite before wolfing down the meat. When Wally dug into the hidden pocket in her shoulder bag to pay for the food—the emergency backup money—she was immediately surprised and pissed off at what she *didn't* find inside: there had been a hundred dollars in cash hidden there, but now there was only forty. Worse, Wally's fake ID—the expensive one that listed her as twenty-three years old—was also missing.

"Shit!" she said, angry with herself for letting it happen.

"What?" Jake asked, looking concerned; it was not normal for the crew to see Wally caught off guard, which she obviously had been.

"My ID is gone, and most of the emergency money."

"How?" asked Tevin. "When's the last time you went in there?"

Wally tried to remember. "Two weeks?"

No one had to say it: two weeks ago was right around the time they had sent Sophie away.

For Wally, the ID was the bigger loss. The expensive fake was like a visa to the young adult attractions in the city—bars, mainly, or maybe the occasional rave if she could scrape the cover charge together—and the times when she hadn't had a good ID she had often felt confined, even claustrophobic. Of course, there were plenty of places where underage kids could talk or sneak their way in, but to Wally that felt too much like asking permission. And she hated that. *Hated.*

"Shit," said Jake. "Fuckin' Sophie."

Tevin opened his mouth as if to object, but changed his mind. There was no defense for the girl.

The crew moved on. Another ten minutes and they were within shouting distance of the 131st Street Smoke Shop, on the corner of Fredrick Douglass Boulevard, where by chance they met up with Panama himself; he was lumbering his way back to the shop, carrying a big greasy bag from the Harlem Papaya, containing at least three hot dogs piled high with onions and peppers and dripping with mustard.

"Little sister," Panama greeted Wally in his low growl, ignoring the others in the crew but taking notice of the two large boxes in their shopping cart.

The man called Panama was large—wide and tall with enormous, powerful hands—and wore short-sleeved Hawaiian-themed shirts year-round, today with a layer of gray, long-sleeved thermals underneath, his long hair woven in a thick braid that ran halfway down the length of his back. Panama stepped toward the shopping cart and, glancing around first in case anyone might be observing him, looked inside both of the cardboard boxes.

"Espresso machines?" he asked Wally.

"Brand new," she confirmed. "Swiss. A complete station, two servers, molded copper casing—that's an upgrade. Retail is seven thousand."

"*Retail.*" Panama snorted, as if offended by the very concept.

"We'll take fifteen hundred," said Wally.

Another snort from Panama.

"Ha. We gonna see," he said. "They can take 'em round back."

The group walked together the final distance to the smoke shop, where Jake, Ella, and Tevin peeled off, wheeling the shopping cart toward an open garage door at the west end of the shop where two of Panama's men waited, ready to take delivery of the machines.

Wally followed Panama into the small smoke shop and all the way through to a back room office, where assorted stolen goods crowded the space in stacks that reached nearly to the ceiling. Panama sat down at a cluttered desk and opened his greasy bag, purring at the sight of the unwrapped hot dogs. Wally sat down on a small folding chair opposite the desk. A second chair, empty beside her, reminded Wally that Sophie had sat beside Wally during most of these meetings. It was Sophie, with three years on the street and all the experience that came with that, who first introduced Wally to Panama.

The big man set his food aside for the moment, picked up his cell phone, and began calling. He carried on brief discussions with several unnamed parties, then set down the phone and picked up his first hot dog.

"Three hundred," he said.

"Hell no," said Wally. "Looks like I'll have to shop 'em around."

"Yeah, guess so," Panama said, speaking through a full mouth. "If you don't mind walkin'. Course, they already in my garage."

"You go to six hundred, that's fair," said Wally, feeling the pressure of having the cash and ID stolen, needing to make up for that loss for both herself and the crew.

Panama didn't reply to the offer. "Where you jack 'em, anyways?"

Wally just shrugged. A restaurant on Columbus Avenue had shut its doors after only a few months in business; Wally and the others had cased the place as a possible crash site and found the espresso machines still sitting inside the gutted shop, unopened. Panama didn't need to know any of that, but this was a chance for Wally to use a strategy she had learned from Nick, a way to avoid getting ripped off by scum like Panama: always dangle the next deal, even if it was total bullshit.

"I can't tell you where I got them," she said, "but there might be more, if you can move these."

"Oh, Panama can *move* 'em. . . ."

"Something else," Wally said, changing the subject. "I lost my good ID, the one your guy Train cut for me last summer."

Panama set down his hot dog, wiped his mouth on his sleeve, and shook his head. "My man Train is unavailable for the next twelve to eighteen months. I got a few good places I use. There a place up in Queens, an old Russian shop in Brighton Beach is pretty good, or these Nigerians in Jersey City . . ."

"Brighton is good."

From memory, Panama dictated an address in Brighton Beach, and Wally jotted it down. She would need to skim at least two hundred dollars off the sale of the espresso machines to pay for a new ID.

"I can't go lower than five hundred on the machines," Wally finally said. "I'd look bad to my crew."

Panama considered this with a skeptical look on his face.

"You take some cards in trade?" he suggested. Panama had a connection for cards that added minutes to prepaid cell phones, something about scamming FEMA disaster relief. Whenever there was a natural disaster in the country, the relief agency passed out prepaid cell phones to victims, plus cards to recharge the minutes. Within days, Panama would have a new shipment of the phones and cards off the black market. He would sell or trade them to Wally and the crew for twenty cents on the dollar, which they could turn around for double on the street.

"Yeah, cards could be part of it . . ." Wally tentatively agreed, already starting to feel the buzz of closing a profitable deal.

"Tell you what . . ." Panama reached inside his desk drawer and pulled a small box with the logo of a cell phone manufacturer on the side. He opened the box and pulled out a shiny new smart phone with a large touch screen in front. He passed the phone to Wally, along with its small portable charger.

"I can be generous, go three hundred on the 'spresso machines," Panama said. "Plus some phone cards that you can bump to two hundred on the street, if you hustle. And you keep that smart phone, thrown in. That a clone, got a thousand minutes on it. You can sell that, get a hundred easy. If you want to keep it, though, I maybe got some business opportunities comin' up in the next few weeks, might be right for you. This way we can be in touch."

"What kind of opportunities are we talking about?"

"Don't worry 'bout it. Good money. I gonna call you when we ready to go."

When Wally emerged from the smoke shop, she found the others waiting on a stoop two doors up.

"We got three hundred cash," Wally said to the group.

"What?" Jake protested. "That's bullshit."

"Take it easy," Wally said. "That's plus phone cards that we can sell for maybe two hundred downtown. All together that's a good score."

They nodded in agreement, though Jake still looked a little ticked off.

"Here's the thing, though," Wally said. "I gotta replace my ID. So that's two hundred of the cash, right there."

The others didn't question Wally's need to replace the lost ID, and they knew the turnover on the cards would be pretty easy. Wally dug into her pockets and pulled out the wad of tens and twenties that Panama had paid her. She kept two hundred and passed the rest to the others, along with the packet of phone cards.

"You guys get started on selling the cards, okay?" Wally said.

"Sure. Where are you headed?" Tevin asked.

"To get the ID. And some personal stuff."

The others didn't object. By now they were used to the boundaries that Wally had erected around her personal history. Everyone in the crew had their own secrets, and they respected hers.

The four of them walked to the subway station at 134th Street and grabbed the C train downtown. As they rode, Jake brought out his MP3 player and, on cue, the others each plugged their own earbuds into the "splitter" that allowed them to listen in on the mix together. The first song was a techno-house remix with a sort of hypnotic effect that almost caused them to miss their transfer at Columbus Circle. Jake realized it first and nudged the others; Tevin, Ella, and Jake waved good-bye to Wally as they hopped off and headed to the 3 train that would take them to Times Square.

Wally stayed on the C. As the train pulled out of the station, leaving her crew behind, Wally sighed, feeling relieved, and even spread out on the bench a little, expanding her personal space. Her crew relied on her leadership so much that Wally sometimes felt trapped under the weight of their expectations. When she was out in the city by herself, Wally reveled in the sense of freedom and possibility. More than once, Wally had imagined where she might end up if, one day, she stepped onto a train alone and allowed herself to keep riding, all the way to the end of the line and beyond.

Wally got off the train at the Port Authority and walked to Harmony House, a resource center for homeless youth on 41st Street. She went immediately to the women's washroom—an impersonal, almost industrial space—and signed in to use a shower. The attendant gave her a clean towel and the key to an individual, prefab plastic stall, fairly clean but water-stained yellow from years of heavy use; the tight space reeked of the bleach that the Harmony staff used every night to fight back the crud. Wally eagerly stripped down and stepped under the strong, hot stream of water, the steam quickly filling up the stall. She soaped and rinsed herself twice, imagining the stink of Panama's oniony hot dog breath washing off her and swirling away down the drain. When the soaping was done, she stood under the hot stream, unmoving, soaking up the heat until the six-minute timer ran out and the water turned off on its own.

Wally dried off, grabbed a clean pair of underwear from her shoulder bag, and put the rest of her clothes back on. At the communal row of sinks, six of them side by side on a sagging fiberglass counter, Wally stood with several other girls—all around her age—brushing their teeth with the plastic-wrapped brushes provided by Harmony and putting on makeup in front of polished metal mirrors that had graffiti messages scratched into them: *Rico does Juanie right, MS13, Sandra is a bitch.* There were dispensers on the wall with free pads, which the girls grabbed by the fistful and stuffed in their bags. From one of the toilet stalls, there came the sounds of a girl quietly weeping. No one paid any attention.

One or two of the girls at the sinks looked fairly healthy and put-together; when they finished with their routines, they could probably pass for regular teens, girls with homes and families and futures. The rest were showing the signs of their difficult street lives. Wally brushed and dried her hair under a hot blower and tied it back in a stub of a ponytail—all her shoulder-length hair would allow—and checked herself out in the mirror. Which one was she, hopeful or hopeless? Staring back at her was a reasonably healthy girl of sixteen, acceptably clean and strong and well fed. Wally could still pass for happy, and she felt encouraged.

Wally's mascara had washed off in the shower. She pulled out her small makeup bag and began with her eyelashes, striving for the same dark, trashy look that she and Ella had so happily perfected. Soon Wally noticed another one of the girls at the sinks was staring at her intently. The girl was big and heavy— she had at least forty pounds on Wally—with a neglected look, her hair greasy, her face clouded over. One of the hopeless.

"What the fuck are you looking at?" Wally said. Hesitation was weakness.

"You ain't buy that," the girl said in a Bronx sneer, nodding at the tube of mascara Wally was applying.

The girl was right. Claire had given it to Wally at the end of their most recent visit, stuffing the tube into Wally's bag as she walked out the door. Chanel. The one tube was worth more than all the other girls' possessions combined, and then some. The girl had to believe that Wally had stolen it.

Wally knew how it would go.

You want it? Come get it, she would say. The girl might hesitate, caught off guard by Wally's aggression, but she wouldn't be able to back down in front of the other girls. She would make a move, and Wally would turn her body to the side, crouching down low into an athletic position as she had been taught at the dojo. When the heavy girl was within range, Wally would throw her left fist forward in a feint, then slam her right fist up into the girl's solar plexus. The girl would drop to the floor of the bathroom, shocked by the terrible pain, panicked and struggling to breathe, afraid that she might be dying.

Imagining the outcome did not make Wally feel strong, only sad for the clueless, desperate girl standing before her.

"Take it," Wally said, tossing the mascara to the girl.

The tube of Chanel was never Wally's anyway, not really. She and Ella found their own makeup in dollar store bargain bins, and that was just fine with Wally. She grabbed her bag and left the bathroom, brushing past the startled-looking girl who now clasped a fancy new tube of mascara in her hand. In the hallway, Wally headed for the exit and was almost out the door when she heard her name called out from behind. She turned to find Lois Chao, one of the Harmony House caseworkers, walking quickly down the hall toward her, waving a small piece of paper in the air.

"Hey, Wally," Lois said, a bit breathless when she caught up with Wally. "How are you doing?"

"I'm good, Lois," Wally answered curtly, hoping to discourage her from offering a pep talk of some kind.

"You look like you're in a hurry," Lois said, reading Wally exactly, "but I told this detective I would give you this. So here."

Wally took the business card from Lois. The name on it was Detective Atley Greer, NYPD, 20th Precinct. Lois watched for Wally's reaction and saw the look of concern.

"It didn't seem like an emergency or anything," Lois reassured her. "He said he just was looking for information on something. You want to use my office phone?"

"No need. Thanks, Lois."

"Okay. Stay safe, Wally." Lois turned away and headed back down the hallway.

Wally's first impulse was to ignore the message—what good could possibly come from calling a cop?—but her curiosity was piqued, and she remembered that her new smart phone was set to block her number, so there was no risk to her. Wally dialed the number on Detective Greer's business card. The phone rang three times on the other end, then went to voice mail.

"Uh . . . hi," Wally spoke into the cell phone. "This is Wallis Stoneman, returning your . . . I mean, responding to the message you left for me at Harmony House. I'm not clear what this is about but . . . maybe I'll try you back later."

Wally hung up, suddenly feeling lame for making the call. *Maybe I'll try you back later?* Her own words sounded weak to her, and that pissed Wally off. There were a bunch of reasons a New York City cop might want to speak with her, and an emergency situation with Claire was far down on that list. Wally put the detective out of her mind and headed back to the Port Authority, where she boarded the Q train for Brighton Beach.

THREE

Everyone in Wally's crew knew she was adopted, but Ella was the first one she'd told about it. On a very hot day in July, Wally and Ella had walked in cutoffs and tank tops to the lake in Central Park, where they climbed down the Hernshead rock to the lakeshore. They took off their shoes and soaked their feet in the cool but slightly algae green water.

"I wasn't cut out for this," Wally said, fanning herself, the fair skin of her cheeks flushed pink.

"For what?"

"Heat. I'm from Russia," Wally said matter-of-factly. "It's always cold and gray there. As far as I know."

"Your parents are Russian?"

"Yeah. Well . . . no. Not my American parents." Wally hesitated a bit, suddenly regretting that she'd brought up the subject at all.

"You mean, you're adopted?"

"Yeah."

"From Russia?"

"Uh-huh."

Ella thought about this for a moment.

"You don't know who your actual parents are?"

"No."

Wally looked at her friend and could see that her imagination was already working overtime. Magical thinking was Ella's specialty.

"Cool . . ." Ella finally said.

"You think so?"

"Oh yeah. You could be, like, secretly a Russian princess or something."

"Hmm. I don't think they make those anymore."

Wally leaned back against the rocks and closed her eyes, happy to let the subject drop. She had spent a lot of time questioning her origins—had once been obsessed with it, even—but dwelling on those issues had never done her any good. The questions that had been swirling around in her brain for the past six or seven years—*Who am I? Where do I belong?*—had never been answered, and the resulting frustration had played a large role in her rift with Claire, her adoptive mother.

"Did you always know?" Ella asked, not ready to let go of the subject. "I mean, your parents told you about being adopted, right?"

Wally sat up straight again. She sighed a little, anxious. It seemed like she and Ella were going to have this talk whether she wanted to or not, but at least it was happening with someone she trusted. The fact that she had been adopted had always felt to Wally like something she needed to defend, as if the world might use that one detail of her history to explain and condemn who she was.

"Yeah, they told me where I came from. I mean . . . I always knew it, in a general sort of way, but it was just an idea, you know? I was a kid and I didn't really think about it."

"You're not a kid now."

Wally looked out over the lake, remembering, figuring she knew the exact moment when her childhood had ended.

"When I was nine or ten," Wally said, "I was watching TV after school. Bored, channel surfing, you know. Waiting for dinner. And I stopped on this story in the local news about a fire in a restaurant or something. In that place, Brighton Beach . . ."

"Out by Coney?"

"Right. Brighton Beach is totally Russian. On the TV news you could see it, the store signs in both Russian and English, people in the background shouting in Russian as the firemen were hosing down half the block. And I couldn't stop looking at all of it. It was totally strange but familiar at the same time, if that makes any sense at all."

"But you'd never been there? Freaky."

"I tried talking to my mom about it, but she got all weird. It was so obvious that she'd be happy for me to just forget that there was that other part of my life. That made me really mad. It was five years—half of my life, by then—and she acted like the whole idea of it was radioactive or something."

"I bet she was scared," Ella said.

The suggestion surprised Wally. "Scared of what?"

"Losing you, I guess. Like you'd decide you weren't really hers."

Wally thought about this for a moment, and the idea of it seemed so simple and true. Of course Claire had been terrified. How had Wally never figured that out on her own? Ella had done it in thirty seconds.

"You're scary, Ella," Wally said.

"True dat."

And isn't that what happened in the end, Wally thought, Claire had lost her? Or maybe that had yet to be decided. Wally didn't know.

"My mother wanted me to stop thinking about the Russian stuff—maybe because she was scared, like you said—but there was no way, you know? The idea of it kept swirling around in my head. There were people in the building who knew me back then, when I first arrived in the States, so I asked them what I was like."

Ella and the others knew Wally came from a wealthy home, but until then she had never shared any real specifics about that part of her life. She told Ella about talking to Raoul, the young doorman who had stood in the front lobby her entire life, and Johanna, who was the super's wife and did almost everything around the house for the Stonemans. The two of them had said basically the same thing: Wally was a totally Russian little kid when she arrived, but she had adapted quickly to her new life; within two or three months she was as American as any kid in the building. Johanna remembered—sympathetically, Wally could tell—a Russian song that little five-year-old Wally would sing to herself in the bathtub, but Johanna said that before long it was replaced with other nursery rhymes in English, and that was that.

"It was like a forced amnesia," Wally said. "That's what my parents really wanted, to wipe out everything that came before."

"Harsh."

"Yeah. When I started figuring that stuff out, it was the beginning of bad times between me and my mother. I guess it was catching, too, because my parents ended up splitting around then."

Wally felt herself getting sad, but she wasn't about to make a big deal about it. Ella had lived most of her life in Queens welfare hotels, the only child of a messed-up drunk of a mother. Her father was serving twenty years in Rahway for armed robbery. Ella had only met him once—on prison visitation when she was seven—and he had told her never to come back. The mother's boyfriend of ten years—a vulgar and violent housing cop from Inwood—would come after Ella hard every night, after the mother had drunk herself into a stupor. He had a small camera that he used to take pictures of Ella and of himself raping her, animal that he was. For Ella it got to the point where she would shut out the pain and just stare at the ceiling, counting the flashes, waiting for them to stop. The most she ever counted was forty-seven.

Compared to that, Wally knew her own history was a carnival ride, and it burned her to think of Ella being so viciously abused. Maybe one day, she and the crew should drop in on the mother's boyfriend and teach him something about accountability. The thought cheered Wally up a little.

"Where's your dad?" Ella asked. "I mean, your adopted father."

"He moved back to Virginia," Wally said, "where he's from. For a while he called a lot and came back here for some visits, but then he got caught up in his life down there. He has a new wife and two new kids—their own. The fact is, he and I aren't really even related. We were thrown together, just an accident like a car wreck. We don't share blood. It's over."

Wally had shocked herself with the coldness in her voice, but obviously Ella could see her friend's pain.

"Don't be so sure," Ella said. "You and I don't share blood, but you're my sister forever."

The two girls shared a look.

"You're not gonna make me cry, bitch," Wally said.

Ella smiled. "What happened after?"

Wally sighed. "Meanness, awfulness. Years of it. By me, by my mom." Wally paused. "I guess I needed someone to blame for Dad leaving, so Mom took the hit for that. It was really bad. It felt like everything in my life was a lie . . . just bullshit, a made-up story. And my mom wouldn't hear any of it, wouldn't talk about it. I think she actually wanted to be closer to me, but at the same time couldn't stop shutting me out. Weird. And I was fucking up in so many ways. At school, everywhere. That went on for a long time. I was spending half my time out on the street when I first met Nick, and then you guys. . . ."

Ella smiled broadly at this.

"Yay," she said, with the kind of glimmer in her eye that she usually reserved for cupcakes and Jake.

"Yeah," Wally said, and managed a smile for Ella. "Yay for us."

For a few minutes, the two of them splashed their toes gently in the water of the lake, cooling down just a little as the summer sun edged lower in the sky.

"And it all kind of started because of that random TV news story you saw about Brighton Beach . . ."

"Yeah," Wally said. "I guess that's right."

"Did you ever actually go there?"

"No. I never did."

Wally rode the Q train to Brighton Beach, a journey of over fifty minutes. She exited the Brighton station—feeling a little anxious—and headed toward the address Panama had given her, the source for good IDs. It was mid-afternoon on a warm day, so the shops on the Avenue were doing brisk business. There were neighborhood grocers stocked with specialty food items from Russia, stores carrying Russian music and books, and several boutiques featuring women's fashions noticeably different from clothing sold in American stores—shinier, with vaguely foreign colors and fabrics. It was a weird experience for Wally. This was her first visit to Brighton Beach, and the place seemed strange and exciting and familiar all at the same time.

She strolled the Avenue, gazing through café windows as some of the locals peered back at her over the tops of Russian language newspapers. She drifted anonymously around the park near the beach, where groups of Russian-speaking men smoked, argued loudly, and played chess. She stopped to watch a pickup basketball game played by teenage boys who looked like they could be her distant cousins. She felt an inexplicable urge to call out to them as if they were old friends she hadn't seen in years, and imagined what it would be like if they turned to see her and smiled with happy recognition.

Wally moved along with the local women as they strolled through an open-air produce market; two old women argued over something, and she understood, somehow, that they were talking about tomatoes. It was only the occasional word that came to her among the flood of an otherwise impenetrable language, but . . . it still felt to Wally as if a hidden part of her mind had been awakened.

After exploring the area for twenty minutes or so, Wally found the shop she was looking for: the sign above the address read MISZIC & SONS. The shop's window signs read CHECKS CASHED, FAX CENTER, NOTARY PUBLIC, and P.O. BOXES AVAILABLE, with Russian translations—in Cyrillic—beneath them. A squat, barrel-chested man seemed to be serving some sort of security function for the shop; he stood outside the front door, regarding every passerby with suspicion. He gave Wally a quick look but otherwise ignored her as she entered.

Inside, there were a few copy machines to one side and crowded shelves of inventory, mostly office supplies. At the back of the shop was a wide counter with a man on duty wearing a green woolen cardigan two sizes too big for his bony shoulders. He was probably no older than sixty, but he looked thirty years older than that, with permanent, dark bags sagging under his eyes, his fingers deeply stained with nicotine. A wall of locked mailboxes stood behind him.

"What you want?" he asked Wally, barely interested.

Wally reached into her pocket and pulled out her legitimate ID—listing her as sixteen years old—and placed it on the counter. She wanted her new, fake ID to contain all the same information except her date of birth.

As the old man looked down at the details on the ID, an odd change in his expression took place. Before Wally could tell him what she was there for, he spoke.

"Wallis Stoneman," he said, reading the name with a thick Slavic accent.

"Yeah," Wally answered, starting to feel anxious; hearing her name spoken aloud by this stranger was frightening in a way that she could not explain.

"*Da*," he said, looking up and examining the features of Wally's face. "I see it. Now you are supposed to tell me your real name."

"Like you said," Wally answered, confused. "It's Wallis Stoneman."

"*Nyet*," the man said.

"Uh . . . yeah, it is," she said. "Maybe I'm in the wrong place. I was told you could—"

"You are in right place, which you know," the old man said with a calm self-assuredness that Wally found annoying.

"I don't know what you want me to say," Wally said, frustrated.

The old man sighed.

"And again," he said, in Russian this time, "I need for you to answer this old man. *A teper skazhi mnye kak tebya po-nastoy-aschemu zovut?*"

Wally almost answered, as if her tongue had a mind of its own. It was an eerie, frightening sensation.

"I'm sorry, but . . ." she said.

"*Dvortchka,*" responded the old man, insistent. "Tell me your name."

Wally felt her face flush with anger; she hated more than anything to be patronized by adults, and something in the old man's tone sounded to her like smugness. When she looked at him again, however, she saw something else in his expression—what was it? Empathy? Concern? Who was this old man and why would he give any kind of a shit about her? Wally was about to repeat her name, stubbornly, but something else happened instead; another answer came to her, a name that seemed to have a will all its own—a will to be spoken—and Wally was unable to resist the force of it.

"Valentina." Wally spoke quietly, with a flawless Russian accent.

"The valiant," said the old man, nodding. "Yes?"

"Valentina Mayakova," Wally said, bewildered by the sounds as they tumbled out from deep inside her. It was a name she had not spoken or heard in eleven years. She suddenly had the feeling that by saying the name out loud, she had betrayed a trust—that at some time deep in her past she had promised to hold the name inside and keep it there.

"*Da,*" the old man said. "Valentina Mayakova."

He rose from his stool and hobbled toward a door behind the counter. He was gone for perhaps a minute, leaving Wally behind, confused. She wanted more than anything to run—her fight-or-flight instincts were telling her to get out of the store immediately—but she could not bring herself to leave before the strange scenario had played itself out. So she waited for only a minute—which felt like an hour. As she stood in confused silence, the security man entered the store from the street and stood near the door, the full weight of his cold gaze directed toward her. Wally wondered what he saw when he looked at her; his expression told her nothing.

The old man finally returned, carrying a large padded envelope. He placed the envelope on the counter and slid it toward Wally. *Wallis Stoneman* was written on the outside and beneath it two more words written in Cyrillic letters. Wally knew— somehow—that her Russian name was written there. There were brownish-green mildew marks on most of the envelope.

"Is for you," the old man said. "In some years past, there was flooding from pipes. Maybe some damage to your things. Cannot be helped."

Again, Wally opened her mouth to speak, but had no words. She slowly reached out and took the envelope, then turned and walked toward the front door of the shop, stuffing the envelope in her shoulder bag as she went. From behind, the old man spoke, and she turned to hear his words.

"Be careful, *vnuchenka*," he said. "This world is a wilderness."

Wally nodded absently and turned back toward the door.

Disoriented, she passed by the security man as she pushed her way out of the shop, making it halfway down the block before she felt faint and realized that she had stopped breathing. She leaned against a store window for a moment, forcing air into her lungs. Wally reached into her bag and pulled out the envelope.

"What the hell?" she said out loud, breathlessly, to herself. How had this happened? She had traveled to this random shop for a new ID and instead come into possession of . . . what? Something with her Russian name written on it; a name that even Wally herself didn't realize she remembered. What were the odds against such a coincidence? It seemed impossible.

The old man had been right about water damage: two edges of the envelope showed dark water stains where the paper had been immersed for some time. The flap was tied closed with string; Wally unwound the string and began to tear open the flap, but then suddenly stopped herself.

Wally had a sense that she was being watched. She looked up quickly and caught a flash of movement on the sidewalk, thirty yards behind her. As a man ducked into a shop doorway for cover, she thought it might be the burly security man from the shop she had just been in.

Wally stuffed the envelope back in her shoulder bag and moved on down the street. She ducked into a large and busy women's clothing store called Notions, its sign written in both English and Russian. Wally began to peruse the racks as casually as she could manage, given the level of adrenaline now surging through her. As she continued to browse, two stern sales-women—mother and daughter, by the looks of them—watched her every move with suspicion, ignoring the six or seven other customers in the store. Wally quickly picked out two blouses and headed toward the aisle of changing booths behind a curtain at the rear of the store. As she approached the curtain, the younger saleswoman followed her, taking note of the blouses.

"Two items," the woman said to Wally in a flinty, Slavic tone.

Wally nodded and stepped into the back room where the changing booths were. At the rear wall there was an exit with a sign that read EMERGENCY EXIT ONLY—ALARM WILL SOUND. Without hesitation, Wally reared back and kicked at the bar lock on the exit door, blowing it wide open and sounding the alarm. Before anyone in the store out front could react, Wally ducked into one of the changing booths, shut the door, and stepped up onto the stool inside so that her feet would not be visible from outside the booth.

Soon came the sounds of the saleswomen, rushing into the changing area and yammering excitedly in Russian, cursing Wally as they spotted the wide-open emergency exit and the alleyway beyond. From the booth, Wally could hear the volume of the women's voices diminish as they stepped out into the back alley, looking for her.

Then Wally heard another set of footsteps—heavier, male—approaching hurriedly from the shop floor and passing through the changing area, also headed for the emergency exit. As the heavy steps passed her booth, Wally opened the booth door just a crack and confirmed the identity of her pursuer: it *was* the security man from the copy shop. He wore an angry expression as he passed through the back room and disappeared through the emergency exit. Wally emerged from the changing booth, leaving the blouses behind as she walked through to the front of the store and out onto the street again.

Wally made her way back to the Brighton subway station, using streets off the Avenue and moving quickly, but not so quickly as to attract attention. She hoped that a train would be ready to go—and it was, the last few passengers trickling on board just as the doors closed. As the train pulled away, Wally glanced back to the platform where the security man, breathless and enraged, had reached the train moments too late. His eyes scanned the windows of the departing subway cars, but Wally leaned behind the solid wall at the end of the car to avoid detection.

She moved toward the back of the last car, choosing a window seat away from the other passengers. She took a moment to catch her breath and collect herself, feeling calmer with every rattle of the elevated subway car that carried her back into Manhattan. She peered into her shoulder bag, where the envelope waited, still unopened.

It was twilight then, and the car's fluorescent panels flickered off and on with every irregular bump on the train tracks below. Wally reached into her bag and pulled out the mildew-stained envelope. She tore through the flap and pulled out two items: a water-damaged manila file folder that was about a quarter of an inch thick and stuffed with documents and a separate brown envelope, small and sealed closed with something rolling around loose inside it.

Wally first opened the small brown envelope, tearing the flap open, and out rolled what looked like a pebble—a single pea-sized stone. On close examination, the "pebble" had a rough outside surface with the slightest hint of reflection coming off it, a faint green glitter. Wally returned the stone to the small envelope, folding it in half twice and then stuffing it in the secure inside pocket of her jacket.

She opened the second item—the manila folder—and saw the extent of the water damage: a collection of official-looking papers, yellowed with age, were almost completely ruined. The ink of the documents had bled away and soaked through all the pages so all that remained were a few scattered words—Russian, Cyrillic—which at first glance meant nothing to Wally. A separate item was a stapled set of papers that resembled an old photocopy of a newspaper article, with only a few sentences still legible.

The file included a single photograph that had survived well. It looked to be a surveillance photo, taken from above, of a man walking across a city street. He was sturdily built, with dark hair and sideburns styled for another era—the eighties, maybe—with dark aviator sunglasses perched on a strong nose. Something about the way the man carried himself was unsettling. Wally looked closely at the man's face—slightly blurred from the poor quality of the security camera image—but his features meant nothing to her.

The final item in the file looked to be completely undamaged. It was a standard-sized mailing envelope, a light blue color that might have been part of a personalized stationery set. There was a faint scent to the envelope. Wally held it to her nose and breathed in, deciding it was an Old World smell, floral and musky. The name *Wally* was written on the outside of the envelope in a woman's handwriting. Wally paused at the last moment before opening the envelope, suddenly feeling a twinge of dread, but then carefully slit open the flap. She pulled out a note, in English, written in the same woman's handwriting as the outside of the envelope. The beginning of the note read *My dearest Valentina*. Skipping down to the bottom of the page, Wally read the closing of the letter: *With my deepest love for you always, Yalena Mayakova.*

"Yalena Mayakova," Wally mouthed the name to herself quietly, in shock and disbelief. At the Ditmas Avenue station, the train dipped down into its dark underground tunnel; by the flickering lights of the train, Wally began to read the letter from her Russian mother.

FOUR

Wally made it back to the bank by dusk. She felt terrible inside and must have looked that way too, judging by Tevin's reaction when he saw her.

"Did'ja see a ghost or something?" Tevin asked, concerned.

Wally had no answer. She was overwhelmed by the events of the afternoon, and the long subway ride home from Brighton Beach had not helped. It had been too much empty time for her to sit alone, struggling to process the events that had the potential to turn her life upside down. She hated appearing vulnerable in front of her crew, but in this situation there was nothing she could do about it.

"Obviously she needs food," said Ella.

Tevin went out and returned fifteen minutes later with two pizzas and a twelve-pack of Dr. Pepper. The crew allowed Wally to eat and relax until she was ready to talk. She forced herself to eat one slice and drink two sodas. The combination of grease, sugar, and caffeine eventually worked for her, and within half an hour Wally felt at least partially revived. She pulled the big padded envelope out of her bag and spread all its contents across the warm marble floor, neatly arranging them in the same order she had found them. The crew knelt on the floor beside her and inspected the items.

First, of course, was the letter. Ella picked it up and, just as she was about to read it out loud, stopped herself and looked to Wally.

"Is it okay?" Ella asked.

Wally nodded yes, actually looking forward to hearing out loud the words that had been crashing around in her head for almost two hours; maybe they would be clearer this way.

"*My Dearest Valentina*," Ella began reading, then gave Wally a questioning look. "Valentina?"

"That's me," Wally said. "My Russian name."

Though all of Wally's crew knew about her adoption, they hadn't heard her other name, obviously.

"You never told us that," Ella said.

"It's new to me, too," Wally said. "Kind of."

"Whoa . . ." Jake said.

Ella began again, this time with a greater sense of gravity: "*My Dearest Valentina. My greatest hope has been that one day, you and I would face each other, embrace each other, as mother and daughter. If this letter has come to you, that dream will never come true. I am gone. Writing this, my heart breaks . . .*"

Ella choked up a little and she paused her reading. She gave Wally a sympathetic look.

"You okay?" Tevin asked.

"I'm okay," Wally said.

Ella continued: *"There are so many things I would like to express to you. I fear that you could never forgive me for abandoning you to this world, but I would happily endure your anger just to be with you, for the chance to explain the choices I have made in my life. You can be sure that I have never stopped loving you, that I have forever hoped for the day that we could finally be together and safe. Perhaps in another life. I am so very sorry."*

Ella paused again, a bit overwhelmed, then went on. *"Certainly you are curious about where you are from and who you were born to be. I have included documents here that will help you to understand all things. It is your right to know why our lives were fated to be separate. Please accept the knowledge here as complete, and search no further. Jeopardy and heartache await you if you do not believe this warning. Please, my beautiful Valentina, accept the miracle of your life and go forward in peace and happiness. With my deepest love for you always, Yalena Mayakova."*

The four of them sat in silence for a moment, considering the contents of the note. Each of the others glanced at Wally to see how she was responding. Though she had already read the note on the subway, the emotional impact of the words was still powerful. She felt stricken by the confusing combination of excitement and doubt.

"Holy shit," said Tevin.

"Where the hell did you get this?" Jake asked.

Wally recounted the events of her afternoon. Tevin, Jake, and Ella took a while to process the story.

"You just walked in there for an ID," Tevin said, "and an old guy you've never seen before gave you this?"

"And his security guy tried to follow me. I don't know why. I don't know anything."

"This is totally out there, Wally," Jake said.

"Yeah," she agreed.

"I'll tell you one thing," Tevin said. "I'd bet the letter is wrong. Your mother—the person who wrote this—the letter makes it sound like she's dead, but I think she's actually not."

"How do you figure that?" Wally challenged him, though she had already reached that same hopeful conclusion herself.

"The envelope has your name on it, so you were meant to get it at some point, right?"

"So . . ." Wally agreed.

"So the way she's written it . . ." Tevin picked up the note and scanned it for the sentence he was thinking about. "Here: *If this letter has come to you, that dream will never come true. I am gone.* See? You're supposed to get this only after she's dead. But you ended up in that shop today by accident, so you got it before you were supposed to."

"How do you know when she was supposed to get it, Tev?" Jake said, always the skeptic. "You're just guessing. We don't know how or when any of this should have happened. And all that shit in there looks pretty old. Anything could have happened to this Yalena woman in that time."

"But what's wrong with Wally believing it?" Ella protested, giving Jake a nudge.

"If it's bullshit, I'd say there's plenty wrong," Jake said.

It was a strange experience for Wally to sit in on this debate, listening to the crew debate the question without her. Part of her wanted to jump in and insist that Yalena was alive, but she didn't know the truth of it any more than the others did.

"I'd bet something else . . ." Tevin said.

"This oughta be good," Jake sneered.

"It is," Tevin said. "I think Yalena is somewhere nearby. Or she was when she wrote this letter."

"Why would you say that?" Wally asked.

"First of all," Tevin said, "how else did the envelope end up in the U.S.? In Brighton Beach?"

"And look what she called you," Ella said, obviously agreeing with Tevin. *Beautiful Valentina.* She wrote that. She's seen you, Wally. How beautiful you are."

"*Please.* Every mother says that about every kid," Jake insisted, but Wally could feel those words hang darkly over the crew—even Jake. Each of them had painful histories with their own parents; kind and loving words were never guaranteed.

Ella shook off the gloom of the moment, defying Jake's cynicism.

"She's alive and she's been watching over you." Ella spoke those words in a whisper, infusing them with a romantic, storybook essence. "That's what I think."

Magical Ella, thought Wally, though she wanted to believe it herself.

"But if you're right," Wally said calmly, determined to be rational, "and she was near, why wouldn't she have contacted me?"

"It's got something to do with the guy in the picture," said Tevin.

They all looked again at the photograph that had been included in the package: the man in aviator sunglasses, crossing an unnamed street in what could be most any metropolitan area in the world. He looked to be about forty years old, though there was no telling how long ago the photo itself had been taken. He had the solid build of a physical laborer and his dark hair was cropped close. Looking at the photograph again now, Wally noticed a dark patch of skin on his neck, partially obscured by the collar of his shirt. A tattoo.

"What about him?" Wally said.

"He's a scary one," said Ella.

"There's something else here," said Tevin, pointing at the underside of the photograph.

Wally took the photo from Tevin and found a faded notation on the underside, in pencil, written in the same hand as the letter from Yalena Mayakova. *"This is a most dangerous man,"* Wally read the note aloud, a chill passing through her as the words crossed her lips. *"He has driven us apart. If you see him, you must run."*

Hours later, Wally lay awake in her sleeping space high above the bank floor, staring up at the dark ceiling. As cars passed by outside, their headlights swept into the bank and flickered on the Trojan War mosaic, briefly giving life to the ancient heroes before leaving them dark again.

Was it possible, Wally wondered, to want something your entire life—desperately—without consciously knowing it? That was how she felt when she first read the line in her mother's note: *My greatest hope has been that you and I would one day embrace as mother and daughter.* Wally shared that furious need for completeness, now more than ever. All her life Wally had felt abandoned, had assumed that she had been an unwanted child tossed aside by unloving parents. Now it seemed—if the letter from her mother could be believed—that the opposite was true. Little Wally—little *Valentina*—had been cherished.

Something else about the Brighton event occurred to her, but only many hours later: when speaking her Russian name aloud—Valentina—Wally had pronounced the *V* sound somewhere between a *V* and a *W*, which she knew was common among some native speakers of Russian. Claire had never really explained why she had chosen the name Wallis, but now it seemed self-evident: Wally was to Wallis as Vally was to Valentina. With the mixed pronunciation of the *W* and *V*, the nicknames were virtually the same in both languages. Claire had chosen the name Wallis as a way of connecting Wally's Russian and American identities, possibly to help give the five-year-old Wally a sense of continuity, easing her abrupt transition from one culture to another. It was a small thing, maybe, but all these years later Wally was grateful for the gesture, and grateful for the reminder that whatever their differences, Claire did love Wally, did care for her in every way she was able.

Wally heard Tevin's footsteps approach on the dark walk-way. He sat down beside her, cross-legged.

"You okay?" he asked. "Long day . . ."

"Yeah." Wally managed a wry chuckle. "It's all so crazy."

"You think it's real? The letter and everything?"

"I don't know," Wally said at first, then, "I want it to be."

"What're you gonna do?"

"I'm going to look for her," Wally said. Just saying the words made her feel warm . . . not quite happy, exactly, but strong.

"Cool," Tevin said. "We'll all look together."

Wally smiled. "Thanks, Tev."

"Maybe we even need it."

"What do you mean?"

He shrugged. "After a while, having something to run away from ain't enough. I think you gotta have something to run toward too. You ever feel that?"

"Yeah, I do," Wally said, and she did. She'd been feeling it herself for some time but never thought it out loud. She and the crew had worked out how to survive on their own, so what were they supposed to do next?

Wally could feel that Tevin had something to say, something important, but didn't know how to begin. Wally searched his eyes, but Tevin broke her gaze. The moment passed.

"G'night," he said. He rose and headed back down the walkway.

"'Night, Tev," Wally said after him, and all at once Wally was exhausted. She wrapped herself tightly inside her wool and flannel bedroll and lay on her back, gazing up at the dark ceiling. A memory crept in slowly, vaguely . . . maybe sparked by the Russians conversations she had heard in Brighton that day. There had been a song, a lullaby. She had once known it by heart, but now it lurked in the distance, teasing her. Where had she heard it? What were the words? The idea of summoning them frightened her, but the impulse was irresistible. She moved her lips and the lyrics stumbled out uncertainly, *"Puskai prïdet pora prosit'sia. Drug druga . . ."*

Wally stopped after those few words, frustrated that she was unable to remember more and left clueless about what the lyrics meant. In the end, she was lulled to sleep not by the song, but by her own exhaustion.

First thing the next morning—Monday—Wally came down from her walkway and woke the others, kneeling down on the floor of the bank beside them.

"I left something out before," she said, and brought out the smaller envelope with the odd, glittery stone inside. Tevin, Jake, and Ella looked at the unremarkable stone on her hand.

"I don't get it," said Ella.

Wally shrugged. "Neither do I, but there's gotta be a reason she put this in with all the rest, right?"

"I guess," said Tevin. "Yeah. Gotta be."

"Anyway," said Wally, "it's a place to start."

The others agreed sleepily. Once they'd gotten their shit halfway together, they took the A train south to the Drop-In Center on 30th Street and 8th Avenue, where they got free coffee and scrambled eggs, then hiked back uptown on Avenue of the Americas to 47th Street. Looking east, they saw the Manhattan Diamond District spread out before them, dozens of gem dealers stretching for blocks. To Wally and the others, all the shops looked the same.

"Where do we start?" she asked.

Ella pointed to a storefront that read HAMLISCH BROTHERS.

"I have always preferred Hamlisch Brothers," said Ella, dramatically raising her hand to her forehead as if she was about to execute a royal swoon. "I simply will NOT wear jewels from any other."

The others agreed and headed for Ella's preferred diamond merchant, ignoring the suspicious looks they received from a klatch of Hasidic merchants gathered on the sidewalk out front, sipping coffee and gearing up for a day of commerce.

Wally tried to open the door of the Hamlisch Brothers shop, but it was locked. At the counter inside, the young proprietor looked up toward the door, appraising Wally and the others and apparently not liking what he saw. He shook his head no.

"Asshole!" Jake said, insulted on behalf of all of them. He grabbed the door handle and rattled it loudly, sneering at the guy. "Open the damn door!"

Wally saw the merchant reach under the counter—for a gun? An alarm button?—and she pulled Jake back.

"Easy, big dog," she said.

"Screw him," said Jake. "There are a hundred other shops here."

"And all their doors will be locked, like his."

Jake heard her and reluctantly shrugged in agreement.

Wally reached into her jacket pocket and pulled out the small brown envelope from the Brighton file. She opened the flap and let the single stone roll out into her hand, then rapped lightly on the glass door. When the merchant looked up again, Wally held the stone up between her thumb and forefinger for him to see. The man squinted, then moved to the door for a closer look.

"Please," Wally said, just loud enough for him to hear from behind the thick glass door.

The merchant considered for a moment, taking another dubious look at the crew, but then made a choice. He opened the door and let the crew in. Once inside, the crew was taken aback by the sheer mass of riches on display, protected by thick glass cases.

"Holy shit . . ." said Jake, and nudged Tevin. "Am I right?"

"Damn," Tevin said in a half whisper. "It's like a museum or somethin'."

Ella pointed out a necklace with a massive emerald mounted on its pendant, surrounded by a halo of identically cut diamonds.

"Was that thing made for me, or what?" she said, without irony.

Facing the merchant at the main counter, Wally held on to the stone. The man was obviously intrigued, looking eager to get his hands on the object of curiosity.

"You appraise stones, right?" Wally asked.

"I do not buy stolen things," he said in a Hasidic accent, almost contemptuous. But his eyes never left the stone.

"I didn't say anything about selling," Wally said to the man evenly. "I asked about appraising."

"Yes, fine," he said, and held out his hand. Wally reached out to place the stone in his palm but at the last moment hesitated—a little taunt—and he gave her an impatient look. She smiled, and finally passed it to him. He put a jeweler's loupe to his eye and held the stone up for close inspection.

"Huh," he said.

The merchant took one more quick, suspicious look at the crew—as if to confirm that they weren't stealing from him while he was distracted—then stepped away from the counter, taking the stone with him to a small, closet-sized work space in the corner of the room. There, he turned on a grinding stone and set to work on the pea-sized stone. The crew waited in expectant silence until the jeweler shut down the grinder and returned to the counter. He now wore a little smile on his face—the smile of an enthusiast who has just solved an interesting puzzle—and looked at Wally with new eyes, reappraising *her* now, as if trying to reckon the provenance of a mysterious gem.

"May I ask how you obtained this stone?" he asked Wally.

"My grandmother left it to me," Wally answered flatly.

The jeweler gave Wally an arch look.

"What you have here," said the merchant, "is a gemstone called alexandrite, quite rare. Named for Tsar Alexander II when it was first discovered in the Ural Mountains in Russia. When this stone is cut, it will be of green color during the day and red at night. Green and red, the colors of Russian royalty.

You see? Some consider it the national stone of Russia. They are quite beautiful when finished properly."

"What else can you tell us about it?" Wally asked, starting to get excited—it felt like her search really *was* beginning.

"They are produced by small output mines mostly, and often the stones from a particular mine will have a signature composition. There is a barely noticeable thread of amber color through this stone. If I am correct, it is from the Lemya Mine, closed now for over twenty years. I am quite sure there have been no Lemya stones on the open market for almost that long, which is unusual," he said. "Very unusual."

"So it's valuable?" asked Wally.

"Yes. I would be happy to take this stone off your hands."

"How valuable, exactly?" asked Jake, obviously surprised. His skepticism about the contents of the Brighton Beach envelope had made him assume that the stone would be worthless.

The merchant leaned against his counter, rubbing his beard, thinking. He went to a laptop computer at the back counter and typed in some inquiries, his eyes searching the results, then returned to Wally.

"One thousand dollars per carat," he said. "Eight thousand."

Eight thousand dollars! Tevin, Ella, and Jake shot each other secret, excited looks, barely able to contain themselves. Ella swallowed a squeal before it reached her lips.

For her part, Wally wasn't really thinking about the impressive dollar number. She hesitated, wondering if selling the stone would be some sort of betrayal. Wally had just received this gift from her mother . . . was she really supposed to just let it go?

Tevin leaned in close, gently gripping Wally's arm. It felt good to have him there, the warmth of his presence beside her. She felt less alone with her decision.

"Whatever you think is right," he said. "But she wanted you to use it, I think, and you'll need money to find her."

Wally thought about this, and reluctantly agreed. She turned back to the jeweler.

"And you'll write down what you know about the alexandrite for me?" Wally asked. Now the jeweler beamed, giving Wally a gratified smile as she exhibited interest in the stone beyond its monetary value.

"Well done," he said. "Yes. I will write it down."

They made the swap, gemstone for cash. The payment was in hundred-dollar notes, and the crew stared wide-eyed at the growing stack of clean new bills as the broker casually dealt them like cards from a deck. For a business transaction of this size, the dealer needed information about Wally, the seller. All of the appropriate paperwork was completed in short order; the merchant jotted down several details about the stone on his shop's letterhead estimate form, and Wally pocketed the note along with the cash. Finally, the jeweler held out his hand for Wally to take.

"I am Isaac Hamlisch," he said.

"Thank you, Mr. Hamlisch," said Wally, feeling good as she shook the man's hand.

"You're welcome, miss," he answered, not even bothering

to verify the name Wally had entered on the provenance forms in front of him.

"And a good day to you, sir," Ella added, affecting her aristocratic tone and giving Hamlisch a curtsy.

Isaac Hamlisch gave Ella a gracious bow of his head, and the four youths exited the shop.

Isaac Hamlisch watched after the four kids as they reached the sidewalk and burst into a victory dance, all of them together jumping up and down with delight, their cheers loud enough to reach him inside the shop.

Isaac smiled, happy to make them happy, and then sat down in front of his laptop computer. He opened his Internet browser and went directly to an international gemstone exchange site, where he entered his user name and password. He clicked over to the open market page and began entering the exact description of his new offering. The gem's recent provenance was listed as "private family estate." With some further research on the site, Isaac confirmed the amber markings within the stone's crystal as characteristic of the Lemya Mine, a small placer mining operation in the northern Ural Mountains—long since closed—and Isaac added that information to the stone's description.

Within milliseconds, all this information would be officially posted on the exchange site, where the stone would appear as "offered for sale or exchange" to thousands of brokers, all over the world.

FIVE

Five hours out of Krasnoyarsk, it had been more than a hundred miles since Tiger had seen any sign of human life. The stolen Benz kept good purchase on the icy road, steam bellowing from its exhaust as it consumed the distance at a hundred and twenty klicks. The gray glow of predawn produced just enough light to reveal an endless landscape of featureless permafrost on either side of the two-lane road. When the sun finally did rise, it would hover low over the horizon for no more than three hours before yielding again the leaden darkness of Siberian winter.

Tiger saw a hint of the compound in the far distance. It was almost time. He wondered if Klesko would even know him, nearly twelve years gone by. He flipped down the sun visor and regarded himself in the small vanity mirror. Seventeen years old only but with the look of a grown man, his maturity and strength already had been proved countless times on the streets of Piter. His eyes were the same deep gray as they had always been, of course, and his thick black hair poured down to his shoulders, just as he had worn it as a child. Klesko would know him . . . if Klesko still knew himself. Twelve years in ITK-61 was a long time to count, and any man could lose his mind in that boundless, frigid abyss.

Half a klick away from the compound, Tiger slowed the Benz and approached at a non-threatening pace. ITK-61 consisted of two cell blocks—one completely empty and dark now—a guardhouse, and two towers. There had once been a stone wall surrounding the compound, but that had largely been eroded by the elements. Three layers of razor wire fence served as the perimeter, but the condemned men within were imprisoned by something far more forbidding: three hundred miles of icy, desolate wilderness and, beyond that, a world that no longer had any place for them. Tiger knew there were only eight surviving prisoners, all at least thirty years older than Klesko, and six resident guards who certainly had been assigned there as punishment.

Tiger pulled to a stop outside the front gate and got out of the car, leaving the engine running. An armed guard inside the wire had stepped to the gate and waited there, his eyes never leaving the young visitor but his gun still holstered. Tiger pulled on his heavy leather car coat as he approached.

"Klesko," he said.

The guard considered the request and waited. Tiger produced a thick wad of bills from the chest pocket of his coat, American dollars, and passed them through the wire. The guard took the bills and clumsily shuffled through them with his gloved hands, counting. He turned and disappeared into the nearest cell block, emerging a minute later with the prisoner, urging the shuffling man along with a swift, painful boot to his hamstrings.

At the first sight of Klesko, Tiger's heart sank. Time, isolation, and brutal confinement had taken their toll on the man, looking as if he had aged two years for every one on the calendar. Gray beard, face creased by exposure and hardship. Klesko had his bed blankets wrapped around him against the bitter cold. On his feet he wore a ragged pair of old boots, three sizes too large, with several layers of rags underneath, wound around his feet in lieu of socks. His breathing seemed labored, uneven.

All at once, Tiger was unsure of his plan, unsure whether he should have come at all. The stories he had heard about Klesko depicted a man of supreme strength and determination, a man who would rather die than give an inch of ground. Stories of fighting his way up through the ranks in Piter and holding point on border runs into Bulgaria and Slovenia, striking fear into the hearts of the local militia. Where was that man now? Everything about *this* Alexei Klesko—the one standing before him now—seemed defeated.

Klesko raised his eyes and stared through the razor wire perimeter. There was a long moment without recognition at first; then it came upon him, his eyes darting over Tiger's features, cataloging and comparing, testing them against an image in his mind of the boy, five years old. Twelve years gone.

"*Tigr . . .*"

Tiger just nodded.

Klesko stood silent and motionless, his eyes still studying the young man before him. His mind raced with questions, with possibilities. With the guard still hovering nearby, the two men spoke in English.

"How much did he take?" Klesko asked. "The guard."

"Five hundred, U.S.," answered Tiger.

Klesko snorted his disgust. *"Hooi morzhoviy,"* he spat the curse.

Tiger could see something emerging behind the man's eyes now, a flicker of life as his mind began to work again. Klesko's back even straightened—just a little—as his eyes scanned the yard around him.

"A stone has surfaced," said Tiger, feeling proud that he could bring this news and wanting Klesko to feel that pride in him also. He watched for Klesko's reaction and was not disappointed; the man's eyes locked on him now, intensely, searching for confirmation that the news was true.

Tiger nodded. It was true.

Klesko was quiet for a moment, and Tiger realized that he was calming himself, controlling his excitement. The moment was everything Tiger had hoped for.

"One only?" Klesko asked with outward calm.

"One," answered Tiger. "In America."

Klesko nodded, absorbing the information.

"These stones," he said, "they are a legacy, yes?"

"Da."

"For you. They belong to you. Understand?"

"Yes," Tiger agreed. "They are mine."

Klesko studied Tiger, as if looking for a sign of something. Resolve? Rage?

"You deserve less?" Klesko asked. "Less than what is yours?"

"No."

Klesko nodded, still unsure. "You have papers?"

"Yes," Tiger answered. "Arrangements have been made."

"Money?" asked Klesko.

"Some."

Klesko nodded.

"Good," he said, meeting Tiger's eyes once more before turning and walking away from the wire. Tiger turned away as well, as if returning to his car, but after a few steps he suddenly turned back toward the perimeter and in a flash his hand was out of his coat pocket, holding a gun. He hurled the weapon into a high arc over the razor wire barriers. Klesko looked up and saw the gun tumbling toward him through the cold air, a beautiful new Pernach.

Klesko threw off his blankets and reached out his hand, finding the grip of the machine pistol in mid-air. He spun toward the stunned guard and within a fraction of a second the Pernach's automatic blasts ripped through the man's throat, decapitating him. Klesko saw the gate guard turn and move toward him, the terrified man now flailing for the sidearm that he had probably not removed from its holster in five years. The delay was fatal; Klesko fired on him, spraying a lethal auto-blast of bullets across the guard's chest.

Just that quickly, Tiger's doubts were answered. The Alexei

Klesko of legend—*of Tiger's boyhood dreams*—had been a dormant spirit all these years, laying low and feigning defeat, waiting for an opportunity to emerge again. Now he was back. Tiger's heart thrummed as he watched Klesko rip a key chain free from the guard's belt and step calmly to the front gate. Klesko used the key to trip the locks and then kicked loose the latch on the counterweight. The weight dropped, drawing down on the pulley and swinging the prison's main gate wide open.

In an instant Tiger was inside the compound, a machine pistol in each hand. Even at his young age, he had already been a street soldier with the Dobriks for years, and he was well prepared for this moment. He charged toward the guardhouse, where two more guards had just emerged, scrambling to lock and load their weapons. Tiger cut them down.

Four dead. Two more guards remained.

Machine gun fire erupted from the nearest tower, strafing the ground at their feet as Klesko and Tiger sought cover behind the corner of the guardhouse.

"Cover," Klesko said—speaking in Russian now—and dashed alone out into the open yard.

Tiger covered Klesko's move by blasting the tower with automatic rounds. Klesko reached the opposite side of the yard, where the prison trucks were parked, and jumped behind the wheel of the nearest vehicle. He cranked the starter but it sputtered, resisting. Now gunfire hit the truck from above, and the bullets ripped down through the roof of the cab in a line, ending with one round tearing into the outside of Klesko's thigh. He growled in pain but continued working the starter until the truck's engine finally roared to life. Klesko immediately threw the gearbox into reverse and slammed his foot down on the accelerator. The truck raced backward, crashing into the tower's support legs with a loud *crack!* The legs bent under the weight of the tower shed, and within seconds the tower reeled and toppled onto the yard with a thunderous crunch, blasting apart and spilling the two remaining guards onto the icy ground, their bodies now broken. They tried to crawl for cover but Tiger was already poised over them with his guns freshly loaded. With a final auto-blast from Tiger's weapons, the last of the guards were dead.

Klesko retrieved a set of keys from one of the fallen guards and turned away from the carnage, ignoring his own bloody bullet wound as he limped across the yard, Tiger staying with him as Klesko entered his old cell block. They opened the cell of Dal Yaminski, enemy of the state, thirty-year resident of ITK-61 and, other than Klesko, the youngest of the inmates.

Yaminski put up no resistance as Klesko herded him out into the passage and into Klesko's own cell. Tiger was shocked at the sight of the space, filthy and cramped and hopeless, only a few spare boards nailed over the open window to fight back the fierce cold. Years spent here would be a living hell; Tiger wondered what kind of damage the experience would do to a man, what kind of father he had been left with.

Klesko shoved Yaminski down onto the rotten old mattress on the floor and, without hesitation, shot the man between the eyes.

Tiger understood. When the prison officials arrived later, Klesko wanted them to find a body in his cell, preferably one that would be difficult to identify. Tiger pulled a lighter from his pocket and lit the mattress in several places. Within seconds the flames began to consume the corpse.

Tiger and Klesko departed the cell and moved through the rest of the block, opening all the doors to release the remaining prisoners. Most hesitated to leave their cells, clearly afraid. Tiger hoped they would eventually begin to disperse from the prison grounds, further confusing the work of the territorial police when they eventually arrived on the scene.

"Not men anymore," Klesko said to Tiger, shaking his head in disgust. Tiger saw Klesko lose focus for a moment, as if forgetting the job at hand. The man's eyes drifted past the fence, to the empty, frozen wasteland beyond.

"Too long in here," Tiger said, his words bringing Klesko's attention back. "They can't imagine freedom."

"*Da,*" Klesko said, then barked, "Move or burn!" He waved his gun in the direction of the prisoners; as smoke from the mattress fire began to fill the block, even the most feeble of them began to run outside and scatter.

Tiger and Klesko left the cell block behind them and walked calmly out through the open prison gate. They slid into Tiger's waiting car—its engine still running—and drove away, Tiger steering them westward along the barren, icy road. The sight of ITK-61 retreated behind them, a column of black smoke rising up into the sky as Klesko's old cell block began to burn in earnest.

"You are ready?" Klesko asked Tiger as they raced onward.

They were headed for a landing strip near the shore of the Kara Sea and from there, in a matter of days, to America.

"*Da, otyets,*" answered Tiger. Yes, Father.

SIX

It was just after six in the evening when Detective Atley Greer arrived at the Central Park West address where Claire Stoneman—apparently a high-end real estate agent—was showing one of her properties. A doorman escorted Atley to a private elevator, swiping his security card to allow Atley access. The elevator climbed thirty floors in eerie silence, finally opening onto the plush, carpeted entranceway of the building's penthouse apartment. Atley found Claire Stoneman there, looking different than she had at their first meeting, seven days earlier. She seemed very professional and well put together now, dressed in an expensive blue-black suit, her hair recently coiffed, stylish but conservative.

Her look matched the setting perfectly: a ten-thousand-square-foot penthouse apartment, directly overlooking Central

Park. The floors were dark bamboo parquet, waxed and polished to a rich, exotic gleam. The great room was two stories
high, its outside wall made entirely of glass, stretching from
floor to ceiling, offering a clear panoramic view of Central Park.
Atley had wondered how Claire Stoneman—a single mother—
could afford the affluent lifestyle he had observed at her own
apartment, and now he understood: the realtor's commission
on a topflight property like this one would be huge.

"Thank you for meeting me here, Detective Greer," Claire
said as she stepped forward to shake his hand. "I've already had
four clients to see this home today, and I haven't been able to
get away once."

"No problem," said Atley. Claire took a deep breath and
steeled herself, out of habit. "You have some news. . . ."

"Just an update," said Atley. "It's a week since we found
the victim in Riverside Park. We've identified her as Sophia
Manetti. Does that name mean anything to you?"

"I'm afraid not. I never met any of Wally's friends—if that's
what the girl was—so whether or not they knew each other, I
couldn't say."

"So far, we don't have much on her," said Atley. "She was
a habitual drug user—a long record of arrests for methamphet-
amine—but we don't have much else to go on at this point.
Her autopsy revealed scars and broken bones that had healed
on their own, over a long period of time. The result of serious
abuse from an early age. Unfortunately, this is common among
the street kids."

"Are you going to ask me if Wally was abused, Detective?"

"No. I'm confident that's not the situation with her."

Claire gave him the slightest nod as a gesture of thanks.

"The girl was frequently seen in the company of your daughter," Atley went on. "Up until several weeks ago, that is, but lately Sophia had been on her own. I made an effort to contact Wallis, in case she might have some information. She called me once, last Thursday, and left a message on my cell phone."

Atley saw Claire's ears prick up at this news, and suddenly he was regretful that he didn't have more to tell her about her daughter.

"But she hasn't contacted me beyond that," he continued. "I can tell you that she sounded completely fine in her voice message. I've waited for her to call me again, but to be frank . . . I doubt reaching out to a cop will rank high on her priority list."

"How did you locate her, Detective?"

"There are a few places where young people in your daughter's situation will appear from time to time. Wallis dropped in at the Harmony House in Midtown last week, and one of the counselors there passed her my card."

Claire was silent for a moment, deep in thought.

"You haven't made much progress, then . . . with the Manetti girl's case? What was her name?"

"Sophia," Atley said. "People call her Sophie, on the street. Unfortunately, most of our leads have gone cold. Our best shot is to have someone come forward with information to trade, and there's a pretty good chance of that. We just don't know if that will happen tomorrow or a year from now."

"If you would keep me posted on her case, I would appreciate it. I realize the girl and I have no real connection, but . . ."

"I understand," said Greer, and he did. The victim was not Mrs. Stoneman's daughter, but she could have been.

SEVEN

It had been a strange week for the crew, beginning with Wally's encounter in Brighton Beach and then their visit all together to the Hamlisch Brothers shop. There had been skepticism about the contents of the Brighton Beach file—on Jake's part especially—but the value of the alexandrite stone had gone a long way toward convincing them that the contents of the file were the real thing. Of course, the specialness of the stone raised more questions than it answered. Why had Yalena included the stone with the Brighton Beach file? Was it just a gift for Wally, or did the stone have some significance beyond its use as currency? Wally had no idea.

Eight thousand dollars. Eighty Benjamins, crisp and clean, far more than any of them had ever seen in one place. Wally was anxious to get started on her search, but the opportunity to spoil her friends was irresistible. Unlike Wally, the others in the crew had led lives full of sadness and violence and deprivation, and Wally now had the means to make them feel special. She decided to put off her quest for just a few days; the four of them would have a weekend full of indulgence.

The surprise was, spending money was harder for the crew than they imagined it could be. They needed almost nothing, day to day, and owning things just slowed them down. Jake and Tevin had ridiculously campaigned for a Wii video game console, and the girls humored them enough to make the trip to an electronics store on Broadway to check it out.

"What are we supposed to do with one of these?" Ella asked as they stood in the video game demo space of the Midtown Best Buy. "Lug it from squat to squat?"

"That's what shopping carts are for," Jake said.

"Actually, no it's not. And that screen is like seven feet across."

Wally stood by and let them duke it out—that was always half the fun, anyway. Ella's common sense won out, of course, and the guys had ended up just playing the demo machine for a couple of hours until a beefy pair of security guards suggested that it was time to move on.

The four of them did make some purchases. Ella had been coveting a pair of shiny new combat boots, and a trip downtown to a military surplus store fixed that, also netting a few thermal layers for everyone's outfits. The girls refreshed their supply of mascara and trashy nail polish. They passed by a western wear store, which Tevin and Jake could not resist. They went inside and both bought real cowboy hats—Stetsons. They made it half a block down the street before Jake saw his own real world reflection in a store window.

"Oh man! I look like a douche!" he howled his buyer's remorse out loud, ignoring the looks of amused passersby.

"Me too!" Tevin had to agree. "That had to be some kinda trick mirror in the store. We were robbed."

"Why didn't you two say anything?" Jake asked the girls with an accusatory look.

"I think you both look great," Wally said with a straight face, but then her eyes met Ella's and they burst out laughing.

"You guys suck," Jake said.

The guys went back and returned the hats to a testy sales-clerk. At a motorcycle-chic boutique in the Village, Ella bought a good-looking leather vest and Jake bought a studded leather belt by the same label. At an expensive outdoor supply shop, Tevin got a stylish messenger bag with reflecting straps. Wally picked up a colorful striped watch cap, very warm, but her big-gest gift came from seeing the glee in her friends' faces as they treated themselves.

They saw a couple of bad 3-D movies and ate like pigs, four meals each day, until even Ella seemed to lose interest. They went ice skating at Rockefeller, which was fun but insanely crowded. By Sunday afternoon, when the weekend of splurg-ing was starting to feel anticlimactic, Wally had an inspiration; they jumped in a cab and headed for Madison Square Garden.

"The Knicks?" Tevin guessed, hopeful.

"Nope." Wally kept them in suspense.

They reached the Garden and Wally led them to the ticket

booth, where a video screen was playing a preview of the Cirque du Soleil show called *KÀ*, which seemed to be about futuristic space pirates. Wally had good memories of their performance called *O*, which Claire and Jason had treated her to for her eighth birthday.

"Oh, hell no," Jake said. "Nothing with guys in tights."

"Trust me," Wally said, and bought four good seats.

The show was mesmerizing. Jake's complaining stopped from the first explosive moment of gravity-defying action, and the staging of the show was unlike anything they had seen before, better than any special effects fantasy film because it was actually happening right in front of them. Even the corny outfits—lots of colorful jockstraps and feathers—seemed appropriate. By the time they walked out of the theater, the four of them were smiling and feeling as though their weekend had been perfect. Wally was grateful for how well things had ended; the next morning her energy would be focused squarely on the search for Yalena, and she was counting on the help of her friends.

Early Monday morning, Wally turned her attention once again to the contents of the Brighton Beach file. She was determined, this time, to keep her emotional responses to the items in check and try to view the file with scientific objectivity. As the others looked on, she laid the items out on the floor of the lobby and went over each piece closely, disappointed again by their terrible condition. In many cases the bad quality was due to water damage, but not all: some of the older documents had faded so badly that they were illegible. Most were in Russian anyway, and although she could afford to hire a translator, she doubted the ancient documents would have much relevance in the search for her mother. If her interpretation of the letter was correct, the contents of the file were meant to fill in blanks in Wally's own history, not help locate Yalena.

Wally came to the two stapled pages that looked like a photocopied newspaper article. "There's stuff still legible here."

"That name . . ." said Tevin, reading over Wally's shoulder. A partial line was still clear and un-smeared on the page, revealing what looked like most of a name: -*amin Hatch*. "I bet that first name is Benjamin. Benjamin Hatch."

"Hold on a second . . ." said Jake, and he disappeared out the emergency exit, returning a few seconds later with a stack of newspapers tied together with string, probably bound for the recycling Dumpster. Jake ripped through the twine—his athlete's muscles kicking in—and went through the pile, pulling out one example of each local paper. "We don't know if the article is from a New York paper, but we can find out."

"Right," said Wally. "Smart, Jake."

"See how much I have to offer, Wally?" he said with a wry look. "I'm not just pretty and powerful. I have a brain, too."

"You've really opened my eyes here, Jake," she answered. "Keep it up."

Wally and Jake were often tied up in some sort of power struggle, but when it was time for him to step up for the group—or her—she had always been able to count on him. It made Wally feel grateful that he was pitching in to help now, however skeptical he was.

She held the fragment of the newspaper article up to each of the local papers in turn—the *Times*, the *Post*, the *Voice*, the *Daily News*, the *Journal*—and the type and format clearly matched one.

"Wa*ll Street Journal*, definitely," Ella declared.

"We can check their archives at the library," Tevin said.

They reached the Bloomingdale Library by ten o'clock and were first in line for an Internet terminal. Jake and Ella went to kill time in the periodical section, while Tevin went with Wally to her assigned computer, where she logged on to the *Wall Street Journal* archives. She searched for Benjamin Hatch and soon there it was, an article in the Small Business section of the *Journal*, May of 1992. It was a human-interest story mostly, relaying the experiences of entrepreneur Benjamin Hatch, who had tried to start an import-and-export firm in the new (back then) post-Soviet Russia. Hatch had encountered many problems, citing outdated business practices and corruption.

Hatch was described as a native New Yorker and former teacher. According to the article, Hatch's business idea was to buy and relabel an inexpensive brand of vodka, popular in Russia but unknown outside the country. The packaging would be upmarket and sexy, and the advertising campaign would play on the idea that the vodka was a fresh, undiscovered treasure from behind the Iron Curtain. By the time of the article's appearance, Hatch's scheme had already fallen apart, though he gave very few details on the causes for his failure.

It was still unclear what connection there was between Hatch and Wally's Russian mother, Yalena, or if he would know anything about how to find her. But there had to be a reason, Wally figured, why the *Journal* article on Hatch had been included in the Brighton Beach file. The only way forward was to find Benjamin Hatch and ask him. A Google search for Hatch yielded no results, other than the same *Journal* article, so Wally made the decision to spend $79.95 at one of the Internet's Friend Search sites, which basically amounted to online stalking. The results came up within seconds, but unfortunately the search located 183 Benjamin Hatches of appropriate age (thirty-five and older) living in the U.S., many in far-flung destinations, including Hawaii and Alaska.

"Too many Benjamins," Tevin said. "Never thought I'd see the day."

Wally and Tevin met up with Ella and Jake outside the library and gave them a look at the long list of Benjamin Hatches.

"Damn," Ella said, perusing the long list. "So many."

Wally pulled out her new cell phone. "Panama says I've got over a thousand minutes on here."

Mentioning Panama's name reminded Wally that he had been her initial connection to the Brighton Beach shop. Panama was wired in with most every black-market operation in the city, so Wally made a mental note to question him about the place later on.

The crew headed back to the bank and began calling all the numbers, the phone's charger plugged into an outlet on the bank floor the entire time. They took turns at it, relay style, reading off a script like telemarketers. "Hello, may I speak to Benjamin Hatch? Hello, Mr. Hatch, I'm calling on behalf of a friend, Yalena Mayakova. No? Sir, by any chance did you ever live or do business in Russia or the Soviet Union? *Hello?*"

The process went on for three full days, not because the actual calls added up to that but because of the inevitable hang-ups, multiple re-calls that bordered on harassment, and extended games of phone tag played back and forth across various time zones. At one point, Wally had to run out to a local cell phone kiosk to buy two thousand more minutes. She found herself fighting a sense of futility—in both herself and the crew—as the process wore on.

In the end, not one of the numbers or addresses had yielded a connection to the Benjamin Hatch they were looking for.

"Shit," Wally had said when they finally reached the last name on the list, a Ben Hatch Jr. in Flagstaff, Arizona. He did not know Yalena Mayakova and had never traveled outside Arizona, though he had plans to do so when he was old enough to drive.

"I'm gonna go to the Sommers-Bausch Observatory in Colorado," said Ben Jr., age nine. "They have a twenty-four-inch telescope and they let people look through it."

"Wow," Ella said, impressed. "Do you watch the sky in Flagstaff?"

"Sure," said Ben. "I have my own telescope, which is

smaller than the Sommers-Bausch, but I can see a lot from my backyard."

"Cool," said Ella.

At that time, Ben's father—Benjamin Hatch Sr.—took the phone from his son and confirmed that he had never heard of Yalena Mayakova, either, and had also never been to Russia. Ben Jr. bugged his father to let him back on the phone with Ella but Ben Sr. said "no" and hung up. That call marked the end of the three-day labor with not a single valuable lead to show for their effort.

The crew put on their coats and headed out of the bank, bound for a Japanese ramen shop on 86th Street, where they were eager to spend more of the money from the gem sale. They ate their noodles at the counter, mostly in silence as they contemplated other ways to track down Hatch.

Wally considered a short list of people who might be able to help with her search, but it was frustrating because each was unacceptable for their own reasons. First there was Claire, who was smart and resourceful but would have a meltdown if she found out Wally was looking for her birth mother. The second person who came to mind was Claire's lawyer, Natalie Stehn, who was the most calm, together person in Claire's life and seemed to be pretty hooked up, resource wise. But Claire brought Natalie tons of real estate business, giving her the kind of income that bought loyalty; Wally figured Natalie would most likely rat her out to Claire.

The last idea Wally had was the best, by far, coming to her

as a slap-on-the-forehead obvious solution. Wally wolfed down the last of her noodles and threw her bag over her shoulder.

"I think I have something," she said to the crew, and they were happy enough to let her go alone. Three days of wasted time on the phone had burned them out.

EIGHT

The address was a third floor walk-up, just across Lexington Avenue from the 92nd Street YMCA. There were several shops on the ground floor, including a mom-and-pop dough-nut shop, so the air carried the delectable aroma of sweet dough being deep-fried.

Wally felt hopeful as she climbed the stairs to the third floor and walked to the last door in the hallway. On the wooden door there was a small logo—the silhouette of a bear—and printed underneath it, THE URSULA SOCIETY. Everything about the location was low-key, nothing that would attract undue attention in this dark corner of the Upper East Side. Wally knocked gently before opening the door and stepping inside the small office, where an elderly man, in his mid-eighties at least, wearing a gray suit and tie, looked up from behind the computer monitor on one of the office's two desks. The second desk was empty.

"Hello," said the man behind the desk, with a slight Australian accent. "May I help you?"

"Uh . . . I spoke to a woman the last time I was here," Wally said, not looking forward to explaining her story to someone new. "An Asian woman. Her name was Carrie?"

"Yes," said the man, and gave a slight nod toward the empty desk at the other side of the small room. "Carrie is in graduate school these days, so her hours here are very irregular."

"Oh."

"I'm sure I can take up where Carrie left off. I'm Lewis Jordan."

"I'm Wally." Wally sat down in the guest chair opposite Lewis. "Wallis Stoneman."

Lewis typed Wally's name into his computer. "We're just beginning the process of digitizing our files, but we've begun with the most recent and are working our way backward, so yours might be on . . . yes. Here it is. Wallis Stoneman."

Lewis was quiet as his eyes scanned the file on his monitor. Wally noted that unlike most folks over the age of sixty, Lewis seemed completely natural using the computer.

"I see you first came in almost three years ago," said Lewis as he continued reading the screen, "and last checked in two years ago?"

"Yeah, two years is about right," Wally replied, suddenly feeling negligent. "Should I have been—?"

"Not at all," Lewis said.

Three years earlier, Wally had read an article about adopted people—of all ages—who were actively searching for their birth parents. One resource mentioned by the article was the Ursula Society, described as a nonprofit organization dedicated to helping adoptees with particularly difficult searches. Wally had come in on her own—without Claire's knowledge, of course—at the age of thirteen. She had met with a young Korean American woman named Carrie, who had taken down Wally's particulars and started a file for her. Carrie's search had come up empty. For several months after that, Wally had called in on a regular basis to check on any progress, but the answer had always been negative and eventually Wally had stopped calling.

"I'm afraid there's been no change to your case," Lewis said. "But I promise we will continue looking. Was there some new information you wanted us to add to your file?"

"I have a name," Wally answered. "Someone who may have known my mother in Russia. The thing is, I've tried every way I can think of but I can't find him."

"I see." Lewis considered this development, a guarded look on his face. "I could use a cup of tea. Black or green?"

"Uh, sure," Wally said. "Black." She had seen a mood change in Lewis and guessed this did not bode well for her.

Lewis boiled some water in a plug-in teapot, then poured it into cups with the earthy-smelling tea bags. Wally watched him. There was a forlorn quality that seemed to hover around him. Maybe it was the work. No doubt the Ursula Society experienced far more failure than success.

"Hot," he said as he handed Wally her tea, then he sat back down.

"Thanks."

"There's a line, Wallis," Lewis began after a moment. "What we have access to . . . the information, the various kinds of resources . . . it's a very sensitive situation."

Wally nodded. Carrie had explained this to her in very vague terms, several years earlier, but the thrust of it was that the Ursula Society achieved its successes through unconventional resources that were outside the boundaries of what was generally available, or even the boundaries of the law.

"Over the years we've arrived at some important guidelines that govern what we are willing to do and what we are not."

"Okay . . ." Wally said, remaining hopeful.

"Here's what I can do in this situation. You supply me with the name of the source; I'll track it down and see if your source is interested in cooperating. If so, then good. If not, we walk away."

Wally considered this, fighting a sense of disappointment.

"I think I get it," she said. "People come in here and make up stories, sometimes? To find someone they're looking for, but for different reasons?"

"It's happened." Lewis nodded. "With terrible consequences. Imagine a violent criminal using us to locate an enemy. Or an abusive husband lying about his situation so that we'll help track down his wife, who is in hiding. These are extreme examples, but—"

"I'm not doing anything like that. . . ."

"I believe you," said Lewis, "but as I say, the rules are strict for good reason."

Lewis read the impatience in Wally's face when he gave her this final word. "This process can be frustrating."

"Yes," Wally said. "It's just, your rules seem pretty unimportant to me right now."

Lewis looked understanding. "I fought with the Anzac Corps in World War II. My fiancée back home, she . . . *we* were pregnant, though she never told me. I heard about the child—my son—from others once I returned home from the war, but by that time my girl had given him up for adoption. It had all been handled through a lawyer who refused to reveal any of the particulars, other than that the family had immigrated to America. Everyone said I should give up on it and go on with my life. Instead, I came here looking for my son. That was sixty-two years ago, and I'm still looking for him."

"*Sixty-two years*," Wally repeated. It sounded to her like forever.

"There are some government records I have never been able to access, despite the connections I've made over the years. I just know his name is in there somewhere, but . . ."

"I'm sorry."

Lewis nodded. "Losing him has been the sorrow of my life, Wallis. So I appreciate your sadness and frustration. But I've handled thousands of cases for the society and there is something I have learned. There are worse things than not knowing, my dear. Answering your question might seem like the most important thing in the world, but it is not. If you place your quest ahead of everything else in your life, you will come to regret it."

Wally thought about this. "Good speech. Does anyone ever listen?"

"No," said Lewis, smiling a little at Wally's feistiness. "By the time people arrive at our door, they are usually hell-bent. Nothing can stop them."

"Like me," Wally said.

"Like you," Lewis agreed.

"I'll do this on my own, but I'm not a detective or anything," Wally said, feeling herself grasping now. "These resources of yours, can you hook me up with some of those?"

"I'm afraid not," he answered, firm but sympathetic. "The situation is this, Wallis: over a long time—more than half a century now—we've helped a great many people, from all walks of life. All professions, all sectors of society. We're a nonprofit organization and don't accept fees for what we do. However, those we have helped often volunteer to become contributors of another kind."

"Oh," Wally said, getting it, "your clients become your sources?"

Lewis nodded. "We have associates inside law enforcement, in the government, the State Department, the judiciary. Intelligence agencies in several countries. Even some in the commercial sector who, in these days of cyber-communities and data mining and so forth, have access to more private information than all the others combined. Those who help us are often taking great risks. They violate laws and oaths and contracts to help in our searches."

"I see."

"We assure complete anonymity to all our sources, obviously. They are like a family to us, really. You understand?"

There was no argument left for Wally to make, and again she fought back her feelings of frustration, determined to show Lewis that this setback would not defeat her. Wally took out a piece of paper and wrote down Benjamin Hatch's name and added, *Entrepreneur. Possibly knew Yalena Mayakova in Russia, in the year 1992, or so*. She passed the note to Lewis.

"You can add this to my file, anyway," she said, "in case something else comes up and you can make a connection."

Lewis took the note and read it. "I'll do what I can, Wallis. I will review your file as well to see if anything can be updated. We will never stop looking."

"Neither will I," Wally said. She walked to the door and Lewis rose from his own chair to show her out. He stayed in the doorway to watch her go, and after a few steps she had a thought and turned back toward him. "I'm sorry about your son." She meant it.

He shrugged. "Get on with other things, Wallis. Choose the life you want. Don't lose yourself in this search."

Wally just smiled, a little sadly, understanding on some level that Lewis's advice was wise and halfway regretting that she would not be able to follow it.

She shook Lewis's hand and left the office, heading back down the stairs and onto Lexington Avenue. Wally was about to turn the corner on 92nd Street when she glanced back at the building she had just left. In a window upstairs stood Lewis Jordan, teacup still in hand, watching her go. They exchanged small waves, and then Wally turned away, headed for her bus stop.

Late that night, Wally was awakened by the sound of her cell phone vibrating on the floor of the walkway, high above the bank. She stirred and checked the phone's display. It read *unknown caller.*

"Hello?"

"Did you know, Ursula is the patron saint of orphans?" It was Lewis Jordan.

"I didn't know," Wally answered.

"I believe she is watching over you."

Join the club, thought Wally.

"That's great, Lewis," she said. "I'll take all the help I can get."

"I shouldn't be sharing information with you, Wally, but it occurs to me that I've been following the rules of this process for fifty years and I am no closer to finding my son. I'm still alone."

"I really am sorry for that, Lewis." Wally could hear the frustration and sadness in Lewis's voice, and sensed that he was struggling with a difficult choice. She remained quiet, hoping he would decide in her favor.

"The Benjamin Hatch you're looking for died three years ago in a traffic accident," said Lewis.

Wally's heart sank. Her best lead for finding Yalena was lost.

"He was survived by two sons from an early marriage," Lewis continued. "Robert and Andrew. Their mother died from ovarian cancer when they were very young. The sons live together in their family home now. It's not far away. I tried to reach them, but they did not return my calls, so . . ." Lewis coughed. "By the society's rules, I should not have told you any of this."

"Thank you so much, Lewis," Wally said, grateful to him and feeling a rush of excitement that she would have a good lead to follow the next day. "I promise you won't regret it."

Wally found a pen and paper in her shoulder bag and Lewis dictated the street address and phone number of the Hatch home, located in a place called Shelter Island.

NINE

Wally tried the number—with her cell set on speaker phone so the others could listen in—and it rang six times before the line picked up.

"Yes?" came a man's voice on the other end of the line.

"Hello. Is this the Hatch home? I'm trying to reach either Andrew or Robert Hatch."

"This is Andrew." The voice was impatient.

"Mr. Hatch, my name is Wallis Stoneman. I'm the daughter of a woman named Yalena Mayakova. Does that name mean anything to you?"

After a brief pause, he answered simply, "No."

"Are you sure? She's from Russia. I'm fairly sure she had some connection with your father, maybe during the time he was doing business over there?"

There was a long moment of silence on the other end of the line.

"He's gone."

"Your father? Yes, I know . . . I'm very sorry for your loss," Wally stammered, feeling a twinge of panic as she sensed that Andrew Hatch was ready to hang up on her. "It's just that I'm trying to locate Yalena, and I was hoping you might have heard your father mention her—"

"We don't know anything about Russia. We have no connection with his business, or any of the Emerson people."

"I understand, but if there's anything—"

"I have nothing for you," the man said, and hung up.

Wally and the others were quiet for a moment.

"That is a guy," said Jake, "who knows an ass-load more than he was ready to talk about."

"No shit," said Ella. "And what's this Emerson thing? He said '*we have no connection with any of the Emerson people.*'"

"I have no clue," Wally said, feeling the rush of having another lead. "That name didn't come up with the article about his business."

"You've gotta confront this guy," said Tevin, "and his brother."

"No doubt," Wally said.

The four of them set off early the next day and rode the J line all the way to Jamaica—the end of the line—where they boarded the Long Island Railroad headed east. The two-hour ride to the Greenport station would leave them just a few steps away from the ferry to Shelter Island, where the Hatches' house could be found. The four of them settled in for the ride, having most of an entire car to themselves so they could all take window seats.

Wally had experience in the Hamptons, having taken several family vacations on the beach over the years, but for the others the train ride was an eye-opener. The view along the way offered glimpses of sprawling beachfront properties and enormous mansions. Jake, Ella, and Tevin jumped back and forth from the right side windows to the left, pointing out homes that seemed to grow more ostentatious the farther up the coast they traveled.

Ella slid onto the seat beside Wally.

"You've stayed in houses like that?" she asked.

Wally looked out the window to what looked like a fifty-room behemoth on the shoreline.

"Maybe not that big."

"That's gotta be insanely nice inside, right?"

"Sure. But do they have a Trojan War mosaic on their bedroom ceiling? I think not."

"Losers," Ella agreed. And then she was quiet for a moment more. "It doesn't take all that to make a home, anyway. Any little space could be one."

"Yeah."

"Maybe we could do something . . . like that."

"Like what?"

"Get an actual place together," Ella said. She made a show of mentioning the idea casually but Wally picked up on it. Ella had given this some real thought. "Not a big deal. Just a place where we paid rent, official-like."

Ella kept her eyes focused out the train window, pretending that she wasn't hanging on Wally's response.

"Yeah," Wally said, caught off guard, a weird little itch of resistance in the pit of her stomach. "We could definitely talk about that."

"If we got jobs, we could do it. I saw at Starbucks that they'll train you to do all those barista things, making the lattes and caps and everything. I bet I could do that."

"For sure you could."

Ella nodded and let it drop. Wally could feel that she had disappointed Ella by not jumping on board, but she didn't know what else to say. Nothing in her life seemed fixed—it all felt like chaos, in fact—and she didn't want to tell Ella any lies. It made Wally sad that she couldn't offer more. She reached out and held Ella's hand, fingers entwined, but the two of them didn't speak again for the rest of the ride.

It was one o'clock in the afternoon when the four of them stepped off the train at Greenport, the small station at the end of the railroad's Main Line. The day was sunny but cool, a chilly wind blowing off the ocean to the east. Wally had checked the ferry schedule online—it ran every half hour or so, starting just before six in the morning and ending before midnight—and their timing appeared to be perfect. The dock was less than a hundred yards away and the small ferryboat was moored there, looking like it was ready to leave soon.

Wally ducked quickly into a gift shop and bought a detailed

map of Shelter Island, then met the others at the dock. There were no other passengers waiting and only one car: a beat-up, weathered old Mercedes taxicab that read FANTASY ISLAND TAXI in faded lettering on its door, with a little plastic hula dancer hanging from its rearview mirror. The ferryman waved the crew on board, and the cab rolled onto the auto section. The ferry tooted its horn and pulled away from the dock, headed off on its short journey across Greenport Harbor. Wally joined the others at the bow. Tevin wore a wide grin as the ferry lumbered across the bay.

"First boat ride," he said.

"Me too," said Ella. "Are we gonna set seasick and hurl?" Her gleeful expression suggested that she might not mind.

Wally saw the excitement in their faces, and it felt good. She was anxious about what would happen on the island, but sharing the simple experience of a ferry ride with her friends already made it seem worthwhile.

The cabdriver got out to smoke. He was a local guy, maybe twenty years old, with curly orange hair, wearing a ratty cable-knit fisherman's sweater under a down vest. The guy had a relaxed confidence to him, and he was clearly in his element. As he smoked, he watched the crew for a moment, then spoke up.

"You need a ride," the cabdriver said in Wally's direction, not asking.

Wally regarded him for a moment and then nodded. The driver nodded back and leaned against the hood of his cab, looking out over the railing as Shelter Island approached just ahead. The small harbor had at least a dozen sailboats moored there, but all of them looked battened down, probably to remain unused for another six months at least. Soon they reached the Shelter Island dock and the crew climbed into the backseat of the Mercedes cab.

"Where to?" the young driver asked.

"You know where Crichton Road is?" Wally asked.

The driver nodded. He steered the cab out of the marina and onto Ferry Road, which would lead them all the way across to the northeast section of the island. They passed through a very small commercial area with a grocery store, a video store, a gas station, and two restaurants. All of it was quiet. Wally followed their progress on the map she'd bought, familiarizing herself with the layout of the island and locating the area where the Hatches' house was.

"You live on this island?" Tevin asked.

The cabbie shook his head. "Nah. My grandmother does, and I come over a few times a week to take her grocery shopping. They don't let her drive anymore."

"It's kinda quiet," said Ella.

"Nine months out of the year, yeah, but jammed during the summer."

"Do you know—"

"The Hatch brothers?" He cut her off. "Not really. They keep to themselves, mostly."

Wally felt a little surge of adrenaline in her system, caught off guard by the cabbie's knowledge that she and the crew were on their way to the Hatch home. She regarded him suspiciously in the rearview mirror, and he read her expression.

"Crichton Road is small," the driver said. "With only seven or eight houses along there. All summer people except for the Hatches."

"Oh."

After just a three-mile traverse of the island, never traveling faster than thirty-five miles per hour, they turned onto Crichton Road, which split off at a Y-intersection. Beside the Crichton Road sign was another sign, pointed in the other direction, which read MASHOMACK PRESERVE ENTRANCE. Wally checked the map and saw that the preserve covered a large swath of land, and it looked as though all the houses on the eastern side of Crichton Road would border up against the preserve grounds. This section of Shelter Island was an especially private place.

The cab turned onto Crichton and drove on for just fifty yards before pulling over on the right side of the road.

"That's it," the driver said.

Wally and the crew looked out at the Hatch home, a large two-story Cape-style home, at least five bedrooms, set back from the road. There was a closed three-car garage set to one side and a gardening shed visible out back. The place was neat and the grounds well tended, but the buildings themselves had fallen behind in upkeep, with a few missing shingles and cracked, weather-beaten paint around the windows. In the back, the property sat against a wide stretch of forest—the western boundary of the Mashomack Preserve, as Wally had noticed on her map.

The cabbie seemed to sense their hesitation as Wally and

the others looked up at the quiet home, which was completely dark.

"They don't know you're coming?" he said.

"Not exactly," Wally said. The situation was not what she had hoped for, obviously, but she was not about to be deterred.

"I can wait," he said. "The brothers might not even be home."

"No, thanks," Wally said. "We appreciate it, but we could end up being here awhile. Fantasy Island cab, right? We'll call if we need a ride back to the ferry."

The driver shrugged and passed her a business card. "Cool."

Wally paid him and the crew climbed out of the cab. The driver did a three-point turn on the narrow dirt road and disappeared back the way they had come.

Wally and the others faced the Hatch home.

"Maybe he was right," said Tevin. "It doesn't look like anyone is home."

They entered through the gate and walked the fifty feet of upward-sloping lawn to reach the front porch of the Hatches' house, then climbed the stairs to the front door. Wally rang the doorbell, which they could hear echoing through the house. When there was no answer, she knocked as well. No one came to the door, and there was no indication that anyone was home.

"Damn it," Wally said.

They followed the porch—which wrapped all the way around the house—to the back deck and peered through

French doors into the back rooms. The place was very sparsely furnished. Next to the kitchen was a family area with an old dining table and a sofa turned toward a TV screen. To one side was a wood-fired heating stove, with the glow of a flame just visible inside. There were no other signs of anyone being home.

Wally tested the handle on one of the French doors, but it was locked. She walked around the rear wall, testing more doors and windows, and found an unlocked window above the kitchen sink.

"We're going in?" Jake asked.

"Just me," Wally said, feeling herself slipping into commando mode, tense in a good way and ready to go. She had work to do inside the house and didn't want to have to worry about the crew while she was into it.

"Why'd we come all the way up here, then?" Jake asked, annoyed.

"I know, but if this goes wrong, I'll need you guys free to help me out. Please stand watch and let me know if anyone shows up, okay? Just pound on the back door or something if you need to get my attention."

Jake was still annoyed, but Wally's argument was reasonable enough. She handed her shoulder bag to Ella and shoved the unlocked window open. She hiked herself up and through the window, supporting her weight inside by grabbing the edge of the kitchen sink and sliding all the way in until she was crouched on the kitchen counter. She then jumped down to the floor, and the sound of her boots echoed through the house. She slid off her boots and left them sitting by the kitchen counter, beginning her quiet search of the house in stocking feet.

Much like the outside appearance of the home, the inside was tidy but run-down. Wally passed through a closed door into the living room, which was a good thirty degrees colder than the kitchen area. Obviously, the only heater being used in the house was the woodstove, and the doors to that area were closed to keep the heat in the essential living area. There was no furniture in the living room. Wally got the sense that the Hatch brothers had been selling off the furniture, one piece at a time.

She returned to the kitchen, where she began checking the cabinets. There she found enough food to last quite a while, but all of two categories: staples like rice and oatmeal in bulk sizes and various foods that must have been foraged from the area: berry preserves, root vegetables. It seemed to Wally that the Hatch brothers were nearly destitute, saving money everywhere they could—they were struggling to hold on to their family home.

Wally found a narrow servant's staircase next to the kitchen and climbed up to the second floor. There she arrived at a long hallway that stretched the entire width of the house, with doors leading into six separate bedrooms, including two "master" suites, one at either end of the house. These two large bedrooms were the only ones with any furniture: each had a bed—mattresses on makeshift platforms—and side tables with lamps. In each closet was a meager but practical selection of men's clothing.

She was just about to exit the second bedroom when she

heard the sharp sound of something hitting the window beside the bed. She stifled a little yelp at the surprise of it. She looked out the window, and it took her a moment to find her crew, crouched beyond the fence at the edge of the property, probably forty feet away from the house. The three of them wore identical looks of alarm, and suddenly Wally heard the sound of a door closing downstairs, followed by the sounds of boots— two sets?—patrolling the first floor of the house. Wally looked at the crew again, and Tevin gave her a signal, holding up two fingers to signify two people downstairs, then changing the signal by pressing the two fingers together until they became the "barrel" in a hand gesture that meant *gun*.

Shit. The Hatch brothers were home apparently, and, for some reason, they were carrying weapons. Had they been alerted that she had broken in? Wally felt a surge of distress but made a sign to the others that they should stay where they were. She thought about calling the police, figuring that getting busted would be better than getting shot by the Hatch brothers as a burglar, but then realized that her cell phone was in her shoulder bag, now outside with Ella. The only phone she had seen in the house was downstairs in the kitchen.

Then Wally remembered her boots. Sitting to one side of the kitchen floor, near the window over the sink. Had she closed the window behind her? Suddenly she couldn't remember.

Possibilities raced through her mind. Should she just call out in surrender? Let the brothers know she was there and apologize, explaining that she was innocently searching for her Russian mother and got carried away when they weren't home and . . . *no*. No way. If she spooked them badly enough, they might take a shot at her—but even if that didn't happen, they would be so angry with Wally for violating their privacy that they would never help with her search for Yalena. So far, the Hatch brothers were still her only decent lead.

Shit.

One set of footsteps—heavy, male, moving at a cautious pace—began climbing the main staircase, headed up in Wally's direction. Wally hustled down the hall as quietly as she could, headed for the back staircase—the one she had used coming up. Though her stocking feet were quiet, the ancient floorboards squeaked slightly under her. The footsteps on the main staircase suddenly halted and remained completely still. Wally slid to a stop and froze. The man on the main staircase didn't move for almost ten seconds—listening?—but finally continued upward, and Wally sped along the last section of hallway until she reached the narrow back staircase. Quickly she hurried downward and then stopped at the bottom of the stairs, alert.

There were still two sets of footsteps moving in the house: the ones upstairs walked the width of the house with occasional pauses and redirections, clearly searching the upstairs rooms. The second set of steps was still downstairs, moving slowly, opening closet doors, searching every inch of the place. From her position at the bottom of the rear staircase, Wally could see her own pair of boots sitting where she had left them on the kitchen floor, undisturbed. She realized that she had placed them mostly out of sight, halfway concealed by the kitchen counter and easy to miss if someone wasn't actually looking for them. Wally also noticed that she had in fact closed the window behind her. So, what had tipped off the Hatches that someone was in their house? Why were they searching for an intruder?

Wally needed to get the hell out of that house. From her hiding place at the bottom of the servant's staircase, she cautiously emerged into the kitchen, making her way quietly across the linoleum toward her shoes, but suddenly the sound of the downstairs footsteps changed direction and headed toward the kitchen, toward her. Wally spun around and raced back to the cover of the staircase, ducking in just as the downstairs man stepped into the kitchen.

Wally heard the man stop and look around the kitchen. She heard a squeak as he opened one of the kitchen cabinets. Wally took a chance and peered out, getting a look at him from behind. He was dark-haired, average height but sturdily built. Salt-and-pepper hair, closely trimmed, wearing jeans and a black leather car coat and carrying an intimidating handgun that Wally recognized as a .45 automatic—Jason, her adopted father, had insisted that Wally take a series of classes on handling guns.

As she watched the man search through the cabinets, Wally suddenly realized that this was not one of the Hatch brothers at all, but an intruder like herself. But if he wasn't looking for her, what *was* he looking for?

The man continued searching and suddenly his attention was drawn toward something Wally had not noticed in the dining area next to the kitchen. He approached a collection of photographs that were pinned to the otherwise empty wall, old black-and-white photos yellowed terribly with age.

The man concentrated his attention on two of the photos. One photo was of a small white rowboat, empty, sitting on a beach at the edge of a dark sea. The second appeared to be of a young couple and—was that a small child with them? The family of three stood in front of some sort of rustic farmhouse. The man reached for the second photo—of the young couple and small child—and pulled it off the wall, looking at it more closely.

"Yalena," he said out loud, with a Slavic accent.

Wally's heart was suddenly in her throat. The stranger had spoken her mother's name.

At that moment the doorbell rang—sounding incredibly loud in the quiet, barren house—and the man turned his attention toward the front of the house, allowing Wally a clear look at his face, in profile. She gasped. The man was older now, a little gaunt, and his eighties-style hair and sideburns were cut back, but there was no question in Wally's mind. This was the man whose photograph was included in the Brighton Beach file: *This is a most dangerous man,* Yalena had written on the back of the picture. *If you see him, you must run.* What had been instantly menacing in his photograph was evident now also, but to a greater extreme: a sense of danger and violence radiated outward from him, merely punctuated by the weapon in his hand. He grabbed the photo off the wall and stuffed it in his pocket.

"Gost!" the man barked in Russian. Visitor, Wally understood.

And now, to Wally's horror, the footsteps upstairs moved to

the rear staircase—the same servant's staircase where Wally was now hiding—and began climbing downward. Toward her.

Shit. Wally had no idea what to do. The man from above was halfway down the stairs when the man in the kitchen began moving toward the kitchen door that led to the entrance hallway and to the front door. Moving cautiously, the man shifted his gun hand behind his back, peered down the hallway toward the front door, then exited the kitchen on his way to check who might be at the door. Once he was gone, Wally jumped out of the staircase and lunged to her left, into a space between the staircase and the refrigerator where a set of old mops and brooms were stored. Wally leaned into the vacant space as far as she could, just barely out of sight, as the second man appeared from the staircase and moved swiftly past her at a distance of less than two feet. Wally held her breath, and thankfully he did not discover her.

The second man was very young—late teens, Wally guessed—taller and slimmer than the other, with long black hair trailing down to his shoulders. In his right hand he held his own weapon, a 9mm automatic. The younger man followed the course of the older, exiting the kitchen in the direction of the entrance hallway, and as soon as he was out of sight Wally sped across the kitchen floor—sliding in her stocking feet to avoid making any sound—to the kitchen counter, where she picked up her shoes in one swooping motion and hustled to the French doors at the rear of the room, unlocking one and fleeing out to the back grounds, careful to close the door quietly behind her.

Once outside, Wally heard a low whistle come from the side fence of the property, where she had seen her crew crouching out of sight. They were still there, motioning for her to hurry. Wally traversed the yard and leapt over the fence, tumbling down in the brush beside her friends.

"Are you okay?" Ella asked in a panic.

"I'm fine," said Wally, breathless but feeling a sense of relief. "That was you guys who rang at the door?"

"Yeah," Jake said. "We did a ring-and-run to distract them."

"Wally," Tevin said, "we're so sorry. Those guys snuck up to the house from the side yard. We didn't see them until they were at the back door."

"It's okay, you did great," Wally assured them. "Let's just get the hell away from here."

The four of them crashed through some brush into a neighbor's yard, staying low, then moved directly toward Crichton Road. Wally got her shoulder bag back from Ella and was just reaching for her phone when the Fantasy Island cab pulled onto Crichton Road and slowed down to park in front of the Hatch home. Wally stepped into the street and waved the cabbie over. He accelerated and pulled up in front of the neighboring house, where they were waiting, and signaled them to jump in. They did, and he drove off.

"Thought I'd check back in case you needed a ride," the mellow young cabbie said. As he looked into his rearview mirror, seeing all four of them breathless and looking spooked, he asked, "How was your visit?"

★   ★   ★

The cabdriver dropped them off at the Shelter Island marina for their return trip. Wally thanked the cabbie and tipped him lavishly.

"Wow," said the cabbie, reacting to the extra fifty bucks. "Are you sure? It was just a few miles."

"I'm sure. Thanks again."

He shrugged and smiled, pocketing the tip. "You've got my card." He gave her a winning grin and drove off.

Within a few minutes, Wally and the crew were at the bow of the ferry again, the chilly wind to their backs this time, looking out over the water and waiting for their heart rates to return to normal.

"It was him, right?" Ella was the first to speak. "One of those guys was the one from the picture?"

"Yeah," Tevin said. "I got a pretty good look. It was him."

"He's looking for her," Wally said, certain she was right, remembering the gratified tone in the man's voice when he had spotted the ancient photograph on the wall of the Hatches' house and spoken her mother's name—*Yalena*—before pulling the photo from the wall and taking it with him. And why was an old photograph of her Russian mother pinned to the wall of that house? Things were all tied together somehow—Yalena, the Hatches, and the two intruders in the Hatches' house.

"He's looking for Yalena," Wally repeated.

"And he's following the same leads that you are," said Jake.

Wally nodded in agreement, feeling a jacked-up sense of urgency.

"I have to find her first."

TEN

The streetlights along Centre Street were just flickering on as Atley parked his car and stepped into Bergin's Pub. He took a table at the back and ordered a beer to nurse while he reviewed Wallis Stoneman's Social Services file. While he waited for his drink to arrive, Atley checked his voice mail and listened to messages from his lieutenant and his watch commander, both curious about why he had nothing to show for all the hours he was putting in on the Sophia Manetti murder. The only other message was the one he had heard two hours earlier from his longtime friend Bill Horst, special agent at the FBI's Manhattan headquarters.

"Yo, Atley," came Bill's voice on the voice mail recording, "I've got something you might need. I'll be at Bergin's around five."

Atley erased the messages and checked his watch, confirming that he had at least fifteen minutes before Horst showed up.

His pint of ice-cold Stella arrived, and Atley took a deep end-of-the-workday drink before finally opening Wallis's file. He could see right off that it would be interesting reading, some of it familiar juvenile stuff, some not so much.

The collection of documents covered the previous two or three years, a time when Wallis Stoneman started acting out in various ways and eventually ended up on the street. There was truancy, of course, and several cases in juvenile court, mostly minor stuff—two instances of shoplifting, a charge for resisting arrest when she and some friends were stopped in the East Village at three in the morning. Wallis was expelled for disciplinary reasons from Harpswell and two other expensive prep schools.

When she finally ran away from home, Wallis's record showed that she was frequently in the company of someone named Nick Pierce and—there she was—Sophia Manetti, recently deceased. Pierce was a runaway minor one year older than Wallis but with a very long record in juvenile court, including drug charges. Apparently the two of them were no longer connected. There were no other mentions in the file regarding the Manetti girl.

According to the file, much of the grief in Wallis's life seemed connected to the fact that she had been adopted, a detail that hadn't come up in Atley's interview with Claire Stoneman. Atley had friends who had been through some of that stuff. The adopted kid reaches adolescence and the usual rebellion issues can get magnified, sometimes to an extreme, as if they wake up one day and they're living in a stranger's home. For the most part, it seemed the mother had done what she could to heal the situation, including various types of counseling, but with mixed results.

There were a couple of special entries in the files by her caseworker that amounted to warnings. In an effort to help her daughter learn discipline and channel her emotions, Claire Stoneman had enrolled Wallis in a mixed martial arts program at a well-known dojo up on Columbus. The girl had kept with it for two years. Wallis was an angry and defiant twelve-year-old when she began the training. After two years of high-level classes she was an angry and defiant fourteen-year-old who now knew fifty different ways to cripple a man. In addition, the mother's ex-husband, Jason Stoneman, was a gun owner, and for safety reasons he had schooled Wallis on the use of various firearms.

Fantastic, thought Atley. Nice parenting. Mr. and Mrs. Stoneman had turned their daughter into a one-teenager wrecking crew, currently at large on the streets of New York City and, apparently, uncatchable. There had been a PINS warrant out on her for a full year, but in that time she hadn't been collared, not even once.

Atley finished the file and his first beer just as Bill Horst arrived.

"Brother Atley." Bill flashed a smile as he sat down and signaled the waitress for two Stellas.

Bill had been a classmate of Atley's back at the academy, almost twenty years earlier. One day during a lecture break, two FBI agents had appeared and stolen Bill away, presumably to be tasked on an undercover assignment that required a face with no law enforcement history. Atley never found out why the feds had chosen Bill—a raw recruit—or what his assignment had been. Bill had been completely off the radar for almost ten years, then shown up in the city again as a regular duty agent in the FBI's Manhattan field office.

"What've you got for me?" Atley asked.

Their beers arrived. Bill nodded thanks to the waitress, then waited for her to leave before continuing. "You put out a BOLO on some girl from the Upper West?"

"I did," said Atley, surprised. He had put out a Be On the Look Out bulletin for Wallis Stoneman but had distributed it to local law enforcement only. He couldn't imagine how the sixteen-year-old could possibly be of interest to the bureau. "Her name is Wallis Stoneman. Street kid."

"She a perp?"

"No," said Atley. "Witness, hopefully. Source, maybe. How'd the BOLO come across your desk?"

"Are you kidding? All of us in the Manhattan field office are huge fans of your work," said Bill. "We have a special bulletin board to keep us up to date on your current cases."

"Fuck off," said Atley.

Bill smiled. "We got a double homicide up the coast yesterday. You know Shelter Island?"

"Heard of it, never been there."

"The victims . . ." Bill paused, clearly trying to figure out how much information to share with Atley, a non-fed. "Okay, so . . . we had a guy on a watch list, just him at first and eventually we added his two sons also. Benjamin Hatch, sons Andrew and Robert. Those names mean anything to you?"

"Nope," said Atley, still perplexed as to how Wallis Stone-man could possibly fit into a federal case.

"Anyway," Bill continued, "this Hatch guy . . . he ran an import business. A few years back the bureau caught word he was sidestepping Customs regs. We ended up plugging his name and his boys' into a watch list, just to keep a heads-up; you know how much of a hard-on Homeland Security has for overseas trade activity. Years go by, no hits ever come up on Hatch or the sons."

"How many years?"

"Ten or more. Hatch croaked three years ago. As for the sons, there's been nothing . . . until yesterday. Apparently, the Hatch boys were out running errands and came home to some surprise visitors. Whoever it was left an awful mess. Andrew and Robert both very dead, very wet. The local cops put the Hatches' names into the system and the case gets flagged on our end 'cause they're still on our watch list. We went up there to show some due diligence."

"Did you find anything?"

"Nope," said Bill. "Nothing for us. Just homicide, far as we could tell. We left the case for the local yokels."

"Okay . . ." said Atley, still waiting to hear what all this had to do with Wallis Stoneman.

Bill pulled out his smart phone and scrolled through the content files for a moment, looking for something. When he found it, he hit play and handed the phone to Atley. It was a color video clip—surprisingly sharp—shot from above by a security camera in what looked like a train station platform.

The footage showed four teenagers on the platform, dressed in emo street attire. Looking closely, Atley identified one of the teens as Wallis Stoneman. As he continued to watch the footage, a train arrived at the station. Wallis and her friends climbed aboard the train and rode away.

"That's her," said Atley, handing the phone back to Bill. "What station is that?"

"Greenport, end of the line. Near the ferry landing for Shelter Island, yesterday. Day of the killings."

Atley considered this for a second and gave Bill a look. "You're not thinking these kids had anything to do with the murders. . . ."

"Nah," said Bill. "The local cops have a pretty solid timeline and a general description of the two unsubs and their vehicle. Plus, your kids left Greenport at least two hours before time of death. We went over the security camera footage from the train station and parking lot, hoping to spot the unsubs in the vicinity—"

"Okay," said Atley. "So, your facial recognition system scanned the faces at the station and ran them against current warrants, and that's how my BOLO popped up. I don't suppose your super-secret software can tell me what young Wallis Stoneman and her friends were doing way the hell up Long Island. . . ."

"I do not know, my friend," Bill said with a cheerful grin, "and as of right now, I consider it your problem, not mine. Cheers."

ELEVEN

The day after the Shelter Island trip, Wally woke up feeling more focused than ever. The quest to find her biological mother had begun with a sort of dreamy, fairy-tale quality to it, but that feeling had evaporated with the sight of the armed men in the Hatches' house, especially the one whose photograph was in the Brighton Beach file. He was the *most dangerous man*, someone whose very presence inspired terror. She suspected—no, felt certain—that she and that man had crossed paths for one simple reason: they were both searching for Yalena. Wally felt just as certain that if she did not find her mother before he did, then she would never find her at all.

Wally joined the others in the bank's employee break room, where they were drinking microwave hot cocoa and eating day-old bagels.

"I'm headed to the library," she said. "What Andrew Hatch

said about 'Emerson' people . . . I'm going to run that down, if I can."

"We're kind of freaked out," Ella confessed to Wally.

"There are guns in this now, Wally," Jake said. "You've run into some serious shit, whatever it is."

"I know."

"You're done with the Hatch brothers, right?" Tevin asked. "You're not going back there?"

"For now I'm just going to try to figure out the Emerson thing," Wally said, wondering if she had already taken the quest too far but knowing that if she gave it up, she would never forgive herself. "I just have to keep moving forward. I'll catch up with you later."

Wally threw her messenger bag over her shoulder and hurried out the bank's rear exit, through the narrow walkway to the street. There she took an extra look around to be sure she was not being observed; the encounter on Shelter Island had put her on alert. If she and those men really were both hunting the same person, they might cross paths again at any time. She scanned 87th Street, looking for anything unusual. As far as she could tell, her exit was safe, and she made her way east to Amsterdam Avenue and had just turned north when she heard footsteps behind her and turned to find Tevin standing there.

"You're okay alone?" he asked.

It was easy for Wally to see that he wanted her to invite him along, that he wanted her to need him. But it was more responsibility than she could handle for the moment.

"Thanks, Tev." She gave him a smile. "Yeah, I'm okay."

He nodded, doing his best not to seem disappointed as he turned around and headed back in the direction of the bank.

The Internet access area of the library had twenty stations running, and Wally had to wait only ten minutes before one came open.

She took her coat off and logged on to her station, opening a search engine on the home page. She typed in the name *Emerson* just to see what would come up: more than four million hits. Wally thought for a moment, then entered both *Emerson* and *Hatch*. One hundred and forty thousand hits. She then entered three terms: *Emerson, Hatch,* and *Russia.* The hits on these terms were equally forbidding—several hundred. The first page of results began with a reference to Cabott Emerson III, former American ambassador to the Soviet Union.

Wally pulled up Wikipedia and entered Emerson's name. The man's full biography came up, revealing that Emerson had served in the Soviet Union for almost twenty years and had been an advisor on Soviet affairs to four American presidents. He had died in the mid-seventies. At the end of the Wikipedia biography was a list of related hits on the search terms, and the third one caught Wally's eye: the Emerson School, named after Cabott Emerson III and located in Moscow.

Hadn't the *Wall Street Journal* article described Benjamin Hatch as "a former teacher"? Wally did a basic Google search for the Emerson School and clicked on the first link. The Emerson School site came up on her screen but immediately presented Wally with a hurdle: the opening page was nothing more than a log-on screen, requesting a user name and password to gain access.

That was strange, Wally thought. The Internet site of most any school, especially a private one, would usually be the equivalent of an admissions brochure, featuring lots of information about faculty, curriculum, campus layout, and admissions procedures. The Emerson School offered nothing. A log-on screen was the equivalent of a sign reading PRIVATE PROPERTY—NO TRESPASSING. Wally tried another tack. She navigated back to Wikipedia and did a search for the Emerson School there. Here Wally had success: the article included a fairly long entry about the school, reviewing its history, the focus of its curriculum, exterior photos of the campus, and a list of notable alumni.

What Wally learned there explained the unfriendly reception at the school's own site. The Emerson School was a private, K–12, American-run school in Moscow that was named after the distinguished American ambassador and geared toward the needs of the Western diplomatic corps living full time in Russia. The student body consisted mostly of the children of diplomats and business executives from the United States and other Western countries; the security of students would be a priority.

Did Benjamin Hatch teach at the Emerson School during his time in Russia? Did Yalena Mayakova herself have some sort of connection to Emerson as well? If she did, then maybe her relationship with Benjamin Hatch had begun there. If so, maybe Benjamin Hatch had helped Yalena reach America. Maybe Wally's best chance for getting closer to her mother was to move backward instead of forward, to retrace Yalena's path to America as a way of finding out why she had left Russia and where she had eventually landed.

It was a lot of maybes. Wally didn't know for sure if learning more about the Emerson School would bring her closer to finding Yalena here in the States, but this string of possible relationships—from Yalena to the Emerson School to Benjamin Hatch to America—was the only real lead she had. She needed access past the firewall of the Emerson School site.

Of the people in Wally's life, she knew only one who had the computer skills to penetrate a secure website; before he began his outlaw life on the street, Nick Pierce had been a computer sciences geek in his suburban New Jersey high school. Nick could help Wally; whether or not he *would* was another question. There was bad blood.

Wally tried a few of Nick's old squats on the Lower East Side but came up empty—two of them were boarded shut, and a third had been renovated from a thrashed old industrial storage space into expensive loft apartments. She walked south on Avenue B and crossed East Houston toward the place that was her last best chance of finding Nick, the Essex Street subway station.

With each step Wally felt more anxious. If she did find Nick, he would almost definitely be doped up—by the time the crew had split from him, his habit had gotten completely out of control, and Wally had heard word on the street that he was still deep into the sickness. His mood would depend a lot on what he was using that day; crack, heroin, meth, and oxy were possibilities, plus anything else he could get his hands on.

Whichever way he was tweaked, Wally figured Nick would still be plenty angry with her. It had been Nick who had initiated Wally into the life of the streets, who had invited her into his crew and taught her much of what she used every day to survive. But in the end it was Wally who proved to be the stronger person.

The two of them had met a year and a half earlier, months before Wally left home. Wally and Darien, a girlfriend from school, had cut afternoon classes and headed down to the area around NYU to check out some of the cool shops. They bought burritos from a food truck on Waverly and were eating them on a bench in Washington Square Park when they were approached by Nick, who was passing out flyers for a rave that night in Chinatown.

Nick Pierce was handsome back then, tall and lanky in a nice way, with untamed curly dark hair and playful green eyes. He wasn't even a year older than Wally, but he vibed a kind of easy confidence—and trouble—that was unlike anything Wally knew from the boys at her uptown prep school.

"Come rave tonight, ladies," Nick said, handing Wally and Darien the flyers, "and your worlds will be rocked."

"Rocked *how*?" Wally said, not giving away any interest in him. "We're gonna need specifics."

"The specifics are that if my friends and I pass out five hundred of these ads, we get into the club for free."

"And what happens inside?" Wally said.

"That depends," he said, looking into her. "What do you want?"

Hmm, thought Wally.

The girls never made it to the rave that night because Darien was, in Wally's opinion, chickenshit. But from that day on Wally made regular trips to the parks—Washington Square or Tompkins Square—to meet up with Nick and his crew: Sophie, Jake, Ella, Tevin, and a rotating group of other strays. Hanging with her new friends was the opposite of being trapped at home with Claire—relaxed, fun, unstructured, and totally without judgment—and her decision to be with them was the first major choice Wally had ever made for herself. It felt good.

Within six months, Wally had left home to be on the street with the crew full time, and the exciting glow of her relationship with Nick lasted a month, maybe two. Then things went wrong.

Nick had always smoked a fair amount of weed, but at some point he had started doing meth—in secret from the crew—and almost overnight he was hard-core hooked. To pay for his fresh habit, Nick began putting the entire crew at risk—especially Sophie—by involving them in street scams and drug rip-offs that would eventually get them busted or worse.

Wally had stood by at first, watching what was going on but without the will to change it. She felt indebted to Nick for welcoming her into the crew and for her "street" education, and at the time she was at least halfway in love with him. For a while those were good enough reasons to stay silent, but Wally had her limits. She reached a point where she even considered abandoning the crew and moving back home with Claire, but things turned out differently.

One afternoon, down in the Grand Central tunnels, Wally discovered Nick sharing a crack pipe with Ella and Jake, their first time doing anything harder than booze or weed. It was a perfect strategy for Nick: if other members of the crew were using with him, they would share his desperation for dope and would go along with his increasingly reckless schemes for making money.

Wally had gone ballistic. In her rage she actually attacked Nick physically and had kicked his ass. Nick the half-gone doper had been no contest for angry Wally and her martial arts training, despite the size difference between them. Wally's defiance forced the rest of the crew to choose between her and Nick, and they didn't hesitate to follow Wally out the door.

"Get clean and you can come back with us," Wally had said, her last words to Nick. Generous, she thought.

"Fuck you, Wally," Nick had answered, his lip bleeding and his ego crushed. "You'll never make it."

Those last words were spoken without conviction; it was obvious to Nick and everyone else what Wally was capable of, and she had proved it every day since then. With the exception of Sophie, Wally had kept the crew clean and safe, and she had long since forgotten the idea of returning to her life with Claire.

Wally made it down to the Essex Street subway platform and—when she was sure she wasn't being observed by any of the IRT employees—jumped off the south platform and hurried into the darkness of the abandoned trolley stop that had stood there empty for decades. The place was dark and filthy with grime, its corroded walls covered with generations of graffiti tags. The acrid smell of piss and shit and vomit hung thick and sweet in the air, and Wally had to suppress an urge to puke.

Wally pulled out a flashlight and made her way toward the old boiler room at the far end of the station. She now felt an eager little rush in her belly to go along with all the anxiety and had to admit to herself that despite the disgusting location she found herself in, part of her was actually looking forward to seeing Nick, to sharing with him her excitement over the search for Yalena. She knew she was being ridiculous, of course, but some part of her held on to the hope that he had managed to turn his life around, that she would miraculously find the old Nick waiting for her.

Wally entered the boiler room, and those foolish, delusional thoughts were chased away. Three or four burned-down candles dimly lit the squalid space. Grimy old heating ducts covered the ceiling and walls, all of them rusted through. Four or five ratty and molded mattresses covered about half of the floor space, surrounded by discarded needles and broken glass pipes. Two young girls in jeans and greasy down parkas were huddled together on one of the mattresses, asleep or drugged out or both, an old moving blanket wrapped around them against the cold air.

Nick was the only other person in the room, sitting upright on one of the mattresses with his back against one of the rotted ducts, smoking a cigarette. His frame was skeletal now, his hair cropped close and those green eyes sunk deep in a perpetual shadow. A ghostly post-binge aura hung off him.

Wally's heart sank at the sight.

Nick stared at her blankly for a moment, looking a little confused before realizing that it was her. He didn't smile.

"Oh, fuck," he said, his voice lazy and hoarse from the pipe. "Are you kidding me? Wallis, you bitch, hello. Please leave now and stay the fuck away from me forever."

"I need something, Nick," Wally said, and Nick laughed out loud.

"Of course you do," he said. "Always the practical one. No social visit, this. How are the kids? Will you grant me visitation?"

"Everyone's good," she said. "Clean."

"Well, good for you. A nice, clean, presentable crew. Hmm . . . have you taken them home yet, to meet Claire? No? Well, then, not *that* clean, huh? Not *that* presentable. But who is?"

The greatest power Nick held over Wally was his instinctive knowledge that her relationship with Claire was the key to everything, the soft underbelly of Wally's well-defended psyche. His remark about the dichotomy of her two separate lives found its target. The guilt over her split from Claire still burned, as did the shame over how she protected that side of her life from the crew and vice versa.

"I think about Claire a lot," Nick said with a playful grin that looked macabre on his sunken features. Whatever dope was still rushing through his system seemed to kick in as he railed on. "That look on her face when she walked in on the two of us, naked on your little twin bed with the frilly pink quilt and that heap of Barbies or stuffed animals or whatever girlish bullshit came with your life of privilege." His expression turned dark as he spoke. "You think I don't know how you'd planned it all, how you worked it out so that Claire was sure to walk in on us there, fucking, and go completely apeshit? You were miserable in that life—alone in that apartment with her—and you wanted an excuse to run. Her rage gave you that excuse, and just like that you were gone."

His words burned all the more in that they were pretty much true; Wally knew that now, even if she had done all of it subconsciously at the time.

"I'm still embarrassed," he railed, "for my role in your chickenshit little drama—"

"Poor Nick," Wally cut him off angrily, almost spitting her words. "You were just a victim, I suppose? Right. As if I could ever make you do something you didn't want to."

"I've thought a lot about that day," he went on, ignoring her, "and I think I get it now. You grew up in a family that was based on lies, Wally, maybe a lot of little ones or even one huge crushing one. I think you were terrified to hear the truth from Claire. Maybe you thought it might tear you both apart, who knows? I swear to God, I would give anything to be there when you finally hear it."

"Congratulations to you, Nick," Wally answered, the words catching in her throat, full of anger and shame. "No one knows better than you how messed up I am. And still you were so careless with me, so willing to shit all over everything we had for . . . what? The pipe? The spike? Or what have we moved on to now? Drain cleaner?"

"There she is," Nick almost shouted, seeming gratified at the acid tone in her voice. "That's my beautiful, angry girl." And at that his head bent down halfway, as if spewing all those accusations had taken every ounce of energy he had left. "Tell me what the fuck you want," he mumbled, "and then get out of here."

Wally wanted to be gone too, and so she quickly explained everything she knew about the Emerson School, their website, how she thought there might be information there that could help her find her Russian mother. Wally watched Nick as he took all of it in, coldly, as if the story was not about her but instead a stranger, someone he'd never cared about. His indifference was heartbreaking.

"Well, I should be flattered," he said weakly, as if he might drift off to sleep at any moment.

"Yeah? Why's that, Nick?"

"Because the answer is so easy. You obviously didn't come all this way for that. You're here because you wanted to see me, even if it was just to find out if I was still breathing. Very sweet."

He managed to raise his head a little, waiting for an answer, and Wally felt those eyes reach out and hold her again, like the old days, a faint trace of life and love still there.

"Yeah, I did," Wally admitted. "I wanted to see you." And

it was true. She felt tears choking up inside her, but fought them back.

"There, don't cry," Nick said with a knowing smile. "Fight it."

She composed herself—as if at his command—and waited.

"Here," he said, and rattled off a list of ten possible passwords, which Wally hastily scribbled on a piece of notepaper.

"You just know it, like that?" she asked, bewildered. "You don't need to hack the site?"

Nick scoffed. "Those sites are designed for stupid people to use. Technology-challenged old people. They would never remember a secure password. I predict the first one on the list will be it."

The first password he had named was EmersonAlum.

"Get the fuck out now," Nick said.

Wally hesitated, thinking there might still be some air to clear between them, but if there was, she couldn't get a handle on it.

"Bye, Nick," she said, heading back toward the open doorway.

"It's Tevin, right?" he said behind her. "Even back then, it seemed like there might be something there."

Nick's perception was sharp, another callback to his old self. Wally was not surprised.

"Not really," she answered, turning back to him. "Not yet."

"Give it time," he said, his eyelids drooping. "I always liked that kid."

And then nothing. Within seconds, he slumped down along

the wall, deep asleep. Wally turned away and left the boiler room behind, making her way through the darkness, back to the Essex Street platform. She climbed the subway stairs into the light of Delancey Street and walked east, no idea where she was headed. Half a block later, Wally was surprised to find thick tears pouring out of her eyes.

TWELVE

Wally rode the subway back uptown, back to the Upper West Side, and walked straight from the station to the Mulberry Street Library. All the way, she struggled with the painful fallout of her confrontation with Nick, unable to shake the feeling that she would never see him alive again. In the end, she decided to set the agony of it aside—she had become good at that—and to move on, to continue driving herself forward, toward Yalena.

All the Internet stations at the library were booked. She signed up for a time slot, but would have a thirty-minute wait. Wally stood in front of the library and dug her "cheater" cigarettes out of one of the deeper pockets in her bag. The habit disgusted her, but sometimes she couldn't help herself. She lit up the cigarette and took a deep drag, exhaling the smoke in the cold air.

Wally shivered. She checked her watch. It was fifteen more minutes until her Internet time began, and with that free time in front of her Wally felt a sense of anticipation in the pit of her stomach. Over the past several days, she had been fighting back a growing need to check in with Claire, and now she decided that this was the time. It had been weeks since their last contact, and for Wally it was almost like an addiction, that feeling she got when she heard Claire's voice, all at once comforting and challenging and maddening.

However tangled their history together might be, Claire was the only mother she had ever known and Wally couldn't imagine a life that did not involve her. Nick's harsh words about how Wally had treated Claire only sharpened her need to renew the connection.

Wally snuffed out her cigarette and pulled out her cell phone. She punched in the code that would block the phone's number from displaying on Claire's caller ID, then dialed. After a few rings, Claire picked up.

"Hello?"

"Hi," said Wally. She heard Claire's tiny gasp over the line.

"Wally . . ."

"Hi, Mom," Wally repeated, speaking evenly and calmly as a cue for Claire to keep her shit together while they were talking.

"Sweetheart—"

"I'm fine," Wally cut Claire off. "I'm fine."

"I . . . I know you are, Wally," and now Wally could hear Claire's throat tighten as she fought away the urge to cry. "I know you are. But I can worry, okay? I'm not going to stop that."

"I know."

"Do you need anything?" Claire asked. "Come home. You can do laundry, I'll make you some food. . . ." She paused. "Bring anyone. I know you have friends—of course you have friends. They need things too. Bring them."

Claire's words were tumbling out quickly, running together. Wally could tell how desperate Claire was to strike just the right note with her daughter, but at the same time unsure how to achieve that.

"And you're okay?" Claire asked again.

"I'm fine." Wally felt herself tensing. "How are you?"

"I'm fine, Wally. Everything is just the same. . . ."

Wally sighed heavily. Here was the problem with all these calls: they pretty much screeched to a halt at right about that spot, after the chorus of "I'm fine's" and Wally's refusal of help.

"Honey," Claire said, hesitant. "Do you have a friend named Sophie?"

Wally was struck silent for a moment. There was no way in hell that this could be a good thing. Wally knew—*knew*—that she had never mentioned any of her crew's names to Claire.

"Why, Mom?" Wally tried not to sound impatient.

"Please. It can't be so impossible to say yes or no."

Wally hesitated. "Yes."

"Sophia Manetti?"

Wally's heart sank. The full name. So official sounding, so clinical somehow.

"What is it?" Wally demanded, feeling the dread.

"Have you . . . have you heard any news about her?" Claire asked.

"Mom, tell me right now . . ." Wally demanded.

"She's gone," Claire said quietly. "I'm so sorry, honey."

"She's . . ."

"She was killed, Wally. She's dead."

Wally's legs suddenly felt unsteady. She sank down to the pavement, leaning against the outside wall of the library. When she hadn't spoken a response after a few seconds, Claire's voice, shrill and panicked now, filled the space between them.

"I'm sorry. She was murdered. In Riverside Park. Over a week ago."

"What are you talking about, Mom? How did you—"

"Wally, do you see how crazy this is?" Claire cried. "Do you see how this ends? What in God's name are you doing out there? I'm sorry! I'm sorry for whatever it was I did to make you—"

"Stop it!" Wally yelled into the phone, her head feeling like it was about to explode. "Stop apologizing for things! You didn't do anything wrong."

"Yes I did."

"No! You didn't do this to me. You didn't do anything to Sophie. It's just who I am. It's how *we* are. There's nothing to fix."

"But we can! Just come home . . ."

"I have to go, Mom."

Wally hung up her phone. She felt sick to her stomach,

but willed herself not to puke right there on the sidewalk. She wanted to cry, but her system was in too much shock to allow that kind of release. She needed to be with her crew, but the idea of facing them with this news was unbearable. What could Wally possibly tell them, other than the truth they already knew: she herself had sent Sophie away. She had done this.

"Oh my God," Wally whispered to no one. She rose and headed toward home, ignoring the subway stops that she passed, determined to walk the entire five miles of cold pavement in a forced march, the city growing colder as the sun set behind the buildings to the west.

Wally found them in the break room of the bank, Ella's mascara running with her tears, her face half-buried in Jake's neck. Tevin sat alone, looking shell-shocked.

"What happened?" Wally asked, dreading more bad news.

The crew hesitated before saying anything.

"It's not your fault, Wally," Tevin said. "You'll say it is, but it's not. . . ."

"We went down to Washington Square to sell more phone cards," Jake explained. "James was there. Greta and Stoney. They all knew about it. Some cop has been down there making the rounds."

And Wally got it, even though the others couldn't bring themselves to say it. They had heard about Sophie on their own.

"About Sophie . . . I heard too," Wally said, and the crushing sadness of it came over her again, images flashing through her mind: Sophie broken and bloody. Sophie alone.

"I did this . . ." Wally began to confess, but before she could say any more, Tevin moved in and wrapped his arms around her. Wally cried at the instant of his touch, just as she knew she would.

"No," Tevin said. "You were right, Wally. What you said before. It was Sophie who turned away from us."

"I sent her away—"

"We know," Ella said. "But you did all you could for her."

It was almost as if the others needed to absolve Wally first so they could also forgive themselves for any way they might have let Sophie down. They cried together in the group embrace for a minute, and then slowly peeled away from each other.

"I loved how Sophie danced," Wally said as she wiped tears away from her eyes, "even when it was embarrassing."

"Which it usually was," Tevin said, managing a little smile.

"I loved how Sophie would be real quiet," Ella said, "then suddenly smile to herself out of nowhere. . . ."

"And never say what it was she was thinking about no matter how much you'd bug her," Jake remembered.

"I loved that she was fierce," Tevin said. "Even if she was wrong." And Tevin thought about it some more. "I think that's why she pushed us away."

They all considered this, and Ella began to cry again, softly, and the others drew her into an embrace again, tightly, until the sound of her tears could barely be heard.

Much later, when the others had settled in for the night, Wally went outside into the narrow alleyway by the rear exit. She dug deep into her bag and found the business card Lois Chao had given her at Harmony House. She held the card up to the street-light and read the name—Detective Atley Greer, 20th Precinct. With all that had been going on, she had forgotten about the cop's message until she heard the news about Sophie.

What had put the cop on her in the first place? Wally remembered her missing ID. If Sophie had been found with Wally's ID on her, Wally's home address would have been on it. That's how Claire had heard about the murder first. Wally dialed the cop's number on her cell, determined to learn what she could about Sophie's death.

"Yeah?" came the voice on the other end of the line, sound-ing busy and distracted.

"Detective Greer?"

"Yeah."

"This is Wallis Stoneman."

There was a pause. "Well. How are you, Wallis?"

"Fine."

"You're fine? Is that right?" In that cop voice, right from the jump. Always questioning, always challenging.

"You called me."

"Over a week ago I called you," Greer said. "Do you know what about?"

"I think I do, now. I just heard about Sophie."

"Right. I'm very sorry about your friend. I'd like us to meet, Wallis. I'm doing my best to find who did this to Sophia, and I think you can help me. You could come in to the station—"

"Ha."

"Right. You still have standing warrants in family court, don't you? I can promise you that I won't try to—"

"Forget it."

"Okay, then. You name the place."

Wally thought about it for a moment. Anything she had to tell the cop she could tell him over the phone, but she considered it an advantage to know what he looked like, for future reference. If Greer was out on the streets, there was a chance their paths would cross.

"Fine. I'll meet you at this address in thirty minutes," Wally said, and gave him a street address on 85th.

"Thirty minutes," Greer said, and hung up.

Atley Greer parked his unit on Columbus and walked west on 85th Street, looking for the address Wallis Stoneman had given him. It was almost midnight and the residential street was quiet; no sign of Wally, no clue why the girl had picked this random location for their meet. Atley was passing by a small public garden—badly overgrown and untended—when a girl's voice sounded his name.

"Greer?"

Atley was startled. He made a quick sideways step away from the garden fence and his hand was halfway to his holster when he made out a young girl's face just behind the fence, almost hidden in the dense, overgrown garden. It was Wallis— an older version of the girl in the mother-daughter portrait hanging in Claire Stoneman's apartment. Greer relaxed, and took a step closer to the garden fence.

"Wallis? You startled me there."

Atley looked the girl over. She was average height with short, tousled blond hair and formidable dark gray eyes that fixed on Atley and did not shy away. She was dressed the way many streets did in dark, practical layers and trashy makeup suggestive of an emo dance-club vibe. The look seemed natural on her.

Atley also made a quick visual reconnaissance of the overgrown lot; it was one of those odd-shaped spaces that had been co-opted for use as a communal neighborhood garden—decades earlier, probably—but had been neglected and was now a wilderness so dark and dense that Atley couldn't see through to its other side. The fence was high and overgrown with vines, and the gate was secured with a rusty padlock and chain. Atley had no intention of trying to grab up Wallis Stoneman on her family court warrants, but if he had, he would have been out of luck: even if he managed to scale the high fence, by the time he did so she would be long gone, presumably through a back entrance.

Atley smiled to himself. He was starting to understand why Social Services had no luck bringing Wallis in.

"You grew up around here," Atley said, putting together how she knew about this spot. The Stoneman apartment was just a block away, on 84th.

"Yeah," Wallis answered. "A friend of mine lived in one of these buildings, back in elementary. We used to sneak in here to smoke."

Atley nodded. "I'm sorry about Sophia. You were close?"

"We were family." The thought was sentimental, but Wally kept her emotions in check as she spoke to Atley. She would not allow herself to look weak in front of the cop.

"Family." Atley ruminated on the word. "Right. But not so much lately, I hear."

"Sophie had a problem with drugs. We have rules about that."

Atley gave her a look.

"Is that right?" he said. "You have rules against dope?"

"That's a surprise? Why? Do you allow crystal meth in *your* family?"

"Uh . . . well, I don't have a family yet, but now that you mention it, Wallis, if and when I get one, I will definitely go for a strict no-meth policy, one hundred percent."

"Are you going to catch who killed her?" Wally asked.

"Yes, we will," he said. "Any thoughts about who that is?"

"Sophie bought from several dealers," Wally answered, surprising Greer with her immediate cooperation. "One was down near Washington Square Park; he calls himself Bright Eyes."

"Bright Eyes?" Atley rolled the name over. "Like Charlton Heston in *Planet of the Apes*?"

"Huh? *No*. Bright Eyes, like the band."

"Oh." Greer got out his notebook and started taking notes.

"There's a guy up in Harlem, too," Wally continued, "calls himself Rage. I think Rage is actually Bright Eyes's supplier. For a user, Sophie was actually pretty reliable, and from time to time she muled for both those guys. That's pretty much all I know."

Wally thought about giving up Panama's name also, but as

far as she knew, Sophie and Panama had been on the outs for months, their connection fucked over by one of Sophie's rip-off schemes. Besides that, Wally's own business at the smoke shop was important to the survival of her and the crew.

"Bright Eyes, Rage. This is helpful, Wallis," Greer said. "So you think Sophia might have been moving drugs recently?"

"I don't see why not," Wally said. "She was using again, so . . . it would make sense."

"If she was holding," Greer said, following the line of reasoning, "that could be a likely cause of her getting attacked. Carrying a package could definitely bring some wolves to her door, so to speak."

"Yeah," said Wally. "That's why we have the rule against dope. Who needs more wolves?"

"*Ha.*" Atley Greer gave a little punctuating chuckle. "Damn right. '*Who needs more wolves?*' I'm gonna write that down. Maybe I'll use that myself, if it's okay with you."

"Knock yourself out."

"Any other thoughts?"

"Honestly . . ." Wally paused here, and Atley could see now that she was struggling to keep her emotions out of her voice. "The thing is, there are just so many things that happen. On the street, I'm saying. I'd guess it had to do with dope, but who knows?"

"Yeah," Greer agreed with a sigh.

There was a moment of silence between them. Atley studied the girl, and she stared right back at him.

"And you're okay, Wallis?"

"Yes."

"Huh," Greer grunted, dubious. "Okay if I ask you one thing, just between us? I'm putting down my pen here." He clicked his pen closed and stuck it in his pocket.

"Whatever."

"What's your plan?"

It was a moment before Wally answered, looking a bit defensive. "What do you mean?"

"I've been learning about you, Wally. I've been studying Wallis Stoneman 101. People say good things about you, which is not always the case with runaway JDs. I hear how smart you are. How resourceful. From what I can tell, whatever you set your mind to, you can do."

Wally sighed impatiently.

"So I've been thinking," Atley continued, "someone as smart and capable as yourself, my guess would be that you have some sort of goal in mind. A plan for your near future."

"Actually, yeah. I'm working on a project right now."

"What about Tevin and Ella and Jake?"

Atley saw just a flash of annoyance in Wally's eyes. She was unhappy that he had gathered even this small amount of intelligence on her.

"What about them?"

"Are they included in this project of yours?" Atley asked. "Because I gotta tell you, Wally, I've read their files too, and their stories aren't like yours. They're vulnerable, always have been. If we're not careful with them, they're gonna end up like Sophie."

"Screw you. We can take care of each other."

"I see," he said. "Hey, here's a question: what were you doing up on Shelter Island last week?"

The question obviously took the girl by surprise. Atley could see the wheels spinning in her head as she tried to figure out how he knew about her trip north. Her inability to fill in the blank really seemed to piss her off.

"Do your job, cop," she said finally. "Find out who killed Sophie."

She turned and stomped off into the dense thicket of brush and vines, vanishing from sight.

THIRTEEN

Tiger exited the package store on Jamaica Avenue and turned south onto a side street, passing through a low-income neighborhood. Some teenage Hispanic kids—with lots of ink on their necks and arms—gave Tiger territorial stares but otherwise let him pass. After three blocks of walking Tiger reached the cheap motel and climbed the outside stairs to the second floor, entering the room at the far end of the building. All the room lights were off and the heavy drapes were drawn closed; Tiger had to wait a moment for his eyes to adjust to the darkness of the room.

"What you get?" Alexei Klesko's voice came from one of the two queen-sized beds—he insisted that the two of them speak English, even between themselves. Klesko was stretched out on the bed, a plastic bag of ice resting between his eyes.

"Pills," said Tiger. "The whiskey you wanted. Some food."

Klesko slid the ice bag off his face and sat up on the bed. Tiger passed him the small plastic envelope of Percocets that he had scored on a street corner. Klesko swilled three of them down with a heavy slug of Jack Daniels, then restored the ice to his forehead and lay back down. His headaches had started almost as soon as they had stepped off the fishing boat in Portland.

"This fucking light," Klesko had raged that first day. "This fucking American light hurts into the eyes."

Tiger pulled some bandages out of his shopping bag and started to work on Klesko's leg wound, where the prison guard's bullet had passed clear through. Klesko had been taking antibiotics, and they seemed to be working despite his daily intake of whiskey. Tiger cleaned both sides of the wound, dabbing them with peroxide before he put on the fresh bandages. Klesko never flinched.

It wasn't Klesko's physical condition that worried Tiger. Aside from the constant rants against the "American light," there were mumbled curses aimed at nothing in particular and long, dark silences that sometimes took hours to pass. Tiger had started to worry that the years of captivity had warped the man's brain; he could not imagine what Klesko had experienced during all that time in the old gulag. If his mind had been bent, though, the damage had done nothing to dull Klesko's ruthless predatory skills; he had proved that during the escape from his Siberian prison.

And yet things were missing, signs of the bond that should have naturally existed between the two of them. Every year on his birthday, Tiger had received a letter from Klesko, awkward sentiments scrawled on a single page in the old man's increasingly shaky handwriting. Those spare gestures had done their work—had kept Tiger hoping desperately for a reunion with his father and vigilant for the reappearance of the alexandrite stones—but the promise of a genuine connection with his father had gone unfulfilled.

In the days since the escape, Klesko had not asked for a single detail about Tiger's life in Piter during the years of his father's imprisonment. Tiger would have told him how he had moved from home to home among the lower echelon of the Dobrik mob, sleeping on floors and in attics, treated not as the son of the fabled Alexei Klesko but instead as a servant, and then, as he grew older, graduated into the role of enforcer, earning his keep on the streets of Piter, intimidating, maiming, and even killing in the name of the Dobriks.

Now, as he thought about the lost connection between himself and the old man, Tiger felt a painful emptiness inside, a sense of anger and resentment that caught him by surprise. Tiger wondered if redemption was still possible, if there was anything he could do to salvage the bond between himself and his father; he didn't know how. Here in this strange country, thousands of miles from home, Tiger's only choice was to keep faith, to hope that recovering the lost stones would somehow, in turn, restore the humanity that was now missing in his cold and distant father.

In the darkness of their motel room, Tiger could sense the painkillers working on Klesko—his breathing had slowed, and he had tossed aside the bag of ice. Tiger would let Klesko sleep for three or four more hours, and then they would be on the move again.

Their first stop in Manhattan—days earlier—had been 47th Street, where the side-by-side row of gem merchants stretched for blocks. Tiger's own information had brought them here, information he had bought from a black market middleman in Prague. The Hamlisch Brothers shop was on the south side of the street, a few doors east of Avenue of the Americas. A red sign hung over the door. By that point, Tiger and Klesko had outfitted themselves in appropriate enough clothing—leather coats, collared shirts, dark blue jeans, and new boots—that the old gem merchant inside buzzed them through the door with barely a hesitation.

The Hasidic merchant had a long gray beard and side curls flowing down his neck and chest. He silently welcomed his customers by spreading his arms to indicate the vast selection of merchandise under his glass counters.

"Alexandrite," said Tiger. "You have a new stone." The old merchant's eyes flickered slightly at Tiger's accent, out of interest but not alarm.

"Ah," said the old man. "Yes. My nephew. He is not here."

"Your nephew?"

"The stone—it is not mine," said the old man. "My nephew Isaac manages his own stock. He is on a buying trip. Europe. He returns by the middle of next week. You come back for Isaac."

Tiger and Klesko stood in silence for a moment, each one processing the man's words.

"You saw who brought the stone?" Klesko asked. "You know who came here with the alexandrite?" Something in his voice—his accent, which was thicker and more parochial than Tiger's—triggered a tremor of concern in the merchant.

"No," said the merchant. "I was not here."

Tiger fixed his eyes on the merchant, considering whether or not the old man was telling the truth. He noticed that Klesko's attention was fixed on the shop's video security cameras—two of them—one high in each corner of the shop's far wall. His father turned his head and looked back through to the shop's front windows: the street outside was busy with foot traffic. Tiger watched, knowingly, as his father's mind performed the cold calculation that governed every action of his life: What did he want? How would he get it? Who would try to stop him?

"These cameras," Klesko said to the merchant. "You have pictures for that day—"

"No," Tiger cut his father off. Klesko was visibly startled as he felt Tiger take hold of his arm with a firm grip, silencing him. "Your nephew returns Wednesday of next week?" Tiger asked the merchant amiably.

"Wednesday." The merchant nodded, with visible relief. "Wednesday or Thursday." The old man passed a business card to Tiger. "You can call first for Isaac, to be sure."

Tiger gave the merchant a smile, then let go of Klesko's arm and turned toward the shop door, opening it for his father to pass through. Klesko hesitated, his pale skin seething red with anger, before finally turning away from the merchant and heading back out to 47th Street, Tiger just behind him.

"He would not give us the video pictures by choice," Tiger said evenly, leaning in close to Klesko, "and then what would you do? You would take them? *Here?*" Tiger gestured to all of 47th Street, its gem shops numbering more than a hundred, security men and cameras and unfriendly faces everywhere. "No. The old man had an alarm button under the counter. We must wait for this Isaac."

Father and son walked westward in silence, side by side. Tiger could feel his father's rage as it surged within him. He knew that every cell in his father's body was aching to punish Tiger's insolence—to make the city a witness to his authority—but Tiger also knew better than to be personally wounded by his father's anger. Klesko had survived all these years, on the streets of Piter and in prison, by being the strongest and most ruthless man in every situation; that instinct could not be turned on and off like a switch. So Tiger waited, patiently, and Klesko's rage gradually subsided. Reason took its place. Tiger was right, after all, and Tiger was his ally.

"*Da,*" said Klesko. "You are right. Good, Tiger."

Tiger flushed with pride but continued walking, making no response. He was warmed by the glow of Klesko's approval, and yet . . . a part of him sensed that this was a dangerous thing to need or want.

From the Diamond District they had traveled directly to the borough of Queens, stopping only to buy a pay-as-you-go cell phone. With Tiger behind the wheel of their stolen Pontiac LeMans, Klesko made calls to several contacts—old business associates. The calls were brief. At the end of the third call, Klesko picked up his street map and found the location he was looking for. Ten minutes later Tiger steered their car into a parking space in a run-down residential area of Queens. The address was a three-story tenement, and Klesko led them down and through an unpromising basement door.

The long, narrow basement space was brightly lit, and along each wall were at least fifteen computer stations, manned by workers of various nationalities, their heads bent low over keyboards, eyes squinting at the computer screens in front of them. To the rear of the basement was some sort of small manufacturing station, and as the men approached that spot, a tall, bony man with a shaved head turned to face them. His face went completely pale at the sight of Klesko, the reaction of a man confronted by a ghost.

"Ramzan." Klesko nodded slightly.

"Klesko . . ." Ramzan mumbled some further response, his eyes flickering in various directions, first at Tiger, with dread, and then to the two exits of the basement, assessing their potential for escape.

"You can help me," Klesko said. He handed Ramzan a small piece of paper. Ramzan nervously reviewed the list of several names on the paper, then regarded the panels of computers, anxious to choose wisely. He finally approached a young Korean man at one of the stations and handed him the paper.

"Find," Ramzan said in English. The Korean kid looked up at Ramzan, glanced once at Klesko and Tiger, then set aside his regular work and began typing furiously on his keyboard.

Meanwhile, Tiger turned his attention back to the small manufacturing station that had occupied Ramzan when they first entered the basement: Tiger could see now that there was a credit-card-imprinting machine, plus shoe boxes full of credit card blanks and stacks of computer printouts full from top to bottom with account-number lists. Tiger gestured toward a side table, where freshly imprinted cards were stacked. Ramzan nodded and, without hesitation, grabbed a handful of the cards, presenting them to Klesko.

"Good limits," said Ramzan desperately, in English now. "Three thousand, five thousand. Three or four days only, then change cards."

Klesko took the cards, not bothering to respond.

"It was so long ago, Klesko," said Ramzan, trying unsuccessfully to disguise the fear in his voice. "It was not me. My deal was ruined also. I had to run also. . . ."

Klesko ignored him, pocketing the counterfeit credit cards. Within minutes, the young Korean operator appeared beside them and presented Ramzan with the same sheet of paper, now with search results jotted down beside only one of the names on the list. Ramzan shot an angry look of alarm at the Korean, but the kid just shrugged; he could do no more. Nervously, Ramzan presented the information to Klesko, who perused the results: an address for Benjamin Hatch, the American teacher who had been Yalena Mayakova's friend those many years ago.

The information had led Klesko and Tiger to Shelter Island, the former home of Benjamin Hatch. Hatch was long since dead, it turned out, but the two of them had waited in the cold, empty house until Hatch's sons had returned home. They'd been very persuasive with the Hatches. Tiger and Klesko had spent the next three days tracking down the woman who the Hatch brothers had given up before they died. Soon, Klesko and Tiger would meet her in person.

FOURTEEN

At the Bloomingdale Library, Wally grabbed an Internet station and brought up the Emerson School website. She typed in the default password that Nick had put first on his list—EmersonAlum—and was granted full access, just as Nick had predicted.

Fortunately for Wally, the school made an effort to help former students and faculty keep in touch, with contact lists and message boards that seemed to get updated on a regular basis. Wally scanned the faculty rolls and found that her hunch had paid off: Benjamin Hatch had in fact been employed at Emerson for three academic years. His last year of teaching coincided with the failed vodka-importing business described in the *Wall Street Journal* article. Most likely, Hatch had traveled to Moscow for the teaching job, but after a few years he had sensed an opportunity to make his fortune in the newly thriving Russian economy, quitting Emerson and setting his doomed vodka import scheme into motion.

The scenario was a guess on Wally's part, and it still didn't explain if or how Hatch had been connected to Yalena. Wally continued searching the site. There was a photo section with class pictures stretching back many years, and Wally spent a half hour scanning the photos but didn't come upon any faces or names that helped her. For one thing, there was no evidence that any Russian students were mixed in with the student body, so it was unlikely Yalena had been a student at Emerson.

Wally continued checking the faculty listings from the time Hatch had been employed at the school—maybe she could track down other former teachers who might have useful information. After a half hour of searching, Wally came upon a listing for a woman named Charlene Rainer.

Charlene Rainer. Wally had the distinct feeling that she'd heard that name somewhere before. She scoured her memory but couldn't pinpoint it. On the Emerson site, Ms. Rainer's position was listed simply as "counselor," and her bio included only her nationality (American) and the span of her employment. Wally immediately noticed that Rainer had left Emerson the same year as Benjamin Hatch, around seventeen years ago. That had been right around the time Wally had been born, and the coincidence was intriguing. If Wally could locate her, Charlene Rainer might have some useful information on Hatch or even Yalena. Wally navigated a separate browser window to the same Friend Finder site she had used to come up with the long list of Benjamin Hatches and, after paying the $79.95 again, entered Charlene Rainer's name.

The results were as daunting as they had been for Benjamin Hatch. There were 141 Charlene Rainers throughout the United States, and many of them were within a realistic age range for someone who might have been working as a student counselor over eighteen years earlier—eighty-seven of them, in fact.

Wally had no luck remembering why Charlene's name rang so familiar for her, and wondering over this question spurred other thoughts. Since opening the Brighton Beach file, Wally had begun to mentally review her relationships with the women in her life, even those with whom she had only casual contact, wondering if any of them could be *her* . . . Wally's real mother. *She's been watching over you*, Ella had said upon reading the handwritten note from Yalena, and Wally had felt instantly that it was true. Was it possible that Charlene Rainer actually *was* Yalena Mayakova? Her heart raced a little at the possibility.

Wally could call all the Charlenes on the list, but that process had not helped find Benjamin Hatch and had taken the crew three whole days besides. No, Wally needed to further narrow down the list of Charlenes . . . but how?

Wally thought about Charlene's position at Emerson: counselor. What did that mean? Was she a career counselor, a college-admissions counselor, or what? Wally reexamined the faculty rolls and found other people specifically listed for those jobs, so the answer was no. Could Charlene Rainer have been some kind of in-school shrink? That seemed like a possibility, since students at Emerson would probably experience some adjustment issues after moving so far from the States. Wally assumed that the Emerson School would only hire a licensed therapist to shrink the children of the American diplomatic corps. A little research on Wikipedia led Wally to the American Psychology Board, a good place for her to start; the APB was the licensing institution that certified the graduates of the nation's best accredited schools.

Wally stepped out of the library and called the APB's public referral number, which was answered by a woman with a business voice that sounded somewhere in between an airline stewardess and an exhausted nurse.

"Referrals," the operator said. "How can I help you?"

"You make referrals for therapists?"

"We offer referrals for licensed members of the American Psychology Board only," answered the woman. "If you'd like to read about the credentials of our—"

"No, thanks, I went to your site. The thing is, my mother is having some issues. A family friend recommended someone, but I misplaced her contact number."

"I can check to see if she is a member of the APB. What is the clinician's name?"

"Charlene Rainer."

"Okay." Wally could hear the woman typing onto her keyboard. "I see we have four members by that name. . . ."

Wally was annoyed. "You wouldn't think there would be more than one."

"What's your geographical area?" the operator asked. "We can probably find her that way."

"Can you give me the contact numbers for all four?" Wally

tried to sidestep the geographical issue, since she had no idea where Charlene might be based.

"Of course. The first is listed in—"

"Actually," Wally cut the woman off as an idea suddenly occurred to her, "sorry for interrupting, but I think maybe I can narrow it down. Do you have information there for specific areas of expertise?"

"Yes, ma'am," said the operator.

"My mother's native language is Russian. That's why this particular therapist was recommended." Wally was taking a shot. If Charlene Rainer spent several years in Moscow, there was a good chance she came away with enough Russian to list it as a marketable skill on her resume.

"In fact," the operator answered after a moment's perusal of the files on her computer screen, "one of the Charlene Rainers is proficient in Russian. Do you have a pencil and paper handy?"

"Shoot," said Wally, and jotted down the phone number and mailing address of the Russian-speaking therapist named Charlene Rainer. When she hung up, Wally looked at the notes in front of her, not knowing whether she should feel lucky or nervous; the address was on West 88th Street, in the Upper West Side between Columbus and Amsterdam, just a short walk from the empty bank where Wally and the crew were squatted.

Atley Greer stood on the balcony of the sixth-floor apartment, looking down on Riverside Drive.

"Can you point out which part of the street you're talking about?" he asked.

Mrs. Dearborn, a bone-thin woman in her mid-sixties, wore a heavy chenille robe, pajamas, and pink ankle-high Ugg boots. She pointed to a spot on the drive just half a block to the north.

"Down there, across from that green mailbox, the kind that you can't put anything in," she answered, and fixed a perplexed look on Atley as she sucked a heavy drag off her menthol cigarette. "What is it with the green mailboxes, anyway? They got no openings to put anything in. What the hell are they for?" She posed the question as if it were one of the great mysteries of the human condition.

"I haven't a clue, Mrs. Dearborn," said Atley.

It had been ten days since Sophia Manetti had been found dead in the baseball diamond—Atley could see the spot from the balcony, less than two hundred yards away—but the case had zeroed out. Atley had worked all possible leads, including the information on Sophia's drug associations that Wallis Stoneman had offered at the community garden, but so far none of it had panned out. Finally the chief of Ds had authorized six uniforms for a re-canvass of the area, and one of the cops had found Mrs. Dearborn.

"So," said Atley, "go over this for me if you would. The officers say you were out here smoking."

"Yeah," she answered, "Mr. Dearborn doesn't let me smoke inside. Even in this cold weather."

"About what time was that, ma'am?"

"Midnight. Ish. It was damn cold."

"So around twelve, and the first thing you noticed was something you saw or something you heard?"

"I heard sort of a yell, an out-of-breath yell of a girl, coming from the park. When I looked down, I couldn't see anything at first, but then this girl rushed out of the brush right over there, right out onto the drive, and the car almost hit her, screeching to a stop, you know?"

"Can you describe the car?"

"A big sedan, American I think, but what do I know from cars?" Mrs. Dearborn snuffed out her cigarette in an over-full ashtray, and the cold morning breeze immediately swept it out of the ashtray and onto the balcony floor. Mrs. Dearborn lit another.

"So the girl just stands there in front of the stopped car," Mrs. Dearborn continued her narrative, sucking on her fresh menthol. "She's sort of frozen in place there, for whatever reason, and that's when the man gets out from the driver's side of the car. Then two guys come out of the park, running like, but then they stop there too, the four of 'em just sort of standing there. Maybe they all said something—I couldn't hear—but after a second they all get into the car."

"The girl's not forced into the car?"

"Not from what I could tell, but who's to say? Three big colored guys there with her? Who's to say what's her idea and what isn't? It's a hard world for a girl."

Atley could not disagree. "And then what happened?"

"The car does a U-turn on the drive and heads back north. I go back inside and watch that Ferguson guy on the TV. He's funny, with the accent and everything. I thought about calling the cops, but . . . she just got right into the car without a fight, you know?"

"I know," said Atley. A 911 call about a girl who had willingly climbed into a car on Riverside Drive would hardly raise any flags. "These three guys . . . what kind of a look did you get at them?"

"My eyes are good," said Mrs. Dearborn, "but that's a ways away and the light's that weird electricity-saving color. Not a very good look, just basic details."

"Okay."

"The big guy driving the car, I'm pretty sure he was a black," she said. "The other two I couldn't say for sure. Probably lighter skin, a little, but both with dark hair. Coulda been Puerto Ricans or even Chinese for all I know."

Atley produced some mug shots for her to look at. One array of photos included a shot of the drug dealer Rage, who Wally had mentioned. He was African American, but very fair-skinned, with freckles, and a puffy 'fro of red hair that was the source of his street name: Rage, for red. None of the lady's descriptions sounded remotely like that, and the other dealer Wallis had mentioned—Bright Eyes—was a blond white kid. Atley showed Mrs. Dearborn their photos anyway.

"Nah," she said with certainty. "Not them."

Atley sighed, tired and discouraged and footsore after almost a full day of canvassing. As Mrs. Dearborn puffed away on her cigarette, Atley leaned over the railing and imagined the scenario as the lady had described it: Sophia Manetti runs out of the park—chased by two men—and onto the drive, where she almost gets hit by a black guy driving a sedan. But she doesn't keep running, because . . . *because*, the driver is someone she knows? That's quite a coincidence. She doesn't even run when the guys chasing her catch up and appear there on the street, next to the car.

Suddenly, it's not a chase and it's not an assault: it's a friendly get-together, right there on Riverside Drive at midnight. They all climb into the car, no drama. The car does a U-ey and heads north on the drive, taking the turnoff that circles back into the park, where the baseball fields are located. Sophia had climbed into that sedan willingly, but her ride—and her life—ended at the hands of someone she knew.

Back at the precinct house, Atley opened the Manetti book to review what he had so far. It did not take long. The biggest boost had been Wallis Stoneman's information about Rage and Bright Eyes—Sophia's drug connections—but if Mrs. Dearborn's eyewitness account could be trusted, then those two were not involved in Sophia's death, at least not directly. Atley had an eyewitness account of Sophia's abduction, if that's what it was, and still the case was dead-ended. He opened the murder book again and reread everything from page one, looking for an avenue he might have missed.

He pored over all the crime scene reports and found nothing productive—no DNA, no fingerprints, no footprints or tire

tracks, no witnesses other than Mrs. Dearborn, nothing interesting in the autopsy other than a slew of drugs in the girl's
system, as expected. Atley moved on to Sophia Manetti's juvie
file. He had been through it already and what was inside added
nothing to the case, just a sad life story with a familiar and
tragic progression: unstable home, parental abuse, drug abuse,
street. Atley continued into Wallis Stoneman's juvie file. The
notes documented Wallis's problems at home, her flirtation
with life on the street, her expulsion from school, etc. Unlike
Sophia, there was no violence documented in Wallis's home,
but the girl had spent the first five years of her life in a Russian orphanage, so who could know what sorts of pain she had
experienced before coming home to America with Claire and
Jason Stoneman?

In the mass of Social Services paperwork was a psych eval
of Wallis, written up when Wallis was just ten. After a single
thirty-minute interview, the Social Services shrink had diag-
nosed Wallis's problem: disruptive behavior disorder. Atley
did a search for the term on his desktop and came up with a
description of the diagnosis: a DBD-diagnosed subject "refuses
to comply with adults," "deliberately annoys people," and "is
angry and resentful." In other words, the subject is exactly like
every teenager Atley had ever met.

"Unbelievable," Atley groaned out loud.

Atley noticed another psych evaluation in Wallis's file, from
when she was even younger, just seven or eight years old. She
had seen a private therapist occasionally over the course of a
few years, presumably paid for by her parents. This shrink's

report contained none of the bullshit psych jargon that had filled the Social Services evaluation. There was only a brief notation by the therapist under the diagnosis heading: "Wally is a lovely girl, intelligent and mature and resourceful and determined. She is also confused and angry, as would be expected. There will be struggles ahead for Wally."

There will be struggles ahead. Strange, Atley thought, to praise the girl so lavishly and then predict struggle. The thing that struck Atley most about the evaluation was the tone—it wasn't clinical sounding, really, but more personal than he had seen in other such files. And one phrase in the conclusion struck Atley as equally intriguing: "She is also confused and angry, *as would be expected.*" Expected why?

It seemed unlikely that the shrink would be able to contribute to his investigation, but . . . *fuck it,* Atley thought. He got on the phone and made an appointment to meet the therapist, Dr. Charlene Rainer.

FIFTEEN

It was already dark when Wally and the crew settled into their seats in the Starbucks coffee place, the four of them lined up shoulder to shoulder at the window counter that gave them a clear view across West 88th. They fixed their eyes on the entrance to the office building on the opposite side of the street.

"So this shrink . . . she was at this Emerson School the same time as Benjamin Hatch?" Jake asked.

"And left the same year," Wally confirmed. "I don't know how well they knew each other. If Hatch had some connection to my mother, maybe Charlene Rainer knew her in Russia too. I don't know."

"And you recognize her name?" Tevin asked.

"From somewhere, yeah, but I can't remember from where or when. But it can't be a coincidence, right? She was in Russia the same time as my mother—all those years ago—and she just happens to have a connection to my life here?"

Wally checked the clock on her cell phone: 5:42. She intended to keep the six o'clock session she scheduled with the therapist—under a made-up name so that Dr. Rainer would not know it was Wally—but was hoping to get a look at the woman's face first; if she recognized Charlene Rainer by sight and remembered their connection, it might give Wally an advantage in their meeting. Dr. Rainer's chatty answering service lady had said the doctor would be arriving at her office from another appointment, so hopefully Wally would get the look she wanted.

Over the next fifteen minutes or so, several dozen pedestrians passed by on the opposite sidewalk, at least half of them women. Wally didn't recognize any of them, and none entered Dr. Charlene Rainer's office building.

"This is brutal," Wally said, struggling to stay cool during this process when in reality she could barely stand the suspense.

"Why are you so stressed?" Tevin asked.

"While I was researching this woman, it seemed like there were lots of overlaps between her history and my birth mother's," Wally said. "It's kind of possible that she actually *is* my mother. . . ."

"Wow . . ." Tevin said, he and the others realizing how easily the situation could tie Wally up in knots.

"Whatever happens," Ella said, "it's better to know."

"Knowing would be nice," Wally agreed with a wry grin.

At that moment a woman came strolling quickly down 88th Street, wearing a knee-length blue overcoat and with a simple leather valise slung over her shoulder. As the woman passed under a streetlight, her features became visible. The woman was in her mid-fifties, most likely, well dressed without trying to make a show of it, a bit of gray peppering her hair.

"That's her," Wally said with certainty.

"How do you know?" Jake asked. "You figured out where you know her from?"

"No," Wally said. "But that's the doctor. I just know it."

Wally stood at the front entrance to Dr. Rainer's building and punched in the code for her office, which was listed on a directory beside the door. The door buzzed and popped open. Wally entered the small lobby and followed a narrow hallway, which opened into a surprisingly large space. It was an atrium, rising up the center of the stylish, turn-of-the-century building. At each level was an overlooking balcony, with a polished wood banister running the full perimeter of each. Wally consulted a directory by the elevator, only to find that Dr. Rainer's suite number was not listed. The whole place seemed strangely quiet; there must have been forty or fifty office suites bordering the atrium, but most of them looked dark.

"Third floor, Suite G," a woman's voice echoed down from up above . . . Dr. Rainer, presumably. Wally climbed into the elevator and rode up to the third floor, then followed the balcony to the left, walking all the way to the suite at the far end: Suite G. The door was slightly ajar. Wally knocked twice, lightly.

"Come in," came the same woman's voice that had called out the suite number from above.

Wally pushed open the door and passed through a tiny waiting room—two upholstered chairs and a small coffee table with a selection of magazines—and then on into the tastefully decorated office space. The woman she had seen on the street, Dr. Charlene Rainer, was at her desk sorting through a stack of mail but looked up as Wally entered. She greeted Wally with a smile.

"Ms. Jones?" the doctor asked. "Welcome. I'm Doctor—" But then the doctor stopped herself and looked Wally over more closely, recognition dawning on her as she focused on Wally's face. *"Wally?"*

"Yes," Wally said, and now—seeing the woman's face up close—Wally remembered. *Shonny.* How old had Wally been? Maybe seven or eight, the first time? She'd been having some problems at the Harpswell School, and Claire had brought Wally in for counseling to a woman who she was supposed to call *Shonny,* casually as if they were friends. The visits had taken place in a different office, and the doctor had aged a bit in the last eight or nine years, of course, but this was unquestionably the same woman. Immediately, Wally remembered feeling safe with her, comfortable.

"Wally." Dr. Rainer's face brightened as she looked Wally over again, taking an inventory of the changes to her former patient. "Look how grown you are. How old?"

"Sixteen."

"Good lord. Can it really be that long?" At that moment

a thought crossed Dr. Rainer's mind—she looked as if she was trying to work out a puzzle. "Are you Ms. Jones? My next appointment?"

"Yes," Wally answered. "Sorry. I'll explain."

"No harm done," said Dr. Rainer. "You're always welcome here, Wally. Please sit down."

Wally chose one of the two guest seats in front of the desk instead of the leather sofa that ran along the opposite wall— she wanted to be up close and personal for this discussion. Dr. Rainer sat down in the high, leather office chair behind her desk.

"It's been how many years?" Dr. Rainer wondered aloud, and then swiveled her chair to face the wooden file cabinet behind her, opening one of the wide drawers. "I'm afraid I never took to the computerized file thing," she said as she searched through the cabinet. "One of these days, maybe . . ."

After a moment of searching, she retrieved a file folder and shuffled through the pages, scanning for the information she wanted. "I can hardly believe it," she said, swiveling back to her desk. "It's been almost eight years since your last visit. I would have guessed four or five, but that's what happens as we get older."

Wally was deeply curious about the contents of that file. She was just about to ask if she could see it—wouldn't happen, probably—when Dr. Rainer returned the file to its place in the drawer and closed the cabinet.

"I've spoken to Claire on occasion," Dr. Rainer said as she turned back to Wally, and the doctor's face revealed a slight look of disappointment. "So I guess I'm at least semi-up-to-date on your current . . . uh, situation."

"I don't want to talk about that now," Wally said, determined to steer the discussion exactly where she needed it to go. No therapeutic bullshit, no recriminations for the choices she had made in her life.

"All right," Dr. Rainer said. "Just . . . you're safe? You're healthy?"

"I can take care of myself," Wally said.

Dr. Rainer smiled. "I don't doubt it. You were always strong."

"I need the truth, Dr. Rainer."

"Of course."

"You were my therapist."

"Yes. Not regularly. We met a few times, when you were having specific problems. Do you want to talk about those issues?"

"No. Back then, when you first started meeting with me . . . you already knew who I was. It wasn't just random that I came to you as a patient. We had a connection already."

"Well . . ." Dr. Rainer shifted in her seat. "I'm not sure in what sense you mean that, Wally."

"You used to live in Russia."

Wally waited as Dr. Rainer remained completely still for a moment, her eyes locked on Wally. The doctor suddenly looked very nervous. She cast an anxious look toward the door of her office, which was still open.

"Wally, are you alone?" she asked warily.

"Um, yeah," Wally answered, wondering what was spooking the doctor. "It's just me."

"Excuse me a moment . . ." Dr. Rainer stepped past Wally, out of her office and onto the balcony hallway. From there, she moved to the edge of the wooden railing, searching the atrium space with her eyes in every direction. Empty. She took a moment and just listened. All was quiet. Somewhat satisfied, Dr. Rainer returned to the office, closing the office door behind her and facing Wally again.

"Wally," she said, exhaling as if she had been holding her breath. "I'm sorry, you surprised me, to say the very least. I'm just a little . . . a little something, today. I'm not sure what. A little anxious, I guess."

"It's okay," Wally said, and forged onward. "You taught at the Emerson School."

"I was there, but I didn't teach," the doctor answered, now making a poor attempt to appear relaxed and casual. "I'd just finished my doctorate at Columbia and I started exploring some of the more exotic job opportunities. I saw that Emerson was looking for an on-staff counselor, and the idea of traveling to Russia for a while was exciting." The answer was longer and more detailed than necessary, and Wally could sense that the woman was stalling, maybe afraid of whatever questions would come next.

"And you knew Yalena Mayakova during that time." A statement, not a question.

Dr. Rainer took a moment. The woman had been uneasy

already, but the mention of Yalena's name took her obvious sense of dread to a new level.

"How do you know that name, Wally?"

"I just know it. Please answer my question, Doctor."

Dr. Rainer took a moment. "Yes. I knew Yalena Mayakova when I lived in Moscow."

"You know that I'm her daughter. You've always known? Back then when you were giving me counseling or whatever . . ."

Another pause. "Yes."

And now Wally had to ask: "Are *you* Yalena Mayakova?"

Whatever question Dr. Rainer might have been expecting at that point, this was not it.

"Me?" The woman was obviously taken aback. "Oh, Wallis . . . *no*."

"You're not my real mother?"

"I am not your real mother."

Wally took a deep breath and let it out in a rush. "Okay. Good," she said. "Nothing personal. I just now realized I wasn't ready for it if you were. Not yet."

"You're not ready because I'm not your mother," Dr. Rainer said kindly. "When you face her, you'll know her. And you'll be ready then. I'm sure of it."

When I face her. Wally's mother was alive. She took a moment to let the reality of it sink in. It was hope that had driven Wally's search forward, but in a corner of her heart she had always held on to a small amount of doubt, a lifeline to protect her in case her search ended in failure. That doubt was gone now, and Wally allowed herself to embrace the feeling of joy . . . and anticipation. The thrill of it raced through her, taking her breath away.

"Tell me everything," she said, barely able to speak the words.

SIXTEEN

Detective Atley Greer pulled onto 88th from Columbus and parked in a loading zone, just a few doors away from the doctor's address. He was seriously dragging after a long day of canvassing on a home-invasion case, and when he spotted a Starbucks across the street, he headed in that direction for a jolt of espresso. He was early for his appointment and had plenty of time.

Atley was halfway across the street, just a hundred feet or so away from the coffee place, when he noticed that the shop was in the process of closing; the manager herded three teenage kids out onto the sidewalk and locked the door behind them. Atley stopped and scanned the street for another nearby source of caffeine but saw none, and was just about to head straight to Dr. Rainer's office when something started to nag at him: hadn't he seen those kids somewhere recently? He turned back

to face the Starbucks and saw that although the shop had been
closed, the teens were staying there, lurking outside the coffee
shop as if waiting for someone. He looked them over again—
still at a distance—and suddenly he realized who they were.
These were Wallis Stoneman's friends, the ones she had been
with in the Greenport train station security camera footage.
This coincidence struck Atley as especially unlikely; he'd been
hunting them for over a week and here they were, outside an
office where he was about to have a meeting that had to do with
Wallis. What did that mean?

Atley looked away from them immediately, hoping they
didn't realize that he'd noticed them. After a few moments the
teens abandoned their post in front of the Starbucks and began
walking together down along 88th Street. They moved casually enough that Atley couldn't tell if they'd made him or not.
Following their movement in the reflection of a shop window,
Atley waited until the teens disappeared around the corner at
Amsterdam and jogged after them. He reached the corner and
stopped there, peering down the avenue to confirm that the
three kids were still far enough ahead of him that they would
not feel him on their tail. They continued casually on their way
down Amsterdam, not once looking back behind them.

Atley checked his watch. He still had half an hour before
his appointment with the shrink and this was too good an
opportunity to pass up. He started walking after the kids, south
on Amsterdam at their same casual pace, keeping the distance
between them consistent. They reached the corner of Amsterdam at 87th and turned left, moving out of view. Atley picked

up his pace and reached the corner in less than ten seconds, but . . . when he made the left turn onto 87th, he looked east down the street and saw no one in front of him, not on either sidewalk. No teenage street crew, no one. Empty.

"You gotta be kiddin' me . . ." Atley mumbled angrily. He hurried along 87th, looking into doorways, scanning the recesses of walk-down basement apartments, but the kids were nowhere to be seen. There were several storefronts nearby, including a dry cleaner, a pizza place, and an empty space that used to be a bank, but a scan of these spots turned up nothing.

"Son of a bitch . . ."

Tevin, Ella, and Jake hunched low and motionless, hidden behind the half-size Dumpster in the passageway behind the bank. Peering carefully out toward the street, they could see the cop looking around, pissed off, wondering how they had lost him.

"How do we know this cop?" asked Jake.

"We don't," answered Tevin. "I don't, anyway."

"Me either. So why is he on us?" Ella asked.

As they considered the question, they watched the cop give up and turn around, headed back to where they had first spotted him: outside the Starbucks, across the street from the shrink's office. Where Wally was.

"This is not good," said Tevin.

SEVENTEEN

"I won't leave here until you tell me everything," Wally said when Dr. Rainer had hesitated to answer her.

"I'll tell you what I can, Wally," Dr. Rainer said. Wally could see that there would be boundaries to this interview; she would have to be cautious not to spook Dr. Rainer any more than she already had.

"You knew my mother very well," Wally began.

"Yes. Since she was your age."

"In Russia. You and Benjamin Hatch both knew her."

Dr. Rainer was surprised to hear Hatch's name come from Wally.

"Yes. Benjamin and I . . . we were together in those days. During our years at the Emerson School. Benjamin and I worked there. For a time, he and I . . ." But the doctor's thoughts drifted for a moment, and she didn't finish her sentence.

"And my mother . . . do you have a picture of her?"

The question seemed to catch Dr. Rainer off balance. Strange, thought Wally, since it seemed like a simple yes-or-no.

"I'm sorry, no," Dr. Rainer finally said.

"But you still know Yalena. She's here."

A pause. "Yes."

"Do I know her?" Wally had a lump in her throat now, her voice cracking a little; she hated being in the grip of something so beyond her control. "Do I know her, Doctor?"

Dr. Rainer shifted uncomfortably in her seat. "I have questions too, Wally."

"No, you don't understand," Wally protested. "I have to find her. Who is she, Doctor?"

"I can't tell you that, Wallis," Dr. Rainer said. "I made that promise. And it wouldn't be safe. If you had that knowledge, there are those who would do anything to make you tell, you see?"

It was obvious that Dr. Rainer would not compromise on this point, and Wally couldn't afford to lose her as an ally.

"Okay," Wally said, trying to hide her impatience. "Then what *can* you tell me about her?"

"What do you want to know?"

"Well . . ." Wally had too many questions. Where to begin? The beginning. "What was my mother like? Back then, in Russia."

Dr. Rainer thought back. "Smart. Pretty." Dr. Rainer looked up and set an appraising look on Wally, obviously making a comparison. "A lot like you, Wallis. Lovely, but . . . more conventional. She had a worldly education; her own mother worked on the staff of the Emerson School, so Yalena practically grew up there, among the Americans. She was athletic. She played the piano well. She was a reasonably good student. Boys liked her, but she was . . . reserved. By nature."

"How did things go wrong for her?" For the past week, Wally had been weaving imaginary narratives in her mind, trying to imagine the sequence of events that had resulted in Yalena Mayakova giving up her own child, her own flesh and blood.

"She had been raised by a single mother," Dr. Rainer said. "And Yalena craved a strong male presence in her life. She was drawn to men, not boys."

"She found someone," Wally said.

Dr. Rainer gave a dreadful sigh. "Someone found her."

"And there was trouble."

"Not at first, but yes. Bad trouble."

"What was the man's name?"

Wally watched as Dr. Rainer wrestled with this question. Did she have to right to reveal the name to Wally? Did she have the right *not* to?

"Klesko." Dr. Rainer spoke the name with reluctance, as if it were a dark spell that she feared might conjure the man himself. "Alexei Klesko."

"*Klesko.*" Wally repeated the name out loud, feeling it. She paused, then asked, "And Klesko is my—"

"Please don't ask me, Wally," the doctor said, insistent. "I'm sorry, but it's not my place."

"It's not your place to keep it from me, either . . ." Wally said, fighting to keep control of her frustration. At that moment she had another thought. She reached into her shoulder bag and pulled out the photo from the Brighton Beach file, the grainy black-and-white surveillance photo of the man she had encountered in the Hatches' house. She held the picture up for Dr. Rainer to see, and the woman went pale.

"Is this Klesko?" Wally demanded. "Is this my father?"

"My God . . ." Dr. Rainer was terrified by the image. "Where was that picture taken? *When* was it taken?"

"Tell me, Dr. Rainer. Is this my father?"

"Yes, Wally," Dr. Rainer relented. "That is Klesko. That is your father."

Wally absorbed this news. She held the photograph before her and looked on it with new eyes. The man whose path she had crossed in Shelter Island—the man who had virtually radiated a sense of menace and violence—was her own flesh and blood. For some reason, the shock of this realization was not as overwhelming as it might have been, and now Wally realized that from the moment she had seen the man's photograph in the Brighton Beach file, there was the smallest voice, deep inside her, that had already told her this truth. The revelation, however frightening, was something Wally was ready to embrace. She welcomed knowledge—even painful knowledge—over the ignorance she had endured for most of her life.

"What happened between Klesko and my mother?"

"Yalena was with Klesko for seven years. In the beginning their relationship was . . . *workable*. But over time Klesko

changed. Something emerged from inside of him, something
dark. It became clear over time that his family's business was
with the Vory—the Russian criminal network—and the deeper
he dove into that world, the more brutal he became. Yalena tried
to leave him, of course, but he never allowed her to escape. By
the time she became pregnant with you, she was resolved that
she would raise you alone, that Klesko would never be part of
your life. This is where Benjamin Hatch became involved. Ben
had some business connections that he used to help Yalena get
out of the country. The cost turned out to be terrible."

"What?"

"It was supposed to be cash. Benjamin's business had gone
to hell; all he had was debt. He agreed to get Yalena out of the
country, but for a price. To pay, she had to use Klesko's money,
and the only way to get away with that was to get him out of
the way. Yalena was privy to details of a deal Klesko and his
associates had put together—some sort of smuggling operation—and she betrayed Klesko to the authorities. She brought
Benjamin with her when she went to where Klesko kept his
reserves—there was a cache hidden on the grounds near his
dacha—which was a mistake. Once Benjamin saw what Klesko
had there—"

"Alexandrite . . ." Wally blurted her guess. It had occurred
to her suddenly, a single critical item that might tie every aspect
of the story together: the gem she'd received from her mother
in the Brighton Beach file. Where had it come from? Had there
been more?

"Yes," Dr. Rainer confirmed. "Once Benjamin saw Klesko's

cache of stones, he wouldn't settle for anything less. Your mother had no choice. She was desperate."

"But Benjamin got the stones, right?" Wally said, trying to piece it all together. "He was paid, and Klesko was out of the way? Then why did she leave me behind?"

"Things went terribly wrong." Dr. Rainer sighed grimly. "Klesko's associates came after Yalena. In their minds, Klesko's money was *their* money. They tracked her down; they would never stop. Yalena was faced with an impossible choice—"

Dr. Rainer was interrupted at that moment by a woman's voice, calling out loudly from the direction of the building's atrium. Her exact words were not clear from behind Dr. Rainer's heavy office door. Dr. Rainer rose from her desk and made her way out of the office, onto the balcony hallway. Wally followed. As they reached the balcony, the woman's call sounded again, and this time they could hear.

"Hello?" came the woman's voice. "Who's there?"

Dr. Rainer and Wally stepped to the balcony and looked up two floors to find a Middle Eastern woman, in her mid-thirties and wearing a business suit, leaning out over the railing. She spotted Dr. Rainer and Wally.

"I hate when they do that," the woman said.

"Do what?" Dr. Rainer asked.

"Some guy rang my line from down at the front door," the woman said. "He said who he was, but I couldn't understand his accent. I shouldn't have buzzed him in, but I figured it was a delivery or something. None of those guys speak English anymore."

Now Dr. Rainer and Wally peered down toward the floor of the atrium, looking for whoever it was who lied his way into the building. The place was quiet and empty.

"Hello?" Dr. Rainer called down toward the ground floor, her voice echoing in the high atrium space. No response. She was anxious now, and Wally was too.

"I've been saying for years that we should have a doorman." The Middle Eastern woman spoke down toward them, sounding put out but not actually worried.

"Call the police right now," Dr. Rainer insisted.

"Oh," the woman said, taken aback by the urgency in Dr. Rainer's words. "You think so? Okay, I—" The woman turned slightly away from the balcony, ready to walk back toward her office, but never made it any farther than that. A thunderous gunshot echoed through the atrium and a bullet tore through the woman's chest, splattering blood on the railing as her lifeless body dropped out of view.

Wally and Dr. Rainer gasped and screamed in horror at the sudden, breathless cruelty of a life being taken before their eyes.

"Oh my God . . ." Wally could barely choke out the words.

"It's him," Dr. Rainer said, her face gone white in terror. She grabbed Wally and pulled her back through her tiny waiting room and into her office, slamming and locking both doors behind them. Within moments they heard someone kicking away at the outside door, trying to get in.

Wally imagined the man from the Hatches' house—a man who radiated terror—and struggled to process the reality of her situation: he was her father, and he was a killer. Was he here for her? For Dr. Rainer? It didn't matter. He was coming in, now.

"The fire escape," Wally said. She rushed to the office window and unlocked it, heaving it up on its tracks. There was an iron security grate attached outside the window, but she couldn't get it open until she figured out that there was a release lever inside the office. Wally pulled the lever and the iron grate swung up and away from the window, clearing a path for escape, but . . . she immediately heard the sound of footsteps coming up the metal stairs of the fire escape. Wally looked down to see someone charging up the steps toward her, his long black hair whipping through the air—it was the younger man from the Hatches' house.

"Shit!" Wally said. Now she tried to close the iron grate, but it had swung completely away from the window and she couldn't quite reach it. When she turned back around, she was surprised to see Dr. Rainer pulling a 9mm handgun from the bottom drawer in her desk.

"For this day," Dr. Rainer said, answering Wally's look.

The doctor reached out the open window and, looking like someone who had practiced on a firing range but never actually shot the handgun in the real world, fired three quick shots downward. The sound of footsteps climbing up from below stopped, at least temporarily, but from the direction of Dr. Rainer's waiting room came a crashing sound—someone bursting through the outside door—and now the second person was in the waiting room area, kicking hard at the door to the inner office, where Wally and Dr. Rainer were now trapped.

"These offices connect . . ." Dr. Rainer whisper-yelled to Wally, and stepped to a closed door on the side wall of her office. She pointed her gun at the lock on the side door, grimacing with both hands on the grip as she squeezed the heavy trigger and blasted the lock with two deafening shots. The side door swung open, revealing a lawyer's office next door.

Dr. Rainer charged into the lawyer's office space and Wally followed her. Wally shut the door behind them and with Dr. Rainer's help tipped a big metal file cabinet down to block it, and just in time. They heard footsteps in Dr. Rainer's office and angry words being exchanged in Russian. Suddenly the door they had just passed through began to shudder as both men heaved against it, each effort shoving the file cabinet back an inch farther. Within seconds they would break their way into the lawyer's office.

"The balcony," Dr. Rainer whispered. She and Wally rushed through the lawyer's waiting room and headed toward the front door that would deliver them back on the atrium balcony, but just as Dr. Rainer's hand reached out and gripped the doorknob, footsteps sounded out on the balcony, arriving outside the lawyer's door, inches from where Wally and Dr. Rainer were standing. This pursuer started kicking at the door from the outside. The two women were blocked in again, this time trapped in the lawyer's office.

Dr. Rainer took a step back and fired two blind shots at the door—some curses in Russian sounded from outside, curses of anger not pain—and soon the kicking at that door began again. By now the first pursuer had shoved the file cabinet a foot back and was just inches from having it open far enough to squeeze through. He grunted like an enraged beast with each monumental effort.

Until that moment Dr. Rainer had held herself together—had been strong on the outside, anyway—but now she began to tremble, and tears flowed out of her eyes.

"Oh God . . ." she said. "He'll make me tell. He'll do anything. . . ."

"There's another connecting office," Wally said, seeing that the office had a side door similar to the one in the lawyer's office.

Dr. Rainer seemed incapacitated by fear at that moment, so Wally grabbed the gun from her hand and stepped to the side door, firing two more shots into the door lock. The door swung open, this time revealing the working studio of some sort of craftsman—a builder of architectural models, which were arranged everywhere in the small space—plus a worktable covered with materials for modeling, including paints and solvents.

The women ran into this next space, where the only piece of furniture big enough to block the door behind them was a huge, metal blueprint locker, too heavy for them to move. Wally looked around and discovered a softball trophy atop the blueprint locker. Wally grabbed the trophy and jammed the narrow top end—the figure of a softball player crouched in a batting posture—in between the door and the floor, like a doorstop.

Wally turned back toward Dr. Rainer, who had flung the craftsman's window up and was now trying to pull the latch under the window that would release the security grate. It was jammed shut. Wally joined in the effort, but the lever would not budge. The fire escape was blocked to them.

There was no second side door to this office, only a front door—where one of the men was already trying to break through—and the door back to the lawyer's office, jammed shut by the softball trophy, but now that door was under assault also, the second man kicking and heaving himself against it, the sharp edge of the trophy digging into the floor but slowly inching backward, giving in to the pressure.

Wally and Dr. Rainer were cornered here, with no way out. In the midst of this storm of violence—the two Russians throwing themselves relentlessly at each door, ready to break through—Wally felt a strange calm come over her. What was that about? Part of her felt that there would be some sort of relief to surrender, that she would give anything for all the fear and doubt she had been living with to simply end, even if that happened through violence and pain. She felt an urge to open the door to the beasts outside and accept her fate. She turned to Dr. Rainer, who was still nearly paralyzed by fear.

"Tell me now," Wally said to the terrified doctor. "I know now who my father is. Who is my mother, Dr. Rainer?"

Dr. Rainer looked at Wally and seemed to understand; whatever fate awaited her, Wally could face it bravely if only she knew the answer to that simple question. The doctor smiled a little, sadly, and opened her mouth to speak.

"Oh, Wally," she said, "you already—"

But those were Dr. Rainer's last words. Four rapid gunshots

sounded from outside the office's front door, the bullets ripping through the lock—an attempt to blow it open. The lock held strong, miraculously, but one of the shots deflected off the metal with a strange, high-pitched *ping* like a sound effect from a Saturday morning cartoon, and Dr. Rainer's voice went silent. Wally looked and saw a bullet hole open up in the doctor's throat, arterial blood spurting out as Charlene Rainer dropped lifeless to the floor.

"No!" Wally howled, and fell to her knees, pulling her scarf off and holding it to the doctor's throat in a desperate effort to staunch the bleeding, but it was a futile gesture: the woman was dead. In a rage now, Wally stood and fired Dr. Rainer's gun into the wood of the front door, with no way to know if the barrage had done any damage. The gun's magazine clicked empty after only four shots.

"Shit!" Wally growled as she tossed the useless weapon aside.

The man out front began heaving himself against the door again, grunting loudly with each effort. The lock and hinges of the door creaked and groaned, ready to give out at any moment, and the same continued from the side door.

Wally looked around desperately for any option, and her eyes fell on the model builder's worktable, where the cans of paint and solvent sat. The label on the solvent can warned that the liquid was severely toxic and flammable. Wally grabbed the solvent and popped the top off. She stepped to the front door and crouched low, setting the solvent can at the bottom of the door so that the nozzle was stuck underneath, facing outward.

Wally stood, pulled a lighter from her pocket, and then, with her left foot, stomped hard down onto the can. The solvent sprayed under the door, and at that moment Wally jumped backward a few steps, lit the lighter, and threw it toward the can.

A flash of light flared from the other side of the door, followed by loud curses from Alexei Klesko. Wally immediately unlocked the door and rushed out, sprinting past Klesko, whose pant legs were now on fire. The enraged man whipped off his leather jacket and started using it to snuff the flames as Wally raced onto the indoor balcony, only to find herself staring straight down the muzzle of a gun held by the other Russian, the young one with the long hair.

"It is over now . . ." the young man said calmly.

In this fleeting moment, Wally's eyes met the younger man's, and between them there was a moment of . . . what? Confusion?

No. *Recognition.*

At this moment Klesko stomped out of the model builder's office, his pant legs blackened but the flames all gone. He raised his gun, and now there were two barrels aimed directly at Wally.

"Fucking bitch . . ." he barked. "You tell me where—"

But suddenly two gunshots exploded from behind them, ripping into the balcony ceiling. Wally and the two Russians looked to discover Atley Greer stalking down the hallway toward them, his service weapon raised in their direction.

"POLICE! NOBODY MOVES!" Atley shouted, but Klesko and the younger man immediately disobeyed, ducking low and using Wally for cover as they turned back down along the balcony and charged in through the door of Dr. Rain-er's office, firing wildly back toward Atley as they went. Wally dropped to the floor as the shots filled the air.

"Stay here!" Greer shouted at Wally as he blew past her on the heels of the two men. He vanished into Charlene Rainer's office and Wally immediately disobeyed his order also: she stood up and ran.

As Wally reached the stairs, there were more gunshots behind her—Atley Greer and the Russians battling it out—but Wally did not turn to look. She hurried down the stairs, and when she reached the second-floor landing, she ran into Tevin, Jake, and Ella, themselves rushing upward, looking terrified.

"Wally!" Tevin shouted, relieved to see her unharmed.

"What the fuck is happening up there?" Jake demanded.

"Come on!" Wally said. "We have to go, now!" She hustled down the stairs at full speed, the others now racing behind her. They made it out the building and ran along 88th Street, but as they moved, they heard a variety of sounds behind them: more gunshots, muffled somewhat because they were going off inside the shrink's building, then the sound of words being barked out in Russian, then the sound of footsteps descending the metal steps of a fire escape.

Wally and the others reached Amsterdam Avenue, more shouts and footsteps echoing along the street somewhere not far behind them. The crew continued south until they reached the corner where their bank building stood. They turned east along 87th and slipped into the rear passageway, where they used the key from the lockbox on the back door to get in their usual way.

Wally immediately dropped down to the cold tile floor of the bank, struggling to catch her breath. The bank was dark; the only light came from the streetlights outside, their glow spilling in through the soaped-up windows. Wally continued to breathe deeply, filling her starved lungs and waiting for the intense surge of adrenaline to drain from her system. She was trembling, and Ella was quick to wrap her in her arms.

"Oh my God," Ella said. "Are you okay, Wally?"

Ella spotted something on Wally's cheek—a spot—and reached to wipe it away. Her finger came away wet with a smear of blood, and Ella gave out a soft gasp at the sight of it. She showed the blood to Tevin, who was sitting right beside them on the floor, waiting for Wally to recover.

"What happened up there, Wally?" he asked.

Before Wally could summon enough breath to answer, Jake spoke—he was crouched near the window of the bank, looking out.

"They're here," he said in a near whisper.

Wally, Ella, and Tevin moved to the window and huddled beside Jake. The crew had scratched a few inconspicuous peep-holes in the soaped-over surface of the glass, through which they could see out onto the street but not be seen themselves. In silence and darkness, they watched the street outside where the two Russians stood now, glancing in every direction, looking for them. The two men stalked about, looking frustrated as they checked some of the dark staircases that led to lower-level apartments and the recesses of other doorways. They looked up and down the street, perplexed.

"Who is this girl?" Klesko shouted with a sense of futility into the cold night air.

The words sent a chill down Wally's spine. As she and the crew sat there, absolutely still and silent, she could not help but wonder what had become of Detective Greer. Wally had no special love for the cop, but he had almost certainly saved her life on the balcony outside Charlene Rainer's office.

As the Russians continued their search of the street, obviously trying to imagine how Wally and the crew had so quickly disappeared, Alexei Klesko stepped to the bank window and pushed right up against the glass, trying to see through the soap into the interior; his face was only inches from Wally. She and the others kept absolutely still, knowing that any movement might catch Klesko's attention. She looked into the man's unseeing eyes, deep gray, just inches away from her own. . . .

"*Ochee chornya . . .*" Wally whispered.

"What?" Ella whispered back. "What does that mean?"

Dark eyes, Wally thought, but did not speak it out loud. *Dark eyes, like mine.*

Police sirens sounded in the distance. The two men abandoned their search and jogged east on 87th, away from the bank where Wally and the crew huddled together, breathless and trembling.

"They'll be back," Wally said. "We can't stay here anymore."

EIGHTEEN

It was just after eight in the morning when Klesko parked
the stolen LeMans on 47th Street, just fifty feet east of the
Hamlisch Brothers storefront. In the passenger seat, Tiger was
about to get out of the car when the door to Hamlisch Brothers
opened and a young man emerged from the shop, setting the
alarm behind him and rolling down the metal security grate
that covered the entire storefront. As the young man proceeded
eastward along the sidewalk, he unconsciously tapped his right
hand on the left side of his chest, indicating that there was
something valuable in the lapel pocket of his simple black suit.

"This must be the young one," Klesko said.

Tiger was concerned about Klesko's mood. Though he
had escaped any real injury, the episode at the Rainer woman's
office—the previous night—had left Klesko in a sullen, sim-
mering rage. The fire that engulfed his pant legs had been more

humiliating than anything else, but the outcome of the event was not at all what they had hoped for: the Rainer woman died before she could tell them anything about Yalena Mayakova's whereabouts, and their pursuit of the unknown girl had ended with her mysterious disappearance into the night.

The failure of all this was not sitting well with Klesko, and Tiger knew that in this state of mind the man was capable of anything, even stupid eruptions of violence that might leave them exposed.

Their greatest hope for finding Yalena had been in finding either Benjamin Hatch or Charlene Rainer; now both of them were dead, and the Kleskos were no closer to finding their target. Their only potential lead was the young girl who they had found at Rainer's office. Tiger and Klesko had no idea how she might fit into their search, but she was intriguing nonetheless. The girl was more capable and resourceful than a normal girl of her age—as demonstrated when she set Klesko on fire and then vanished without a trace—and there was the sense, on Tiger's part anyway, that the girl was familiar in a way that he could not quite explain.

Did the girl have some connection to Yalena Mayakova? Tiger and Klesko did not know yet, but one possible source of information was Isaac Hamlisch, the young diamond merchant who had been gone on a buying trip to Europe when the Kleskos first visited his shop. It was Hamlisch who had listed the alexandrite stone on the international market—only two weeks ago, but to Tiger it felt much longer—and he could reveal the identity of the person who had brought him the stone. Now

Hamlisch was back in New York, and walking alone on 47th Street toward the Diamond Buyers Club, one block away.

Tiger stepped out of the car and followed Hamlisch as Klesko started the engine of the car and pulled out into the street, which had almost no traffic at that hour. Once Klesko had pulled the car even with the young merchant, Tiger moved swiftly; he pushed up against young Hamlisch from behind, sticking the barrel of his gun into the man's ribs.

"Easy," Tiger whispered into the stunned man's ear, and steered him onto the street, into the open door of the waiting car. Klesko had shoved the front passenger seat forward, so Tiger and Isaac slid straight into the back of the two-door muscle car. With the car door closed and the front seat folded back into place, the now terrified Isaac Hamlisch was secured beside Tiger in the backseat of the car.

"Oh God," Hamlisch muttered.

"Relax," Tiger said.

Klesko steered down 47th Street and turned south on Fifth Avenue, the muscle car's powerful engine growling hungrily, even at the slow pace of Manhattan traffic.

"You are Isaac?" Klesko asked, peering back at the merchant with the rearview mirror.

"Y-yes . . ."

"You did purchase alexandrite, yes?"

The question clearly caught Isaac by surprise. "Oh . . . yes. One stone."

"Look up with your eyes," Klesko ordered him.

"Two weeks ago I bought the stone," Isaac continued, but

kept his eyes down, terrified of meeting Klesko's penetrating gaze. "I took it with me to—"

"Look to me!" Klesko barked. Tiger encouraged Isaac's cooperation with a gentle jab to the ribs with the muzzle of his gun, hoping as he did so that the man would not piss himself.

Isaac wisely raised his face so that Klesko could read his eyes.

"Tell who was it that brings you the stone," Klesko demanded.

Isaac opened his mouth to speak but then hesitated, and no words came out of his mouth. Tiger saw this as an interesting development, and knew his father would also. Even with a gun placed squarely against his rib, Isaac Hamlisch was defiant. What would inspire this simple businessman to be so reluctant, so careless about his own safety? His hesitation could only mean that the identity of the person who sold him the stone was worth protecting.

A child, perhaps.

"Ah," Klesko said, apparently agreeing with Tiger that Isaac's hesitation was an answer in itself.

"A girl?" Tiger asked, his greater ease with English obvious as soon as he spoke up. "A young girl? Short blond hair?"

Isaac did not answer.

"There is nothing you can do for her," said Klesko. "We already know, you see?"

"A girl," Isaac confirmed, "and three others."

The man's eyes dropped down again, not in fear now

but in an obvious gesture of shame for having given up the information.

"One stone?" Klesko asked. "Not cut?"

"One stone, uncut."

"She said from where?" Klesko asked.

"From a family estate, she said."

Klesko did not understand the term. He asked Tiger for a translation.

"Estate," Tiger said. *"Naslyedstvo."*

Klesko snorted contemptuously.

"And what did you pay for this stone?" he asked.

"Eight thousand dollars."

"That is fair for market?"

"Yes."

"Where can we find this girl?"

"I have no idea."

Through the rearview mirror, Klesko's eyes burned into Isaac, Klesko deciding whether or not Isaac was lying.

"She will come back to you?"

"I don't know if she has more stones."

"She gives you her name?"

"She signed documents. It's the law."

"Yes?"

"The name was Aretha Franklin."

Tiger could not suppress a wry laugh. He could not help but feel a certain amount of admiration for the cunning of the mysterious girl, this petite, blond-haired *Aretha.*

"Not the real name?" Klesko asked Tiger.

"No, Father," Tiger said, careful not to make Klesko feel mocked for his ignorance of popular culture. "Not her real name."

They drove in silence then for nearly a minute, continuing south on Fifth, making better progress than usual in the sparse pre-holiday morning traffic. As the seconds ticked by, Tiger knew that Klesko was making a decision about the diamond merchant's fate. It seemed to Tiger that Isaac knew this as well, but the young Hamlisch remained stoic.

"You will buy more stones if we bring them?" Klesko asked Isaac.

"Y-yes," said Isaac, stammering a little. "Yes, I will buy more stones."

"You will not speak of us to police?" Tiger asked.

"No."

"If you speak," Klesko said, "we will know this. We will find your family and kill them all. Look at me with your eyes . . ."

Looking sick with dread, Isaac lifted his eyes and met Klesko's in the rearview mirror.

"You believe we will do this?" Klesko asked. "Kill them, every one?"

"I believe it," Isaac said.

After a moment more of consideration, Klesko pulled the car over to the curb.

"Go," said Klesko, reaching over to open the passenger side door. With a sense of relief, Tiger shoved the passenger seat forward with his foot and climbed out of the car, allowing

Isaac to climb out as well. Tiger got back into the front seat and Klesko steered them back into the traffic, leaving Isaac Hamlisch behind.

"We find the girl," Klesko said.

"*Da,*" Tiger agreed.

They turned west and drove to Tenth Avenue, then pointed north and headed all the way to 87th Street and Amsterdam, the corner where they had lost track of the girl and her friends the night before.

They scanned the area—this time in full daylight—trying to figure out how the children had escaped them.

"How do they disappear into the air?" Klesko asked as he and Tiger continued their search of the corner where the four teens had eluded them. "These are magic children?"

They had been forced to abandon the previous night's search as the police descended on the area, but now it was daylight and the streets were back to normal business. As he had the night before, Klesko soon focused on the empty bank on the corner. He tried again to peer through the soaped windows, but without satisfaction. Tiger followed as his father moved to the narrow service walkway at the rear of the bank building, finding the rear fire exit. The men found something curious there: on the door handle hung a small combination lockbox, attached to the handle tightly enough so it could not be removed.

"There is a key," said Tiger.

"Eh?"

"If you open the box with the code, there will be a key inside."

And then Klesko understood: the bank space was empty and available for lease. The key was for realtors to gain access to the property. Klesko tugged at the lockbox, confirming that it was still fully attached and unbroken.

"If they entered here, they have the code," said Tiger.

"How?" Klesko asked.

Klesko stepped to the first Dumpster near the door and lifted its top. The bin was less than half full. At least a dozen empty pizza boxes were stacked inside, plus three plastic grocery bags piled near the top, filled with trash. Klesko tipped the bags open and found crumpled wrappers for various kinds of snack food: chips, candy, popcorn, etc. He closed the Dumpster again and the two men moved out of the walkway, back to the sidewalk.

"This was her place," Klesko said.

"No more," said Tiger. "They would not stay."

"They are gone," Klesko agreed. "So. Why throw garbage away? They will never come back. Why make it clean? Who has code for getting this key and also makes this place clean?"

Tiger considered the question, but suspected that his father already knew the answer. Tiger followed Klesko to the front entrance of the bank space, where inside the window a placard was mounted. It read:

For Commercial Lease—7,000 sq. feet
Desmond & Green Realty

NINETEEN

The phone picked up on the first ring.

"Yeah."

"Hey. This is Wally."

"Little sister," Panama purred. "What up?"

"You had another place for me to get an ID," said Wally. "Could you give me that?"

"Not the Brighton?"

"No. The other one you said."

"What? They mess with you in Brighton?"

Wally considered the question: *Did they mess with me in Brighton Beach?* They changed her life in Brighton Beach. Did that count?

"Long story," she answered. "It's fine. The other one?"

"Jersey City," answered Panama. "You don't like Russians, then fine, I give you some New Jersey Nigerian motherfuckers, see how you like that. You ain't never find no Africans blacker than these. These motherfuckers *black* . . ."

Wally waited out Panama's diatribe on the abyssal blackness of Nigerians until he finally coughed up the Jersey City address.

"What else goin' on?" he said once he had dictated the address. "You gonna bring somethin' in? More o' those shiny *expresso* boxes?"

"That was a onetime thing," said Wally. "But I need to ask you something about Rage."

There was a moment of silence on Panama's end of the line, and then a sigh. "I'm disappointed, little sister, you wanna get in some shit with Rage. You too good for his business, you want my opinion."

"I'm not going to do business with him."

"Then good."

"He's still moving party supplies to the clubs downtown?"

Another moment of silence on Panama's end. "Who the fuck is askin'?"

"I am," Wally said. "Do you remember Sophie? She used to be with us?"

"Little Sophie ain't welcome aroun' here no more. Used to be sweet, now crystal got her all fucked up. Think maybe she mulin' for Rage these days."

"She's dead. Killed."

"Okay," Panama said after a pause. "That ain't exactly shockin' news, you see what I mean. *'Tweaka chick goes into business with Rage, nex' thing you know she found dead.'*"

"Yeah," said Wally. "Doesn't mean I can't be curious. You've got nothing for me on this?"

"What I got is a big slice o' Panamanian wisdom: let it the fuck *go*. You hear me, little sister? Nothin' good gonna come out of you holdin' on to that kinda shit."

The trip to Jersey City went smoothly enough. Tevin and Wally traveled alone, taking the New Jersey PATH train to Journal Square and walking two blocks to a warehouse doorway on Sip Avenue. The Nigerian crew lived together in their warehouse space, and a few of them were still asleep on cots when Wally and Tevin arrived at nine o'clock. The transaction was simple, especially compared to Wally's experience in Brighton Beach: the Nigerians delivered a first-rate fake ID for two hundred dollars, no questions asked and no lives changed.

The deal included a musical bonus: ten tracks of music performed by the Nigerians' own band, a Palm Wine combo called the Ghosts of Ilorin. The Nigerians downloaded the tunes onto Wally's cell phone so she and Tevin could use their earphone splitter and listen to the tunes together on their ride back to Manhattan.

Wally leaned into Tevin as they listened to the music, resting her head on his shoulder, wanting to feel him next to her. It had been rising for days, this sensation. Something to do with . . . *everything*—hearing from Dr. Rainer that her mother was still alive, witnessing the bloodshed on the same night, staring directly into Klesko's eyes through the window of the bank. All of it had shaken something loose inside Wally, opened her up to sensation and emotion in a way she couldn't remember experiencing, ever. It was almost overwhelming. Wally wasn't sure what any of it meant, but she knew that having Tevin close answered a yearning inside her that she was no longer willing to deny.

Tevin sensed the change, clearly. He tapped Wally on the shoulder and she pulled out her earphones. They could still faintly hear the the Ghosts of Ilorin leaking out of their earbuds as they spoke.

"You're okay?" he asked, searching her eyes with a look of confusion.

Wally couldn't blame him. How many different signals had she sent him over the past months?

"I'm good," she said, and smiled.

Tevin chuckled a little at the enigma that was Wally Stoneman and shrugged. They put their headphones back on and listened to the music for a while, but then Wally pulled her buds out and yanked Tevin's out as well.

"That's your way of saying you want to talk?" Tevin said. "Real subtle."

"Do you think about what will happen if I find my mother?"

"What do you mean?"

"I mean to us," Wally said. "You and me. Jake and Ella."

Tevin considered the question, looking reluctant.

"We'll work it out," he said, sounding confident, though Wally sensed that he too was concerned about their fate.

"You don't think I would just, like, run off with her and

ditch you guys?" The question had been preying on Wally's mind, and even she didn't know the answer, so how could the crew? The tension among them had ramped up since Wally's search had begun, and she figured the doubt about their future together had something to do with it.

"It's crossed my mind." Tevin shrugged. "Jake and Ella too."

"Yeah."

"What's the answer?" he asked.

Wally thought about the right thing to say, something that would be honest but also convey how much she herself had suffered over all the doubt that surrounded them.

"You guys are my family," she said. "I can't imagine my life without you. But if I said I knew everything coming our way in the future, that would be a lie."

Tevin nodded. "Okay." But he looked like he had something else to say, so Wally waited him out. "You could stop all this," Tevin finally continued. "I'm not saying you should, but . . . who would blame you? Those men . . ."

"They're looking for Yalena too." Wally spoke with absolute confidence. "You see that, don't you, Tev? We're following the same trail. If they find her first . . . I'd never be able to live with that."

Tevin nodded but didn't respond. Wally could see that he had hoped for another answer.

"The way you guys came into the building last night," she said, "all that shooting and everything, and still you were coming up. That was unbelievable and totally brave. I'll never forget that."

"I'll always protect you, Wally," Tevin said, shyly now, not meeting her eyes. Wally could see that he wanted to say more.

"I know," she said. Again, she leaned her head against Tevin's shoulder.

Wally wanted to tell him more. She wanted to share what she had seen as she sat behind the darkened bank window and looked into Klesko's dark eyes; Wally had seen herself, had seen both her past and her future contained in the singular features of Klesko—her father—and her unalterable connection to that monster was almost more than she could bear. She tried to put it all out of her mind, if just for a few moments. She leaned closer into Tevin and he wrapped his arm around her shoulders.

"We'll find a new place to crash," she said. "And then I have an idea for something nice."

They met up with Jake and Ella at the Bloomingdale Library. At one of the Internet stations, Wally worked at finding the crew a new place to crash. She found the online site for Desmond & Green Realty—the top Upper West Side agency that Claire Stoneman worked with—and logged on, entering the password that she was not supposed to know. She filled in some search parameters, and a list of housing possibilities immediately appeared on the screen, along with an interactive street map that showed their locations. Wally sent the list to the library's printer, and within a few minutes they were off together, house hunting.

The first place on the list wouldn't do. It was a neighborhood video store on 100th that had gone belly-up. The shop's rear walkway was shared with several businesses that had deliveries coming in at all hours, so access would be limited. The windows hadn't yet been covered, either; the crew could do that themselves, with soap or paper, but the management company might notice the changes.

The crew migrated south for a few blocks, to 94th Street and West End Avenue, and this second spot was an absolute score. The building was a twelve-unit, turn-of-the-century apartment building that was being renovated into six big luxury condominium units. The documents Wally had accessed online told her that the development company had gone into receivership halfway through construction, and the lawsuits could go on for years. Until a settlement was reached, the building would stand empty.

Wally punched the code into the lockbox and got the key to the space. The crew entered at the basement floor, which had once been a dry cleaner's shop. It was now empty and was a perfectly discreet squatting place for the crew. The spot included a bonus that was almost too good to be true: one street north on 95th Street was a public high school that shared a back alleyway with the empty dry cleaner's. Teenage school kids would be a common sight in the neighborhood, so the crew wouldn't attract unwanted attention.

As they explored the space, Wally heard Ella give a delighted shriek and followed the sound to a full bathroom in the back, which included a shower and a vanity mirror with a ring of makeup lights around the edge. Nirvana. The boys could squat—literally—anywhere, but for Wally and Ella, a decent bathroom was essential. This one was way more than decent.

"Why haven't we been living here all along?" Ella asked.

"Just got listed." Wally shrugged and smiled. "Welcome home."

TWENTY

That first night in the dry cleaner's was warm and quiet, and the exhausted crew slept in late on Thanksgiving morning, almost till noon.

"We slept through the parade," Ella said, yawning.

"Good," Jake said. "That thing gives me a headache."

"We have other plans, anyway," said Tevin.

Wally got up and went to the ironing room, coming back with a full paper bag, which she emptied on the floor in front of the others. Clothes.

"Tev and I stopped at the Salvation Army on the way back from Jersey," Wally said. "We've spent hardly any of the money, even on our fun day. We figured a Thanksgiving dinner would be good."

"A real one?" Ella said, lighting up.

"Sure," Wally answered. "Turkey, stuffing. The whole deal."

They picked through the items and matched the second-hand clothes with their sizes: a couple of colorful, funky ties for Tevin and Jake, new plaid schoolgirl skirts for the girls to wear over their leggings, and some accessories like junk jewelry and skinny scarves.

"Thirty bucks for all this stuff," Tevin said.

Layered on top of their usual clothes, the crew radiated a sense of urban chic. The only resistance came when Wally pulled out an old British public school blazer with red piping on the seams and a bona fide crest sewn onto the front pocket. She handed it to Jake.

"Oh, hell no," Jake said.

"C'mon," Wally said. "You'll look totally hot. . . ."

"No fucking way—"

"Oh my God, Jake!" Ella objected. "Put it on, right now. I don't wanna see that varsity jacket at our fancy table."

Jake remained indignant but caved in to Ella's command. As Jake put on his jacket, Ella took a couple of the varsity pins off his letterman jacket and attached them on the lapel of his new blazer.

"That actually works," Wally said.

Jake looked at himself in the mirror. "It does, doesn't it?"

The crew hoofed it to the subway stop and caught the B train south, toward SoHo. Wally had called around the good restaurants in that part of town the night before, and she'd been lucky: Balthazar had a cancellation on a table for four at three o'clock.

"Do we need, like, special manners for this place?" Ella asked as they walked.

"Nope," Wally said. "You know how to eat, right?"

"I do."

"Besides," Wally said, "you and I are ravishing, and our men are breathtakingly handsome. Our biggest problem will be the envy we inspire in those less fortunate than ourselves."

They found Balthazar on Spring Street and—just as Wally predicted—there were no hassles. The maitre d' did give them a halfway curious look, but that probably had more to do with their age than anything. Style-wise, the fashion-forward crew fit in nicely with the upscale, quasi-bohemian crowd in the busy restaurant. The only hiccup came with Ella's first reading of the menu.

"Uh, where's the turkey and stuffing?"

"This is a bistro," Wally said. "French style. But look toward the bottom of the second page: *turkey leg confit.*"

"What's that?" Tevin asked.

"It'll be yum, I promise."

And Wally was right. The turkey was "insanely tasty," according to Ella, delivered to their table with deference and efficiency by a flock of hovering waiters who never even let a water glass dip below half full.

"Best Thanksgiving turkey ever," Jake said as he wolfed down the huge leg on his plate, with in-between bites of fried herb potatoes and wild mushroom sauté.

"Yeah, by far," agreed Tevin. "Like, *another-planet* far."

Most of the other guests in the café were youngish, upwardly mobile types, with only a couple of real families dining together. The parents of those families barely noticed Wally and her crew at all, but their children were fascinated. Obviously jealous, they stole sideways glances at the four teenagers and fantasized about a world devoid of embarrassing parents, itchy sweaters, and flatulent great-aunts with untrimmed whiskers. Ella was the first of the crew who noticed this attention, so of course she gave the kids furtive waves and sympathetic smiles.

Wally felt good for the first time in days. Seeing the delighted faces of her friends as they ate and laughed, their faces glowing in the candlelight as they toasted each other with wineglasses full of sparkling water, Wally knew she had done the right thing in bringing them here. And something else, the warm feeling at their table—and in the room—gave her kind of a flashback to an earlier time. A bittersweet memory.

Tevin noticed that something was on Wally's mind.

"What?"

"I don't know," she said. "I was just reminded. One of the last dinners I had with my folks, before they split, was Thanksgiving out. Sort of like this."

"Wally—" Ella wanted to console her.

"No, it was good. Really. Maybe the last nice time we had together." She looked at the others with a warm smile. "We're having a nice time too, and that's how I'm reminded. Thanksgiving dinner with two happy families, both of them mine."

They toasted each other again, just as their waiter arrived with a dessert cart full of the most indulgent pastries any of them had ever seen. Wally again observed the looks of wonder on their faces, but now focused especially on Tevin. He was as thrilled as the others with the sight of the treats, but Tevin observed the desserts as if through the window of an elegant shop that he was forbidden to enter, as if these special things were there for him to witness but not taste for himself. Even as he was deciding which pastry to order, Tevin looked as though he was doing something that he would later be punished for.

Wally's heart broke a little at the sight of this.

"You know what?" Wally said. "Let's hold off on dessert. We can do better."

The others gave her skeptical looks.

"Better than this?" Ella said, crushed that she would not be tasting the towering, gleaming wedge of lemon meringue pie that she had already selected.

Wally just nodded, confidently, and looked to the waiter. "We'd like the check, please."

The crew followed Wally out of the bistro, obviously curious about what she was up to.

"What's on your mind, Wally?" Tevin said.

She took out her smart phone and did a local map search, coming up with a place called 60 Thompson, described as a "chic boutique hotel that brilliantly reflects the refined, artistic sensibility of SoHo." There were several dollar signs attached to the review, meaning it was expensive even by Manhattan standards. Wally enjoyed keeping her friends in suspense as she led them the few blocks to Thompson Street and in through the front door of the hotel.

The lobby was hushed and stylish in a restrained way, lit to a sort of muted glow that gave the place an intimate feel. Wally felt a rush of guilty excitement as she stepped up to the front desk and placed a credit card on the counter. It was a Platinum American Express card with her name on it, given to her by Claire "in case of an emergency." Wally had never used the card and was determined that she never would, but at that moment she felt driven by an irresistible compulsion.

A young woman with beautiful, dark skin—Indian, Wally thought—attractive in a well-tailored dark blue suit stood behind the counter. The name tag on her lapel read *Chantra*. She leaned over and examined the credit card without touching it, then stood back and took a long look at Wally and the crew, clearly trying to reconcile what she perceived as a mixed message.

"Yes, ma'am?" she said to Wally.

Wally pulled out her good fake ID and set it next to the AmEx card.

"We'd like a suite," Wally said casually, "if one is available."

Chantra arched one eyebrow. She took another look at the crew and another look at Wally's cards. Finally she picked up the Platinum card and moved toward a back office.

"Just one moment, please," she said with an enigmatic smile. She disappeared into the back office for a moment but returned promptly, still holding on to the AmEx card.

"What type of suite do you require, Ms. Stoneman?"

"Two bedrooms, please."

"Yes, very good. We have a two-bedroom suite on the 16th floor with an excellent perspective of the park," Chantra said.

She placed a price sheet on the counter for perusal, but Wally did not look at it.

"I'm sure it will be fine," Wally said.

Through all this, the crew stood behind Wally, biting their tongues, determined not to break whatever insanely reckless and generous spell their leader was under.

"Excellent," Chantra said, sweeping the price sheet out of view and setting the paperwork into motion.

Soon the bellman was ushering the crew into the elevator— "No luggage, then?"—up to the 16th floor and into a suite so luxurious that it took their collective breaths away, even Wally's. The bellman opened the curtains to reveal a large picture window with an expansive view of downtown, to the south.

"Would you like turndown service, ma'am?" he asked as Wally slipped him two twenty-dollar bills for his trouble.

"Not necessary, thank you," she said, and the bellman was gone, leaving the stunned crew alone in their suite, the air redolent with the scent of the two dozen fresh white roses arranged in a crystal vase on the side table.

Wally reached for the hotel phone and dialed for room service.

"What can we offer you this evening, Ms. Stoneman?" asked the voice on the other end of the line, no introduction necessary.

"We'd like two of every dessert you have," Wally said, "and one bottle of champagne, your choice."

Alone in the bedroom with Tevin, Wally turned to face him and saw that his body was very tense, his fists clenched at his sides and his jaw fixed. At first Wally mistook his posture for anger, but then discovered from the look in his eyes that Tevin was consumed with anticipation, his body vibrating with intense animal energy, raw and barely restrained.

"Tev," she said. "Your eyes . . ."

"What?" he asked, breathless.

"I know them, but I don't."

He moved toward her and wrapped her in his arms. Wally tilted her chin toward his, and they kissed passionately for the first time, locked together. Wally thought the closeness would calm him, but instead his excitement spread from every inch of his hot, sweaty skin to her own. And then she was trembling also and she lost her breath, feeling like his body was water flooding all around her and she was drowning.

"It's okay," she said, struggling to catch her breath. "Everything is okay." Wally wasn't thinking clearly, or even thinking at all, and didn't know if the words of reassurance were meant for Tevin or herself. She understood in that moment how much of themselves they had held away from each other.

A blur of uncontrollable thoughts rushed through Wally's mind, memories of her first time with Nick—so different, intense but contained—and she realized that she had no idea what it would be like to experience another human heart this way, with no calculation.

They began undressing each other, fumbling, not willing to fully release their hold as they did it so they had to pull and slide the clothes off between their bodies and immediately reestablish contact before any air could rush in between them.

"Don't let me go," she said.

"I won't."

When their bare skin touched, they settled into a flow of actions and reactions that happened naturally, and Wally could feel herself casting away all control and getting caught up in the irresistible force of it. Before it could happen—with their clothes off now—Wally pushed him away, needing all of her strength to do it, and looked at him naked in front of her. She decided he was perfect, and that once she reached out for him again, she would not be able to let go, but Tevin suddenly looked troubled. Wally pulled him even closer, sensing his distress and afraid that the spell between them would be broken.

"What is it?" she asked him gently.

"I haven't"—he hesitated—"I mean, I don't know anything. I know I love you, but I don't know anything else."

"That's what I want," she said.

She reached out and pulled him toward her, both of them falling back together onto the bed.

Later, between the crisp white sheets, they lay side by side, their bodies touching but otherwise just . . . still. Wally thought it might be the quietest room she had ever been in. She wondered how deeply she would sleep, whether it would be easier or harder after so long in spaces that were not her own, that were full of the sounds of others.

"I think a lot . . ." Tevin began, and then stopped himself, organizing his thoughts. "I think about . . . after I'm gone. Like, who will remember me? Will anyone think that the world was a different place because I was in it?" He paused. "It sounds kind of dumb now that I say it out loud."

"It's not dumb."

"I guess," Tevin said, "what I'd like, when that time comes, I want to belong to someone. So at least one person will look back at the memory of me and think, *he was mine*."

It made Wally's heart ache to hear those words from Tevin. He had been alone in the world, set adrift by those who were supposed to take care of him, and now Wally and Jake and Ella were all he had.

"Could you and I belong to each other?" Tevin asked.

It was a moment before Wally answered.

"Yes," she said.

For that night they did belong to each other. Wally was glad for it, glad for Tevin that he was able to experience that closeness with someone who loved him and glad for herself that she had something so powerful to give. Before very long he was sound asleep. Wally listened as his breathing settled into a deep, peaceful rhythm before she quietly whispered the familiar lullaby to herself . . .

> *Puskai prïdet pora prosit'sia,*
> *Drug druga dolgo ne vidat?*
> *No serditse s serdtsem, slovno ptitsy,*
> *Konechno, vstretiatsia opiat . . .*

Halfway through the last verse, she was asleep as well.

TWENTY-ONE

Atley was home alone with three-day-old spaghetti, watching the Michigan–Ohio State game and trying to put the events of the previous twenty-four hours out of his mind. He leapt on his cell phone when it rang, glad for the interruption.

"Detective, this is Claire Stoneman."

"Oh. Mrs. Stoneman . . . is something wrong?"

"No no, not an emergency at all, Detective," she said hurriedly, hearing urgency in Atley's voice. "Damn it. I'm sorry. It's strange for me to call, I know. This was inconsiderate; I'll call you on Monday instead—"

"You're not bothering me. I'm enjoying a very low-key Thanksgiving this year."

"Okay. I was just . . . I was hoping for news, anything."

Atley wasn't sure what to tell Claire Stoneman about her daughter and the Manetti murder case. Atley himself was on indefinite leave following the shoot-out in Charlene Rainer's building, pending the outcome of an OIS report on the incident. If his superiors had asked Atley to grade his own performance during the gunfight, he would have said that he failed in every way, and it would be hard to argue: shooters were still unidentified and had escaped, Wallis Stoneman was still running free, and two women—including Dr. Charlene Rainer—were dead. Not Atley's fault, but all of it happened on his watch.

The Sophia Manetti case was on indefinite hold, and the higher-ups in the precinct had decided that the two shooters in the Dr. Rainer incident had no connection to the Manetti murder. Atley disagreed. There was nothing random or arbitrary about the two shooters' actions on that day. The men were obviously there for either Wallis Stoneman or Charlene Rainer—or both. The likelihood that in the space of ten days Wallis would be connected to two completely unrelated murders seemed very slim.

Now, on the line with Claire Stoneman, Atley was sure of one thing: he would not be mentioning the shoot-out to the distressed woman. She was desperate for news about her daughter, but even the tamest description of that violence would leave her with terrifying images of Wallis in danger. There was no point in that.

"I have nothing specific to tell you," Atley lied, "other than that the investigation is ongoing."

"I see," Claire said, clearly disappointed. There was silence on the line for a few moments, and Atley could feel her anxiety over the line.

"We're still working the case and we're still determined to bring your daughter home," Atley said. "No one is giving up."

"I appreciate that," she said. "I'm sorry for bothering you, Detective—"

"Tell me something about Wally," Atley said, feeling that he had let the woman down. He didn't want to end the conversation that way. "Anything about her."

There was quiet on the line for a moment.

"Sometimes we'd have help come in," Claire began. "When she was little and already a real handful, very defiant. So we'd bring in babysitters or nannies when I was down to my last nerve and just needed a few hours away. One of them was named Helen . . . she was Honduran, I think. Wally was a terror with her, of course, testing her like she tested everyone, but somehow Helen seemed to take it in stride. Late that first night, she was trying to get Wally in bed and Wally was fighting her with everything she had. I hovered at the bedroom door, curious to see how Helen would handle her. In the middle of Wally's worst tantrum, Helen remained completely calm. She leaned in close to Wally until the two of them were face-to-face, and in this cold, powerful voice she said, *'Listen to me now, little girl . . . if you do not behave, The People will come for you.'* Wally went absolutely silent, and I saw something on her face I had never once seen before: fear. Wally was terrified."

The line went quiet for a moment. Atley could hear the tinkling of ice as Claire took a drink—he hoped there was something strong in her glass. As she continued, he could hear the quaver in her voice.

"I've thought about that night," Claire continued, "again and again over the years, trying to imagine what thoughts haunted Wally at that moment, what faces she imagined. *The People.* Who did she think they were?" Claire paused, but Atley did not interrupt her. "I know that whatever her nightmares are, none of us can rescue her from them. I suppose it's the same for all of us."

Claire Stoneman went quiet again. For Atley it was almost too much to bear, the image of the woman sitting in her apartment, waiting, he assumed, with a full Thanksgiving meal for a child who would not be coming home. At least not today.

"I told you I would find Wallis," Atley finally said. "And I will."

"Thank you, Detective," Claire said, genuine gratitude in her voice. "Happy Thanksgiving."

"Same to you, Mrs. Stoneman."

Atley had been pulled from the Manetti case and was technically on leave, but it was a holiday weekend and his time was his own. Department resources would be off-limits to him until his shooting case was cleared, but other avenues were available if he could dig up a lead to pursue. His first thought was Bill Horst—the FBI had its hooks into the city better than anyone.

TWENTY-TWO

Wally and the crew slept late—the two couples in their own rooms—and then ordered a room service breakfast in the last hour before checkout. They were mostly quiet with each other as they ate omelets and drank orange juice, all of them experiencing some afterglow from the night before. Wally and Tevin were also a little awkward with each other, adjusting to the sudden change in their relationship.

For Wally—in the light of day—the new phase of her relationship with Tevin felt a little like an unwelcome complication. She did love Tevin, and their experience the night before had been important to her, but Wally was still driven by a powerful sense of purpose and didn't want to be thrown off her quest. She knew this was selfish, but at the same time she didn't want to end up resenting Tevin for distracting her. The choices in front of her were all so confusing.

They checked out of the room and walked back across Central Park, Ella and Jake in the lead with Wally and Tevin just behind. Wally could feel Tevin's uneasiness, could sense that he was trying to play everything cool but didn't quite know what Wally expected of him, or what she would allow.

"We're good, right?" she quietly asked Tevin.

"Yeah, of course," he answered. "Always."

"What's that?" Ella asked from up ahead, picking up on the curious change in chemistry between Wally and Tevin. Wally made a show of ignoring Ella's question, but Ella seemed to know everything anyway and shot Wally a playful smirk. Apparently, Wally and Tevin becoming an actual couple was something Ella could really get behind. Wally didn't feel ready for that level of sharing yet—she felt like it would just be more unwelcome distraction.

As they walked on, Wally began plotting the next step in locating Yalena. The events that had taken place at Charlene Rainer's office had terrified her, but Wally's level of determination was unchanged. She thought again about those terrible events—the deafening echoes of gunshots, Charlene's blood splattered everywhere—and Wally suddenly felt guilty for her next thought: she was frustrated that Charlene had taken so much critical information with her into the next life.

Or had she? Wally thought about all the potential information contained in Dr. Rainer's office: patient files, medical insurance forms, contact numbers, bookkeeping information. As they reached Central Park West, the crew headed north toward their new crash pad at the dry cleaner's, but Wally paused at the corner of 88th Street.

"I'm gonna swing by the doctor's office," she said.

"The shrink's?" Jake asked, surprised. "Why would you ever want to go back there?"

"I think I have to," Wally said.

"It's a bad idea," Tevin said. "There's going to be cops there still."

"Uniforms, maybe, but not anyone who knows me, I'll bet. If it looks wrong, I'll just beat it."

Wally could feel from the crew's vibe that they were disappointed, the three of them realizing that her need to find Yalena hadn't been diminished by the special time they had together on Thanksgiving day . . . and night.

"Please just come home with us," Ella pleaded.

Wally bristled at Ella's needy tone. They were going to make her feel guilty for doing what she needed to do.

"It's not home, Ella. It's an empty dry cleaner's." Wally's tone was cold—even harsh—and she instantly regretted it.

"Wally . . ." Ella looked hurt.

"Ella, shit . . . I'm sorry. I didn't mean—"

"This mystery mom you're working so hard to find," Jake said angrily, "she threw you away. Don't forget that."

"Easy, Jake . . ." Tevin reproached him.

Wally opened her mouth to reply angrily, but stopped herself. They were having a bad moment already and she didn't want to make it worse.

"You know I'm right, Tev," Jake said. "And so do you, Wally." He turned away and continued walking north. Ella gave Wally a sympathetic look, smiling a little to let her know that there were no hard feelings, but then hurried to catch up with Jake.

Only Tevin remained.

"Jake is being a dick, but he's not wrong," Tevin said to Wally. "I know you've got some idea in your head, how Yalena is some heroic person who made a huge sacrifice for you, but you need to be honest about it, Wally. She did leave you behind. And she said in her letter that you should go on with your life and not look back. Remember that the next time you put yourself in danger for her."

Wally knew Tevin's heart was in the right place, but at that moment his calm, reasonable tone just pissed her off.

"Yeah," was all Wally said, and forced a little smile for him.

Tevin leaned in to Wally and gave her a gentle kiss on the cheek, then turned and hustled after Jake and Ella, leaving Wally behind on the corner of 88th and Central Park West. She suddenly felt chilled and deeply alone.

She forced herself to shake off the dark feelings and headed west, quickly covering the three blocks to Charlene Rainer's office building. There was one police cruiser and a couple of workmen's pickup trucks parked in front of the office building, including a locksmith's truck. The front door was kept open with a doorstop, and workers were shuttling through the front entrance, carrying hardware and replacement doors for the wrecked offices upstairs.

Wally strolled inside with confidence, as if she owned the place. There was still no doorman in the lobby, and Wally noticed that the workers were using the elevators in the atrium to move their gear up, so she headed straight for the empty stairwell and climbed up to the third floor.

More workmen were on the third floor. Wally walked slowly as she approached the three office doors that needed repair. The closest of the three was the third office she and Dr. Rainer had entered as they tried to escape—the model builder's studio—and that was the door the workmen were repairing first. The next door—the lawyer's—had already been removed and was set leaning against the wall, at least ten splintered bullet holes clearly visible on its surface. The third doorway was Suite G—Dr. Rainer's—and there was yellow NYPD crime scene tape stretched across it. A folding chair sat just outside the door, and Wally figured there must have been a uniform cop assigned to protect the crime scene. He was gone from his post . . . for now.

Wally headed for the second door—the lawyer's—still walking casually as if she belonged in the building. Casual was the last thing Wally was feeling inside, though, as evidence of the violence two nights earlier was obvious in several places. The pool of blood from Charlene's wounds had been mopped up but not very thoroughly, and blood splatter was everywhere on the surrounding walls, marked by circles drawn in red grease pen by crime scene investigators. There were smudges of black fingerprint dust on the walls, especially around the area of the doorways, and several sections of the wall plaster had been removed, for what reason she didn't know. Looking up to the hallway above and across the atrium space, Wally could just make out evidence of blood splatter from the unlucky woman who had died first.

Wally shuddered at the visual memory of both women's deaths, and thought about the handgun stashed in Charlene's desk drawer. *For this day,* Charlene Rainer had said, as if she had expected that one day Klesko would emerge from the past and come looking for her. Wally could only assume that her own mother lived just such an existence, trying to carry on with her new life but never quite able to feel safe, never free to make contact with her own daughter for fear that she would endanger her.

As Wally reached the empty doorway of the lawyer's suite, she glanced behind her to find that the workers were focused on hanging the first door and were not looking in her direction. She slipped inside the lawyer's office and, once inside, noticed that the doorway between that suite and the next—Dr. Rainer's—had been filled and hung with a brand-new door, but the new lock had not been attached yet. A piece of the yellow crime scene tape was stretched across the doorway, but Wally simply ducked under the tape and pushed through the unlocked door, stepping into Charlene's inner office space and closing the door behind her. Charlene's office was a total mess, not just from the battle, but from the army of crime scene techs who had obviously tromped through, dusting every surface for prints and leaving chunks of plaster on the floor from where they had cut away pieces of the wall. Charlene's laptop computer was gone from its spot on the desk.

The disturbance that caught Wally's attention most, however, was the open drawers of Charlene's file cabinet: someone had been going through the files. Wally headed straight for the cabinet and rifled through the alphabetized files, and her heart sank when she discovered that her own file was missing. *Detective Greer must've grabbed it,* Wally thought. Wally searched under two other names—Valentina and Yalena Mayakova—just in case, but there were no files under either name. Wally shifted her focus to Charlene's desk, sifting through all its drawers for anything that might be relevant. As she looked, Wally became aware of footsteps approaching from somewhere out in the hallway. They stopped outside Dr. Rainer's door—just a few feet from where Wally stood—and there was a metallic scraping sound as the person sat down in the folding chair. The cop was back.

Even more quietly now, Wally looked through Charlene's desk, but she found nothing, and turned back to the file cabinets. Wally remembered how cautious Charlene was about sharing information that had to do with Yalena Mayakova and thought maybe her file had been intentionally filed under a different name or in an unlabeled file folder. Wally returned her attention to the file cabinets and worked her way through them but found nothing of use except that once she had run through all the file names, to the end of the alphabet—Charlene had a patient named Zahan—there was still another file cabinet left that she had not explored. The doors of this extra cabinet were unlocked, and Wally immediately set to scanning her way through them.

The individual files bore client names, as with the case files in the larger file cabinet, but this second group of files contained only billing documents. Again, Wally found no file with her name on it but kept scanning all the way to the end—Zahan again—only to discover a single unlabeled folder *after* Zahan. Wally pulled the file out and spread it open on Charlene's desk. The records on this anonymous account matched Wally's history with the doctor, the last official visit logged being eight years earlier. This anonymous client had never once been billed for his or her visits. Reaching the end of the file, Wally found a standard contact sheet. The first address listed, with no name attached, was Wally and Claire's home address on 84th Street. The second address was for the Harpswell School. Under the "Emergency Contacts" heading there were four phone numbers: Claire's home and cell phone, the general number for the Harpswell School, and, unexpectedly, a fourth phone number that had been completely covered over with permanent black marker, with no name given next to it.

Wally held the paper at an angle to the daylight coming in through the window and discovered that the redacted phone number had been written in a hard-tip pen and made an impression in the paper just visible when read from an oblique angle. It turned out not to be a phone number at all, but a PO box address on Myrtle Avenue in Brooklyn, completely unfamiliar to Wally. She copied down the address and looked at it again, feeling a quick thrill of adrenaline rush through her. A voice inside her told Wally that she finally held in her hand a direct connection to her mother.

Wally secured the address inside her shoulder bag and then scanned the room, looking for a way out. She now noticed that the office's window—looking out at the fire escape—had been completely removed. Her luck was turning. Wally unlatched the iron security grate from the empty windowsill and stepped out onto the fire escape. She climbed down to the alleyway below, and she was gone.

TWENTY-THREE

It was early evening—dark outside—when Wally slipped through the back entrance of the old dry cleaner's and found Tevin asleep—he had dozed off on a rusty cot that had been left behind in a back room of the cleaner's. She was changing out of her Thanksgiving clothes and into her warmer street threads when he stirred awake.

"Wha—"

"It's okay, it's just me," Wally said.

"Hey. You're going out again?"

"Yeah. Where are Jake and Ella?"

"Times Square. Figured the holiday crowds would be a good time to get rid of the last phone cards."

"Why didn't you go?"

"I was worried . . . the way we all split up today. I wanted there to be someone here when you came back."

"You guys said what was on your minds, Tev, and I have no problem with that."

"But what I wanted to say is that you being happy is the most important thing to me. I'm going to help any way I can until you find what you want."

"That means a lot," Wally said, and it was true. "I felt bad about today too, especially after . . ."

"Yeah, *especially after*. I know. Is this going to be weird?"

"I don't know. I mean, not necessarily . . ."

They looked at each other and cracked up just a little, embarrassed.

"Oh man," Tevin said. "Maybe if we just ignore it for a while, see how it sits?"

"I vote for that too," Wally agreed, and Tevin seemed relieved.

"Where are you headed now?"

"A place near the Brooklyn Navy Yard," she said, and recounted the lead she had found in Dr. Rainer's files.

"You're taking a cab?"

"Nah, there may be someone waiting. I rented a car."

Tevin beamed at this news. "Seriously?"

Wally shrugged. "The new ID is good, and I used Claire's AmEx again. I mean, at this point why not?"

"Wait . . . can you even drive?"

"Really badly. I barely made it out of their parking lot."

Excited, Tevin rose off the cot and began lacing his shoes. "I'm killer behind the wheel. Leave a note for the others so they don't stress, okay?"

Wally was about to object, but she could see that Tevin would not be denied this adventure.

Tevin was beyond psyched to find that Wally had rented a Lincoln Town Car; he'd expected something boring and beige—an anonymous Toyota sedan—and instead found himself behind the wheel of a classic American whip, cruising the streets of Manhattan.

"It was the only car they had left," Wally said.

"Now I am truly happy," Tevin said, unable to stop smiling. "This is better than the—"

"Better than the *what*?" Wally cautioned him. "If I were you, I would choose my next words very carefully."

"Better than the turkey. Duh."

"*Whatev*," she said. They both smiled.

Tevin drove downtown and onto the Williamsburg Bridge, crossing the East River to Brooklyn and exiting at Broadway.

"Broadway south and down around Flushing Avenue," Wally said, and Tevin followed her instructions. This route led them south of Williamsburg toward the Brooklyn Navy Yard, but they turned off Flushing before then, heading toward the intersection of Myrtle Avenue and Carlton in Fort Greene.

"*Mail boxes*," Tevin read out loud, pointing to a sign over a small storefront on Myrtle.

"That's the address," Wally said. "Park back there . . ." She pointed to a spot on Carlton where they could park with a good view of the PO box store but remain out of sight. Tevin did a U-ey and grabbed the parking spot, then shut off the engine.

It was just after noon by then, and the neighborhood shoppers were out on Myrtle, many of them seniors pulling their little rolling shopping carts and ducking into the bodegas that lined the street. The PO box store had an all-glass front, with several hundred mailboxes covering the walls of the main room and a service desk to the side with one clerk sitting by, a smallish freckled woman with short-cropped red hair and a tat creeping up from under her shirt collar—a club chick daylighting as a store clerk.

"Stay with the car, okay?" Wally said to Tevin. "I'm going to check the box." She climbed out of the car, buttoned her coat against the cold air, and crossed Myrtle, walking straight into the shop as if it was a part of her daily routine. She headed directly to Box 310. Wally had to bend down a bit to get a look and was disappointed to find that there was no small window on the box to reveal whether or not there was mail waiting inside. The space behind the boxes was lit, however, and in the light squeaking through the side of the box door, Wally thought she could make out the shadow of at least one letter inside.

"Can I help you with something?" the clerk asked, bored as she looked up from some ink drawings she was scribbling on an art pad. "That's not your box, right?"

"No," Wally answered, and turned to the clerk without hesitation. "It used to be a friend's and I haven't been able to figure out if she's still in town. . . . The thing is, she was with this guy who was hitting her and all of us kept saying she should get a restraining order and she kept saying she would but in the end she would just go back to him and—"

"*Christ . . .*" moaned the clerk, exasperated already, "tell me what box number."

"310."

The woman typed into her computer monitor. "What's your friend's name?"

"Oh . . . it's Yalena, but she was having her mail sent care of a friend so the asshole who was beating her wouldn't be able to—"

"*Stop.* Do you at least know her friend's name?"

"Uh . . . no," Wally said.

"Then I can't help you," said the rocker clerk, and returned to her artwork. "Have a nice day."

Wally sighed and walked out of the shop, crossing back over Myrtle and sliding into the Town Car again.

"What happened?" Tevin asked, and Wally explained the situation. "So," said Tevin, "we just figure that it's still her box and wait her out."

"And hope she checks her mail more than once a month," said Wally.

"Friday is a big day for people to get stuff done," Tevin said confidently. "Before the weekend, you know? Something will happen."

"Then we need to get closer," Wally said. "We can't pick out the individual box numbers, and we need to be sure if someone is using the right box."

"I don't think so. If we get closer, we might spook her."

"Yeah," Wally agreed.

"You know what they do in the movies?" Tevin said with a

mischievous grin. "They send a huge red box to the person at the box number so it's obvious who picks up the mail."

Wally smacked her forehead with the palm of her hand. "I can't *believe* I forgot to bring a huge red box."

Tevin laughed. "I have an idea," he said, then reached into the seat well for his backpack, rifling through the various contents until he found a cheap ballpoint pen. He opened his door and climbed out of the car. "What's the PO box number again?"

"310," Wally said. "What're you doing?"

"Workin' it out." Tevin shrugged with that mischievous grin again.

Tevin crossed Myrtle and entered the store, walking straight up to the clerk, who looked up from her "artwork" with her standard expression of annoyance. "Yeah?"

"You got a piece of notepaper?" Tevin asked. "I need to leave a message for my friend Sisco."

"*Sisco*," the woman repeated in a snide tone, annoyed again at the interruption of her work. She pulled out a piece of notepaper and slapped it onto the counter in front of Tevin. He scribbled some words onto the paper and then folded it in half, writing *Box 617* on the outside. He held the note out, and the clerk took it without looking up at him but made no move to actually deliver it to the box. Tevin remained at the counter.

"What?" the clerk said.

"The message is really important."

"*Oh my God.*" The clerk groaned the words, as if being subjected to torture. She slammed down her art pen and rose from her stool. With Tevin's note in hand, the woman left her post and walked back around behind the wall of PO boxes to place the note in the appropriate box. As soon as she was out of sight, Tevin scrambled across the floor of the shop and headed straight for Box 310. Once there, he jammed the tip of his pen into the box's keyhole and twisted it hard to the side, breaking the tip off inside the keyhole.

"Thank you!" Tevin called out to the clerk as he turned and left the store.

TWENTY-FOUR

Near the corner of 94th Street and West End Avenue, a gypsy cab was pulled halfway back into a service alley, its nose poking out far enough to allow the passengers a full view of 94th Street. In the backseat of the cab sat Klesko and Tiger. Behind the wheel of the cab was Ramzan, the Bulgarian from the basement credit card shop in Queens, fidgety and sweating despite the cold of the day. Klesko and Tiger kept their eyes on the abandoned dry cleaner's on the first floor of an empty building, half a block away.

Within an hour, they spotted three of the four teens arriving—none of them *the* girl—and watched the youths as they snuck in the back entrance of the dry cleaner's, using their own key.

Locating the new hiding place had not been difficult; once Klesko had figured out the girl's scheme with the empty commercial space, it had been a simple matter of obtaining the real estate listings from the same company—Desmond & Green Realty—and searching for the empty location that best suited the girl and her crew.

Soon afterward, two of the kids had reemerged and walked off, leaving the black one alone in the dry cleaner's.

"We wait for the girl," Klesko said, and Tiger nodded.

Tiger watched his father, anger and impatience growing in the old man with each passing hour. So far, Tiger had been able to rein Klesko in, to keep him focused on their goal so that his thoughts would not drift back into the vortex of rage that was clearly swirling inside the dark recesses of his father's mind. The violence at the office building of Charlene Rainer had done nothing to appease Klesko's need for vengeance. If anything, the urgency of his need had been whetted by spilling all that blood.

Tiger wondered how long it would be before his father's actions surpassed reason, surpassed the man's ability to control himself or to be influenced by his son. What would Tiger do then?

The men's patience was rewarded when the blond girl—the one they had encountered at Dr. Rainer's office—arrived on the scene by herself and behind the wheel of a large American sedan. She proceeded to park on the street in front of the cleaner's, a very bad parking job in fact, and entered the cleaner's. Within minutes, she reemerged with the black kid. The two of them climbed into the Lincoln and drove off, the boy behind the wheel.

Within thirty minutes the three men in the gypsy cab were

parked half a block up from Carlton Street in Brooklyn, watching the two teens. The men had a clear view of the Town Car but were still partially hidden behind a red-and-white-striped tow truck parked just in front of them. Behind the wheel of the cab, Ramzan was anxiously alert to the mood and movements of Klesko, seated directly behind him.

"Klesko," Ramzan whined, "I say it again. So long ago, Klesko, troubles came to you in our deal, but it was not me who brought them."

"No, not you," Klesko grunted.

"I offer to help because we do business over many years, trusting each other. Making each other much money. That day . . . the police were there already . . . twenty Darzhavna and there was nothing I could do—"

"A truck full of Abakan rifles and nothing you could do?"

"By myself and just the two Serbs? Just muscle, a couple of *patsani* only?" Ramzan could see that Klesko had no appetite for his arguments. He mumbled a lament, mostly to himself: "It was so long ago."

Bringing Ramzan and his gypsy cab with them had seemed like a good idea at first—the girl did not know Ramzan's face at the time, so having him behind the wheel would be good cover—but after several hours in the Bulgarian's presence, Klesko was tiring of his incessant mewling and the sour smell of fear that reeked from the man's pores.

"Something . . ." said Tiger, who had a pair of binoculars trained ahead on the Town Car. "The black one is doing something."

Klesko took the binoculars and watched as the girl's companion entered the postal shop, the same shop the girl had visited just a few minutes earlier. The boy ran some sort of game on the witless girl behind the counter, getting her out of the way with a ruse and then fouling one of the box locks when she wasn't looking.

"A plan," said Klesko. "They are watching one of the boxes."

"I want to smoke," said Ramzan.

"So smoke, *pizda*," said Klesko.

"Outside," he pleaded. "I need air."

Klesko stared for a moment at the back of Ramzan's head, boiling up with irritation. Every sound and smell and motion of the man seemed to inflame Klesko's wrath, and finally he was unable to contain it. Tiger kept one eye on his father and recognized his mood.

"No . . ." Tiger began to urge restraint.

Too late. Klesko reached forward and with his left hand grabbed hold of Ramzan's thick, wiry hair, pulling the man's head back as Klesko drew an ice pick out of his coat pocket and thrust it into Ramzan's neck, slipping it with a discernible crunch between his vertebrae. Ramzan's body went slack.

"Father . . ." Tiger began, betraying his thoughts with a look of disapproval.

"Yes?" Klesko growled. "Something to say, *Tigr*?"

But Tiger changed his mind and remained silent. Klesko reached to Ramzan's face, closing the dead man's eyes and gaping mouth. He turned Ramzan's head to the side, shielding his seeping wound from view in case any curious pedestrians should pass by. Tiger wanted to speak but waited a moment, listening to his father's breathing to determine when calm had been restored to the man.

"What after this, Father?"

"Eh?"

"We will find the stones."

"And the whore," said Klesko.

"And then?"

"She dies."

"Of course. What then?"

Klesko gave Tiger a look of incomprehension.

"America is big," said Tiger. "Many places to go when we have what we need. Yes?"

Klesko just shrugged and returned his attention to watching the street, waiting for the girl and her black boy to make their next move.

TWENTY-FIVE

In the four hours that Wally and Tevin had been waiting, at least three dozen customers had come and gone from the PO box shop. No one had tried to access box number 310. The interior of the rented Town Car kept going icy cold, and each time, Tevin had fired up the engine to reheat the air so the two of them wouldn't freeze solid.

"I don't know," Wally said. "What are we going to do? Stay watching here for days? A week?"

"She'll come," Tevin said.

"Eight years," Wally said. "That's how long it had been since I had my last appointment with Dr. Rainer. The address has got to be at least that old."

"If the address is no good, then that's what you'll find out today. An answer you didn't want is still an answer."

They had been waiting for almost an hour more when a

woman entered the shop from the east, wearing a knee-length French army surplus woolen overcoat, with mismatched knit gloves and a rainbow-striped scarf wrapped around her neck. On top of her head was a bright orange hunting cap with earflaps that flopped down. The overall effect was artsy bohemian. The woman moved directly to a different section of the PO boxes and removed some mail, shuffling through it casually and tossing the junk in a blue recyclables container. Wally sighed and checked the car's clock for the twentieth time that hour. It was a quarter to five and almost completely dark outside.

"Shit," she said.

"Hold up a sec," Tevin said, his eyes still focused on the shop. Wally looked ahead and saw the woman with the rainbow scarf move to another section of the boxes—somewhere very near box 310—and shuffle through the keys on her chain until she found the one she was looking for. She tried to stick the key into the lock but failed and tried again, pushing harder and twisting at different angles. The lock wouldn't take the key. The woman bent over and seemed to be looking at the box's keyhole, and then she turned away and stepped to the service counter. From their watching post fifty yards away, Wally and Tevin could see the shop attendant leave her post to walk around behind the mailboxes. She returned a few seconds later with a small collection of envelopes—maybe three or four— and handed them to the rainbow scarf lady.

A surge of adrenaline jolted Wally awake, her eyes now fixed on the woman.

"Do you recognize her?"

Wally had shared with Tevin some of her conversation with Dr. Rainer; Wally had come away from their meeting with the sense that Yalena Mayakova was already a part of Wally's life, at least peripherally, that her Russian mother was someone she would recognize.

"I don't know . . ." Wally said, a little frantically. She couldn't get a good enough look at the woman's face. "She looks like she might be around the right age."

"So we stop her?"

Wally's mind was spinning now. The woman took mail from two different boxes. The mail from box 310 might be hers, or someone else's.

"No, not yet," Wally said. "First we follow."

They had already worked out their plan: Wally would get out of the Town Car and pursue on foot while Tevin stayed behind in the Lincoln and followed close by, ready to pick Wally up in case the subject moved to a vehicle or bus. If the pursuit led to a subway stop—the G line stopped two blocks away at Clinton and Washington—then Tevin would hurry to park the car and join Wally on foot.

The woman in the scarf left the shop and walked out onto Carlton. Wally climbed out of the Town Car as Tevin started the engine.

"Don't get too close," Tevin said. "She might be spooky."

Wally nodded and shut the car door behind her, heading immediately toward the corner of Carlton, keeping pace with the woman as she headed north. The woman walked casually, not in any hurry. On the first block, there was a housing development on the left side of the street, a full square block with a handful of eight-story apartment buildings, but the woman passed those by and continued on. The next intersection was at Park Avenue, where the noisy Brooklyn-Queens Expressway passed high overhead. The woman walked under the expressway, crossing Park and continuing to the north.

Wally noticed that almost no one else was on the sidewalk other than herself and the woman, so she slowed down a bit, wary of revealing her presence. Wally glanced behind her to confirm that Tevin was still in contact and found that he was, driving slowly up Carlton with the Lincoln's headlights off, pulling into open spaces against the curb whenever he could in order to stay out of sight.

The woman continued onward until she reached the end of the block, where Carlton ended in a *T* at Flushing Avenue and the broad fenced-in lot just adjacent to the dark Brooklyn Navy Yard. The woman crossed Flushing Avenue to use the opposite sidewalk, which ran along the high cyclone fence that surrounded the lot, a dense thicket of razor wire at the top. Wally followed from the opposite sidewalk, keeping her distance. Within a hundred yards the woman came upon an entrance in the fence—a driveway with a motorized gate. The woman must have held a remote control unit in her pocket because as she approached, the gate began to open for her, its old motor grinding into action and rolling the gate to one side.

Wally watched all this from across the street, where she was able to get a good view of the area the woman was entering. The lot contained a village of rusted old Quonset huts—perhaps fifty in all—arranged in a grid with barely enough space in between them for a small vehicle to pass. A few of the huts had lights on inside. Wally watched as the woman headed into the yard and toward the huts. As she moved onto the site, the motorized gate automatically began to roll closed behind her.

Wally raced across the street and, as she ran, spotted an empty malt liquor bottle in the gutter. Wally bent down to grab the bottle and reached the driveway opening before the gate was fully closed. She set the bottle down lengthwise in the gate's track, and the mechanism came to an abrupt halt as it bumped up against the obstacle, leaving an opening in the gate wide enough for Wally to squeeze through. Wally stopped and looked west on Flushing, spotting Tevin in the Lincoln and signaling for him to park the car. Tevin found a parking spot and jumped out of the Town Car, joining Wally outside the front gate.

"She's in *there*?" he asked, scoping out the village of metal huts on the other side of the fence. "What is this place, anyway?"

"Don't know," Wally said. "C'mon." Tevin followed Wally, both of them turning sideways to shimmy through the narrow gap in the gate. They began to walk slowly among the huts, hearing the woman's footsteps somewhere nearby but unable to tell which direction they were headed.

"Which way did she go?" Tevin asked.

"I lost her." Wally shrugged, frustrated.

Wally and Tevin began to move crossways through the huts, checking down each lane as they went, hoping to spot the woman. At the third lane they finally spotted her—she had stopped in front of a hut down toward the far end and was pulling out her noisy key chain. She unlocked two heavy bolts and swung the metal door open, its rusty hinges squeaking loudly. She reached inside the doorway and turned on an inside light, which spilled out of the hut and illuminated her for a moment.

Before entering her space, the woman paused and looked down the lane in the direction of Wally and Tevin, as if sensing that she was not alone, but Wally and Tevin ducked behind a corner just in time to avoid being seen. The woman entered the hut and closed the door behind her. Wally and Tevin could hear the woman locking the door behind her, both heavy bolts sliding into place with a secure *ka-chunk*.

Tevin turned to Wally with a questioning look. "The light from inside the hut . . . it showed her face."

"I saw," Wally said, "but we're too far away. . . ."

"Okay." Tevin shrugged. "Then let's go see her up close."

Wally nodded and the two of them moved down the quiet lane, tense with anticipation. As they walked, they noticed that many of the huts had interesting items arranged outside them: sculptures, engine parts, paint-splattered benches.

"I think they're art studios or something," Tevin said. "They're using this old place like some kind of artist's colony."

They finally reached the door to the woman's hut and Wally reached out, knocking twice. Tevin took two or three steps backward and stopped halfway across the lane; he wanted to be close enough to support Wally but not so close as to spook the woman in any way.

"Who is it?" came a woman's voice from inside the hut.

Wally hesitated. "It's Wallis," she said, loudly so her voice would reach through the door. "Wally."

"Who?"

"It's Valentina," Wally said after a pause. "I'm looking for Yalena."

"Valentina?" came the woman's voice.

The two heavy bolts of the door were unlocked from inside. The door creaked partially open to reveal the woman, looking hesitant and wary. Her rainbow scarf was gone now, revealing her to be about forty years old with long dark hair just beginning to go gray, and a somewhat plain face but arresting green eyes, which were now peering through the narrow opening in the doorway. The woman cast a glance over Wally's shoulder to where Tevin stood—he took another half step backward and looked away, determined not to be perceived as a threat that would cause the woman to retreat.

"Who are you again?" the woman asked Wally.

"I'm Wallis," Wally said, her voice suddenly tremulous. It was clear by the confused, emotionless look on the woman's face that she had no idea who Wally was. The woman was obviously not her mother, and Wally felt this latest disappointment deeply. How many more of these letdowns would she need to endure?

"My name is Wallis," she said. "You collected the mail from Box 310 . . . at the postal shop?"

The woman's brow furrowed as she reassessed the situation. "Wait . . ." she said, "so you *followed* me? From the boxes? Who do you think you are? I want you to leave now or I'll call the—"

"Please," Wally said as the woman began to close her door, and the genuine distress in her voice gave the woman pause. "I just need to speak with her."

"Wallis, is it?" the woman began, keeping her voice calm and even. "Wallis, this is really none of your business, but I check the mail at Box 310 for an old friend of mine—"

"Yalena?" Wally offered. "Or . . . no, she uses a different name now."

"No, dear, it's a gentleman," she said, softening, but then she stopped herself. "It really doesn't matter. He's had the box for just a few years. I'll tell you what, if you want to leave a note, I'll pass it along, but I really think there's been some sort of mistake."

The woman waited for a response, but Wally seemed more at a loss now than ever. Tevin stepped forward and placed a supportive hand on her shoulder.

"You should leave the note, Wally," he said gently. "Maybe there's still some sort of connection."

Wally just nodded. The woman disappeared for a moment, her door swinging open just enough to reveal the artist's studio inside, with several worktables stacked with various types of white paper—some vellum, some rice paper—plus large rolls of wire and some gleaming steel cutting tools. Hanging everywhere from the ceiling was the woman's artwork: strange, ethereal shapes constructed of white paper pulled over thin wire frames, like oddly shaped kites.

The woman returned with a sketch pad and a charcoal pencil, which she handed to Wally. Wally kept the charcoal poised over the paper for a moment, unable to decide what to write. Then she scratched several sentences and signed the bottom with her name and telephone number. She tore the page out of the pad and folded it, scrawling *To whoever . . .* on the outside, then handed the pad and the note back to the woman.

"Thanks," said Wally in a hollow, desolate voice. "I'm sorry that I bothered you."

"Oh . . . no, I'm sorry I couldn't help you more," said the woman as she took back the pad and note. She sounded genuinely sympathetic, and her eyes were filled with pity. "I really hope things work out for you."

Wally nodded blankly and turned away, Tevin joining her as she retreated back down the empty lane.

"I'm really sorry," Tevin said.

Wally nodded. They had almost reached the end of the lane when they heard the woman's voice behind them.

"Wait," she said. Wally and Tevin turned back around to find her still standing in her open doorway, Wally's note unfolded in front of her, a dawning awareness in her expression. "Are you really her daughter?"

"Yes," Wally said urgently. She hurried back down the lane to face the woman again, who was now looking troubled and conflicted.

"When was the last time you saw her?" the woman asked.

"Never," Wally said.

"Oh." The woman was taken aback, the wheels of her mind spinning as she tried to decide the right thing to do. "The thing is . . . it actually *is* a woman who I collect the mail for, not a man. I'm sorry. I was being protective, I guess. I really don't know her very well. We met by chance around the time we were both starting our leases here—"

"Here?" asked Tevin, who stood back over Wally's shoulder. "She has one of these huts?"

"Yes," the woman answered hesitantly. "Like I said, we barely knew each other, but she was nice, and since she wasn't around very much I started picking up her mail for her. There's no mail service here, so most of us use that same postal shop."

"Which hut is hers?" Wally asked, her heartbeat quickening again.

The woman hesitated, torn between obligation and instinct. Should she help, and how much? She faced Wally, looking into her eyes in an attempt to reckon the truth of her story.

"You really are her daughter, right?" the woman asked. "You wouldn't lie to me about that?"

"No," Wally answered. "I mean, yes. I'm just trying to connect with her."

Wally stammered a little in her excitement, struggling for words, but the woman seemed satisfied.

"One row over," she said. "The number on the door is 27, about halfway down the driveway. I already dropped off her mail, through the slot. I haven't seen her in person in a few weeks, but I know she still comes around."

"Thank you so much," Wally said. "It will be okay, I promise." Wally turned to go but the woman held her up for a moment, holding out the note she had written just moments before.

"Give this to her yourself," she said, and Wally answered with a smile as she took the note.

TWENTY-SIX

Wally and Tevin made their way through the colony of huts, finally arriving at the one marked 27. By this point, Wally's heart was truly racing. She dropped down to the floor and peered under the door of the unit. There was only a very faint light in the room, but it was enough illumination to reveal a small stack of mail that had clearly been shoved under the door and collected there, perhaps several weeks' worth.

"Who knows when she'll be here," said Wally. She checked every possible hiding place in the vicinity of the door but found no hidden keys. She and Tevin walked the perimeter of the hut, finding several large windows cut into its corrugated metal skin, but they were covered with steel grates, which made it nearly impossible to break in. They returned to the front door, where they both sat down, needing a breather.

"I can barely even stand this," Wally said. "I'm so close."

"All we need to do is wait," he said. "As long as it takes." He looked at Wally and saw she was shivering a little. He took off his bomber's jacket and wrapped it around her shoulders. Wally wanted to object, but she looked in Tevin's eyes and saw that the gesture was important to him.

As the evening grew later, several other tenants of the colony closed up their units and left for the night. On their way to the main gate, they cast wary glances at Wally and Tevin, who remained loyally at the door of hut number 27. The air was getting much colder, and it seemed like just a question of time before the two of them would have to give up for the night. It was almost eight o'clock when the door of the hut directly across the lane creaked open, and a man in his late forties exited, getting ready to lock his door behind him with a clangy set of keys that hung on his belt. He wore canvas carpenter's overalls splashed with a rainbow variety of paint colors and a worn chambray shirt under a ratty old fisherman's sweater. His salt-and-pepper hair was longish and a bit unkempt, but his beard was well trimmed and he had the deep and perceptive eyes of a practiced observer.

Before he locked his door, the man noticed Wally and Tevin sitting against the opposite hut, watching him. He studied Wally's face for a moment.

"Ah," he said casually. "So you're the daughter? Wally, right?"

For a moment Wally and Tevin stared blankly at the man—his words had caught them off guard—but then they clambered to their feet and faced him. As she spoke to him, it took all of Wally's self-control to match the man's casualness.

"Yeah, hi," she said. "Mom mentioned you, but I can't remember your name. I'm sorry. . . ."

The man waved off her apology. "Please. Forget it. I'm Phil. How's your mom? I haven't seen her this week. I miss hearing her music."

"Mom is fine," Wally replied. "Just busy, I guess."

Phil nodded his understanding. "C'mon in," he said, motioning for her to follow. "Let me show you something."

Phil opened the door to his hut and turned on the overhead lights, six large fixtures hanging from the ceiling that provided a soft, even light for the room. Tevin and Wally—still taken aback over this sudden development—followed him inside to find a well-supplied painter's studio with a full-size easel at the center. Tackboard had been attached to the sloping walls of the hut, and hundreds of charcoal sketches filled every spare space of it, newer sketches pinned right on top of older ones. Phil scanned the walls, racking his brain, then finally moved to one section of the wall and peeled away a few sketches. There, a few layers deep, he found two or three rough pencil sketches of a young girl, perhaps eight or nine years old, staring straight at the viewer with her deep, dark eyes. Wally.

"See?" said Phil. "I knew it was you right off. You have beautiful, mysterious eyes, Wally. An artist's dream."

"Uh, thanks. So, wait . . ." Wally's mind raced. "Phil. Did we ever—"

"Meet? Oh, no. Your ma brought in some snapshots and I used those."

"Oh."

"So you're meeting your mother here?"

"Yeah," Wally said casually. "She got held up, so we're just hanging. Oh, I'm sorry . . . Phil, this is my friend Tevin."

"Hey, Tevin," said Phil, and the two men shook hands. "Well, shit, you shoulda just knocked. No reason to sit out in the cold . . ." Phil pulled open a drawer in his paint cart and fished through hundreds of random items before finding the key chain he was looking for—a miniature Statue of Liberty with just two keys attached. Phil exited his hut with Wally and Tevin close behind. He stepped across to the door of hut 27 and used the two keys on the chain to unlock both bolts and then pushed the door open in front of him. Phil reached inside the hut to hit a light switch, and a set of hanging ceiling lights similar to those in his studio came on, illuminating the space.

"I gotta run out," Phil said, stepping aside from the doorway so that Wally and Tevin could enter, "but it was good to finally meet you, Wally, and you as well, Tevin."

"Thanks so much," Wally said, muting her excitement as she shook his hand.

Wally closed the door behind Phil and faced the room. It was very different from Phil's hut or the one belonging to the sculptor woman: instead of a crowded and unkempt artist's space, hut 27 was very spartan, dominated by a single major item: a baby grand piano stood at the center of the room, a deeply polished black with *Steinway & Sons* written in gold lettering on its face board. Wally regarded the piano for a moment, then slowly stepped to the instrument and sat on its bench. She carefully, almost shyly raised the fall board to reveal the keys. Wally played a scale. The piano was perfectly in tune.

"She's a musician," said Tevin.

"She was, back home," Wally answered, somewhat sadly. "Dr. Rainer said that."

"And there *you* are," said Tevin, nodding toward the far corner of the room. A single bed was placed in the corner, neatly made with a heavy woolen blanket on top and two pillows aligned. On the wall above the bed was an oil portrait of Wally at age eight or nine, obviously painted by next-door neighbor Phil, based on the sketches he had shown them. The painting was a mostly straightforward portrait, not stylized in any way, but with a slight emphasis placed on Wally's most remarkable features—her well-defined cheekbones and dark, focused eyes. Phil had added a delicate substratum of red to the eyes that brought the portrait to life with a fiery intensity.

"Wow," said Tevin.

Wally recognized her own face, but was taken aback by the underlying combination of sadness and anger that was so stark in the portrayal. There was accusation in the girl's eyes.

"Is that really me?" she asked.

Tevin could see that Wally was disturbed by the picture. "It's beautiful, Wally. Like you are."

Wally turned away from the portrait and inspected the rest of the room. There were three other objects of note in the room: a two-drawer metal file cabinet, a paper shredder standing beside it, and a plain wooden wardrobe. Wally first opened the file cabinet—it was unlocked—and discovered the basic financial documents of a relatively small life: lease payments and utility bills associated with the studio—the Quonset hut— plus financial records of several bank accounts and credit cards. The accounts were flush, with a total of assets nearing three hundred thousand dollars and credit limits exceeding twenty thousand dollars on all the credit cards. Every document listed two authorized account holders: Ellen and Kristen Whitney.

"*Ellen Whitney,*" she said out loud. "*Kristen Whitney.*" Tevin looked over her shoulder as Wally leafed through the documents, which covered many years.

"You don't know the names?"

"No."

"One of them's probably just an alias for her," Tevin said. "And you, I bet. Your mother has an alias, makes sense she'd have one for you too. So this is all yours too. That's how she wanted it."

Wally moved to the wardrobe, which stood about six feet tall and four feet wide, with a mirror in front. Wally swung the doors open and made an inspection of the contents. On the floor of the wardrobe were two small, identical black suitcases, the kind with a handle and rollers and of a size that could be carried on board an airplane and stored in the overhead racks. On top of the suitcases were two pairs of leather walking boots, both new and both black. They were an expensive Scandinavian brand name that Wally had seen for sale in nice Manhattan shoe stores, designed to be the most practical all-situation footwear possible, stylish but with the practicality of a soldier's combat boot.

Wally checked out the boots and found that one was size

seven—the most common woman's foot size—and the other a size eight: Wally's size. She took off her own worn boots and slipped on the new ones. Perfect. Next, Wally checked out the clothes hanging in the wardrobe. There were only a few items: two warm, knee-length woolen overcoats in dark blue; two gray cashmere V-neck sweaters; four pairs of new denim jeans; and several basic T-shirts, crew neck, white and dark gray. A pull-out drawer contained half a dozen pairs of women's underwear—basic black—plus several unopened pairs of panty hose and calf-high woolen socks that would be a perfect match for the boots. Every item was brand new, never worn, and sized medium, just right for Wally.

"What do you see here, Tev?" Wally asked.

"This is a safe house," Tevin said. "And a jumping-off point for . . . wherever. For escape."

"For the worst-case scenario," Wally agreed. "If every precaution had gone to shit and danger was close." It was a sanctuary—Wally understood—ready to handle the needs of a mother and daughter who had finally been reunited, after many years of separation, and were ready to venture into the world. *Together at last.* Wally allowed herself to imagine this for a moment, and the thought of it was exciting but . . . also something else. Sad? Why sad? The answer came to Wally immediately. She imagined Claire, alone and left behind. It *was* a sad thought—Wally hated it—but at the same time she resented the intrusion, resented her sense of obligation to Claire.

As Wally's thoughts drifted, some movement outside the window caught Tevin's attention. He stepped to the glass and scanned the area, catching sight of a person moving quickly between two huts at the far end of the lane and then disappearing from view.

"Wally . . ." he began, but hearing the wary tone in his voice Wally was already at his side, staring out the window as well.

"What did you see?" she asked.

"I don't know. A guy, maybe one of the tenants."

Wally moved quickly and hit the light switch, throwing the hut into darkness. The two of them stood silent, not moving. Waiting. Moments passed with no more evidence that someone was outside the hut. Wally was about to turn the lights back on when she heard an unexpected sound: a key sliding into one of the door locks. The dead bolt of the first lock clicked open, and then the key worked on the second bolt.

Wally stood motionless and held her breath, as if any act or motion, no matter how small, might somehow upset the sequence of events that was about to unfold: she was about to face her mother. As the second dead bolt slid open, the front door of the hut swung open. At the doorway stood a woman lit in silhouette by the outside lights, her features not yet visible. She took half a step into the hut, flicking on the lights as she closed and bolted the door behind her. The woman then turned to face the room and froze there, stunned at the sight of Wally standing before her in the center of the floor, Tevin just behind her. The woman remained silent and still for what seemed to Wally like an eternity.

"Wallis?" the woman finally said, surprise—and dismay—in her voice.

TWENTY-SEVEN

"Johanna?" Wally said, her mind racing.

Standing before Wally was a woman she had known for . . . how long? As far back as she could remember, Johanna had been a constant in Wally's life. She was the wife of Vincent, the live-in building superintendent, and had been helping Claire around the house forever. There were the mundane things, of course—shopping, cleaning, and sometimes laundry—but those tasks described a housemaid, and Johanna had been much more than that within the Stoneman household. She was someone who Claire trusted implicitly, a friend and confidant more than an employee.

It was Johanna who had chaperoned Wally to school whenever Claire was unable to, making sure Wally had everything she needed in her book bag and that her jacket was buttoned up tight. When the lifeguard for the rooftop pool missed his afternoon shift, it was Johanna who had stood silent watch as Wally and her friends swam. On days when Claire had been at work late, Johanna happily stepped in, taking Wally to the playground near Strawberry Fields and pushing her on the swing for over an hour, making her feel cared for and safe.

And something else. As Wally and Johanna faced each other now, a specific memory forced itself into Wally's consciousness. After a particularly bad fight between herself and Claire—how old had she been then? Twelve? Thirteen?— Wally was charging out of the building in a tearful rage when Johanna blocked her way, ushering her into the tiny employee lounge, where they sat together in silence, for hours it seemed, until Wally had calmed down. They hadn't really talked, but Johanna had held Wally tight and rocked her gently, her arms wrapped all the way around her as if afraid she might float away and never return.

Wally looked at the woman before her with new eyes, cataloging specific details as if for the first time. Johanna was in her early forties with blue eyes and light-colored hair that now had hints of gray throughout. She was somewhat petite but wiry and physically tough, and possessed a quiet nature that belied her obvious inner strength. The woman had a slight accent that Wally had never thought much about; she'd always assumed for some reason that Johanna had Scandinavian roots.

"It's you?" Wally was in a daze, her heart and mind reeling as she tried to come to grips with this new version of reality.

Johanna was still confounded by Wally's appearance there. As her mind processed the situation, the woman suddenly looked very much alarmed, in much the same way that Dr. Rainer had when Wally appeared at her office.

"Wally, you should not be—"

Johanna's words were interrupted by the sound of racing engines and the strobe of flashing blue lights just outside the hut. Tires screeched as at least two vehicles came to a stop. Within seconds, there came the sound of rushing footsteps and a loud knock on the metal door of the hut, the sharp sound echoing almost painfully against the inside walls.

"Federal agents!" boomed a voice from outside. "Open the door!"

Wally stepped toward the window to look outside, but Johanna grabbed her by the shoulder and pulled her back.

"No," Johanna said. "This could be anyone. Stay back."

Both Wally and Tevin moved back, farther away from the front door of the hut.

"Federal agents!" the call came again, with another round of loud knocks. "Open the goddamn door or we'll tear it down!"

Johanna stepped to the tall wooden wardrobe at the far end of the hut. She lowered her shoulder and pushed into the large, heavy piece of furniture, shoving with all her strength. Her force moved the wardrobe away from the wall until there was enough separation to reveal a semiautomatic shotgun with a pistol grip and .45 automatic handgun mounted to the back panel of the wardrobe. Wally and Tevin stood by, stunned by Johanna's swift action as she retrieved both weapons, sticking the handgun under her belt at the small of her back as she moved to the front door. With her right hand Johanna raised the shotgun, and with her left she unlocked the door and slowly pulled it open.

Standing outside the door was a white man in his mid-forties, dressed in civilian clothes but with a nylon-shell jacket that had *ATF* printed across its chest in bold yellow letters. He held a handgun trained squarely at Johanna's chest. His eyes fixed immediately on her shotgun, which was raised and pointed directly at him.

"Stay cool," the man said evenly, his words obviously meant for Johanna but also for the other agents behind him. He never took his eyes off Johanna and her shotgun. "You're gonna want to put that down. We're ATF. We're here to help you."

Johanna looked behind the agent and saw two more of them—a short but sturdily built black woman and another white guy, tall and fit. Both were armed, their handguns raised at Johanna. Two unmarked sedans were parked on the lane, one to either side of the hut, both with flashing light panels in their grills that splashed the colony with hypnotic blue.

Johanna wasn't ready yet to let her guard down.

"I want to see your ID," Johanna said.

"Yalena Mayakova?" the first agent asked Johanna as he flashed his ATF credentials.

Johanna crept forward just enough to get a clear look at the man's ID, then leaned out just a little farther and scanned the entire area outside the hut, looking beyond the two ATF cruisers. Just the three of them, as far as she could tell. Wally and Tevin exchanged looks of shock and bewilderment; layers of intrigue were unfolding before them with no time to process.

Wally had finally found Yalena, but the moment of mother-and-daughter reunion—dreamed of, prayed for—had barely happened at all, and now it seemed to be morphing into something else entirely.

"What do you want?" Johanna barked at the agent.

"We need all of you to come in for questioning," the agent said. "We'll move to our field office. This is in your best interest. Your life and the lives of these two young people are in danger."

"What danger?" Johanna demanded.

"Klesko," Wally blurted. She looked directly at the agent. "This is about Klesko?"

Hearing the name shocked Johanna. She kept her eyes on the agent as she questioned Wally.

"*Klesko?*" Johanna said, alarm in her voice. "How do you know that name, Wally?"

"I . . . I started looking for you," Wally said, confused. "Klesko is looking for you, like I was. And—"

"Everything will be explained in due time," the agent said. "Now we need to move. Lower your weapon and step out, all three of you."

Johanna remained silent, still considering her next move.

"Stay behind me," she said to Wally and Tevin.

The two of them obeyed her, following as she slowly stepped outside the hut and into the lane, her shotgun still raised in front of her as she continued to scan the area with her eyes.

"Everything is secure," the agent assured Johanna as she

emerged from the hut. "Lower your weapon and set it down on the ground in front of you."

Johanna appraised the agents standing before her, all three of them with their weapons still raised in her direction, holding their positions at separate firing angles that had her and the two teens squarely in their sights. Johanna took a quick glance behind her, meeting Wally's eyes.

"We'll go with them," Johanna said.

Wally nodded in agreement. "No choice."

Johanna turned back toward the agents and lowered the muzzle of her shotgun.

"Good. Now set the weapon down," the agent said again.

Johanna carefully bent forward, her arms extending outward as she prepared to set the shotgun down on the ground. She had almost done this when the sound of racing engines came again, this time from the direction of the front gate. Johanna straightened, the shotgun still in her hands, as the three ATF agents all turned in the direction of the engine sounds.

"What the hell—?" The black female agent began to speak but was interrupted by a squeal of tires and then a crashing sound: the colony's security gate behind torn out of its track by a charging vehicle. This all took place out of their line of vision—the group's view was blocked by the Quonset huts surrounding them—but the sound of the approaching vehicles grew louder . . . closer. The female agent turned to Johanna and yelled at her.

"Drop your weapon NOW and get in the vehicles—!"

Before Johanna could respond, a cab swerved around the

corner at the far end of the lane and raced toward them at full throttle.

"What the hell?" the older agent growled.

With a clear shot at the agents and their waiting vehicles, the cab gave no sign of slowing or stopping but continued on its collision course, hurtling toward them, faster with each passing second. The agents raised their weapons and all fired simultaneously but with no effect; even as the bullets tore into the taxi's windshield, the driver—Klesko—kept the vehicle on course. The taxi plowed head-on into the first ATF cruiser. The cruiser lurched backward and slammed into the second male agent, rolling over and crushing him beneath its weight. Within seconds, the wreckage burst into flames.

The two surviving agents—the older man who had first appeared at Johanna's door and the younger black woman—now fired on the taxi as Klesko ducked down low behind the dashboard to shield himself from the barrage.

"We're going NOW!" Johanna said to Tevin and Wally, grabbing Wally by the arm and leading them both down the lane in the opposite direction, toward the area where the gate had stood. Wally spotted a Glock 9mm handgun on the ground—it must have belonged to the fallen agent—and grabbed it as she moved.

The gun battle continued behind them as Johanna and the teens made it about halfway down the narrow lane, and they stopped only when they became aware of some loud noises ahead of them. With a terrible screeching of tires, a red-and-white-striped tow truck rounded the corner at the far end of the lane and hurtled straight toward them at high speed. The truck was too wide for the lane, and as it moved forward, it plowed aside whatever was standing in front of the huts: wooden porches, sculptures, and plants.

"Shit!" Johanna hissed.

She shielded Wally and Tevin with her body as she fired her shotgun at the charging tow truck. The truck continued barreling forward, its heavy steel body unaffected by the barrage of gunfire. Wally grabbed Tevin and Johanna, pulling them away from the lane and toward a walking passage between two of the huts. The tow truck—with the younger Russian from Dr. Rainer's office clearly visible behind the wheel—tried to follow them, but the passage was far too narrow. The truck tried to power its way through, but it only succeeded in tearing away the corner of one of the huts.

Wally and the others raced away as fast as they could run, the enraged howl of the driver following them.

Back in front of hut 27, there was a break in the gunfire as the two ATF agents reloaded. Klesko took advantage. He threw open the door of the taxi—now riddled with dozens of bullet holes—and rolled out onto the pavement. He jumped to his feet and charged forward, slamming a new magazine into his gun as he ran. He was quicker than the agents—they were still reloading when he sidestepped the burning cruiser and leapt up on top of the second vehicle, standing tall as he gunned down the frantic agents below him with successive shots to the head.

Wally led Johanna and Tevin in a zigzagging pattern

through the colony of huts, crossing the lanes that ran north and south and dodging in between the huts in places where the spaces were not blocked. Even as they made progress, they could hear the two vehicles now scouting the colony, patrolling the grounds like circling sharks. Occasionally they caught a glimpse of the vehicles, the taxicab now rolling along the north end of the lanes, closing off that direction as the tow truck swept through the lanes behind them, driving them forward.

"They're trying to cut us off," Wally said, and the three of them pushed their pace, hoping there was a way out at the far end of the colony. They finally reached the last lane—and the last row of huts—at the northeast corner of the Navy Yard. Just past the huts was another tall cyclone fence with at least four feet of razor wire looped at the top, virtually impossible to surmount.

"Damn," Johanna said. "Back this way."

They turned and ran the opposite direction down the lane, the last row of huts on their right and the cyclone fence on their left, the south corner of the lot a hundred yards away. The tow truck—Tiger behind the wheel—pulled into their lane behind them and sped in their direction. Johanna backpedaled as she squeezed off a few shotgun blasts in the direction of the truck, and Wally did the same with her handgun, but the young Russian swerved side to side in the lane just enough to avoid a direct hit from any of the shots.

The others followed Wally as she ducked between two of the huts to make it over to the next lane, sidestepping a half Dumpster and a pyramid of potted plants to make it through, but as soon as they emerged, they found the taxi there—Klesko behind the wheel—already racing in their direction. The taxicab would easily cut them down if they tried to cross his path.

"Back!" Wally barked.

She reversed course, Tevin and Johanna following as she sped between the next two huts, headed back in the direction of the perimeter fence, where the tow truck was still patrolling. As they ran, Johanna blasted two more shots at the taxicab, but then the chamber of the shotgun rang empty. Johanna tossed the useless weapon aside and continued after Wally.

In the cab of the tow truck, Tiger scanned the row of Quonset huts to his right, where the three had disappeared. He slowed the truck but kept moving forward; he knew Klesko was defending the next lane over, and he expected their quarry would be herded back in his direction soon.

Suddenly there was a blur of motion directly ahead of him as a half Dumpster came wheeling out into his path, the girl and the two others pushing it with all their strength. Tiger had no time to react and blasted into the Dumpster with the crash bumper of his tow truck. It was a major jolt, but the truck was clearly the winner. He accelerated and turned his wheel to the right, plowing the Dumpster out of the lane and into one of the Quonset huts amid a shower of sparks. He backed the truck up ten feet, then surged forward again, wheeling around the Dumpster and racing after the three fleeing figures as they sprinted toward the perimeter fence.

As they moved, the girl and her friends hurled various loose objects into the truck's path, hoping to slow Tiger's progress as he hunted them down. They rolled a round metal picnic table with a large sun umbrella into his path. The massive truck plowed it under. Tiger was only slightly inconvenienced by the umbrella, which became stuck on the hood, blocking his view. He never even slowed down but reached out his window and tossed the umbrella aside.

More obstacles stood in his path—large earthenware pots with plants in them, large plastic garbage bins, a wooden trellis, a big barbecue grill on wheels—but none of it was anything more than a minor annoyance as Tiger charged on, the corner of the perimeter fence looming closer. Looking forward, Tiger beheld an unexpected sight: the young "Aretha" girl was standing fifty feet ahead in the lane, directly in his path, her handgun raised in his general direction—but not exactly. Her gun was pointed lower, toward his front wheels. Tiger wondered briefly what the girl was thinking; the truck's crash bumper would protect the engine, and even a tire blowout would not slow him down enough. Then he knew.

"Shit!" Tiger growled.

Wally stood her ground in the lane, aiming her gun carefully at the barbecue grill that was half-plowed under the tow truck's nose and dragging on the ground. Attached to the barbecue was a medium-size propane tank, and Wally had the tank in her sights. The driver of the truck seemed to realize the danger at the very last moment, and he swerved the truck directly into the row of huts, running over a pile of lumber scraps that were stacked outside one of the dwellings. As the truck ran over the pile, the loose boards dislodged the barbecue from underneath it.

Wally took her shot at the propane tank—now rolling away just to the side of the truck—and the tank exploded in a fireball. The blast did not blow the truck into the air as Wally had hoped it would, but the ploy succeeded anyway: to avoid the explosion, the driver of the truck veered hard to the right, plowing right through one of the Quonset huts and into the next lane over.

"Yes!" Tevin whooped.

But there was little time for celebration. Apparently the taxicab had abandoned its patrol of the next lane, because it was now barreling at them in their own lane from the same direction the tow truck had taken. A crazed-looking Klesko was behind the wheel, plowing aside any remaining obstacles as it sped toward them.

"Come on," Wally commanded, and the three of them raced on to the end of the lane, where the fence surrounding the Navy Yard came to a corner, forbiddingly high and with the same barrier of razor wire on top. The taxi was closing fast on their position.

"There!" Johanna pointed ahead to the last Quonset hut, which had a ramp out front for wheelchair access. "We can use that. . . ."

The three of them set upon the wooden ramp—fifteen feet long, at least—dragging it away from the hut and over to the fence. They struggled to tilt the heavy wooden structure straight up to its full height and then tipped it over, toppling the ramp like a felled tree. The ramp crashed down heavily onto the fence, and it sagged a few feet outward under the weight.

Before Wally could react, Johanna reached out and grabbed the Glock out of her hand.

"What are you doing?" Wally asked. "Let's go—"

"I'm right behind you!" Johanna shouted back. "Go now!"

She turned toward the approaching taxicab and blasted away with the Glock. Klesko ducked down beneath the dashboard to avoid the shots and the cab careened into a hut, coming to a crashing stop.

As Johanna continued to fire—making sure Klesko stayed pinned in the cab—Tevin pushed Wally ahead of him and up the ramp, its slope steep enough that Wally had to grip the handrail to pull herself up. As she climbed upward, she looked back over her shoulder, panicked that Johanna was lingering too long as she tried to cover Wally and Tevin's escape.

"COME NOW!" Wally shouted at Johanna, with no response.

"Keep going, Wally," Tevin shouted, and continued to push her from behind. "Get over the fence and she'll come."

Wally understood that Johanna would not make her own escape until Wally herself was free, so she scampered up the last few feet of the ramp and dropped down over the side of the fence, where a row of Dumpsters made the distance easy to jump. As soon as she had touched down safely, Wally called back to Johanna.

"NOW! PLEASE!" she yelled.

Johanna tucked the Glock into her belt, then turned on her heels and scrambled up the ramp. Tevin waited at the top to help her over, reaching out as she approached. Johanna was within an arm's length of Tevin when a mighty roar came from the direction of the next lane over. The tow truck came blasting through the last hut at full ramming speed, tearing the hut off its cement foundation.

The entire hut bent in half from the impact and surged forward with a thunderous sound of tortured metal. The hut collided with the escape ramp, driving it off the fence and crashing it down. Johanna and Tevin rode the ramp to the ground, still inside the Navy Yard and on the wrong side of the fence from where Wally now stood.

"Run!" Wally implored them from over the fence. She grabbed onto the fence desperately, wishing now that she was still on the other side so she could help her friends or share their fate. "Get away!"

But there was nowhere Johanna and Tevin could go. Wally watched helplessly as they tried to pick themselves up from the wreckage, but now Klesko and Tiger emerged from their vehicles and rushed forward, their guns drawn. Wally could only look on in horror as disaster unfolded.

Johanna saw the two men coming toward them and reached back for the handgun under her belt, but . . . it was gone. Dazed, she looked around the wreckage of the ramp and the destroyed hut, desperate to find her weapon. She could not find it, but Tevin did; the gun sat on the ground before him. He stared at it for a second as if examining a foreign object. He picked it up, and from the first moment of contact, it was painfully obvious that he had never held a gun before. He awkwardly raised the gun and steadied it with both hands, then took aim at the approaching killers.

"NO!" Wally shouted, but it was too late. As Tevin raised the barrel of the gun, a barrage of gunfire came from Klesko and Tiger, cutting into the boy. He dropped to the ground, instantly lifeless.

"TEVIN!" Wally wailed in agony as she watched her friend die. She truly felt at that moment as if the bullets had entered her as well, ripping through her own flesh as they had ripped through Tevin's, tearing away whatever it was that held life and love. For what seemed like forever she stood motionless, staring with horror and disbelief at Tevin, waiting for a sign of life that in her heart she knew would never come ever again.

"Oh, Tevin . . . oh God. . . ." Wally mouthed the words, but there was almost no sound, the air finding no way out of her clenched chest.

But Wally's anguish did nothing to stop the violence from continuing.

Within seconds the two Russians were on top of Johanna. Klesko pistol-whipped her and she dropped to the ground, barely conscious as she groaned loudly in pain. Klesko did not slow his pace but kept moving forward, stepping over Johanna and charging the fence toward Wally, his gun still raised.

Wally stood frozen there for just a moment, still shocked nearly senseless by Tevin's slaughter and the sight of Johanna brutally struck down, her unconscious body now under the control of the two killers. The sight of Klesko raising his gun toward her now, however, stirred her primal sense of survival; she ran, her escape shielded by the Dumpsters against the fence. Klesko threw himself at the cyclone fence and climbed just high enough to get a shot at Wally as she retreated, but when he drew her into his sights and pulled the trigger, the hammer clicked harmlessly. His mag was empty.

"Fuck!" Klesko howled, dropping to the ground and pounding furiously against the fence as Wally made her escape.

TWENTY-EIGHT

It had taken Atley more than a day to find Special Agent Bill Horst. There had been half a dozen unreturned phone calls to the Manhattan field office and Bill's home, and finally a drop-in visit to the field office, where he never even made it past security. Atley had no luck at all until late the following night, when a call went out over the cop channels about a gun battle in Brooklyn that had involved federal agents.

Atley took a chance and made the drive over the bridge, headed for the Brooklyn Navy Yard. He was en route when some details about the battle came over the radio.

Holy shit, Atley thought, listening to the police broadcast. Wallis Stoneman, the runaway, already being sought for questioning in the murder of Dr. Charlene Rainer, had been present at the Navy Yard shoot-out as well. Now an APB came over the radio and it was official: every law enforcement agency in

New York was actively looking for Wally. Atley still had no clue what Wallis was up to or how the Sophia Manetti murder figured into it, but he felt vindicated that he had spent so much of his time tracking the girl. Whatever was going on, Wallis Stoneman was in the middle of it.

It was almost nine o'clock that night when Atley arrived at the old Brooklyn Navy Yard, where a fleet of police cruisers and emergency vehicles and news vans had the traffic completely blocked. He double-parked a few blocks away and walked to the yard, badging his way through two Brooklyn police lines. On the way, Atley used his cell phone to dial Special Agent Bill Horst—his fourth try in the past hour—and Horst finally picked up.

"Where are you?" Bill greeted the call.

"Near the gate," Atley said.

"Here at the yard?" Bill sounded unhappy. "Shit. Stay where you are, Atley. I'll find you. Do NOT come through the gate."

Bill hung up before Atley could reply. Atley obeyed Bill's instruction, hanging back from the broken gate at the yard and waiting for Bill to emerge from the crime scene chaos across the street. Bill Horst finally appeared at the gate of the Navy Yard. He spotted Atley on the opposite sidewalk and crossed over to join him.

"Why are you here?" Bill demanded brusquely. "We got three dead ATF agents over there—I personally knew two of the guys more than ten years—"

"Shit, Bill . . .I'm sorry."

"It's a bad scene in too many ways, Atley. All the agencies want to keep this federal."

"I get it," Atley said, "but you have an APB out for Wallis Stoneman. That's all I need to know about."

Now Bill looked even more exasperated. Before speaking, he steered Atley halfway up Carlton Street, away from any curious feds who might spot him talking to an NYPD suit cop.

"So what the hell?" Atley asked.

"Your BOLO was here," Horst said. "The street girl. That's confirmed. You're not hearing this from me, but these three agents? It's looking like they were off the res, running their own thing. None of their ACs have any idea what they were doing down here."

"Running what? What were they into?"

Bill Horst hesitated, struggling with the decision. He snuck a look over his shoulder, back in the direction of the Navy Yard crime scene, still anxious that someone from his team would spot him talking to a local cop.

"It's just you and me here, Bill," Atley reassured his friend.

Bill sighed and began to talk. "Atley, you remember back all the way to when I got pulled out of our academy class? I know you guys resented it, how I was picked like that, like the feds thought I was the ace of the goddamn class or something."

"And you weren't?"

"They basically picked me for body type. You believe that shit? There was a joint FBI and ATF unit that joined an Interpol operation in Eastern Europe—Bulgaria—and they were looking for guys who fit the genetics. Plus, I speak German from my folks. And I was a clean face."

"Okay," Atley said, surprising himself that he was in fact relieved, a little, to hear this. Had he really been holding that bullshit grudge all these years?

"Make you feel better?" Horst said with a weary smirk.

"A little. Yeah."

"So I'll spare you the long story that mostly has nothing to do with this case," Bill continued. "Just know it was about Russian guns—*everything* moves through Bulgaria—and we were on it for two years. There was this one mover that we spent a lot of time trying to nail, name of Klesko. Came up with the Dobrik mob as a fixer, moved up to bigger things. Nasty motherfucker, highly productive. The international task force—including us—nailed him fifteen years ago on a tip about an arms exchange. The legend on the street was that his girlfriend was the one who tipped us and took off with his entire negotiable stash, worth millions in cash and precious stones. Over the years, a lot of folks have been looking for the girlfriend—"

"Meaning they've been looking for Klesko's stash." Atley was slowly putting it together.

"More than ten years and they've never stopped."

"So how the hell does Wallis Stoneman figure into all this shit?"

"We don't know yet, Atley, but the two shooters you faced off with? The other night at the shrink's office?"

"You know about all that?"

"I told you, Atley," Bill said with a wry grin, "we're all big fans of your work."

"Funny."

"No, we got called in when the two shooters were ID'd. It was Klesko and his son. The kid is a chip off the block, an experienced fixer already at the age of seventeen. Came up on the streets of Piter, just like his father. Between the two of them, they're not known for missing what they aim at. You're a lucky son of a bitch to still be breathing. Plus, it looks like they were the doers tonight on these three ATFs."

"I thought you said this Klesko was locked up."

"Yeah, he was"—Bill shook his head in dismay—"but not anymore. Two years ago he was transferred out of a high-security facility and put out to an old-school Siberian *re-education* camp, not quite so secure. The sentence was for life, but it didn't work out that way."

"He escaped?"

Bill nodded. "Yeah, and here's how good a getaway he made from the Siberian camp: it was *us* that told the Russians he was gone, once we ID'd him here in the States. They didn't even know. Apparently, there was a fire. . . ."

"So we've got the father and son Kleskos in town looking to recover what was taken from them years ago," Atley said. "Which means they think the girlfriend . . . ?"

"Yalena Mayakova was her name back then," said Bill.

"The Kleskos somehow figured out that this Yalena Mayakova is in New York somewhere. . . ."

Bill Horst nodded and continued the thought for Atley, "And some ATF agents—who were part of our task force all those years ago—seemed to figure out the same thing."

"Ten years go by"—Atley was still putting it all together— "and now everyone gets the scent again, at the same time? The ATF guys and the father-and-son Kleskos?"

"We have no idea what set it off, but it's all coming down now. Two bloodbaths and your BOLO was right in the middle of both."

"Why were they all here in the yard?"

"I'll tell you when we know, but so far we've come up with squat. Look at the place. Like a goddamn tornado hit it and now half of it is burning."

There was a long moment as Atley continued to process all the new information. There was one detail he'd expected to hear from Bill at some point in the narrative, but he hadn't; once Bill brought the subject of the Russian mob into the story, Atley expected him to say something about Wallis Stoneman being a Russian adoptee. Either Bill didn't know about Wallis's Russian origins or he did know and was just holding that detail back. Whichever it was, Atley could tell that something was on Bill's mind that he hadn't spilled yet. For a guy who had survived undercover for more than five years, Atley found him pretty easy to read.

"There's something else, right?" Atley said. "What are you not telling me?"

Bill hesitated again but finally continued, leaning in close to Atley and speaking quietly though no one was near them. "Obviously this is all a huge embarrassment across all the feds, and the sooner the file is closed the better. . . ."

"They're gonna sweep it all up in a tidy package." Atley understood. "They're gonna say it's over, that these three agents had gone bad and now they're dead, end of story. But you don't think so."

"I don't know."

"You have an idea."

"And no one wants to hear it right now," Bill said. "And especially not from me. Not from inside their own house."

"So?" Atley waited. Horst was being shut down by his command and he resented it.

"There was another guy," Bill said, forcing the words out as if he was pulling his own teeth. "ATF also. He's been working an undercover assignment on a local arms trade, in Manhattan, for the past two years. I know him—he was part of the Bulgarian thing with us years ago, and he was tight with those three who are now dead over there in the yard. He's smarter than the others put together, and he's ruthless. Always gave me a very dark vibe. If you're going to keep looking for the Stoneman girl, Atley—"

"I am."

"Then you might just end up face-to-face with the guy. If that happens, Atley, you shoot. Don't stop shooting until your clip is empty. That's how he'll do you if he gets the chance."

"Who is he, Bill?"

"His name is Cornell Brown."

TWENTY-NINE

With a glass of red wine in hand—her second—Claire leaned back in the sofa and watched the talking heads on TV. The local public station was rerunning the evening news, a panel of experts talking about multi-national relief efforts in Africa. Claire muted the sound but let the pictures roll on, the silent flickering of the screen imbuing the desolate apartment with a gloomy blue glow. The apartment was so quiet now, and empty.

Another weekend alone. When would change come? she wondered. How much of her old life would she have to let go of before she could move ahead?

The house phone rang and Claire picked up the portable handset.

"Yes?"

"Mrs. Stoneman?"

"Is that you, Raoul?"

"Yes, ma'am. Uh . . . Mrs. Stoneman? Your Wallis is on her way up."

Claire's breath caught in her throat.

"She's very upset, Mrs. Stoneman," said Raoul hesitantly. "There is . . . she has blood on her—"

Claire was out of the sofa at that very moment, tossing the telephone aside and rushing out her door to the elevator landing. The nearest elevator opened to reveal Wallis, in much worse condition than Claire had ever seen her: she wore a too-large army-surplus bomber jacket that made her look like a wounded bird, and underneath it her sweater was torn halfway into shreds. Wally's eyes and cheeks were smudged with mascara from crying, and her neck . . . there was some sort of splatter there. Blood? Wally's face seemed frozen in a look of torment.

"Oh my God . . . Wally . . ." Claire wanted to rush and embrace her daughter, but it had been so long since Wally had welcomed her affections that she held back.

"Mom . . ." Wally's tearful voice was angry and woeful at the same time as she stepped slowly out of the elevator and stood before Claire. "I've been strong, Mama. I have. But I don't know what to do now."

Claire couldn't resist any longer; she reached out for her daughter, wrapping her up tightly and leading her back to the apartment. Once inside, they both slumped to the floor, still embracing.

"It's all gone so bad . . ." Wally sobbed.

The entire battle at the Navy Yard had lasted no more than two minutes, but it had been the most disastrous event of

Wally's life. Once she had leapt the fence and escaped Klesko's gunfire, Wally lurked nearby in the shadowy perimeter of the Navy Yard, looking on helplessly as Klesko grabbed up Johanna and beat her with the butt of his handgun before heaving her limp body into the cab of the tow truck. The Russians jumped into the truck and raced away from the scene, taking Johanna with them but leaving Tevin where he lay, motionless and gushing blood on the tarmac, so alone. Wally's first instinct had been to run to Tevin's side—hoping against reason that he had somehow survived—but before she could reach him, the sirens of cop cars and fire trucks could be heard closing in on the scene, a swarm of them.

Wally knew that if she stayed at the site, she would be taken into custody, and she didn't trust the police to believe her story or take the immediate action that would be needed to save Johanna. As Wally walked quickly away from the Navy Yard, she discovered that the army-surplus jacket she was wearing—Tevin's jacket—held the keys to the Lincoln in the front pocket. She was at the wheel of the Lincoln and driving away when she realized that there was only one place she wanted to be, only one place where she would feel truly safe and sane and cared for.

"I went looking for my mother," Wally began, Claire's arms still clutched around her as they sat on the floor. "My Russian mother."

"You did *what*?"

"I'm sorry if that hurts you, Mama, but I had to."

"But how could you possibly—"

"And now Tevin is killed."

Claire was in shock, trying desperately to process what Wally was telling her. "One of your friends? *Dead?*"

Wally nodded, the tears now pouring down again.

"My God, Wally . . ."

"All he wanted was to take care of me," Wally said. "And now he's gone, and they took her. They took Johanna."

Claire eased her embrace and held Wally by the shoulders, looking into her eyes with piercing intensity.

"Johanna?" Claire said. "I don't understand. *Who* took her?"

"It's too much to tell," Wally sobbed. "I found a place, in a part of Brooklyn, the Navy Yard. It was like . . . like a safe house or whatever, a place set aside by my Russian mother in case something bad happened. You see, she's been here all along, watching me. It's Johanna, Mom. Her real name is Yalena Mayakova. My Russian mother."

"Wally—"

"Then everything went bad, so bad," Wally went on. "First there were three agents, ATF or FBI or something. But then the two Russians came. They're the ones who killed Dr. Rainer—"

"Dr. Rainer? Charlene Rainer? She's *dead?*"

"And the men came to the Navy Yard too. They killed Tevin and took Johanna. One of them, Mom, he's my father. My Russian father. He took Johanna."

"Your *father?* What are you saying?"

The barrage of information stunned Claire speechless for a

few moments—she struggled to process all that Wally was telling her.

"I could see it," Wally said. "He has the same dark eyes, like mine."

"Oh God."

"I'm sorry, Mom. It's all my fault. I had to go looking and I made all of this happen."

"There were two?"

"What do you mean?"

"You said there was the Russian man and another."

"A young one. With Klesko."

"Klesko."

"My father. The two of them took Johanna and now she's gone. I don't know where."

Claire closed her eyes for a long moment, as if in silent prayer, and when she opened them again, she spoke:

"I know where," she said.

THIRTY

"What do you mean, *you know where?"* Wally demanded. "How is that? *How* do you know where they're taking Johanna?"

"I'll explain on the way," Claire answered, still distressed but keeping herself together. She looked at her watch. "We have time."

Bewildered, Wally stared at her mother and realized something: Claire was appropriately shocked to hear about the violent tragedy at the Brooklyn Navy Yard—and the murder of Charlene Rainer—but the news about Johanna's true identity didn't seem like a surprise to her. And the fact that she knew where Johanna was being taken . . . Wally almost got the sense that events were playing out in a way that Claire had anticipated. Or dreaded.

"Mom? You knew about my Russian mother all along? You knew that Yalena was right here, all the time?"

Claire released her answer with great difficulty, as if breaking a vow.

"Yes."

"You know that she's been watching over me?"

"Yes."

"How could you let it be?" Wally demanded, hurt and anger in her voice. "How could you know that and keep it from me all this time?"

"It's so complicated, Wally," Claire said. "Right now, Johanna is in trouble and we can help her. We have to get ready. Right?"

Wally couldn't argue the point; Johanna needed their help now. Everything else could wait.

"And you know where they've taken her?" Wally asked.

"It's *she* who will take *them*," Claire said with certainty. "The men are after something, something that was taken from them—"

"The alexandrite?"

The name of the stones—coming from her daughter's mouth—shocked Claire again.

"My God, Wally . . . what have you been doing? Who have you been talking to?"

"There are more of them? That's what my father is here for. Johanna is taking them to the stones?"

"Yes, but we can be there first. Understand? We have time, but we have to get ready. All right?"

Wally was suddenly too tired to argue. Claire ran a hot shower and helped Wally peel off her torn, bloody clothing. Wally's eyes had a vacant look now, her eyes—and heart—cried out and empty. She stepped into the shower. Immediately, the pulsing hot water began to soothe and revive her.

"I'll find you some clean clothes," Claire said as she disappeared from the bathroom, "and put on some coffee."

Wally turned the outer ring on the showerhead until the pulses were slow and heavy. There was a small tile bench at the back of the shower stall and she sat down on it, bowing her head low so that the rhythmic bursts struck directly at the back of her neck and sent a tingling sensation down the sore muscles of her back. She would allow herself ten minutes in the shower—just long enough for calm to take hold. Physical and emotional exhaustion was lurking just beneath the surface of her disturbed consciousness, and Wally could not allow herself to give in, not yet.

Anyway, it was absurd to imagine how she could possibly sleep with the images now coursing through her mind: Johanna being struck down and tossed into the cab of the tow truck. The sight of her best friend, Tevin, dead and alone on the tarmac of the Navy Yard because he insisted she leap the fence first. Dead, in defense of her, the same boy she had slept with just two nights before. Was he still lying there on the ground of the Navy Yard, even now? Or had he been removed, shipped off to a cold slab at the city morgue?

Wally knew that all these tragedies had taken place because of her, because she had placed the goal of finding her mother above every other concern, and when that moment had finally arrived, it was a disaster. But Johanna was still out there, somewhere, and still alive. Wally needed to focus not on the past but on what would happen next. Any hope for saving Johanna seemed to hinge on Claire. She claimed to know where the two men would be going with Johanna and seemed determined to do what she could to save her. This of all things was no surprise; over the course of Wally's life, Claire had proved that she would willingly sacrifice herself to protect someone she loved.

Oh no, Wally thought, struck by a sudden realization.

Wally bolted out of the shower, running out of the bathroom and back into the apartment. The place was silent and empty. Wally cursed herself. Still naked and dripping wet, Wally jumped to the front door and flung it open, revealing an empty hallway.

"SHIT!" Wally grabbed the house phone and the doorman downstairs immediately picked up the line.

"Miss Stoneman?"

"She's gone?" Wally barked into the phone. "My mother left the building?"

"Well . . .yes, Miss Stoneman. About five or six minutes ago."

"She took the car?"

"Yes, she did. Is there anything I can—" Wally threw down the phone in a rage and stomped around the living room, pacing in circles, directionless and frantic. "Shit!" It was a few moments before Wally noticed the single piece of notepaper on the dining room table, held there in place by a small glass paperweight. The note read:

You'll be safe here, Wally. I'm sorry and I love you, more than I can ever say, or prove. Love, Mom.

"Shit!" Wally shouted again, then retrieved the phone she had thrown to the floor. She hit the speak button and heard the dial tone. *Good*, she hadn't broken it. Wally dialed Claire's cell phone number, but after seven or eight rings the call was patched over to Claire's voice mail. Wally hung up and redialed three times until Claire finally picked up. . . .

"Wally . . ."

"Mom! Whatever you're doing—"

"Wally—"

"No! This is MY life, Mom! I made this happen! This is something for me to fix. Tell me where you're going."

"No, Wally. I'm sorry. I love you." And then Claire hung up her line.

"DAMN IT!" Wally hollered to the empty apartment; she barely resisted hurling the phone down again. Instead she hit redial once again, but now the line went straight to voice mail; Claire had turned off her phone.

Wally paced through the apartment, frantically trying to think through the problem. As her mind spun the possibilities, she went to her room and put on some jeans and a turtleneck, readying herself to head out into the night as soon as she had figured out what to do, what move to make next. She realized that she would have to calm down if she had any hope of solving the problem.

She took several deep, cleansing breaths, the way Claire had taught her when she was a frustrated, angry little girl. *Breathe in through the nose to the count of four, hold for seven seconds, then out with a whoosh to the count of eight.* After three or four of these breaths, Wally felt her thinking gradually came back into focus.

What did she know? Wally thought about the brief phone call with Claire; there had been sound in the background, but nothing specific, just a constant, relatively high level of background noise. What did that mean? Claire's car was an Infiniti SUV, low to the ground and powerful but with good sound insulation and with a hands-free cell phone system that had noise canceling built in. To produce engine sound that noticeable, the car would have to be traveling at speed. That probably meant that Claire was not driving on city streets. No, Wally guessed that the Infiniti was on an expressway.

So, which one? Since she'd needed to get herself ready and then have the valet get the car out of the basement garage, Claire had only had a few minutes' head start. So the road had to be a close by, no doubt the West Side Highway, but that didn't narrow down the possible destinations really; it only suggested that she was headed away from Manhattan.

What *else* did Wally know? Not much. The more she pressed herself to think through her situation, the greater her sense that she was completely in the dark, and had been in the dark her entire *goddamn* life. Sheltered, coddled, appeased . . . *lied to*. Shit.

Stop being angry, Wally silently commanded herself, *and think*.

What else did she know? She reviewed the few moments she and Claire had shared in the apartment. What else had Claire said? She had been shocked, certainly, by Wally's hastily reconstructed news about all that she had been through that night, ending with Tevin's death and Johanna's abduction.

"The two of them took Johanna and now she's gone. I don't know where."

Wally had grieved, the image of Johanna being thrown into the tow truck still painfully fresh in her mind.

"I know where," Claire had replied, and it had not been a guess on her part; it had been a statement of fact. She *did* know where. What else did she say? Wally ran through their brief exchange, trying pick out anything useful but not coming up with anything. Claire had run a hot shower for Wally, and she was going to put out some clean clothes for her. Claire also said was going to make coffee, but that was obviously just a misdirection to set Wally at ease and give Claire time to get away.

"We have time," Claire had said confidently. *We have time?* How could that be? The men had taken Johanna away and were guaranteed to hurt her if she did not give them exactly what they wanted. Obviously, Klesko was convinced that there was still some money and stones remaining from the cache that Yalena had taken from him. Where had they been kept all these years? A bank? Some sort of storage facility? Either of those might explain the "we have time" comment; a bank vault or storage facility would operate on a preset schedule, accessible only at a certain hour the next morning. That made sense.

Claire must have known exactly where the remaining stones were kept and when they would be accessible.

How could Wally figure out where that hiding place was?

Wally continued her frantic pacing, trying to stimulate some sort of eleventh-hour epiphany. She had only one thought and picked up the phone again, hitting redial.

"Yes, Miss Stoneman?" came the doorman's voice.

"Raoul? Sorry I hung up before . . ."

"That's okay, Miss Stoneman."

"Can you tell me what was my mom was wearing?"

"Uh . . ." The doorman considered, then answered uncertainly. "A jacket, I think? A warm one? And a cap. Boots, maybe?"

"Thanks, Raoul." Wally hit the end button on the phone. Claire's choice of outdoor clothing did not suggest a bank or other indoor location like a storage locker. As she ran through the possibilities, Wally had a thought. She was staring at the portable phone in her hand. The LED panel was lit up with the last number called: the phone number of the desk downstairs. Wally hit the down arrow button and the screen scrolled down to the list of the numbers called last, past the calls Wally herself had made to Raoul at the front desk. Wally saw the number listed for the last phone call Claire had made—she had called outside the building just five minutes before she left. The phone number looked vaguely familiar, but it took a minute or so before Wally finally recognized the area code and then the full phone number. Wally herself had dialed that number just a few days earlier. She hit redial and the phone rang through. Voice mail picked up on the other end of the line and a message played. Now Wally knew where Claire had gone and where Johanna would be found.

Wally went to her room and quickly dressed in warm clothes, including Tevin's jacket and the good boots she had found in the Quonset hut. Once she was ready to go, a quick calculation told her she had time to make one important stop before driving north to Shelter Island.

THIRTY-ONE

Ella and Jake heard the key in the lock and bolted up from their makeshift bed. They didn't dare use their flashlight to see who it was, for fear of giving themselves away in case it was not either Wally or Tevin, coming home.

"Guys?" Wally's voice, quiet.

"In here, Wally," Ella said.

Wally moved into the back room of the old laundry, where an ancient steam-press bench had been left behind and where the crew had set up their bedrolls. Ella and Jake greeted Wally, sleepy-eyed.

"What time is it?" Ella asked with a little yawn.

"Just after two," said Wally.

"You were gone so long," Ella said. She studied Wally for a second, noticing that she was wearing Tevin's jacket. "Where's Tevin?"

Wally hesitated. She used her flashlight to dig around and find the bag of cheap tea candles they had bought at a discount import store. She lit three candles, which gave the room a warm, flickering glow.

"Where's Tevin, Wally?" Jake asked warily, sensing something ominous in Wally's manner. On the drive there from Claire's apartment, Wally struggled over what she would tell Ella and Jake about Tevin.

"He's gone," Wally said finally, because she knew no other way. "Tevin is dead."

Ella and Jake stared at Wally in disbelief, needing a moment to process her words. Silent tears began to stream down Ella's face, while her features remained frozen.

"What?" Jake looked like he had been kicked in the gut.

"Those men . . ." Wally said. "We went to a place to find my mother, and they were there."

"*Oh no . . .*" Now Ella shook her head, almost violently, trying her hardest to deny what she was hearing.

"Tevin protected me."

"Of course he did. This was all for you, Wally," Jake suddenly blurted, enraged. "This was your own private party. You should never've taken him with you."

"I know."

She kept herself as emotionless as she could, refusing to cry, not allowing herself the privilege of grieving with her friends precisely because she was the one responsible for this terrible thing.

"He loved you, Wally," Jake went on, caught between sorrow and anger. "Is this how you love people back?"

"Jake, stop it . . ." Ella pleaded with him, grabbing him by the arm. "She didn't mean it. . . ."

"And all for what?" Jake would not be dissuaded. "Did you get what you wanted? Did you find her?"

Wally paused before answering, feeling ashamed. "Yes."

"Oh yeah?" Jake almost laughed. "How'd she stack up? Was it a good trade?"

"Jake!" Ella pulled at him.

"Damn it!" Jake shouted. He jumped up and kicked at the plasterboard wall, caving it in again and again and then punching it with his bare fists as well, a dozen violent strikes at least, until he was exhausted and gasping for air. Overcome, Jake dropped back down to the floor and buried his head in his arms, his body trembling. Ella slumped beside him and wrapped him in a tight embrace. For several minutes Wally kept her distance, allowing them their grief, then sat down beside them on the floor. She reached out carefully and laid her hand on Jake's back. He sobbed as he felt her touch. After a moment, Wally spoke.

"I could never explain how sorry I am," she said.

They did not answer, and after a moment Wally continued.

"The thing is," Wally said, "I've been lying about something, to myself and to you. The lie was that we were all in the same situation, but that's bullshit. You two—and Tevin—you've been through so many hard things in your lives. I was feeling sorry for myself and pretending that it was the same for me, but it wasn't. I've had some pain, but I've been loved and supported too, and had so many advantages. I don't really understand why I've made the choices I have, but it's time for me to put things in order, you know?"

"We've been a family," Ella said. "That was never a lie."

"No, it wasn't," Wally said. She looked hopefully at Jake, hoping to see some sign that he might forgive her, eventually. He managed a small, sympathetic smile, and Wally smiled back gratefully. She reached into her bag and pulled out a letter-size envelope, setting it down in front of them.

"There's two thousand dollars in here," Wally said. "That's for both of you. You know Lois Chao, at Harmony House? She's been telling me for a long time about this place upstate, called Neversink Farm. It's a bus ride, maybe three or four hours. The directions are inside there with the money. It's a different kind of residential setup—a working farm. You help out around the farm and do a couple of hours of school every day so you can get a GED." Wally paused. "I'm not telling you what to do, but it's a chance for you both to start again. The money is yours, for a nest egg, for whatever."

Ella and Jake didn't know what to say, not sure at first whether they were being given a gift or brushed aside. The two shared a look for a moment, and Wally thought she could see a sense of relief pass between the two of them, a sense of willingness to give themselves over to something new and hopeful.

"What about you?" Ella asked.

"I have to see this through," she said, struggling not to break down. "Just me. I'm already responsible for what happened to Tevin. If anything happened to either of you . . ."

Ella reached out and took Wally's hand, holding it close to her. Wally squeezed her hand back, grateful. She checked the time on her phone.

"I can take a few minutes," Wally said to Ella. "Let's do our thing?"

"Okay."

Jake looked on quietly as Wally and Ella hurriedly performed their nail-painting ritual, in silence. When they were done five minutes later, Wally gave Ella and Jake each a quick hug and a smile, and walked out the door.

THIRTY-TWO

Wally made her way through town to the Queens Midtown Tunnel and drove east onto Interstate 495, where she would stay for the next two hours until the Long Island Expressway came to an end. She checked the car's clock, which read 1:30 A.M. Good. She had a full tank of gas and had picked up three cans of Red Bull to keep her going. She plugged her music player into the car stereo and blasted a mix that Tevin had put together a few months ago. There were some fierce dance tunes by the Swedish singer Robyn, who Wally loved, with some ballads mixed in and some old-school rap. One of the songs was Tevin's favorite, "Concrete Schoolyard," a soulful old rap by Jurassic 5.

Wally listened to the song three times, all the way through, and cried during the last one. She then unplugged the player and put the radio on scan until it found a station with good dance music. She left it there, the music cranked up loud enough for passing cars to hear, and swilled down the first of the Red Bulls.

She thought again of Johanna, grateful that Klesko needed her to find the stones or she would certainly be dead already. A feeling kept nagging at Wally; it had been since she encountered Johanna face-to-face at the Navy Yard. Their reunion had been strangely anticlimactic, and not just because it had been followed so closely by Klesko's violent attack. She had expected that the first encounter with her biological mother would be transformative, an event that would somehow explain and excuse and put to order all that Wally had experienced in her young and stormy life. Dr. Rainer had predicted an intuitive response for Wally when she finally met her mother, a sense of instant recognition that Wally could hold up like a mirror and truly see herself for the first time.

That had not happened. Wally felt as confused as she ever had, as alone as she ever had. Why? Since her earliest years, Wally had been looking to others to inform her sense of self, to provide her with an authentic image of who she was and where she belonged. Now, after the disastrous events of the previous days, Wally saw this quest—directed outward—as childish and futile. To have any meaning, her search for identity would have to be focused within. Claire, Johanna, her adoptive father Jason, that monster Klesko, even her crew—these people were all essential to Wally's life in one way or another, but they did not define her.

Understanding all that finally, Wally was more determined

than ever to save Johanna from Klesko; her search for her biological mother had brought violence and heartache to everyone
in her life, and Wally could not allow one more person to suf-
fer for her own recklessness. Within hours, Wally would prove
her place in the world the only meaningful way she knew how:
through her own actions. This hope for some sort of resolution
gave Wally an unexpected feeling of calm. She listened to the
music on the stereo and let her mind go numb, just for a while,
to shore up her mental strength for all that awaited her.

Two hours passed in what seemed like no time at all. She
reached the end of the interstate and veered onto Old Country
Road, headed northeast. In less than twenty miles, she arrived
at the small marina in Greenport, which she and the crew had
visited just days earlier. The ferry to Shelter Island stopped service at midnight, meaning that Klesko and the younger Russian—and their hostage, Johanna—could not have made the
previous night's boat. They might try to find an alternate way
onto the island, but Wally guessed they would take the less
complicated option and wait for the first morning boat, just
before 6 A.M.

Wally turned off her headlights and eased down Wiggins
Street, which led toward the train station and the pier for Shelter Island's North Ferry. The setting was much different than
during Wally's last visit to Greenport; it wasn't quite 4 A.M. yet,
so the town was in darkness except for a half-dozen dim overhead streetlights that were positioned around the pier and parking lot area. Wally pulled to a stop about three blocks away from
the pier, unwilling to get any closer for fear that Klesko and the

younger man—almost certainly waiting near the ferry—would spot her.

Wally quietly slipped out of the Town Car and headed down a side street toward the train tracks—where she was less likely to be seen—then walked toward the pier from the southwest. This approach would bring her through the empty train station and right behind the ferry parking lot. From there she could mark any vehicles that were already in line for the ferry or waiting nearby. As she reached the lot, she saw that there were no cars in line, which was not surprising since the first ferry wouldn't set off for nearly two hours. About halfway up 3rd Street, however, Wally spotted the Russians' tow truck. The truck was parked facing the pier, away from the direction of Wally's approach, so they would not have seen her arrive. Just behind the dark windshield of the truck, Wally could make out the embers of two burning cigarettes. There was only a narrow rear section to the cab—barely room enough to stash a toolbox—and Wally flushed with rage at the thought of Johanna crammed into the space, bleeding, terrified.

Wally briefly thought she might call the local cops, right then, and have them converge on the ferry landing, forcing a standoff with the Russians. She dismissed the idea immediately. Wally had witnessed Klesko and the younger man in battle up close; Greenport's cops wouldn't have a prayer in that fight, and Johanna was more likely to be killed in the crossfire than rescued.

Wally remained hidden in the shadows and continued scanning the area, looking for Claire's Infiniti SUV, but after thinking about it for a while, Wally realized how unlikely it was that Claire would come directly to the ferry landing. Claire had known—how?—that Johanna would lead the Russians to the Hatches' house on Shelter Island. Claire would also know, then, that Klesko and the younger one would be there at the boat landing, waiting for the first ferry of the morning, armed and vigilant, with Johanna under their control.

So what sort of plan did Claire have in mind and, just as important, what was Claire capable of? Wally was forced to ask herself, for the first time in her life, exactly what sort of person Claire Stoneman really was. Did Wally even know? Wally was forced to consider that there was a hidden side of her adoptive mother that Wally herself was clueless about.

Wally left the pier area quietly and walked back to the Town Car. She turned on the engine to heat up the car and considered her next step. Did Claire and Johanna have some sort of plan in place, something they had figured out in advance? It seemed possible. There was clearly some sort of bond between Claire and Johanna that Wally had never had a clue about. Wally finally decided to make an assumption: Claire would do what Wally herself would do, which was try to gain some sort of strategic advantage over the gunmen. The best way to do that was to reach the island first and be waiting for them when they arrived.

Wally needed a boat, at 4 A.M. in Greenport, Long Island. This sounded like an impossible task at first, but then she got an inspiration. She did a Google search on her cell phone and when the directory turned up what she was looking for, she hit the call button.

"Fantasy Island Taxi." The voice on the other end of the line was very groggy, fresh out of a deep sleep.

"Hi. Uh . . . I'm so sorry to call you at this hour," Wally said. "I'm the girl you drove to the Hatches' house? Last week?"

"Uh . . . oh. Yeah. Hey. You need a ride? I'm not on the island, and the ferry doesn't run for another . . ." There was a moment of silence as he checked his clock. "*Christ*. It's four in the morning."

"Yeah, sorry again. And, actually, I do need a ride, but the boat kind. I have to get to the island right away. Do you have any ideas?"

"You're going back to the Hatches' place?" the guy said. "Even after everything that happened?"

Wally didn't understand what he meant by *even after everything,* and she didn't really have time to figure it out.

"I still need to go there, yes," was all she said.

There was a moment of silence on the other end of the line.

"You're an interesting girl," said the cabbie. "I'm going to call you back in like two minutes."

True to his word, he called right back and gave Wally driving directions to a different part of the marina. He also gave her the description of a particular lobster boat at that wharf.

"Guy is about to go out for the morning. He's expecting you."

"Thanks again," Wally said, "and sorry for being a pain."

"Forget about it."

Wally put the Lincoln in gear and did a U-turn, heading

back up to Front Street, which followed the Greenport coast-line but was out of sight of the ferry landing area. She drove northeast, searching along the waterline for the wharf the cab-bie had described. Soon she came upon a small working marina where a lone lobsterman was rigging his one-hand-trap boat for its morning tour. Wally parked the Lincoln on the nearby street, grabbed her messenger bag, and walked down to the pier, where she and the lobsterman were the only living things in sight.

"Good morning," Wally said.

The lobsterman—mid-fifties, wrinkled from a lifetime of squinting, wearing yellow-slicker overalls and a heavy sweater—looked up at Wally, appraising her briefly before returning to his work. If encountering an emo-dressed teenage city girl on his fishing marina at four o'clock on a November morning was a unique experience for him, he did not let on.

"Yep," was all he said to Wally.

"Our mutual friend says you might be able to take me across to the island?"

"Ferry leaves in a few hours."

"I can't wait that long."

"I got traps to check, dearie."

The lobsterman was giving Wally his gruff down-easter act, and she didn't have time for it. She pulled a fistful of twenty-dollar bills out of her bag.

"This is around five hundred dollars," she said. "Please. It really is an emergency. No one else can help me."

Now the lobsterman looked up, the authentic desperation in Wally's voice getting his attention.

"Please, sir," she repeated.

The lobsterman took a moment to reappraise Wally.

"Keep your money. Where on the island you need to be?" he asked with an exaggerated sigh.

Wally pulled out a map of Shelter Island—the one she had bought on her first trip there—and studied it for a moment under the single, dim light hanging over the dock. "It's a house on a place called Coecles Inlet—did I say that right? I really have to get there now. It's an emergency, I swear to you."

"That's near ten miles," mused the lobsterman. "We'd best take the whaler."

Within minutes, Wally and the lobsterman were aboard a twenty-one-foot Boston whaler, making the Shelter Island crossing at a crisp thirty-three knots. The water was quiet, and the air was cold but still. Sunrise would not come for another couple of hours, but there was enough ambient light to read the heavy, looming clouds above.

"Snow coming soon," the lobsterman shouted over the growl of the outboard, and he was right. Ten minutes into their run, snow began to fall in the still air; large dry flakes fluttered down slowly, only to disappear in the ocean waters.

Wally was grateful for the speed of the whaler. It was probably only three or four miles from Greenport to the Hatches' house as the crow flies, but the route to the beach on Coecles Inlet followed a circuitous course around two points on the island, and the total distance was every bit the ten miles that the lobsterman had said. Twenty-four minutes into the crossing, the lobsterman rounded the spit at Ram Island—Wally followed their progress on her map—and steered the whaler southwest, into the narrow mouth of Coecles Inlet. The waters of the inlet were shallow and calm, and stretched out to a full five square miles. There were no houses at all on the beaches of the inlet since it was protected land, which belonged to the Mashomack Preserve. The only signs of habitation were at the farthest reaches of the inlet, where they were headed now at a reduced speed, around twenty knots.

Wally pulled a flashlight out of her bag and held the map up for the lobsterman, shining the light to illuminate their destination: it was the beach closest to the Hatch home, which was the last private property abutting the virginal conservancy land.

"This spot here," Wally said. "I think there's a dock."

As he steered the boat across the dark waters, the lobsterman took just a quick glance at Wally's map, confirming the destination.

"The Hatches' house?" he said.

"Yes."

"Shame what happened."

"What's that?" Wally asked. The lobsterman looked at Wally and saw that she had no idea about the murders of the Hatch brothers. He briefly ran down the information for her, not having to shout quite as much since their speed had now reduced to ten knots for their final approach to the dock on the Hatch property. Wally did her best to process the information without emotion.

"How long ago was that?" she asked, and when he told

her, Wally realized that when she had seen the Russians in the Hatches' house, ten days earlier, they had been there to kill the brothers. The thought made her sick. Should she have done something differently? Should she have called the police to report a break-in?

"It ain't just you this morning, dearie," the lobsterman said, nodding in the direction they were headed.

Wally looked ahead to the dock, now just fifty yards away, where the falling snow had blanketed the shoreline of the inlet in white. Wally could see the outline of a small skiff, maybe fifteen feet long, tied off at the dock. Had the skiff brought Claire here? Wally wondered how Claire had found a boat in the middle of the night, but the more she thought about it, the clearer it became. This sequence of events—from the appearance of Klesko in America to, Wally anticipated, a showdown at the Hatches' property—was a worst-case scenario that Johanna had prepared for and shared with Claire. The boat was part of the plan, stored somewhere near Greenport and standing ready. Whatever their plan was for this worst case, Wally hoped it was a good one.

The lobsterman's Boston whaler slowed to a drift as he steered it parallel to where the skiff was tied off. Wally hopped out of the boat and onto the weathered gray boards of the dock.

"You sure you know what you're doin'?" the lobsterman asked.

Wally nodded and held out the five hundred dollars, but the lobsterman waved the offer away.

"You kids, you grow up too fast," he said.

"Yeah, we do," Wally said, mustering a smile to thank the man.

The lobsterman gave her a little salute and gunned the engine of the whaler. Within ten seconds he was out of sight, just the fading growl of his outboard to mark his departure across the inlet.

Wally crept quietly through the Hatches' house and found Claire in the kitchen, almost scaring her mother out of her skin.

"Mom?"

"Wally!" Claire stifled a scream. "Oh my God!"

Wally saw immediately why Claire was so spooked, and it wasn't just because of her own surprise appearance there. The inside of the house had been violently torn apart, from closets and cabinets to floorboards and furniture cushions. In the kitchen where they stood, blood was splattered everywhere, and a large pool of it stained the center of the floor. There were outlines within the blood pool indicating that two bodies had once rested there.

"How did you find this place?" Claire said, terrified and angry all at once.

"I was here before."

"*What?* When was that?" Claire demanded. "Why did you come?"

"I came to meet the Hatch brothers—I guess it was the day they died."

"I didn't know anything about this." Claire gestured toward the bloodstains, still coming to grips with the gruesome evidence before her. "How did you know I would be here?"

"I figured it out," Wally said. "You and Johanna have a plan, right? She's supposed to bring them here for the stones?"

"Please don't do this, Wally. Leave now, I'm begging you. I did everything I could to make sure this would never happen."

"And it happened anyway," Wally said. The sight of all the blood was terrifying to her as well, but in a strange way Wally was feeling vindicated by everything she saw, by everything that had happened up until that moment. Her search had brought her there for a reason, she was sure of it. "I belong here, Mom. My whole life, everything has been leading to this. We're going to save her."

Claire opened her mouth as if to object again but must have read the determination in her daughter's eyes. She sighed deeply and finally surrendered to the inevitable.

"Shit," Claire said. "That's the way it has to be?"

"Yes, Mom. We both know that."

"Okay," Claire said. Wally could see the wheels turning inside her mother's head as she assessed the challenge before them. "He's strong, Wally. And ruthless."

"I know."

"Our only chance is to catch him by surprise."

"Good," Wally said. She looked at her cell phone to check the time. "The first ferry sails in fifteen minutes. What do we do?"

THIRTY-THREE

Claire led Wally to a covered woodpile at the back of the Hatch home. She reached in back of the pile and retrieved a small bundle wrapped in plastic and fastened with duct tape. Claire tore through the wrapping, including several layers of yellowed old newspapers, to reveal three handguns, looking fairly well preserved. There were half a dozen speed loaders of ammo for the guns.

"Benjamin's stash," Claire said.

Claire was about to pass one of the guns to Wally, but at the last moment held it back.

"It's been a long time, Wally," said Claire. "Can you still use it?"

"Not as long as you might think," Wally said. She confidently took hold of the gun and two speed loads, sliding one into the barrel and flicking the mechanism shut, ready to shoot. "I always thought it was weird, Mom," she said. "A mother and her eleven-year-old girl together at a shooting range, blowing away targets."

"And what do you think about it now?" Claire asked.

"All things considered, not so weird."

With their weapons ready, they turned and faced the ground behind the Hatches' home. There was a stretch of open ground, about fifty yards, before the low scrub began and, beyond that, the forest of the Mashomack Preserve. All of it was covered in white, with more snow still falling.

"There are three buried caches," Claire said. "The first is about two hundred yards away, inside the preserve. The next is about two hundred yards beyond that. The third is farther, almost back to the shore."

"But why out here at all? If Yalena—"

"Benjamin took the stones, Yalena the cash. That was their bargain. But when they—she and Benjamin—first arrived by boat from Russia, Yalena stayed here. She kept a close eye on Benjamin and followed him late at night, through the dark woods, when he dug his hiding places. Just in case."

"In case this day came?"

"Yes. Yalena wanted to take the stones back from Benjamin and return them to Klesko's associates in Russia," Claire said, "in the hope that they would stop looking for her. But Benjamin made it clear that if she tried anything like that, he would reveal her new American identity—and yours, Wally—to those same people. There was nothing she could do."

"What about after Benjamin died? Did his sons know where the caches were?"

"From the looks of that house," Claire said, "I would say not."

"Probably drove them crazy," Wally said. "Thinking about the stones somewhere out here, just waiting to be found."

"You're probably right. But it didn't matter, for Yalena. She still couldn't risk trying to retrieve them, however many of the stones were left. The brothers knew about her new identity, so she couldn't do anything to anger them."

Claire stopped in the snow and faced Wally. "Klesko will never let us walk away. You understand? No matter what we do or what we give him. If we want to live, we have to win."

"I understand," Wally answered.

"Good. The snow will show our tracks, so we'll take an indirect path to the first cache."

Wally nodded in agreement and they began to walk, heading off to the side of the Hatches' property, where their tracks in the snow would be less obvious.

"You know a lot of Yalena's story," Wally said.

"Yes."

"Please tell me what you know about her," Wally asked as they walked along. Claire was silent for a long while before she began.

"Your mother was young when she got together with Klesko. It was a terrible mistake, and she realized it too late. It will be hard for you to hear this, Wally. . . ."

"I may never get another chance."

"Yes, okay," Claire said, and gathered herself to continue. "Yalena tried to get away from him several times over the years, but he tracked her down and brought her back. The last time, he beat her mercilessly, almost to death, and raped her. That is how you were conceived." She paused, and the full weight of the message hit Wally all at once. "I'm sorry," Claire said, reaching for her hand.

Conceived by rape. The shocking story—Wally's own cruel history—was a savage body blow, striking Wally with a depth of pain she didn't think she was capable of feeling anymore. She looked to Claire, wanting to be assured by her loving gaze that life was not always this cruel, that there was still peace and goodness in the world. Claire had always been able to make Wally feel safe that way, but instead Claire turned her head away from her daughter, avoiding Wally's glance as if it might burn her.

"Mom . . ." Wally's voice quavered.

Claire steeled herself to continue. "When Yalena learned that she was carrying you, she was determined that Klesko could never be a part of your life. She never told him about you."

"He doesn't know about me?"

Claire shook her head no.

Wally considered this for a moment. Her path had crossed Klesko's three times so far, and he had been following her when she finally found Yalena's safe house. Who did Klesko imagine she was, anyway? Probably it made no difference to him, as long as Wally led him to Yalena, to the stones.

Wally and Claire walked in a wide arc away from the grounds of the Hatches' property and past small signs that marked the edge of the Mashomack Preserve. Claire continued to tell Yalena's story, the first part mostly covering what Wally already knew.

"So Benjamin Hatch took the stones in exchange for getting Yalena to America," Wally said, still needing to understand. "What went wrong? Why did she leave me behind?"

"The problem was," Claire said, "Klesko's associates—powerful men—figured that with Klesko in prison, his riches belonged to *them*. After your mother made off with everything, they hunted her relentlessly, knowing she would try to escape the country. It was too dangerous for Benjamin to try to get her out at that point. So they waited. With the help of family and friends, she stayed hidden for six months, long enough to give birth to you. She and Benjamin thought that enough time had passed for her to make her break, but as soon Yalena came out of hiding—with you—she was spotted. Your mother was certain she was going to be caught and both of you killed. She had an old family friend—Irina Ivanova—who was a nurse at a children's home. Your mother made the hardest decision of her life."

"She left me behind."

"She did. She left you behind to save you. She never expected to escape Klesko's associates, but fate surprised her. Benjamin got her out of the country alive."

"And eventually she found me again." Wally filled in the logical progression of events. "In the U.S., with you."

"She never gave up," Claire said.

The woods became denser. Claire pointed to a small clearing with two red maple trees at its center, bare of foliage now.

"Between those two red maples is the first cache," Claire said. "That's our moment, okay?"

Wally nodded. "Yes."

"We'll find a place with cover and wait."

Claire led the way as they marched past the first cache, finding a spot among some snow-covered scrub brush just thirty yards beyond the cache. They both knelt down on one knee and waited, their eyes focused on the woods beyond the clearing, where Klesko would most likely appear.

"In all this time," Wally said, "why didn't Yalena ever reveal herself to me? Why didn't she tell me our story?"

Claire considered this. "She was ashamed. She had abandoned you."

"But it was to save me."

"Yes, but that truth was not enough for her to forgive herself. She had left you behind—alone and an entire world away—while she made her own escape."

Wally sensed a note of judgment in Claire's voice and objected.

"She had no choice."

"No, and she hoped that one day you would be able to hear everything and understand. But by the time you were old enough, you were so very angry, Wally. Angry at everything and everyone. It wasn't your fault; there were lies in our home, and unhappiness. You took all of that on your own shoulders, especially when your father left. Yalena thought that if you heard the truth, about her decision to leave you behind, your anger would fall on her. She was afraid you wouldn't be able to forgive her."

"I would have," Wally insisted.

"Are you so sure?"

They were silent for a long time after that. A full hour passed, there in the cold woods, and Claire wrapped Wally up in her arms to share her warmth. They almost didn't hear it—quiet footsteps approaching in the snow—but the sound of a branch snapping alerted them. It was still a few minutes before the sun would rise, but there was enough ambient light in the woods for them to make out two figures approaching the clearing: one was Klesko, still limping but moving ahead with a sense of purpose, a handgun in one hand and a small shovel in the other. Beside him was Johanna, looking barely alive. She walked gingerly and off balance, with her hands fastened behind her back, and there was dried blood around her nose and mouth.

Claire let out a quiet gasp at the sight of Klesko.

"Goddamn it," Wally whispered. "They've beaten her more."

"It's just Klesko?" Claire whispered. "I thought you said . . . didn't you say there were two of them? Klesko and another?"

"There *are* two . . ." Wally answered, and both of them began to scan the woods, looking for signs of the younger Russian. There was nothing. No sound and no movement, only the gentle snowfall.

"He's here somewhere," Claire said, frustrated. "Following them, protecting against an ambush. We can't make a move until he shows himself."

Klesko and Johanna reached the center of the small clearing, where the two red maples stood. Johanna made a gesture toward the two trees, and Klesko drew a huge combat knife from under his belt, cutting the tape around her wrists and freeing her hands. He shoved her down to the ground and tossed the small shovel down beside her. She began digging. The ground must have been nearly frozen, because her progress was slow. Impatient, Klesko reared back and kicked her in the ribs, sending her tumbling with a sharp cry of pain.

Wally flinched and almost stood up, but Claire grabbed onto her and held her down.

"Faster!" Klesko barked; his voice carried a little in the woods but was quickly muted by the snow that surrounded him, in the air and on the ground. Johanna crawled back to the cache site, leaving a trail of blood in the snow, and resumed digging. She stopped at the sound of her shovel striking something hard about a foot and a half belowground. Johanna brushed away some more dirt with her hand, then rose to her feet and stood back, waiting for Klesko to step in and claim his prize. Klesko took one step toward the cache but then stopped himself, suddenly wary. He shoved Johanna back to the ground and motioned for her to open the container while he kept his gun pointed at the back of her head.

Claire's hand gripped Wally's arm tightly. "Be ready," she whispered.

They watched as Johanna reached down into the cache slowly, but then suddenly spun around with a gun in her hand. Johanna squeezed off one quick shot at Klesko—the bullet missed its mark, and Klesko immediately dropped onto Johanna, struggling for control of the gun in her hand.

Wally began to stand, but Claire held her back.

"No," Claire insisted. "The other one is here somewhere."

At that very moment, they spotted a blur of motion off to one side of the clearing. It was Tiger, flying out from the forest like a bolt of lightning, dark hair flowing behind him as he covered the distance to the cache and struck Johanna with his fist, freeing his father from her grasp. He grabbed the handgun from Johanna and tossed it aside.

Claire and Wally were poised to jump out when a chance presented itself, but even through the struggle Tiger seemed to sense the possibility of an ambush; his eyes darted into the surrounding woods and he never lowered his gun.

"*Damn!*" Wally hissed.

Now Klesko, in a rage, stepped to the fallen Johanna—her head bleeding from Tiger's blow—and held his gun to her head, ready to kill her. Before he could shoot, Tiger lunged at his father and knocked Klesko's hand aside just as he squeezed the trigger. The shot plowed uselessly into the snow beside Johanna.

"Not yet!" Tiger yelled. He reached down into the hole and pulled out the cache box—a watertight plastic container the size of a coffee can. Tiger turned the box upside down to reveal that it was completely empty. He held the empty container up in front of Klesko. "We still need her, you see?"

Klesko howled with frustrated rage.

"*Bitch!* I will cut out her fucking heart. . . ."

"Not yet," Tiger said again, and hauled Johanna back up to her feet. She wailed in pain.

"There are more places, yes?" Tiger growled into Johanna's ear. Johanna nodded yes. Tiger shoved her forward, and she began stumbling through the woods again, headed in a northeast direction. They passed within twenty feet of Wally and Claire, who stayed hidden and silent as the men continued on, following Johanna as she struggled onward to the next cache.

Once Johanna and the two Russians were out of sight, Wally and Claire hustled through the woods as quickly as they could.

"We'll arc around from the south," Claire said. "They're moving slowly. We can still beat them to the second cache."

"How will we stop them? Is there anything in the next one?"

"Yes," Claire said. "I don't know if it will work, but we need to be ready."

Within a minute, they passed a small pile of mossy fieldstones, now covered with a thin layer of the falling snow.

"The cache," Claire said. "It's there, beneath the middle rock."

At that moment they heard Klesko's voice barking out behind them; he was not yet visible in the dense woods but not far away, growing closer.

"Keep moving," he commanded. *"Which way?"*

Wally and Claire moved to a crumbling stone wall, fifty feet away from the second cache, and ducked down out of sight behind the rocks. They watched as Johanna appeared again; she slogged through the snow, unsteady on her feet and looking only half-conscious as Klesko prodded her on with his gun barrel. Tiger's head was on a swivel and his gun raised, as if he sensed a threat nearby.

Soon they reached the cluster of fieldstones that Claire had pointed out as the second cache. Klesko shoved Johanna forward onto her knees and Johanna pulled three of the stones away from the cluster, exposing a patch of open ground. It took just a few sweeps of her hand to clear the thin layer of soil, revealing the top of a plastic container exactly like the first.

Tiger stayed vigilant, scanning the surrounding woods.

Johanna reached to pull away the top of the cache container, but Klesko grabbed her by the shoulder and heaved her aside. He stepped up and reached for the lip of the container to pull it back, but then suddenly stopped himself.

"What?" Tiger asked.

Klesko took a few steps back from the plastic container and prowled the area nearby until he found what he was looking for: a fallen branch, about eight feet long, barely visible under the layer of freshly fallen snow. Klesko picked up the branch and stripped away its smaller limbs.

"Step away," Klesko commanded Tiger.

Tiger obeyed his father, pulling Johanna with him as he moved away from the cache. He continued to scan the surrounding woods like a well-trained soldier.

Fifty feet away, Wally and Claire huddled behind a ruined stone wall, watching in dismay as their plan unraveled.

"*Damn it,*" Wally whispered.

Klesko crouched low and kept his distance from the cache. He reached the long stick toward the cache container, placing the tip of the branch under the lip of the plastic container's lid and raising it. Nothing happened. Klesko took a cautious step forward, close enough to see that the cache was completely empty. Klesko stepped back and crouched low again, then reached the tip of the branch under the bottom part of the plastic container and lifted it, upsetting the cache container from its spot in the cold earth.

There were two old, rusted soup cans dug in underneath the container, each covered with a layer of aluminum foil and attached to a small wire. The cans were only visible for a second before they exploded, sending their double-powered pulse of light and sound in every direction as Klesko and Tiger shielded themselves from the force of the blast.

THIRTY-FOUR

"Bitch!" Klesko howled into the frigid morning air. Klesko stepped up to Johanna and kicked her hard in the gut.

Behind the stone wall, Wally and Claire cringed at the brutal punishment.

"Shit," Wally whispered desperately. "We have to—"

"No," Claire said, trying to keep it together. "Not yet."

Klesko shouted at Johanna. "How many more?"

"One more," Johanna said, her voice gone so weak that Wally and Claire could barely hear the answer.

"So we stop playing this game, yes?" Klesko said, trying to temper his voice to sound reasonable. "Any stones in the last?"

Johanna, obviously feeling hopeless, just shook her head no.

Klesko chuckled darkly and gave Johanna another merciless kick to the ribs. The woman was so weak and beaten that her body did not even flinch at the punishment.

"*Tigr*, your birthright is no more."

Tiger didn't want to believe it, but the reality of it seemed clear.

"*Da*," he agreed. "Gone."

Klesko chambered a round into his gun, the sharp mechanical sound echoing out into the surrounding trees.

"You make games for us?" Klesko crowed into Johanna's ear. "Here is how you pay. . . ."

Klesko raised his gun and pressed it to Johanna's head.

"No!" Wally cried out, unable to stop herself. At the sound of her voice, Klesko and Tiger became hyperalert, anxiously scanning the forest around them to determine which direction the call had come from.

"Who is here!?" Klesko shouted, keeping his gun trained on Johanna. "Show yourself or this one dies!"

Wally made a move to stand up, but Claire held her back.

"I have to do this," Wally said.

Claire looked into Wally's eyes with an expression that seemed fearful and brave at the same time.

"It's not you they want, Wally," Claire said.

"What do you mean?"

"They want Yalena."

"But they have her," Wally pled. "And they'll kill her."

"Trust me this once," Claire implored her daughter. "You said you could forgive her, your mother. Did you really mean that?"

"Yes. Of course," Wally said, confused.

"For everything? For leaving you behind?"

"Yes."

"For being too much of a coward to tell you the truth? You could forgive her for that?"

"Yes," Wally insisted, tears of confusion and fear now welling in her eyes. "Why are you asking me this?"

Claire gave Wally a sad smile. "I never stopped loving you," she said.

She lovingly caressing Wally's face and hair, as if committing the feel of them to memory, then kissed Wally on the forehead.

"My beautiful Valentina," Claire said, then repeated in flawless Russian, *"Moya prekraasnaya Valentina."*

Those few words, spoken fluently by Claire, stunned Wally silent. Claire reached back and hid her handgun under her belt at the small of her back, then stood straight up. Fifty feet away, Klesko and Tiger immediately focused on her, raising their guns in Claire's direction. She held her hands up high, palms open, empty.

"I'm here, Alexei," Claire said.

Claire stepped purposefully toward the two men.

Wally took all this in, paralyzed with confusion. She sat motionless on the frozen ground, watching as Claire—the only mother she had ever known—walked unflinchingly toward the Russian killers. In a flash Wally's mind raced with all that Claire had told her about her Russian mother: her betrayal of Klesko, her abandonment of Valentina to the orphanage, her flight to America, and finally her determination to reunite herself with her child.

The story had been her *story.*

"Oh my God," Wally whispered. She could barely breathe.

As she struggled to process all this information at once, Wally was struck by the terrible realization that Claire was now willing to sacrifice herself yet again, all for Wally.

"Yalena?" Klesko said dubiously as he watched Claire approach. He wasn't sure it was her at first, but then recognition came to him. "Yalena." He spat her name, cold rage in his eyes at the sight of Claire. *"Yobanaya sooka . . ."*

Fucking bitch.

Klesko charged at her, drawing his gun up and pointing it at her face as they neared each other.

"Mom! No!" Wally's voice shot out from the woods.

She rose from her hiding place and vaulted the stone wall. She raced up behind Claire, her own gun drawn and pointed at Klesko's head.

"Don't you touch her, you son of a bitch!" Wally barked at Klesko, who suddenly looked confused, the aim of his gun flashing back and forth between Claire and Wally. Tiger raised his gun as well, pointing it at the girl stomping quickly through the snow toward them.

"No, Wally!" Claire cried. "Go back!" But seeing her daughter's resolution, Claire quickly reached behind her back and drew her own gun; all four of them—mother and daughter, father and son—converged at a point near the empty cache, four guns raised and shifting their aim from person to person. The confusion was undeniable in all their faces as they looked to each other, back and forth, trying to make sense of everything.

"M-Mom?" Wally stammered, unable to give voice to all the questions swimming through her mind.

"It's okay, Wally," Claire said. She kept her gun trained on Klesko as she knelt down to Johanna—slumped on the ground near the cache—and checked her pulse. "Johanna's still alive, barely."

As Claire stood upright again, Klesko studied Claire's face closely, squinting. He traced her features in the air, with the sight of his gun, trying to recognize the woman all over again.

"Yalena, but not Yalena," he said. "The nose, the eyes. Doctors did this. And . . . this is ours?" Klesko indicated Wally with a nod, but did not wait for an answer from Claire. "I see it," he said, studying Wally's features as he had Claire's. He laughed, almost giddy at the irony—he had been hunting his own daughter.

"Ochee chornya," he said. "Dark eyes, like me."

"Never yours, Klesko," Claire said, turning to give Wally a reassuring look. "You were never his, Wally. Do you understand?"

Her thoughts still reeling, Wally answered her mother with a quick, uncertain nod. Claire turned her focus to Tiger. She studied his features, lovingly but sadly.

And she never lowered her gun.

"So grown," she said to her son, struggling to keep her voice from cracking. *"Tigr.* My boy. I'm so sorry."

The young man glared at her. For once, his unassailable composure revealed some cracks, betraying a deep sense of rage as he looked upon Claire. When he spoke, however, there was unexpected vulnerability in his voice.

"Was it so easy to choose?" he asked Claire. "One child for the other?"

"It was impossible," his mother answered, her words barely a whisper as her thoughts took her back to that terrible time. "His family had taken you away from me, would barely let me see you. All I wanted was to be a mother to you, but they never allowed it."

"I was lost to you," Tiger said with pain in his eyes.

"Not in my heart," Claire said. "I never stopped thinking about you, never stopped loving you. I'm so sorry. . . ."

Claire regretted the inadequacy of the apology, even as she spoke it. She waited, hoping for some sort of response from Tiger, but he remained silent, his unforgiving stare hanging on her. Wally took all this in with both fear and wonder, the tangled mess now unraveling.

"Tigr." Wally said her brother's name out loud, with a natural Russian inflection, just to hear it from her own lips. The siblings' eyes met, as they had outside Dr. Rainer's office, and that same sense of recognition was there again. Claire observed the exchange between brother and sister, her heart breaking over everything that had been lost.

"I'm sorry," Claire said again, weakly. *"Prosti menya. . . ."*

"Bitch!" Klesko howled as if in pain, the sentimentality of the moment an offense to his sensibilities. *"Prekratyi!* Where is my money? My stones! I will have them, Yalena, or you die today."

"We'll die anyway, won't we, Alexei?" Claire said.

A malevolent smile crept onto Klesko's face.

"Yes," he said with a look of satisfaction. "Good. We all die today."

A sudden barrage of gunfire erupted from the woods around them. One bullet ripped into Klesko's back, spinning him around, while a shotgun blast peppered Tiger from the side, several pellets tearing into his face.

"*Sookin syn!*" Klesko howled in pain and rage.

Claire dove for Wally and pulled her to the ground, covering her.

Under heavy fire from gunmen they could not see, Tiger and Klesko staggered into the woods, leaning against each other and seeking cover as they returned fire. Soon they had disappeared and the gunfire continued, with one man's voice calling out.

"Finish them off! I have the women," the voice shouted.

Wally and Claire could hear the footsteps of at least three men trotting into the woods, hunting down the two Russians. More gunfire sounded in the near distance as Klesko and Tiger fought for their survival.

A single set of footsteps approached Wally and her mother, Claire still lying halfway across Wally in the snow, protecting her. The man's voice sounded again, nearby. Wally looked up and was surprised to see a familiar face looking down at her, a smug grin on his face and a sawed-off shotgun in his hands. He reached down and grabbed the women's guns, hurling them off into the woods.

"Little sister," he purred at Wally.

Claire gave her daughter a questioning look. "Wally? Who—"

"His name is Panama," Wally finally said. "He buys and sells things."

"Not Panama, actually," said the man, his voice suddenly without the street inflection that had seemed so natural to him before. Now he sounded more like a cop. He reached into his lapel pocket and pulled out a leather ID holder, flipping it open to reveal an ATF badge and then shutting it again.

"Cornell Brown," he said, grinning at Claire. "And you would be Yalena Mayakova. I've been looking a long time for you, Yalena. A very long time. Now, you needn't be concerned with the Kleskos anymore. My men will take care of them."

If Brown was expecting any gratitude from Claire, he was disappointed; she fixed a murderous gaze on him.

"Please get up now," Brown spoke reasonably, "and let's go have a look at your other stashes. And don't tell me there are no more stones. I would know very well if you had unloaded them, so don't waste my time. Take me to the stones, now."

With Brown's shotgun pointed at her face, Claire struggled to her feet. Wally rose along with her, helping her mother up. As her body moved, Claire groaned in pain and grabbed her stomach.

"Mom?" Wally opened Claire's parka, to discover that Claire had a gunshot wound to her abdomen, blood soaking her clothes deep red.

"Mom!"

"Let's move, then," said Brown, looking at Claire's wound. "Not much time for you, Yalena."

"Fuck you," Wally said.

"Okay," said Brown, pushing the barrel of his sawed-off against Wally's forehead. "Then let's get it over with."

"No!" Claire cried out. "I'll take you."

"Good," said Brown.

"Johanna . . ."

Brown looked down at Johanna, looking completely lifeless in the snow beside them. He nudged her body with the toe of his boot, and there was no response.

"No longer your problem, I'd say," said Brown.

Claire pulled Wally close and kissed her.

"I'm sorry," Claire said.

"We're moving," Brown said. "Right now."

He followed as Claire led them through the woods, in the direction of the beach; Claire was in great pain and needed Wally's support to keep upright.

"I'm the only one who figured it all out," Cornell Brown congratulated himself as they pushed through the woods. "Everyone had a theory about Yalena Mayakova, but I'm the one who put it all together, and it only took me fifteen *goddamn* years. That you were pregnant when you ratted out Klesko and left little Valentina at the orphanage. How you made it to the U.S. with the help of the scumbag Hatch—all that. Of course, I never quite figured *who* or *where* you were, Yalena. Little sister here, she helped me with that last step."

"What do you mean, I helped?" Wally asked, but in fact she was already putting it all together herself.

"I got hold of your adoption records," said Brown smugly.

"How?" Claire wanted to know.

"I have a source," Brown answered. "A good one. And I tracked you down in the city. Yalena wasn't gonna show her face for me, that was for sure, but she might if her girl came looking for her." Brown let that thought hang there, his eyes beaming at Wally as she figured it out.

"The file from Brighton Beach," Wally said. "The note from my mother . . ."

"What note? What are you talking about?" Claire struggled to follow the exchange between Brown and her daughter.

"Oh, Mom. I'm sorry," Wally said, in anguish now. "It was me. I ruined everything. I went to Brighton Beach and there was this package for me, and it had a letter and papers and . . . it was all a fake?"

"All fake, all bullshit." Brown chuckled. "Not bad, right?"

As the three of them made their way to the beach, another barrage of gunshots was exchanged back in the woods, just a *pop, pop* sound like fireworks from that distance, no way to tell who was winning.

"I had little Sophie—poor little Sophie—steal your ID," Brown continued, "so you'd need a new one. Even gave you a choice where to go, but I knew you'd choose the one in Brighton Beach 'cause of the Russian thing. I had that file planted and waiting for you. And the letter from Yalena—that lit your fire right up, didn't it, little sister? Once you started looking for Yalena, it was just a matter of time before she poked her head out. And she was your American mother all along!" He shook his head and whistled through his teeth. "Never saw that coming. She was right there the whole time."

"And Sophie?" Wally said, seething. "It was you who killed her?"

Brown shrugged as if the decision to take Sophie's life was nothing remarkable, the cost of doing business. "Remember who it was that first brought you to me? Sophie. Girl with a habit is easy to use that way. But she started missing her crew—by then you'd kicked her out—and it made her a little crazy. She was gonna track you down and tip you off to what I was doing, so . . ."

"You fucking asshole," Wally seethed.

Brown ignored Wally's rage. He stopped for a moment and listened. The sounds of gunfire from the woods had stopped. He continued walking, urging Wally and Claire along with him. Claire was in terrible pain, the blood from her wound now dripping down onto the white snow. The three of them reached the beach of Coecles Inlet; the Hatches' dock was far off to the left and the pristine sand of the Mashomack Preserve to the right.

"Where?" Brown demanded.

Claire weakly pointed to the spot where a stone jetty reached into the inlet. The three of them slogged along the sand, Claire struggling even more now. Brown was oblivious to her suffering.

"You know what I'm most proud of?" he said. "The stone—the alexandrite. I pocketed that when our ATF team tore through Klesko's St. Petersburg apartment, long ago. I'd been holding on to that for sixteen goddamn years—little bit of a retirement bonus for myself—but then I realized what a fine investment it would be to put it in that file, Wally—to get your imagination going. That hurt, but it was worth it. Just like the picture of Klesko, the psycho bad guy, to add a sense of urgency. Of course, I had no idea he'd actually show up, but that worked out fine too. Klesko lit a real fire under your ass, am I right? Had to get to your mama before he did?" Brown chuckled again, immensely proud of himself. "And all along you had the cell I gave you—with GPS. I've had my crew on your ass for weeks; of course, never close enough for you to spot them."

When they reached the jetty, Claire steered them inland again, following the line of the jetty to the denuded brush just ten feet from the edge of the beach. Partially buried in the sand was a woven steel cable, rusty from decades of exposure, which had once been the anchor of an old pier. Claire traced the cable for ten more feet, then got on her knees and began to dig underneath it. The ground was frozen on its surface and brutally difficult to penetrate. Claire was struggling for breath now and ghostly pale.

Wally dropped to her knees beside Claire to help dig. As she dug, Wally observed her mother and became even more anxious.

"Mom?"

"I'm okay," Claire said, and tried a reassuring smile for Wally, unsuccessfully.

"Keep going," Brown said. "Slow and easy. I saw that shit you pulled with Klesko. One goddamn twitch and you are both dead." He scanned the woods, now growing anxious as the moment he had been working toward drew near. It had been several minutes since there had been gunshots behind them.

Wally kept digging, and within five minutes she was over two feet down in the soil and sand mixture. Her fingers scraped on the top of a plastic container.

"Easy . . ." Brown cautioned her.

Wally reached down into the hole and grabbed the plastic container, then stood up with it in her hands. It was not large—a pint at the most—but through the translucent blue plastic it was easy to see that it was almost full of pebble-size stones.

"That's what I'm talkin' about, little sister," he said, his voice reverting to the Harlem street accent he used for his role as Panama. "Gimme here."

As she stared at Brown, a strange smile came to Wally's face—as if she had a secret. She raised the container up, holding it beside her ear, and slowly shook it. It made the sound of a large baby rattle, hundreds of pebbles *plock*ing loudly against the walls of the plastic. The sound seemed to mesmerize Brown, for a moment. Wally went on, shaking the container harder, filling the air with the rumbling of the stones.

"Enough," Brown commanded her, and reached out for the container.

Suddenly he felt the muzzle of a gun against the back of his neck and heard the *click* of a hammer being drawn back. He stopped speaking.

"Agent Brown." Atley spoke calmly. "Detective Atley Greer."

"Listen, Detective," Brown said in a reasonable voice, Atley's gun still pressed into his neck. "Maybe we could discuss an option that would benefit both of us. . . ." Atley quieted him by jabbing the muzzle of his gun more insistently.

"Don't make a stupid mistake," said Atley. "I've called it in . . . it's over." Atley looked past Brown to Wally and Claire. "Is she all right, Wallis? I've called her injury in too—they're scrambling a medevac."

Wally tossed the cache aside and knelt down by Claire, who was looking worse now.

"Mom," Wally said, "you're going to be okay. . . ."

For just a moment, Atley was distracted by the interaction between mother and daughter. Brown took advantage and spun suddenly around, whipping Atley's gun aside with the barrel of his shotgun, which he then pointed at Atley's face. He was ready to blow Atley away, but a gunshot rang out from behind Atley. A bullet hole appeared in Brown's forehead and the life was gone from him instantly. As Brown dropped to the ground, Atley spun around and raised his own weapon again, but two more shots came, striking him in the arm and his ribs on the left side. Atley dropped to the ground, still alive but clenched in pain as he gripped his own wound.

It was Alexei Klesko who stood above Atley, gun in hand,

winded and with fresh wounds, but still alive. Tiger was at Klesko's side, also hurt; he bled from gunshot wounds near his ribs and lower leg.

"Daughter," Klesko said to Wally, pleased with himself despite being in obvious pain, "tell your American friends: never fight a Russian in the snow. You see? How many empires of the world must learn this hard lesson?" Klesko gave a swift kick to the body of Agent Brown. "ATF? Kiss my ass . . ."

Klesko stepped to where Wally was crouched at her mother's side.

"Give them," Klesko said, his voice a primal growl as he pointed at the plastic container

In sudden burst of rage, Wally grabbed the container and hurled it at Klesko. It hit his chest and the impact popped the lid open. Several hundred small stones flew out of the container in every direction, with a few dozen dropping to the ground at Klesko's feet. He bent over painfully and pulled up a handful of them, examining the treasure with emotionless objectivity. They were clearly just stones from the beach, worthless.

"Of course," he said with a strange sort of resignation, and passed the handful to Tiger. "My son, I leave you this. Your future."

Klesko chuckled. Tiger let the stones spill through his fingers and glared at Klesko.

Turning away from his son, Klesko took a deep, slow breath, relishing the feel of the cold air in his lungs, then stepped forward until he was standing above Claire.

"Yalena . . ." he said, then raised his gun at Claire, pointing it directly at her face. "Now, *your* future . . ."

"No!" Wally shouted, positioning herself between Klesko and her wounded mother. "It's over! Leave her alone!"

Klesko barked a sardonic laugh.

"You think I cannot kill my own blood?" He pointed his gun straight at Wally's face, but at that moment Atley rose from where he lay bleeding on the ground and launched himself desperately at Klesko. The two men struggled for a moment, but Atley's wounds were greater and he didn't have the strength to take Klesko's gun away. Klesko freed one arm and elbowed Atley in the solar plexus, dropping him once again to the ground. Klesko used the butt of his gun to knock Atley unconscious.

Klesko raised his gun once more, aimed it at Claire, and was about to shoot, but a blast sounded beside him and the left side of Klesko's chest exploded from the single shot, close range. The woods were silent for a moment as Klesko remained standing, looking startled. He gazed down at the gaping wound to his chest, now spurting blood. With disbelief, his eyes followed the only possible trajectory of the shot to Tiger, who stood beside him with his smoking gun still raised. The young man stared unapologetically at his father, watching almost without expression as Klesko dropped to the ground beside Agent Cornell Brown.

Sirens could be heard in the distance. Wally turned to Claire, whose face was now a ghostly white. She was barely holding on to consciousness.

"Mom!" Wally cried, wrapping her arms around her mother's neck.

"My girl." Claire smiled weakly. "We're together." Claire looked up and her eyes met Tiger's. He stood six or seven feet away, keeping his distance. Claire raised a hand and waved Tiger over to her. For a moment he did not move, but then slowly he shuffled over, shy and awkward, and knelt down beside his mother and sister. Something had changed Tiger; like a revelation, his anger had melted away. Tiger seemed suddenly to be no more than a boy, the sad and lonely child who had been left behind so many years ago.

"I can't believe it," Claire said, beaming. "I never thought this could come true. We're all here. *Moyi dyetki . . .*" My babies.

"Mama. . . ." Wally was barely able to speak, tears spilling down her face.

"No, baby," Claire said. "I'm so happy."

With all the energy she had left, Claire began to sing softly, in Russian. As she sang, she cast her eyes back and forth between Wally and Tiger. *"Puskai prïdet pora prosit'sia, drug druga dolgo ne vidat. . . ."*

Wally began to join in, singing quietly along with Claire, *"No serditse s serdtsem, slovno ptitsy, konechno, vstretiatsia opiat . . ."*

Claire smiled as she heard the words of the song from Wally's lips. "I sang the song the day I left you, Valentina. Do you remember what the words mean?"

"No."

Claire looked from Wally to Tiger. "Your brother will tell you," Claire said confidently, and then she began to sing the song again, one line at a time, *"Puskai prïdet pora prosit'sia . . ."*

Tiger sat motionless and quiet for a moment, overwhelmed. Claire waited.

"How swift the hour comes for our parting," Tiger translated, the words barely more than a whisper as his eyes met Claire's as she sang on.

"Drug druga dolgo ne vidat?"

"No more to meet—or who knows when?"

"No serditse s serdtsem, slovno ptitsy . . ."

"But heart with heart must come together."

"Konechno, vstretiatsia opiat . . ."

"And someday surely meet again."

It was there now in Claire's eyes, a look cast lovingly between her two children that told them who they were and where they belonged; they were hers and she was theirs, all together finally. Reflected in her mother's gaze, Wally saw herself, as if for the first time.

And then Claire was gone. Wally dropped her head to Claire's chest and wailed, grasping her dead mother in her arms desperately, as if struggling to pull her back into life. She stirred from her grief only when she became aware of the sirens in the near distance and then the approaching thunder of the medevac helicopter that flew low beneath the clouds overhead. Wally lifted her head, her eyes red from crying, her shirt stained and wet with Claire's blood. Tiger stood frozen in place, overwhelmed and feeling every kind of pain at once. Wally looked Tiger in the eye with desperate urgency.

"My brother . . ."

"*Sestryichka*," he answered. Little sister.

"Run," she said.

With those words, Tiger's awareness of his surroundings—and his situation—came rushing back, and reality took hold again. Tiger stuffed his gun under his belt and, with one last glance to his sister, bolted into the woods. Within seconds he was out of sight, disappearing under the dense curtain of snow that continued to fall.

THIRTY-FIVE

Wally stayed home alone at the 84th Street apartment for three days. She slept a lot, ate almost nothing, and cried her share. In between, when she felt strong enough, Wally went slowly through her mother's private things, looking for any information about the woman she had known as Claire Stoneman. As Wally reflected on the last eleven years of her life, she assumed there must have been clues that Claire was not who she claimed to be but also—in the great irony of Wally's young life—*exactly* who she had always claimed to be: Wally's mother. But there were no clues. Yalena Mayakova's transformation into Claire Stoneman had been complete, leaving no traces at all.

At four o'clock in the afternoon, on her third day alone, the house phone rang and Wally picked up, surprising herself.

"Yeah."

"Miss Stoneman—"

"Stop it, Raoul. I'm still just Wally."

"Okay. Wally, someone named Natalie Stehn is here."

"Yeah, okay. Thanks."

Wally didn't feel like company, really, but she was grateful to Natalie—her mother's and now Wally's lawyer—for all the things she had done and was still doing on Wally's behalf. After the incident on Shelter Island, Wally had been questioned by both local and federal authorities for over twelve hours, with a Social Services caseworker waiting in the wings to take Wally into custody. Natalie Stehn had shown up and bulled her way into the interview room, armed with a document that declared her to be Wally's legal guardian, signed and notarized several years earlier by Claire Stoneman. Once her custodianship had been established, Natalie had demanded Wally's release and had brought her home to 84th Street. Natalie had offered to stay with Wally, but Wally had insisted on being alone.

The doorbell rang and Wally opened the door for Natalie, a smallish woman but very forceful and direct. She gave Wally her own version of a sympathetic smile, but touchy-feely was not Natalie's style.

"How are you, Wally?"

"I'm okay. Come on in, Natalie." They sat on the soft couch in the living room, Wally tucking her legs up under her robe, Natalie sitting squarely upright. "I want to thank you again for the other day," Wally said. "I'd be in juvie right now if you hadn't shown up."

"Just my job, but you're welcome. Is there anything you

need right now? Money? You still have the credit card, right? You can get cash with that?"

"I'm good."

"Okay," Natalie said, and pulled a file from her valise. "Any order you want this stuff?"

"Johanna."

"Right," Natalie said, and leafed through the file. "The doctors still have her in a medically induced coma while she recovers from massive trauma. As I said before, the staff say it's a miracle she's still alive, but at this point they're fairly optimistic about a recovery."

"When can I visit her?"

"They're going to wake her up in two days—probably—depending on her progress."

"Okay. I want to be there when that happens."

"Right, I'll keep you posted as I keep in touch with the medical staff."

"Jake and Ella?"

"My guy found them." Natalie leafed further into her reports. "It looks like things went pretty much the way you hoped, the two of them together at that residential facility, Neversink Farm."

"Good," Wally said. "And the place is okay?"

"Yeah, my guy says it checks out. Nice clean farm, animals, a lake. Here's a random detail: apparently they've already put Jake in charge of a pig named Titan, a massive boar, and the kid seems happy about it. Ella is learning to cook."

Wally was pleased with this outcome. She figured these

were perfect assignments, a recalcitrant beast to match Jake's own aggressive nature and Ella in a kitchen with lots of food.

"It sounds like a good situation," Natalie continued. "I think my guy halfway wanted to live there himself. So, how would you like to proceed, as relates to those two?"

Wally had given this a lot of thought. "Jake and Ella deserve a chance to make their own way," she said. "That's what I want to happen. And we can be, like . . ."

"A safety net?"

"Yeah, a safety net. I like that." Wally smiled, imagining Ella and Jake on a flying trapeze, Jake hurling Ella up in the air and catching her again. *She's watching over you.* . . . That's what Ella had said about Wally's Russian mother, and she had been totally right about that. Magical Ella.

Natalie turned a page in her file and sighed. "Tevin."

"Tevin." Wally nodded, her smile evaporating.

"My guy has looked everywhere, and the only relative he's found for Tevin is an aunt whose last known residence was in Nashville. No current address for her yet. Tevin's remains are still in the city morgue, but the coroner has released them to be claimed."

"We can claim them?"

"We can get a court order for that. My suggestion? I can make arrangements to have his remains cremated, and you can take custody of him. That way, over time, you can decide how you want to memorialize him. Maybe at some point with your friends Jake and Ella, maybe with Tevin's aunt when we find her . . ."

"That sounds right, Natalie. Let's do that."

"Good. Now, we haven't talked about this yet, but on a hunch I set the wheels in motion for you to petition for emancipated minor status."

"Yes."

"That's what I thought. So we'll set aside the estate issues until after you're emancipated; that'll make things simpler. As executor of your mother's estate, I've done some preliminary work with an accountant. I can tell you that your mother was a very successful woman, as you know. Once everything is settled, you'll assume ownership of this apartment—it's paid for in full—and of various assets, both onshore and off. Claire was a shrewd businesswoman. Money will not be a problem for you, Wallis, unless of course you go *meshugeh*, which, once you're emancipated, will be entirely up to you. Good?"

"Yeah, good. Thanks, Natalie."

"So, I know this is a difficult subject for you. I had a fairly long conversation with your father." There was an awkward pause. "Jason, I mean. Obviously."

"Okay." Wally's heart hardened at the mention of his name.

"You know he's been here in town since he heard about everything. You haven't returned his calls."

Jason had called the apartment dozens of times, but Wally had ignored the messages. He had also shown up at the apartment building, but Wally had told the doormen to turn him away.

"It's up to you, Wally," Natalie said. "You're a big girl. But . . . for all his flaws and transgressions, I do believe Jason cares about you very much. He did let you down, but also remember that Claire's secrets were kept from Jason as well as you. With no trust in the marriage, the cards were stacked against him. Anyway, as I say, it's up to you. He wants to come to Claire's service, but he'll stay away if you say he's not welcome."

Wally considered this. She wondered if there was still any room in her jaded heart for trust, for faith.

"Let him come," she said.

Natalie could not suppress a hopeful smile.

"Way to go, Wally." Natalie gathered her things and stood to go. "I'm going to head out and give you some time."

"Thanks. Sorry to be so—"

"Are you kidding? Wally, I would give anything to be as strong as you are. Truly."

Wally nodded her thanks.

Natalie hovered for a moment, looking anxious, as if debating something in her own head. Wally could see the woman struggling.

"What is it, Natalie?"

"I just couldn't figure out if I should wait on this or what. Your first few days, you were pretty raw. You still are, I know."

Wally tensed again. "God, Natalie," she said. "What next?"

Natalie pulled out a letter-size envelope and passed it to Wally. *For Wally* was written on the front, in Claire's hand. The envelope was sealed.

"Your mother wrote a new note to you every six months or so and asked me to hold it . . . you know, just in case. I have the old ones in a file back at my office, if you ever want them."

Holding the letter in her hand, Wally almost laughed.

"The real thing," she said.

"What's that?"

"Nothing," Wally said. "Thanks again for everything. I'll see you at the service on Saturday?"

"Of course," Natalie said. "I'll see you Saturday, but no doubt we'll talk on the phone before then."

"Thanks again, Natalie."

Natalie gathered up her things and showed herself out of the apartment, leaving Wally alone, the envelope from Claire sitting unopened on the coffee table in front of her.

Wally found Atley Greer at Pier 63 in Chelsea, his left arm in a sling, struggling mightily to wrap a tarp around some sort of boat, a long and sleek craft that barely looked big enough to float a full-size man.

"What the hell is that thing?"

"It's an outrigger canoe," Atley said. "It's taken apart right now, but the hull, right there, and the float connect together. Then you've got a helluva boat."

"This is the end of your season?"

Atley nodded. "I've been so busy chasing miscreants around the city, I never had my last paddle." He looked out over the water of the Hudson, sparkling in the bright midday sun. The current was slack and the wind gentle. "Damn. Look at that water. Today would have been it, but not with my busted wing." He held up his broken arm, worthless for paddling as long as the cast was on.

"Nice water to look at, though."

Atley gave her a look and shrugged. "You gonna help me with this, or what?"

Wally pitched in and the job went much faster. They zipped the canvas tarp around the boat and its elements to make a long narrow package, then carried it together to a boat rack, where they locked it down.

"I got your invitation for the service on Saturday," Atley said. "Thank you."

"You'll be there?"

Atley nodded.

"I was wondering—"

"About your brother."

"Yes."

"Long gone. He left a blood trail that disappeared at the Hatches' house, and after that . . . we got nothing. Every local and federal agency on the eastern seaboard is looking for him. Three days and not one sign."

Good, Wally thought. She didn't say it out loud, of course, but Atley caught the look on her face and knew.

"And my mother. Is anyone trying to put together her story? I guess the details don't matter much now, but . . . you know. I'm thinking about her a lot, everything she went through."

Atley nodded his understanding. "The FBI is piecing her timeline together. A friend of mine is heading up that side. They've got a good handle on her, I think."

"All the way back to Russia?"

"To when she was a kid, yeah. Your grandmother worked in the dean's office of the Emerson School for over twenty years.

Yalena attended the school for free and pretty much grew up with American kids."

Wally considered this. "That's why the good American English. I don't remember ever hearing an accent in her voice."

"Not just the language," Atley said. "Seems like she learned most everything about American culture. That's gotta be the main reason the transition to her American identity was possible."

"My grandmother . . . the one who worked at the Emerson School?"

"I'm sorry. She passed on about ten years ago. We're not sure how much family you have left back there, if any."

Wally nodded stoically.

"Yalena made her way to New York with Hatch's help," Atley went on. "Because of his import business, he had some bent contacts at Customs. She stayed in the Shelter Island house with him before moving off on her own. Claire Stoneman came into being then, with the help of some minor facial surgery to be sure, and Yalena Mayakova disappeared for good. Her first months here—staying at Hatch's, healing up from the surgery—Yalena used that time to practice her English until she could completely pass."

"That's impressive, I guess. . . ."

Atley nodded. "From then on, Yalena's life reads like a perfect American resume: husband, real estate license, successful career, high-rise apartment on the Upper West Side . . . and all in record time." Atley paused for a moment. "You know why, don't you? Why she did all that?"

"She was creating a character," Wally said. "Someone who could return to Russia and bring me back."

"Yes. The family friend she left you with, at the orphanage, her name was Irina Ivanova. She made sure you wouldn't be adopted by anyone else. She actually became the director of the orphanage. Do you remember her?"

"I don't know," Wally said. "Maybe. How did Johanna get involved in all this? She wasn't Russian."

"Apparently, she and your mother formed a strong bond after you moved into that building. Yalena certainly needed someone she could trust, and Johanna obviously became a good friend; she knew all your mother's secrets and held them close. When Johanna showed up at the Quonset-hut safe house—it seems she did that from time to time as a favor to Yalena, to pick up mail and so forth—Klesko obviously knew she was not Yalena, but she was the only resource he had, and Johanna gave up the information about the Shelter Island caches. It seems like that was their plan all along, Yalena and Johanna: if the worst-case scenario ever happened and Klesko came looking for Yalena, she would lead Klesko to the caches. The first one they'd booby-trapped with a homemade aluminum flash grenade. It sounds kind of harebrained now, but it could have worked if Klesko had come alone."

Atley could see Wally struggling with all the information.

"I'm sorry," he said. "I'm sure it's all too much."

"Yeah, it is. But I need to hear it anyway."

"Well, there's something else you need to know."

"What?"

"Klesko . . ."

Wally's pulse quickened at the mention of the name. Tiger's bullet had barely missed Klesko's heart, and, against all odds, the bastard had survived. Apparently the cold and snow of Shelter Island had been the deciding factor, preserving the man's vitals until the medevac arrived.

"You're not going to tell me he escaped," Wally said. "I saw the size of the hole in the man's chest."

"Not escaped, exactly. Vanished is more like it. Call it extraordinary rendition, or whatever term the feds are using these days. Klesko knows too much about the international arms trade to let him ever appear in a regular American courtroom. They grabbed him right up. No doubt he's already overseas in a secret detention facility. I hear the one in Thailand is a favorite these days. But this is not something you should worry about—even if he survives the interrogations, they'll put him in a hole so dark and deep he'll be lost to the outside world forever."

The idea of Klesko alive and on the mend—no matter how far away or how securely held—was chilling to Wally, and Greer's assurances meant exactly nothing to her. Alexei Klesko would haunt Wally's thoughts forever.

After a few moments of quiet, Wally looked up and was surprised to find Atley smiling at her.

"What?"

"You get the prize, Wallis," Atley said. "You're about the only person involved in this case who didn't ask about the goddamn stones. That's what they usually want to know about *first*."

Wally shrugged. "I don't care about the stones."

"That's good, 'cause they're all gone. Have been for almost fifteen years, as close as the feds can figure."

"What happened to them?"

"In the end, Yalena ended up splitting them evenly with Hatch. They both needed money but knew that if they put the stones on the market, they would be traced back to them. Hatch found a dealer in precious stones—a guy in Atlantic City, we think—who agreed to list them by a slightly different description. Turns out there's a mine in Madagascar that turns out alexandrite with a similar vein of amber. Not exactly the same, but close enough. They gave the guy a twenty-percent discount on their value if he listed them as coming from the Madagascar mine. Your mother was sensible and invested her money well. Hatch wasn't so smart and, over time, blew most of his money."

"So much damage caused . . ." Wally began to say, but didn't finish her thought. None of it seemed to matter anymore. She and Atley stood together in silence for a while, their eyes on the Hudson River, flowing by.

"I like this better, Wally," he said. "With no fence in between us."

"Whatever, Cop," she said, then gave him a little smile before walking away.

THIRTY-SIX

Wally slept. She was out for six or seven hours, feeling disoriented when she woke on the living room couch in the small hours of the morning. *Home*, she reminded herself as she had the previous three mornings, taking a moment to remember where she was and the wild series of events that had brought her there. She got up and peed and washed her face, then went to the kitchen and started boiling water for coffee. She watched the pot until it boiled and took her coffee into the living room. She sat down on the sofa, where she had slept, and wrapped herself inside her mother's favorite blanket. Halfway through her coffee, Wally finally reached for the letter from her mother and opened it.

The letter was dated just a month earlier and could not have been more different than the flowery missive from the Brighton file.

My Dearest Wally, the letter began. *Mostly, these days, I'm just worried and angry. Where are you? Why won't you come home to me? I know I am to blame for this situation we are in. The lies I told, the truths I held back. The only peace I find comes from this knowledge: whatever mistakes I have made, whatever wounds I have caused, the result of everything—good and bad—is you, my Wally, and I can say without doubt that you are perfect as you are. I have never known anyone as strong or smart or capable of giving love. Do you know that about yourself? I hope you find out before it is too late. What you are doing with your life now is something I cannot condone or understand, but my grief about that does not change my certainty that it is within you to make a difference in this world. Please find a way to share your gifts with people you care about. If you do that, all that has come before will have been a journey worth taking. I am only sorry I will not be there when you reach your destination. I hope there is a heaven, for one reason . . . so that I can witness what you become. All my love, Yalena.*

Wally read it all the way through, twice, then returned it to the envelope and set it back down on the coffee table. Under any other circumstances, the contents would have brought her to tears, but on that dark November morning they did not. The main reason, Wally knew, was that no emotional outpouring could possibly match the farewell scene in the snow on Shelter Island, where Wally and her mother had been reunited and said goodbye forever, all at once. That experience and the subsequent days of solitary mourning had wrung her out. The grief and the tears would no doubt revisit her in days and weeks and years to come, but for now Wally Stoneman was done crying.

Wally's other reaction was to remember the poetic, emotional letter in the Brighton Beach package and wonder where exactly it had come from. Wally tried to imagine ATF Agent Cornell Brown—the man she had known as Panama—sitting down and composing a letter so authentic and emotionally complex, but she simply could not wrap her mind around that possibility. But if Brown himself had not written the note, who had? One of the corrupt hatchet men on his ATF team? Doubtful as well. Wally could not shake her instinctual response to the note: it had been written by a genuinely passionate person who had firsthand experience of loss and grief.

If this doubt about the Brighton Beach letter were the only issue bothering Wally, she probably could have overlooked it. In the truth, however, she had felt a nagging doubt during the previous few days, and the letter question only added to her anxiety.

Cornell Brown's boastful narrative, as he marched Wally and Claire through the woods to the site of the last cache, did not really hold together. If Wally believed his version, he had singlehandedly solved the Yalena Mayakova mystery, right down to the exact orphanage where Wally had been raised and her eventual destination in the United States. From her earlier efforts to unravel her own personal history, Wally knew that that information was heavily protected by privacy laws—in both Russia and the United States—sometimes buried so deep that the answers were lost forever. Even with the government resources available to him, it was highly unlikely that Cornell Brown had suddenly, after fifteen years of fruitless searching, come upon all the answers at once.

Then who had? Who had the massive resources to unlock the Yalena Mayakova mystery? If someone had helped Cornell Brown with his scheme, it seemed probable that the same person had also composed the deeply affecting Brighton Beach letter. Did Wally know anyone even remotely capable of accomplishing all that? For the next few hours of the morning, Wally remained folded up in the sofa, staring out the apartment window until the first hint of sunrise spread a peach-colored glow to the east. She wondered if there really was someone out there who could explain how and why her life had been torn apart.

It was just a few minutes after seven that morning that Wally came up with an answer. She had a good idea who had revealed her identity to Cornell Brown, and she thought she knew why. Wally brewed a fresh pot of coffee to help keep her awake and got dressed. The thermometer on the balcony window read twenty-one degrees, so Wally dressed warmly, wrapping up in Claire's favorite cashmere overcoat. It was still early, so Wally decided to walk across the park. By nine o'clock, she had made it to Lexington Avenue on the Upper East Side, her cheeks pink from her long walk in the cold morning air. She found a coffee shop at the corner of 91st Street that gave her a good view of the building across the street, and she waited.

At 9:23 that morning, Lewis Jordan finally appeared, walking north on Lexington Avenue. He wore a dark blue overcoat and a wide-brimmed black fedora, his breath fogging in the cold air as he moved up the street with a wariness that was not surprising for an eighty-five-year-old man on an icy morning. As she watched his approach from the window of the coffee shop, it seemed to Wally that there was something less vital about the man—out in the open air of the city—than when they had first met inside the Ursula Society offices.

Wally watched Jordan enter the society's building and then paid her bill with the coffee shop cashier. She exited the shop and jaywalked across Lex, entering the building just two minutes or so after Jordan. She climbed to the third floor and walked down the long hallway to the office door that said THE URSULA SOCIETY, the logo of a bear silhouette underneath. Wally entered without bothering to knock. The office was the same, nice enough but nondescript, with a wooden desk on either side of the room that each held a computer monitor. Wally was confused, for a moment, to find no one in the office, but she soon became aware of noises coming from behind a door, slightly ajar, at the back wall of the room. Within just a few seconds, the door opened all the way and Lewis Jordan emerged, a short stack of file folders in his arms.

Wally watched the man closely, wanting to mark the exact expression on his face once he saw her. He was startled at first to find someone else in the office with him, but once he recognized Wally, he seemed gladdened.

"Oh, Wallis! Good to see you. I didn't realize we—" But Lewis soon cut his cheerful greeting short. He read Wally's expression and understood that a shift had taken place. His face lost much of what little color it had, and the smile fell away from him.

"What happened?" he asked.

"Tell me what you did, Lewis."

Lewis sighed deeply and shuffled over to his desk, setting down the stack of file folders and then sitting down himself. The old, wooden swivel chair creaked loudly beneath him as he reached out and held the edge of his desk, bracing himself. Lewis looked up to meet Wally's relentless gaze.

"I made a choice," he said. "There's a man, an agent for—"

"The ATF? Agent Cornell Brown. Tell me what you did, Lewis."

Lewis took a deep breath. "Agent Brown is a source of ours. Some years back we helped him locate a nephew, his sister's child that she had given up for adoption. As a result, he offered himself as a resource for us, in future searches. Two years ago, when you first came in with your situation, I knew that Brown had served in Eastern Europe as part of some sort of criminal task force and might have connections in that part of the world."

"It was *you* who brought attention of my case to *him*?"

"I thought Brown could help you." Lewis nodded. "As soon as he read your file, he recognized your situation. The time frame of your arrival at the orphanage, the lack of documentation. Somehow he figured out that you were the daughter of Yalena Mayakova and Alexei Klesko. He told me that his team had been putting together a case against arms dealers in the former Soviet republics and that if they found Yalena—your mother—she could testify for them. He said the arms people would find her eventually anyway and kill her, so really I was protecting her by helping Brown and his team find her first. Initially, I refused, of course. All my rules, you see . . ."

"But eventually you changed your mind. Why?"

Lewis shook his head ruefully, clearly ashamed of what he had done.

"Brown said he had access to some immigration documents that would help locate my son in America—the very documents I had been trying to find for decades. Harvesting the information would be a great risk for him, he said, because of where the database was located. He would do it for me, but only in exchange for my help in locating your mother. He said he would protect Yalena when he found her, and the two of you would be reunited, just like you wanted so badly. I ignored our rules, I know, but my own desperation blinded me, Wallis. To die without knowing my son . . . I was too weak to resist the opportunity."

"So the Brighton Beach file was your idea?"

Lewis nodded yes. "I knew that with just a small amount of inspiration you would begin your search, and that sooner or later Yalena Mayakova would reveal herself to you."

Wally realized now how perfect the plan had been. A little thread of hope had been offered to her and she had pulled it, unraveling her own life and the lives of those she loved most. She could blame Lewis, certainly, for helping Cornell Brown set all of it into motion, but Wally felt responsible as well. She had been willing to risk anything in the search for her mother, and in the end she had lost it all. She expected to feel hatred and rage for Lewis, but instead all she felt was pity.

"And Brown was lying?" Wally said to him. "He never told you where to find your son?"

"No. I haven't heard from Brown in days."

"You won't," Wally said. "He's dead."

"Oh God." Lewis was stunned. "What happened, Wallis?"

Wally wondered if Lewis Jordan—looking older and weaker by the moment—would survive the guilt he would feel when he had heard about all the grief that had resulted from his mistake, but she couldn't bear any more secrets. Wally sat down beside Lewis and calmly told it all as the old man wept—for Wally, for her family, for the sorry state of the world, and for his own fall from grace.

When the story was over, Wally felt exhausted but also strangely lighter, unburdened. She moved to the side table and turned on the electric teapot that was set up there, then placed tea bags in two mugs and waited for the water to boil. There was a draft in the room and Wally noticed the open door in the back of the office. She walked through the doorway and found herself in a large, musty room with three rows of industrial file shelves rising all the way to the ceiling, bolted there to prevent them from toppling under the weight of all the paper. A label hanging from each shelf read OPEN CASES. Every shelf was full.

Wally marveled at the sheer numbers. The Ursula Society held thousands of open cases—thousands of unanswered prayers. Some files were recent, but many looked very old, their edges frayed and yellowing, untouched for decades, maybe.

She walked slowly among the stacks and experienced a strange and chilling sensation, as if she could actually hear the voices of longing whisper in her ear: *Come find us.* She thought of Tiger, her brother, a lifetime of distance between them and yet they shared an undeniable bond. Could she hear his voice as well? Was his among the chorus of others, calling out to her? The old man from the shop in Brighton Beach, he had spoken the truth: *This world is a wilderness*. Tiger was out there now, alone. She could feel him thinking of her, even at that moment, and she knew what she had to do.

She would find him. She would find them all.

ACKNOWLEDGEMENTS

I am grateful for the endless care I received from Ben Schrank, Anne Heltzel, and everyone at Razorbill/Penguin. Kari Stuart, Robert Lazar, and the folks at ICM made everything possible, and none of this would have happened at all without the faithful and formidable Christine Cuddy.

I have been blessed with family and friends who have long stood by me despite my general crustiness and variously offensive personal behaviors, for which I now apologize. Foremost among my supporters are my loving parents, Ann and Mike Richter, who have been in my corner forever and without fail.

The list of friends who have aided and inspired me would challenge the space available here, but I received special help with *Dark Eyes* from Catherine Meyers, Kate Story, Vera Blasi, Peter Maduro, Susannah Grant, David Sanger, Roxanna Badin, Geoffrey Sturr, Hailyn Chen, Sandy Kroopf, Marischa Slusarski, Claire Bidwell Smith, Leslie Rainer, Arlen Heginbotham, Laura Richter, Sarah Richter, Ricardo Mestres, Jodie Burke, Lisa Bromwell, Elizabeth McQueen, Brian Tudor, Liz Macfarlane, Diana Mason, Nan Donlin, Nina Frank, and Steven Rapkin, plus all my cheerful neighbors, both human and animal.

My heartfelt thanks to all of you.

---

* The song "Strain of Guitar (on the River)"—words by A. Oshanin, music by A. Novikov—appears as translated in *A Russian Songbook*, edited by Rose N. Rubin and Michael Stillman (New York: Dover, 1989).